Falling Home

KAREN WHITE

CENTER POINT PUBLISHING
THORNDIKE, MAINE

This Center Point Large Print edition
is published in the year 2010 by arrangement with
NAL Signet, a member of Penguin Group (USA) Inc.

The text of this Large Print edition is unabridged.
In other aspects, this book may vary
from the original edition.
Printed in the United States of America
on permanent paper.
Set in 16-point Times New Roman type.

ISBN: 978-1-60285-907-4

Library of Congress Cataloging-in-Publication Data

White, Karen (Karen S.)
Falling home / Karen White.
    p. cm.
ISBN 978-1-60285-907-4 (library binding : alk. paper)
1. Life change events—Fiction. 2. Georgia—Fiction. 3. Domestic fiction.
    4. Large type books. I. Title.
PS3623.H5776F35 2010b
813'.6—dc22

2010035113

To Wendy Wax Adler and Susan Crandall—for your friendship and fierce support over the years. And for reading this book in all of its versions without complaint. Thank you.

ACKNOWLEDGMENTS

This publication would never have happened without the many letters from readers asking for this book years after the original version was out of print. So thank you, readers, and thanks to my agent, Karen Solem, and my publisher, New American Library, for making it happen.

AUTHOR'S NOTE

About ten years ago, I sat down at my computer to write my third novel. I didn't have a publisher for it, but I felt compelled to write the story about two sisters who'd been estranged for fifteen years. It was a fish-out-of-water story, too, about a woman raised in a small Georgia town yet firmly entrenched in her New York City lifestyle who's suddenly forced to ask the question of whether you can really go home again.

That book, *Falling Home*, was published in the summer of 2002 in mass-market format and with a cover depicting a glass of pink lemonade with a lipstick mark on the top. It wasn't the cover I'd envisioned for the book, yet I was pleased to have the book out on bookstore shelves so I could share the story with readers. And readers seemed to love the story as much as I had, so much so that when the book disappeared from bookstore shelves a short while later, I continued to get mail from readers desperate to find it. Those letters have continued ever since, especially as used copies were the only ones available and were being sold for really silly prices.

Fast-forward seven years, and the rights to the

book belong to me again. My current publisher, New American Library, repurchases the rights and schedules publication for November 2010. They give the book a beautiful new cover, and then I'm given the opportunity to revise the book.

I was hesitant at first. After all, readers loved the story and they loved Cassie, Harriet, Maddie, Sam and the rest of the inhabitants of Walton, Georgia. But then I realized that I didn't need to change any of that at all. Instead, I wanted to enhance the book by challenging myself to write it *better*. After all, since *Falling Home* was originally published, I'd written nine more novels. From experience, my writing had become tighter, more observant, more concise. I wanted to use this experience to make a better book. And I think I've accomplished this with the 2010 rendition of *Falling Home*.

To readers familiar with the older version, the most obvious difference you'll notice is the addition of two more points of view. Whereas the original story was told only through Cassie's eyes, the new version is also told from Harriet's and Maddie's points of view to give the reader more insight into the characters and their motivations. What might not be so noticeable is the "tightening" of the words. I've tried to rewrite scenes using fewer words, realizing I can get my point across more quickly if my readers aren't stumbling over a whole lot of words that are saying the same thing.

Ultimately, I still love this book as much as I did when I originally wrote it. I laughed at the funny parts, and cried at the sad parts, and sighed happily when I finally reached "The End." And that, to me, is the sign of a good read, whether it's old or new.

CHAPTER 1

Cassie was dreaming again. It was of old summers: the summers of bare feet, skinned knees, and homemade peach ice cream that dripped down her chin and made her fingers sticky. Aunt Lucinda rang the supper bell, and Cassie and Harriet raced each other past the gazebo toward the back porch, their sun-kissed legs pumping under white sundresses. The jangling of the dream bell seemed so real, Cassie felt she could touch the cold brass and make it stop.

Her fingers touched Andrew's arm instead, his skin warm under her hand, and she jerked awake, the smells of summer grass and Aunt Lucinda's lavender perfume lingering somewhere in the back of her mind. But the jangling continued, filling Cassie with dread.

She held her breath, looking at the glowing numbers on her clock, and listened for the next ring of the telephone. Only bad news came at three in the morning. Births and engagements were always announced in the bright light of day. But bad news came at night, as if the sun were already in mourning.

Andrew stirred briefly, then rolled over, away from her. Rising from the bed, Cassie stumbled across the darkened bedroom and into the living room so as not to awaken him. She hit her little toe on a chair leg and let out an expletive, her choice of words the only thing still reminiscent of her background.

"Dangnabit!" she muttered, reaching for the phone and knocking it off the table. She grappled with it on the floor before finally placing it to her ear. "Hello?"

There was a brief pause, then, "Hi, Cassie. It's me. It's Harriet."

Cassie's blood stilled as she gripped the receiver tighter. "Harriet," she said, her voice sounding strained and unsure to her ears. "How are you?"

The words were so inadequate and stupid that she wanted to bite them back as soon as they left her mouth. It was three a.m., her estranged sister was calling after nearly fifteen years of silence, and she was asking about how she was in the same kind of voice in which she would ask a coworker if she liked sugar in her coffee.

"It's Daddy. He's dying."

A siren screamed outside in the dark beyond Cassie's window. She reached across the table and flipped on a lamp. "What happened?" The brilliant-cut diamond in an antique platinum setting on her left hand sparkled in the dim light. Andrew came and sat next to her, his forehead creased with a question. Cassie put her hand over the receiver and mouthed, *My sister.*

"Hang on a second." Harriet's phone clunked as

12

the sound of a baby's crying trickled through the line. It must be Amanda, Harriet's new baby. Cassie knew each child from pictures her father sent. There were five of them—spread evenly over fifteen years of marriage. Each birth announcement from her father had opened the old wounds, scraping away the scabs, making Cassie bleed again.

Harriet came back. "I'm sorry. The baby's been fussy all day."

Cassie swallowed. "What's wrong with Daddy?"

Harriet sounded as if she'd been crying. "He's had a heart attack. It was during his annual physical so he was at the hospital when it happened, and they were able to treat him right away. We didn't think it was so bad, but he says he's dying. And you know he always means what he says. He's in the hospital now, but he wants us to bring him home tomorrow. It was his idea to call you right now, in the middle of the night. He says he won't rest in peace until both of his girls are here. He wants you to come home."

Cassie didn't say anything but listened to the sounds of the phone being put down again and of the fretting baby. She glanced over at Andrew, who had put his head back against the sofa and closed his eyes. Her gaze wandered the living room of the Upper West Side apartment they'd bought together as an engagement present to each other. Nothing in the cool, crisp space, with its black-and-white checkerboard of color and harsh angles, resembled the old house in which she had grown up. The house with porch swings, ancient oaks, and screen doors. Just as the woman she had become no longer resembled the girl of twenty who had left the small town of Walton, Georgia, fifteen years before without a backward glance.

Then a man spoke, his words deep and resonant. "Cassie? It's Joe."

She looked away, trying to focus on the abstract splotch of color in the painting behind her sofa, wanting to block out the memories his voice stirred. The memories of moonlit nights and serenading katydids in the gazebo behind the old house, and of Aunt Lucinda's gardenias, drooping in the heat, spreading their seductive aroma.

"Cassie? Are you there?"

"Yes." Her voice cracked, so she said it again, firmer this time. "Yes. I'm here."

Andrew sat up and took her hand, his eyes guarded.

Joe spoke again. "Are you coming home?"

The receiver slipped in her sweaty palm. Every day she handled difficult clients, the bread and butter of the ad agency, but nothing had ever made her as unsettled as the sound of Joe's voice and the mere thought of returning to the place she swore she would never set foot in again.

"I am home," she said, defiant.

"You know what I mean, Cassie." She could

barely hear him, he was speaking so low. "Harriet needs you now. As much as you need her, I suspect. Your daddy's dying and he wants his girls to be with him."

She looked over at Andrew. He wore only boxer shorts, his skin pale in the glare of the lamp. She stared at the contours of the muscles on his chest, every ridge etched in her fingers' memory. Cassie had worked for Andrew Wallace for five years, been his lover for three, and his fiancée for one. Like her, he was a transplant to New York, all the way from Newport Beach, California.

Cassie reached for his hand resting on his thigh. He jerked awake, his eyes meeting hers with a question. She squeezed his fingers, feeling the bond between them, the bond that made her regard them as wild hothouse flowers, uprooted from the tropics and moved to an intricately landscaped formal garden. They understood each other, sharing a mutual passion for their work, and never talking about how very far from home they both were.

Cassie blinked hard. "I'll come. For Daddy."

Joe sighed into the phone. "Whatever it takes to get you here, Cassie. Just come as soon as you can."

Cassie heard whispering on the other end of the phone; then Harriet spoke again. "Let me know which flight you'll be on, and I'll pick you up."

"No." She said it too quickly. She wasn't ready

for an hour alone in a car with Harriet. "I mean, I think I'll drive. I'll need a car while I'm down there, and . . . I'd like the time to think. If I drive straight through, I can be there by tomorrow night."

"You be careful—the roads aren't safe for a woman driving alone."

"Really, Harriet. I can take care of myself."

Harriet breathed into the receiver. "I know, Cassie. You always have."

Cassie waited a moment, then said, "Tell Daddy . . . tell him I'm coming."

They said good-bye, and Cassie hung up, staring into space for a long moment. Finally, Andrew stirred next to her and she pulled her hand away. "I've got to go back to Walton. Daddy's sick and wants me there now. He's dying."

Andrew looked down at his carefully manicured hands, and drew in a deep breath. "I'm sorry." He looked up. "I'd like to come with you, but I can't right now."

Cassie regarded him calmly. "I know. That's fine—I think it's better you stayed anyway. Walton's not your kind of town. You'd be screaming to leave after five minutes."

He set his mouth in a straight line. "It's not that. It's just that one of us needs to stay behind to see to business. The BankNorth campaign is scheduled to hit next month, and we've got lots of work to do. But I want you to stay as long as you think you need to."

16

She touched his shoulder. "Really, Andrew. You don't need to explain. I understand. And thanks."

He nodded, then looked away.

Cassie rubbed her face, trying to scrub away old images. "It's so hard to believe. I just spoke to him on the phone last Sunday. He was telling me yet again that it was time to come home." She smiled at the darkness outside the window. "He said the most peculiar thing."

Andrew flipped off the lamp, then stood, pulling her into his arms. "What did he say this time?"

Cassie nestled into the soft spot below his collarbone, wrinkling her nose at the tang of stale cologne. "He said that Georgia dirt would always stick to the soles of my shoes, regardless of how many elocution lessons I took."

Andrew snorted softly. "The old judge never gives up trying to argue his case, does he?"

Cassie shook her head. "No, he doesn't." She closed her eyes, knowing her Italian pumps would never have the patience for the clinging red clay of Georgia.

They stood in their embrace in front of the large plate-glass window. The never-ending traffic below pulsed and vibrated like an electronic serpent, moving with the city's energy. Cassie lifted her chin and stared out at the glittering city skyline, the hulking outlines of the surrounding buildings like the bruises on her memory.

Without being conscious of it, she lifted her

hand to the frail gold chain on her neck, and placed her fingers around the four small charms that hung from it. The gold was cool to the touch, but it comforted her, just as it had done many times since her mother had given it to her.

Andrew's voice sounded muffled. "You're nervous."

Cassie lifted her head and looked up at him. "I am not. Why would you say that?"

"Because you always play with your necklace whenever you're nervous. It's your only annoying habit."

She pulled away. "I'm not nervous. Just . . . thoughtful."

Cassie dropped her hand, and Andrew bent to kiss her neck, his lips warm and lingering on her skin. He lifted his head. "How long do you think you'll be gone?"

She felt a prickle of annoyance. "I don't know, Andrew. As long as my father needs me, I guess."

He rubbed his fingers through highlighted hair. "I'm sorry; I don't mean to sound callous. Stay as long as you need to," he repeated, as if trying to convince them both that he really meant it. He sent her a dim smile. "And don't forget I'm only a phone call away if you need anything."

Placing her hands on his chest, she fixed him with a steady gaze. "Actually, there is something. I'm going to drive. And I was wondering if I could borrow your car."

She could see the hesitation in his eyes by the glow of the lights outside.

He dropped his arms from her shoulders. "My car? You want to drive my car?"

Cassie could almost hear his internal struggle. Nobody she knew in the city needed or wanted a car, much less had a place to put one, but Andrew had a house in Connecticut, complete with horse barn and garage.

His shoulders slumped slightly. "Couldn't you rent one?" She could tell he wasn't completely joking.

She took a deep breath, wondering if he would be as protective of her as his wife as he was about his car. "I want something safe, reliable—and fast. You know I'll take good care of it." Trying to add some levity, she said, "And it *is* insured, right?"

"Very funny, Cassandra. But what if it breaks down? I don't know if I want a redneck grease monkey under her hood."

Cassie put her hands on her hips, reminding herself of Aunt Lucinda. She quickly dropped them. "Just because they have accents doesn't mean they're ignorant, Andrew. Most of the boys I grew up with could rebuild your car from a junk pile and it would perform better than it does now." Cassie chewed on her lip, wondering why she had jumped to the defense of Southerners. It wasn't like she was one anymore. She had rid herself of her accent along with her long hair and penchant for fried foods—although she still couldn't bring herself to wear white shoes after Labor Day or before Easter.

Andrew sighed. "All right. You can borrow my car. But you have to promise me you'll take care of it, and have it waxed at least once."

She pulled him closer and kissed him. "Thank you. I promise I'll take care of it."

Several hours later, in the predawn morning, they caught the first train to Greenwich, Connecticut, and took his car out of the garage. Andrew loaded her luggage into the small trunk of the compact Mercedes, and spent twenty minutes going over things she could and couldn't do with his car.

When there was nothing left to be said, he took her in his arms and kissed her deeply, his hands sliding down her back in the practiced way he knew she liked. "I'll miss you," he murmured into her neck. "And I hope all goes well with your father—call me and let me know how things are going."

"Thanks, and I will." She brushed his lips with hers. "I'll miss you, too," she said, as she pulled away and settled into the front seat.

She shut the door, put the car in gear, and sent him a brave smile. She couldn't shake the feeling that this parting was somehow permanent. Swallowing the thick lump in her throat, she shouted, "I'll call you," then pulled away.

Her glance in the rearview mirror revealed Andrew standing in the parking lot, staring after his car until it rounded a corner and he disappeared from sight.

CHAPTER 2

It was nearly nine o'clock in the morning by the time Cassie started out, the late June sun not yet warm enough to burn the dew off the grass of the immaculate yards she passed. If she drove fast, she'd be in Walton around midnight. She knew the directions by heart. Shortly after moving to New York, when the pull of things familiar was almost more than she could stand, she had stopped at a AAA office and received a TripTik. The pages were now worn and crinkled, the holes around the plastic binding torn in places. Despite the car's built-in GPS, the TripTik lay on the passenger seat, unopened, just in case she got lost.

She fed CDs into the stereo, singing aloud to keep her thoughts at bay. She would have to deal with them soon enough. The little red car took her first through New Jersey, then Pennsylvania, then across the Mason-Dixon Line and into Virginia. As the sun slipped behind the painted edges of clouds, she swung through North Carolina, the smudge of the Blue Ridge visible on the far horizon. The temperature and humidity rose in steady degrees the farther south she drove, but she was somehow loath to raise the windows and turn on the air-conditioning. Feeling the dampness on her skin and hearing the screeching of the summer insects brought her closer to home faster than the steady roll of road under her tires. She thought of her father, but dared not think of anything beyond that: not of seeing her sister again, nor of Joe. Instead, she studied the endless asphalt stretched out in front of her, the dotted line like a yellow brick road to follow home.

After nightfall, she clipped the northwest corner of South Carolina and entered Georgia. She wasn't sure if it was her imagination, but the air seemed to change. It was as if the red dirt permeated the air, altering it somewhat, distinguishing it from the more ordinary air of other states. She could almost smell the Confederate rose and jasmine that clung to the back porch of her father's house, and a longing to be there, to see her father, consumed her so fiercely that she pushed the gas pedal down further.

She had just passed the Walton welcoming sign, WHERE EVERYBODY IS SOMEBODY, when the gas indicator light blinked on the dash, then glowed a solid red. She was sure Andrew had told her how much reserve was in the tank once it hit empty, but she didn't remember. There were no other cars on the road, just hers, and the black stretch of lonely highway. She spotted a small reflector sign that said, GAS—24 HOURS, then followed the arrows off the interstate onto a road that led through the small-business district of Walton, Georgia. The road seemed familiar to her, but not the landmarks. Things had changed. She recognized the corner where Virgil's Soda Shop and the drive-in theater had once been, and blinked hard. A carpet warehouse and a fast-food restaurant, in squat, square buildings, stood there instead.

The streetlights were the only illumination, all of the businesses shrouded in darkness at the late hour. A flickering sign guided her down the street toward the gas station, and she paused in front of it, almost smiling as she read the neon lettering: BAIT. GAS. CAPPUCCINO. The cappuccino part was new, but Cassie knew the gas station well. It had been a high school hangout and owned by the father of a boy she had gone to school with. She couldn't think of the boy's name, but remembered how he had hung around the fringe of their group, as if basking in the light of Harriet's glow, but afraid to get too close.

Cassie pulled up to a gas pump and jumped out of the car, eager to be done with it and on her way. She was so close now. A handwritten sign was duct-taped to the front of the pump: AFTER DARK, PLEASE PAY INSIDE FIRST. She opened the car door, yanked out her keys and purse, then locked the door with a quiet beep from the remote. Squinting to see in the dim yellow glow of outdoor lighting, she spied a large plate-glass window and door, with a man standing inside behind a counter. She walked across the parking lot and through the door.

Cassie crossed the cracked linoleum tiles, passed the racks of Moon Pies, breath mints, and chewing tobacco, and handed the man her American Express card. "I'd like to fill my tank with premium, and get a cup of cappuccino, please."

Deep blue eyes stared back at her from a face of well-worn leather surrounded by a cottony strip of white hair on top and a beard. The face looked vaguely familiar, but she preferred to remain incognito. She was back in town to see her father, not to stage an embarrassing homecoming. A homecoming that would surely dredge up unwelcome memories.

He smiled, then handed back her card. "Sorry, ma'am. I cain't take American Express."

She frowned. She'd meant to stop at an ATM on the way to get more cash but had been reluctant to delay her arrival any more than she had to. "Oh. Would you take a personal check, then?"

"Sure can. I'll just need to see a driver's license."

A chair skidded behind her, and she whirled to see a tall man unfolding himself from a stool to stand. He wore jeans and cowboy boots, and his button-down shirt had the sleeves rolled up above his wrists, exposing tanned forearms.

"I'll fill your tank for you, ma'am."

Cassie stalled, not sure whether Andrew would approve of this man's being near the Mercedes. "That's all right. I can manage."

Blue eyes regarded her, and she realized they were the same deep hue as the old man's. The younger man sent a look toward his father as a smile warmed his mouth. She had the distinct impression she was being laughed at.

"The pump's a bit stiff, and you need a big grip to hold it down." He leaned an elbow on the counter. " 'Sides, I wouldn't feel right makin' a lady pump her own gas while I sit inside here. Don't worry—you won't need to tip me."

She narrowed her eyes at him, trying to ignore the handsome crease lines around his mouth when he smiled. She wasn't wild about standing outside and being eaten alive by mosquitoes as she filled her tank anyway. If he really wanted to, then he was welcome to it. "All right. I just need to unlock the gas tank first."

He followed her outside, and she fervently wished she had worn jeans instead of the short skirt she had pulled from her closet. He moved around the side of the car near the pump as she unlocked the tank. "It takes premium."

"Got it," he said with a smile that made her wonder whether she should hang out a little longer to make sure he knew what premium gas was. The man just stared back at her and she had a feeling

25

that he knew exactly what she was thinking.

She turned to go back inside, then called over her shoulder, "Thank you." The words seemed unfamiliar, but somehow necessary. She didn't wait for him to answer before returning inside.

Facing the older man, she asked, "Could you please tell me where the cappuccino machine is?"

The white-haired man stood with a grunt, and came around from the back of the counter. "The dang thing's over here. Haven't had too much business for it—but it was my son's idea. He goes away to college and comes back with all sorts of crazy ideas. So I'm cleaning and filling this here machine every day." He hitched up his overalls over a considerable mound at his middle, and ambled to the back of the store. "Don't tell anyone, but now he's got me drinkin' it, too. Helps me stay awake when the late-shift help don't show up and I need to fill in. Course, I add a drop of JD to sweeten it a bit." He winked and reached for a stack of Styrofoam cups.

Cassie looked out the large window at the younger man. He stood next to the car, waiting for the gas to finish pumping, tossing a coin in the air and catching it. His sandy-colored hair was a bit longer than she was used to, just brushing the back of his collar, but it suited him. He was probably like an Italian sports car: nice to look at but not much under the hood. She wondered what his major in college had been. Probably phys ed.

Their eyes met through the glass. *Darn.* She'd been staring. She quickly took a sip from her steaming cup of cappuccino, immediately burning her lip and tongue.

"Dangnabit!"

The older man slipped her a glance. "Careful— it's hot."

"Yeah. I noticed." She pulled her checkbook out of her purse. "How much do I owe you?"

He lowered his eyeglasses on his nose and examined a small monitor. "That'll be thirty-nine seventy-five."

The bell over the door rang and she felt the younger man enter, but didn't turn around. She placed the cup on the counter and wrote out the check, then slid it over.

The older man examined it closely, then slid it back to her.

"Sorry, ma'am. Cain't take an out-of-state check, and this one says you're from New York."

She held back an exasperated sigh. "Fine. Do you have an ATM machine nearby?"

The man sent her a blank stare, then handed the check to his son. She noticed the young man's hands as he bent over the check: long and tapered, the knuckles bony ripples under the smooth skin. No car grease staining the nail beds, either.

His eyes met hers, lighting with some sort of amusement. "We can take her check, Dad. I know her."

"Oh, really?" Cassie resisted the impulse to put her hands on her hips.

"You're Cassie Madison. We went to high school together, and the first two years of junior college."

She examined him closely, an alarm starting to go off inside her head. Instinctively, her hand flew to the charm necklace around her neck.

"I was with you when you heard the news about Joe running off with Harriet the night of our sophomore fall formal in college. I held your head over the bushes while you threw up."

Cassie realized the sound of a deflating tire was coming from her own mouth, and she closed it. She should have figured it out as soon as the old man had said the word "son," but she'd been too preoccupied with getting out of there as quickly as she could. She remembered a young man of twenty with braces and thick glasses that magnified his eyes until they seemed to cover most of his face. Sam Parker: the third-to-last person on earth she ever wanted to see again.

"You've . . . changed." Those were the only words she could force out.

His eyes brightened. "So have you."

"I'm surprised you remember."

Half of his mouth turned up. "It's not something a person forgets."

She dug in her purse to find her keys, trying to hide the flush rising on her face. "Well, you have my permission to forget it now."

As she'd tried to do for years. But the recollection of her waiting for Joe on the front porch of her daddy's house wearing her purple taffeta dress and the promise ring Joe had given her was written in indelible ink on the creases of her memory. She could still see Sam's face as he walked up the porch steps and handed her the note from Joe and Harriet. The urge to throw up had hit her as soon as she saw both their names scrawled at the bottom of the letter.

Mr. Parker came around the counter. "I guess you're here to see your dad. I'm real sorry to hear the judge is doing so poorly. The sight of you should perk him right up."

His eyes warmed her, his sympathy sincere. For some reason, she wanted to cry, and quickly blinked away the tears.

"Thank you." She swallowed. "I have to go now. They're expecting me."

Sam spoke softly. "You can't—you're leaking transmission fluid. Didn't you feel the engine jump a little bit?"

She stared at him blankly. "Not exactly."

"Well, we don't have the right kind, but we can get it for you. Just not tonight. Dad'll take care of it tomorrow. For now, let me drive you home."

She wanted to decline, since every time she looked at him she relived the biggest humiliation of her life. But she relented, realizing her options were limited. "All right."

He didn't move, but seemed to expect her to say something else.

"Thank you," she added. "But it's not my home anymore. I'm just here for a visit."

Sam sent her a sidelong glance before stepping outside, holding the door for her as she followed him to the extended cab of his pickup truck.

He moved her luggage to the truck, and then held the passenger-side door open for her to get in. She looked at the big step up, and wondered how she would climb up in her short skirt.

Sam turned his head away, and she hoisted her skirt up around her hips to climb up, then settled it back down as she backed into the seat. The truck appeared to be new, the aroma of leather still strong inside.

Sam closed her door, then approached the driver's side, pausing at the open door as his cell phone beeped with a message. He looked down at the screen, his eyebrows tucked into a slight frown. "Looks like I'm heading in your direction anyway."

Sam slid easily onto the bench seat of the truck. Cassie had half expected to find a gun rack or a Confederate flag in the rear window and was almost disappointed to discover the window empty and nothing in the backseat except for a black bag.

He shifted the truck into gear and moved it out onto the road. "You've been gone a long time, Cassie."

She turned away from him, looking out the side window. "People call me Cassandra now, and yes, I have."

He seemed intent on ignoring her body language, and filled the empty air with questions. "Sounds like you've made a pretty big name for yourself in New York. Your daddy's real proud of you. All he talks about these days are his girls and his grandkids."

Cassie only nodded her head.

He was silent for a moment. "I just never figured you to be the type to run away from things."

She whipped her head around to stare at him, sure she could see the trace of a smile on his lips.

"Now don't you go and be getting all mad at me. I'm just stating a fact. I never thought I'd see the day when Cassie Madison let a situation get the best of her."

Cassie sat up straight in the seat. "I didn't. I always knew that this town wasn't the place for me. The timing just seemed to work out, that's all. I'd always planned to leave."

"And never come back—even for holidays? Did it never occur to you that there were people here who loved you and missed you?"

She turned to look at his strong profile, the passing street lamps casting mottled light on his face. The man had certainly changed since she'd last seen him—and all for the better. The fact that he'd given her disappearance any thought at all surprised her. She hadn't thought about Sam Parker once in the fifteen years she'd been away.

Squirming in her seat, she turned away. "I meet my daddy every year in Atlanta and we do all our catching up then. That's enough." Folding her arms across her chest, she added, "I'd rather not talk about this now."

He leaned forward and turned on the radio to a country station with a man singing a song about his dog Jake. Cassie gritted her teeth, wishing for the soothing New Age tones Andrew liked to pipe through the hidden Bose speakers in their apartment.

"I guess not talking much is another thing you learned up north."

"What do you mean—another thing?"

He shrugged his shoulders, stretching one arm along the back of the bench seat. "Well, I don't remember you being so snooty before. But I do recall how you always got mean when you were scared."

She glared at him. Then, without speaking, she reached for the volume control on the radio to make it louder so she couldn't hear him. She was already riddled with guilt and Sam was only making her feel worse.

With the radio blaring, they drove back to the interstate and took the next exit. It was then that she noticed her teeth were chattering, even though the night was warm, balmy almost. Within ten minutes they were passing Walton First United Methodist on the left, the illuminated sign outside offering up its message from Reverend Beasley. NEED A NEW LOOK? HAVE YOUR FAITH LIFTED HERE. She remembered Reverend Beasley putting up a new sign every week, and wondered if he still did.

Sam stopped at a deserted intersection, where a corner of the high school was visible two blocks down. He turned right onto Orchard Street, and past the familiar houses of the Ladues, the Pritchards, and elderly Mrs. Harris. Then another right on Madison Lane, the ancient oak trees creating a veil over the street. The houses were more sparsely set here, getting farther and farther apart until all that was left was the end of the street and a long gravel driveway. Cassie turned her head, staring at two under-contract signs at houses on either side of her father's property. Sam turned off the radio, and the night sounds buzzed all around them.

Slowly, they bumped over the gravel road, the only light that of the moon drifting through the lane of oaks, stealing the colors from the land-scape, turning the red hood gray. The large white house loomed before them, the sight as comforting to her as her mother's arms, and the old memories hit her again. She felt a gentle touch on her forearm.

"Are you all right?"

She nodded, suddenly not trusting her voice.

He parked the truck in the circular drive, then reached into the backseat and pulled out the black bag. He got out and walked to her side of the truck as Cassie tried to let herself out. But her efforts were hampered by her short skirt, and she would have fallen out the door if it hadn't been for Sam's arm guiding her down. His hand held hers for a moment, his palm surprisingly soft and warm.

"It'll be fine, you know," he said softly, his Southern accent soothing to her ears.

Cassie removed her hand. "I know. It just takes a little getting used to. I can handle this." She shut her mouth abruptly, cringing at the quavering of her voice. Her hand reached up, her fingers hugging the charms on the necklace tightly.

He watched her hand with a small smile, but didn't say anything more.

They walked up the porch steps centered between two of the six fluted columns. Cassie stopped, her confidence sagging. Sam walked ahead of her and put his hand on the doorknob of the screen.

"Shouldn't we knock first?" she suggested, trying to buy time.

He tugged the door open, releasing the poignant aromas of furniture polish and old wood. "I usually don't. Besides, they're expecting me."

She sent him a quizzical look. "What?"

Before he could answer, the patter of running

feet on wood floors cascaded toward them, the sound of shouting children reaching them before anyone came into view.

A towheaded boy of about five ran toward Sam, his head bent like a rampaging bull's. "Dr. Parker!" he screeched as Sam lifted the little boy high over his head.

"Doctor . . . ?" Cassie stopped as the sound of more little feet brought her head around. A small girl with red braids ran pell-mell toward her, shrieking, "Aunt Cassie," at the top of her lungs. Her arms were outstretched, and Cassie quickly stretched her arms wide, too, to catch the little girl.

Cassie stood there, awkwardly hugging a child she had never seen before in the foyer that had lived only in her dreams for over a decade. She watched the slender figure of a woman appear at the top of the staircase and then gallop down the wooden stairs, another familiar sound that twanged on the strings of Cassie's memory.

The woman stopped in front of her and smiled her toothy cheerleader smile, the smile that had always reminded Cassie of their mother. She smelled of roses and talcum powder and baby spit-up, and Cassie felt disoriented for a moment, looking at this grown woman she knew but didn't know.

Harriet's smile never wavered. "Welcome home, Cassie."

CHAPTER 3

Harriet reached for her sister, but Cassie stiffened in the embrace, the ghost of forgiveness long absent. Harriet pulled back, her smile fading slightly. "It's good to see you. You look just wonderful." She placed the flat of her hand against the blunt edges of Cassie's chestnut bob, making it bounce. "You look so . . . sophisticated." She dropped her arm, feeling suddenly shy. "It suits you."

Harriet stared up at her sister, only fifteen months older, and still a full head taller. Cassie's strength and confidence had always made Harriet feel protected, even before their mother's death when Cassie was eight and Harriet was seven had forced Cassie into the role permanently. They had been the best of friends ever since Cassie could pick Harriet out of her crib when she cried. Cassie hadn't even minded when their mother held her back a year in school so she and Harriet would start kindergarten together. They had shared everything. Until Joe.

Cassie spoke slowly. "You look . . . well, you look the same."

Feeling self-conscious, Harriet touched her shoulder-length hair she still wore pulled back from her face with a fabric headband, realizing how unstylish she must look now to her glamorous sister. And how really wonderful and nearly unrecognizable Cassie now appeared.

The child at Cassie's knees began hopping up and down, her arms reaching up for her to be held. Harriet swooped down to pick up her daughter as her words spilled out in a rush. "We let the kids stay up tonight at Pop-pop's house because they were so excited about seeing you. That's Joey, by the way," she said, indicating her son, being jostled up and down on Sam's back. "And this is four-year-old Knoxie—we named her after Grandma Knox on account of the red hair. We've just been hoping she didn't get Grandma's foul temper, too, although the old woman did have a lot of sweetness in her when she wanted to—"

"How's Daddy?" Cassie interrupted.

Harriet closed her mouth, feeling chastised, and wondering why she'd been rambling in the first place. She handed Knoxie to Cassie, then went to pry Joey off of Sam. "He was complaining about not being able to sleep, so I paged the doctor. You remember Sam Parker, don't you? Saved me and a bunch of us seniors from failing biology and algebra. He was with us at the junior college, remember? Then, I guess it was after you left, he went away for school, and we're just all so grateful to have him back."

Sam relinquished the squirming boy on his back and headed for the stairs. "I certainly remember

37

Cassie. Didn't recognize her at first, though, until I saw the back of her head."

Cassie's cheeks pinkened. With a tight smile, she said, "Funny, I hardly remember Sam at all." She turned back to Harriet. "Can I see Daddy now?"

Harriet nodded, reaching for Knoxie. "He's . . . he's not at all like you saw him last time, so try not to be shocked when you see him."

"I can handle it," Cassie said, and followed Sam up the stairs.

After quickly sitting both kids in front of the Disney Channel with strict instructions not to move, Harriet went upstairs to try to interpret the undercurrent between Cassie and Sam, and wondering why all of the "I'm sorrys" she'd planned on saying when she'd seen her sister for the first time had remained unspoken.

She caught up to them as Cassie and Sam reached the dark double doors at the end of the long upstairs hallway. Harriet's two oldest daughters, Madison and Sarah Frances, sat cross-legged on the floor outside the door, leaning against the hallway wall, their heads propped against each other, their eyes closed, and apparently sound asleep. Sarah Frances had honey-colored hair like Harriet, but Madison's hair was two shades darker—not dark enough to be brown, but not light enough to be called dirty blond. It was no-man's brown, as Cassie used to lament over her own hair, hair that now glinted with highlights that hadn't been put there by the sun. Harriet paused for a moment to study her girls, struck by how much they resembled her and Cassie before more than just their hair color had changed.

Sam tapped lightly on the door, then pushed it open. He stepped back, allowing Cassie and Harriet to enter first.

Cassie paused on the threshold. Sam seemed to sense her hesitation and rested his hand firmly on her shoulder as Harriet tried to see the room through the eyes of someone who hadn't seen it for over a decade. The dark hues of the room, the burgundies, navies, and forest greens, underscored the fact that there had been no feminine influence on the decor for more than twenty years. An old man, his emaciated frame barely making the covers rise, rested in the imposing four-poster bed. It stood high off the floor, a family heirloom in which generations of their family had slept. The man was barely recognizable as the robust father of their memory, but when he opened his eyes, almost black against the pasty white of his face, Cassie's face showed recognition and relief. Straightening her shoulders, she walked toward the bed.

A pale hand, the blue veins visible beneath the paper-thin surface, reached for her, and Cassie held it, cupping it gently between hers like a child holding a butterfly. Harriet looked away, feeling the ever-present guilt at having been the one partially responsible for Cassie's long absence, and for separating her father from his favorite child. But not for anything else; she would never feel regret or guilt for anything that had transpired all those years ago. It was the only way, especially in the beginning, in which Harriet could face each day.

"Hi, Daddy. I'm here," Cassie said. "It's about time," he said, then closed his eyes. His hand went slack in hers, and she turned to Sam in a panic as Harriet stepped closer to the bed.

"Is he all right?" Cassie asked.

Sam stepped closer, pulling a stethoscope from his bag. "I'm sure he's fine. He was just waiting up for you to come home before he could go to sleep. Sort of like when you were a teenager."

Cassie stroked their father's cheek before moving back from the bed to allow Sam to examine their father. "Not likely. I wasn't the one with a different date every night of the week." She sent a sidelong glance toward Harriet. More softly, she said, "He'll even tell you that most of his gray hairs weren't caused by me."

Sam gave her a disbelieving stare before he leaned over the old man with his stethoscope. "That's not how I remember it."

"Me neither," Harriet said quietly, although she was no longer sure of how much truth was in either statement.

Cassie crossed her arms over her chest. Ignoring both of them, she asked, "Is he okay?"

Sam straightened, taking the stethoscope from his ears. "He's just sleeping." Sam fixed her with a steady gaze. "And when he awakes, we can talk about that unsolved incident our senior year in high school when somebody painted Principal Purdy's front porch hot pink while he slept."

Harriet stifled a laugh as she watched Cassie's ears turn red, remembering how she'd lied straight to her father's face for the first and only time in her life so Cassie wouldn't get in trouble, and how the memory of the pink porch still made her smile.

Cassie squeezed his arm. "Oh, Lord, Sam. You're not going to tell anybody, are you?"

His shoulders shook with laughter as he put the stethoscope back into his bag. "Cassie, that was more than fifteen years ago. Do you think anybody still cares?"

Cassie's chin jutted out in the direction of the old man on the bed. "He would." She swallowed thickly. "Is he . . . is he going to be all right?"

Sam sent a glance toward Harriet before taking Cassie by the elbow and leading her toward the door. He leveled his gaze on her and spoke quietly. "I'm going to be blunt with you because Harriet wants me to and because I know you want to hear the truth. No, he won't. You're probably not aware, but this isn't his first heart attack, and his heart is too weakened now to fully recover. I'm afraid it's only a matter of time." He paused for a moment. "I'm sorry."

Harriet watched as Cassie pulled back her shoulders, reminding her for the first time since her return of the old Cassie. "Have you considered anything else? What about surgery or a transplant?"

Sam shook his head. "I've exhausted all viable options, Cassie. He wouldn't survive surgery, and a transplant is out of the question at his age. I'm sorry, but there's nothing we can do."

Cassie's eyes glistened with unshed tears. "If you don't mind, I'd like to get a second opinion. Not to sound rude, but where did you get your medical degree, anyway?"

Harriet closed her eyes briefly, waiting for Sam's response. The undercurrent between Sam and Cassie remained thick, like molasses in January, and Harriet was no longer sure whether Sam's usual gentle bedside manner would work on her sister.

Annoyance flickered in Sam's eyes. "Harvard. Perhaps you've heard of it."

"Oh." Cassie's shoulders slumped as if her fighting spirit had deserted her. "May I stay with him for a while? I promise I won't wake him."

Sam paused for a moment. "Sure. Harriet knows what to do if he awakens, and I'll be back in the morning to check on things. You try to get some rest." He opened the door, then turned back toward

Cassie. "And I'd bet my best hunting dog that the judge has known about the pink porch all along." With a wave toward both of them, he stepped into the hallway and closed the door behind him.

Harriet felt momentarily unsure of her position, a feeling she'd grown unfamiliar with as the years of being a wife and mother had rendered uncertainty obsolete. "Do you want me to stay?"

Cassie looked at her as if becoming aware of her presence for the first time. Harriet's unspoken words of apology dangled on her lips, but she still couldn't say them, knowing that they would never be the exact words that Cassie would want to hear.

"I don't care," she said as she turned toward the bed just as their father's eyes opened. Cassie walked closer and sat on the bed, while Harriet remained where she was by the door, unable or unwilling to leave.

His voice sounded small and distant. "You've cut your hair shorter since I last saw you. Makes you look more like your mother." He sighed softly. "Sure wish she was here. Then she could give you a dressing-down, since I don't have the strength right now."

"Thanks, Daddy. It's good to see you, too." Cassie kissed him on his withered cheek, then bent her head as if she were trying to hide the tears that fell down her cheeks. Their father patted the mattress next to him, and she collapsed beside him, her head sharing his stack of pillows. She looked like the terrified child Harriet felt like, faced with losing one of the last remaining anchors to their childhood.

Cassie reached for his hand and held on tightly. "I miss Mama. I wonder . . ." Cassie sniffled, then snuggled closer. "I wonder if things would have turned out differently if she had been here."

Harriet stiffened, wondering if her father knew she was in the room, and waited quietly for his answer.

The judge spoke with his eyes closed. "If you mean she might have known about Joe and Harriet and stopped them, I don't think so. Even you can see now that they were meant for each other."

Cassie turned away. "He was mine." She sounded childish, as if they were talking about a favorite doll, her voice at odds with the image of the sophisticated woman with the expensive clothes and shining hair.

"Yes, Cassie. He was yours. But that was a long time ago. He and Harriet have a wonderful marriage now, and five children." He paused, taking deep, labored breaths. "It pains me to see how in all these years you haven't even tried to make peace with your sister. Harriet's tried so many times to reach out to you. And you've made no effort at all to get to know your nieces and nephew. They're fine children, Cassie. You'd be proud of them."

Cassie couldn't hide a sob. "I know—and I'm

sorry. I've kept all their pictures in my photo album, and I do think about them all the time. But it still hurts, Daddy. It still hurts. Sometimes I don't know if I'll ever get over it."

Harriet's own eyes stung with tears and she wanted nothing more than to slink out of the room, but she had the sensation that Cassie had forgotten she was even there.

"What still hurts, Cassie? The fact that you lost Joe, or that somebody got the best of you?"

Cassie's eyes widened, as if she were only then realizing the possibility of truth in his words. "I don't know anymore. I honestly don't know. Maybe it's just an old habit that I don't know how to break. Or maybe I just can't get over the fact that you were on her side. You didn't do anything to bring them back."

Harriet shook her head, remembering the blistering words her father had delivered to both her and Joe on their return to Walton as a married couple, and the feeling that never went away that something precious and irreplaceable had been lost forever.

The old man shifted in his bed. "It wasn't a matter of taking sides. I didn't like the manner in which they let their feelings be known, but I knew deep down that they were meant for each other. And that, in time, you would forgive them and find somebody who was really yours."

His voice sank to barely a whisper. "It's been

fifteen years, Cassie. It's time to get over it. Get on with your life."

Abruptly, Cassie left the bed and went to the window. "You always took her side. I guess that will never change. But I am over it." She paused. "I'm thirty-five years old, Daddy. I've outgrown all that. I have a new life, and none of that matters anymore. This town, these people—I've left it all way behind me." She sighed, pressing her forehead against the glass. "And the more I've stayed away, the easier it became to not come back."

The judge struggled to sit up on his elbows. Harriet took a step forward to help him, but Cassie was faster, steadying him and then propping the pillows behind him.

His voice sounded strained. "You can go to the moon, Cassandra Lee Madison, but this place, these people, will always run in your blood. You can't get away from it, so you might as well come home."

Cassie helped him lie back against the pillows, the bright spots of pink slowly fading from his face. Harriet stepped forward to help, knowing that Cassie had never been able to back away from a fight with their father. He was stubborn, but it was a trait Cassie had inherited from him. Harriet's eyes met Cassie's and she shook her head to get her to stop, but Cassie looked away as if she hadn't seen her at all. Firmly, Cassie said, "This isn't my home anymore."

His long, bony fingers tightened around Cassie's forearm as Harriet placed a hand on his shoulder, his voice quiet but still just as forceful and fearsome as it was when they were little and Cassie had been caught telling a lie. "The hell it's not. And there's nothing you can do that'll change that. If I have any say in the matter at all, you'll come back to stay."

Cassie surprised Harriet by leaning forward to kiss his forehead. Gently, she said, "You don't have any say. I'll stay here until you get better, but then I'm going back home—to New York."

He didn't answer, and his eyelids fluttered closed. Harriet and Cassie stood on opposite sides of the bed for a long moment, staring down at their sleeping father while years of unspoken words nestled beside him.

Harriet spoke quietly to her sister. "Let me get you something to eat and walk you to your room. I'm sure you're exhausted from the long drive."

"No," Cassie said, the word sharp. "I want to stay here with him." She lay back down beside him, her hand folded around his, and closed her eyes. Long ago, when they were still children, Cassie had told Harriet how for about a month after their mother died she'd spent nights under their father's bed, listening to his breathing. Their mother had given up her long fight with cancer in this room, and Cassie as a little girl had thought that if she had been there, she would have heard the moment her mother stopped breathing, and been able to awaken her. But she had died, and Cassie had vowed to herself that she wouldn't allow the same thing to happen to her father.

The story saddled a young Harriet with guilt, knowing that as she had slept peacefully in her own room down the hall, Cassie had kept vigil over their father, dozing off and on, and pinching herself awake as the night wore on, until gray dawn eased its way through the dust ruffle. When her father rose to take his shower, Cassie would escape into her room to sleep for two hours before Aunt Lucinda jerked open her curtains. She had done that until one morning her father had stuck his head under the bed and told her she was too old to be sleeping there.

Harriet was about to ask her again if she wanted something to eat when she saw their father's hand squeeze Cassie's. With his eyes still closed, he said, "I think painting Principal Purdy's porch showed a lot of spunk, you know. I just hope that by now you've learned there are better means to get your point across."

Cassie's eyes widened in surprise. "So you really did know. Why didn't you tell me?"

He shifted under the covers. "Because then I would have had to punish you, and you didn't deserve it."

Cassie stuck out her chin, reminding Harriet so much of the old Cassie that she almost smiled.

"You're damned right I didn't. He wanted to cancel prom because of some silly food fight in the cafeteria—and not even everybody was involved. It just wasn't fair."

The judge let out a soft grunt. "It was a damned fine stunt. And you should know that I laughed for about an hour straight after I saw it."

They laughed quietly together for a moment. Finally, Cassie said, "Thanks, Daddy. For not getting me in trouble."

"You're welcome." His voice sounded tired. "I'm glad you're home." He looked at Harriet and held out his other hand toward her. "We both are."

Cassie said nothing, but squeezed his hand. Knowing she wouldn't leave, Harriet bent down to kiss her father's forehead before leaving to retrieve an extra blanket from the cedar chest in the hall to put over Cassie.

When she returned she saw that Cassie had found a spot on the floor, a pillow from the bed tucked under her head, sound asleep. Harriet gently laid the blanket on top of her, then flipped off the light before gently closing the door behind her.

THE FOLLOWING MORNING, Maddie stood at the door to her grandfather's bedroom as her mother pressed her ear to the door. Turning back toward Maddie, she whispered, "Your aunt and grandfather are still sleeping, and you may not disturb them. I'm sure Aunt Cassie is dying to see you, too, but she's exhausted from her long drive. Just give her time to get up and dressed, and I bet she'll even tell you stories about New York City."

Maddie looked at her mother, wondering once again how this small, blond woman could really be her mama. The only thing they had in common was their green eyes. Even her mother commented frequently about how much Maddie was the spitting image of her Aunt Cassie—right down to the long legs that allowed both Cassie and Maddie to make her mama look shorter than she already was. Sometimes her mother would say that Maddie and Aunt Cassie shared more than just a physical resemblance, whatever that meant.

"Well, butter my butt and call me a biscuit."

Her mother made a sound like somebody sucking on a straw in an empty glass. "Madison Cassandra Warner! I'm going to wash your mouth out with soap if I ever hear you use that expression again."

"But it's already ten o'clock! Is she going to sleep forever?"

Before her mother could answer, the door opened and Aunt Cassie stood there, blinking in the bright light and staring at them with brown, puffy eyes. As she shut the door behind her, she gave them a funny smile, as if all of her face muscles weren't awake yet.

"So, you must be my namesake."

Maddie stared at the stranger in front of her, the

face familiar only from pictures. She noticed how Aunt Cassie's hair was lighter now instead of the yucky shade of brown her own was, and how cool it looked even though she still had bed-head. She felt a prod from her mother's knuckle in her back. Feeling suddenly shy, she said, "Yes, ma'am. I'm Maddie." She gave her aunt an awkward hug, then stepped back.

Maddie watched as her mother looked at her and then at Cassie, as if seeing them together for the first time was like scoring a touchdown. In a funny-sounding voice, her mama said, "I know you two have a lot of catching up to do, but I've seen Cassie before she's had her coffee and it's just plain nasty."

Aunt Cassie yawned and wrinkled her nose at Maddie's mama, making Maddie smile because it reminded her of something she and Sarah Frances would do.

Squeezing Maddie around the shoulders, her mama said, "You, missy, need to go eat your breakfast and I'll go round up some coffee."

"I'll get it." Maddie ran to the kitchen. After finding two clean mugs in her grandfather's cabinets and filling them with black coffee, she carefully headed back upstairs to her aunt's old room. When Maddie came to stay with her grandfather, this was the room she used. The pink canopy bed and rose wallpaper with matching bedspread and curtains were the same ones Aunt

Cassie had had when she was a girl. Sleeping under the tiny roses had always made Maddie feel a connection to the aunt she'd been named after but had never met.

She was about to enter the room when she heard her mother's voice and she stopped, afraid she might interrupt. Especially if it meant her mama and Aunt Cassie were going to talk about why her aunt had been gone for so many years, and why there was that look on Aunt Cassie's face that reminded Maddie what her little sister Knoxie looked like when she couldn't find her favorite blanket.

"It's so good to see you here again. I guess I never gave up hoping."

Aunt Cassie laughed, except it didn't seem like a real laugh. "Just don't get used to me being here— it's only until Daddy gets better and then I have to go back."

"And if he doesn't? What then?"

Maddie bent her head into the steam from the mugs, not wanting to hear the answer.

"He will. People survive heart attacks all the time."

"I'm glad you're back," Maddie's mama said again. "There's been lots I've wanted to say to you over the years and I finally have the chance."

The mugs were beginning to feel heavy in her hands, but Maddie wasn't leaving now.

"If this is about you and Joe, I don't want to talk

about it. It's over and done with and I can't see any good coming from it if you drag it all out now."

Maddie jerked her arm, spilling hot coffee on her hand, but she forced herself to remain quiet. *You and Joe.* What did she mean?

She had to strain to hear her mama speak. "I never wanted to hurt you. I don't know if you can believe that any more now than you could then, but it's true. And I need you to know that."

"If you think that little apology can erase fifteen years of humiliation and hurt, you're wrong. Which is why I don't want to discuss it."

Maddie heard the squeak of bedsprings and quickly ducked into the next bedroom, somehow managing not to spill any more coffee. Footsteps emerged from Aunt Cassie's room, then stopped. And when her mother spoke again, Maddie thought she might be crying.

"You were my best friend, Cassie. My hero. And I want you back in my life. In all our lives."

Aunt Cassie didn't say anything. Finally, Maddie heard her mother say, "I love you, Cassie. I'm glad you're back." Maddie listened as her mother walked across the hall and then down the stairs.

Aunt Cassie didn't move for a long time, and Maddie stayed where she was, afraid to make a noise, the coffee cooling in her hands. She was about to tiptoe from the room when she heard her Aunt Cassie say, very quietly, "I love you, too, Harriet."

CHAPTER 4

Cassie's luggage had already been brought up to her old room, and she grabbed her overnight bag with shampoo, conditioner, and razor, then stumbled into the bathroom.

She showered quickly, using a trick she had learned in graduate school of keeping the water cold. Not only did it cut down on showering time, but it also made one alert and ready for the morning. Cassie was pretty sure she'd need every ounce of alertness she could muster. The thought of seeing Joe again made her hand tremble, and she cut her leg with the razor.

She turned off the water and opened the curtain, realizing there were no towels on the rack. Shivering, she remembered a clean towel someone had put on her bed. "Dangnabit," she muttered under her breath. She grabbed a wad of tissue and stuck it to her cut knee. Then, with wet hair dripping down her face, she stuck her head out the door. The hallway was blessedly deserted. She clutched her clothes in a ball in front of her and took two quick steps across the wood floor before her wet heel slid out from under her and she landed with a loud thump on her bare backside.

To her horror, she watched the door to her father's bedroom open, and Sam appeared in the doorway. His gaze scanned the hallway until it finally rested on her.

Cassie held her underwear to cover her breasts, the other hand clutching the rest of her clothes in her lap.

Sam cleared his throat. "Is that a New York thing?"

Her voice was unnaturally high-pitched. "Is what a New York thing?"

"Doing yoga while naked and dripping wet in the middle of a hallway."

She narrowed her eyes. "I slipped."

Sam left the doorway and began walking toward her. "Are you hurt?"

Cassie held her hand with the panties in front of her, then quickly pulled it back. "I'm fine. Please go away."

She could see he was trying to hide a smile. He turned back to the door. "You haven't changed as much as you think you have, you know."

"What's that supposed to mean? Besides, I'm two dress sizes smaller than I used to be. And I don't wear glasses anymore."

"That's not what I meant. But don't worry—it's a good thing. You were a pretty neat kid." He twisted the knob and opened the door. "Now go put some clothes on before somebody sees you."

She heard the laughter in his voice, but before she could reply he had closed the door behind him.

As soon as she heard the latch click, Cassie

bolted into her room and got dressed as quickly as she could. She dried her hair, taking care to curl the ends under, and put on her makeup. She'd need all the defenses she had to get through this day.

The smell of frying bacon wafted up to her, causing her stomach to rumble. She stalled in her room, hoping Joe and anybody else would be gone by the time she got downstairs. She certainly couldn't face him on an empty stomach.

As she walked toward the stairs, she saw that her father's door was open and approached, wanting to see if he was awake. She paused on the threshold, seeing Harriet sitting by the side of the bed and holding his hand. Cassie turned to go, but was called back by her father.

"Come in, Cassie. I'm not so sleepy now and I want to see my girls together."

She walked over to the other side of the bed and sat on the edge, digging her heels into the side rails like she'd done as a child. She slid her hand into his, and watched his face break out in a broad smile.

"I can die a happy man now." His hand squeezed Cassie's, the pressure so faint she cast a worried glance at her sister.

But Harriet was leaning forward, smoothing the hair off her father's forehead. "Don't say such things, Daddy. You're going to be just fine; you'll see."

Harriet turned away to pour water into a cup

from the bedside table, and Cassie's eyes met her father's. She read the love in them, and the fading strength. She also saw the good-bye.

The judge took a sip of the water, Harriet holding up his head. When she put the cup down, he put his hand in hers again. "My girls," he said, his eyes moist. "You've given me such joy all these years. Your mother would have been so proud."

Cassie looked down at a spot on the Oriental rug, blinking rapidly.

"Tell us about this Andrew you're thinking about marrying, Cassie. Is he planning on coming down for a visit? Because if he wants to ask my permission, he'd better hurry."

"Daddy," Cassie started to protest, then stopped when she noticed he had closed his eyes

"How many kids are you going to have?"

Her hand felt sweaty, trapped in the warm cocoon of her father's big fist. "We, um, we haven't really talked about that yet."

Her father nodded, his eyes still closed. "They'll need to know their cousins and their aunt and uncle."

"We'll visit." Cassie used her other hand to wipe her eyes. She caught her sister's gaze, then looked away.

Her father's voice had sunk low in his chest, his breathing raspy. "Do you still laugh a lot, Cassie? I've missed that the most." He swallowed deeply, then continued. "It was like that rush of popping bubbles after you pour a Coke. Effervescent. Yes, that's what he called it."

Cassie waited for him to catch his breath before asking, "What who called it?"

When he didn't answer, Harriet spoke softly. "Sam. He and Sam talk about you a lot."

Cassie flicked her sister a questioning look, and was about to ask why Sam would have any interest in her, when their father spoke again, his voice so low that Cassie had to lean down to hear.

"So, Cassie—do you still laugh?"

She sagged against the bed. "Sometimes, Daddy. Sometimes."

His eyes flickered open briefly, then closed again as he set his mouth in a stubborn line. "Mm-hmmm," he muttered, and Cassie squirmed. That had always been his sign that he was about to mete out punishment following a confession he had forced out of her. When he didn't say anything else, Cassie relaxed, feeling the stress leave her shoulders.

Harriet smoothed the hair off his forehead again. "You need to rest now, Daddy. I'll stay here in case you need anything."

He nodded, and Cassie leaned over to kiss him again, holding her head near his for a moment longer, feeling his breath on her cheek. "I love you, Daddy." Her voice cracked, and she bent her head close enough for his hair to rub her face.

"I love you, too."

Harriet looked at her sister. "You go get some breakfast. Aunt Lucinda is aching to see you. She's been frying up a storm all morning, waiting for you to come down."

Cassie nodded. "Okay. But call me if . . . if you need anything." As she turned to go, she thought she saw the trace of a grin on her father's lips, the type of grin he had always worn when he had a surprise for her. She turned back again, but his expression had gone slack, and his breathing held the steady rhythm of sleep.

Slowly, Cassie walked down the stairs, her stomach rumbling at the enticing aroma. As she descended, she paused at each portrait of her long-gone ancestors, naming them in her head, and stopping completely in front of the painting of old Great-great-great-grandfather Madison, who had built the home in 1848 to attract a bride. It must have worked, because the man had had four consecutive wives, giving him a total of nine children. Cassie stared into the dark brown eyes, recalling how she used to scare her sister with stories about how those eyes would watch Harriet as she walked up the stairs. Cassie smiled, remembering how Harriet wouldn't walk up the stairs alone for years.

She reached the kitchen and paused at the familiar sight of Aunt Lucinda's back. Her father's younger sister had been like a mother to her, moving in when Cassie's mother got too sick to get out of bed. She had been there for all of Cassie's milestones: the birthdays, the recitals, the academic awards, and, later, the tears. Aunt Lucinda now stood before the stove, her knobby shoulders more bent than Cassie remembered, wearing her standard uniform of a bright red housedress and high heels. Cassie was suddenly taken back fifteen years to the morning she had last seen her aunt standing at the stove, peach oven mitt tucked under her arm as she kneaded biscuit batter with one hand and fried eggs with the other.

"Aunt Lucinda?"

The older woman turned, her bright red lips parted in an "O." She walked toward Cassie and squeezed her tight, the familiar smells of Youth Dew bath oil and bacon grease oddly comforting.

"My goodness, Cassie. It feels good to hug you again—but you're all skin and bones. Don't they eat in New York?" Her words couldn't hide the warble of tears.

She kissed Cassie's cheek, but Cassie didn't have the heart to rub off the inevitable red mark. Just as she had as a little girl, she would wait until she was out of Aunt Lucinda's eyesight.

As Lucinda released her, Cassie noticed for the first time the two men sitting at the table. Sam had paused over a heaping plate of grits and sausage, and the man across from him sat with a baby on his lap, feeding her a bottle. Gentle slurpings filled the suddenly silent room as Cassie realized the dreaded moment had arrived.

Aunt Lucinda squeezed her around the shoulders one more time, then nudged her forward. "You've already seen Sam, and here's Joe." She turned toward the men. "Doesn't she look fine, y'all? Just as pretty as her mother, don't y'all think?"

Cassie blushed to the roots of her hair, suddenly reduced to age twelve and the time she and Harriet had come home from school and interrupted one of Aunt Lucinda's bridge parties. All the ladies had fawned over Harriet, with her gold hair spilling over her sweater. Aunt Lucinda, striking her mother-hen pose, had stood and pushed Cassie forward, telling everyone how smart she was, and how she hadn't quite grown into her looks yet. Cassie cringed at the memory.

Sam swallowed a mouthful of food. "You're right, Aunt Lucinda. She sure is. The new hairstyle threw me at first, but I would have recognized her anywhere."

She forced her gaze in Joe's direction, concentrating on the baby in his arms. It was swaddled in pink, the color setting off the baby's rosy cheeks. Slowly, Cassie raised her eyes. Her gaze swept over Joe, looking for the boy she had once loved with all her young heart, and waiting for lightning to strike her, leaving nothing but an outline of ash on the ceramic tile floor of the kitchen. But nothing happened. She felt nothing.

No spark, no tightening in the chest, no tingling in the belly. Joe Warner no longer made her mouth go dry. He looked like the high school football coach and science teacher he had become, complete with red marker stains on his fingers and a shirt pocket bulging with pens, pencils, and a pink pacifier. He was still drop-dead gorgeous, with laughing brown eyes that narrowed to slits when he smiled, but he'd lost the power to suck the air out of her lungs with just a look. He was her sister's husband, an old friend, and nothing more.

Still, the old ache, hinting of hurt and humiliation, throbbed in the back of her heart. She smiled tentatively, putting her hands in the pockets of her linen walking shorts. "Hello, Joe. It's been a while."

She became aware of Sam watching the exchange, his back rigid in his chair.

Joe stood, awkward for a moment, then smiled back. "Yeah. It sure has. How've you been?"

She took a step forward, close enough to smell the peculiar mixture of baby powder and formula. The baby's blue eyes opened wide, and then she smiled, making milk drip down her chin.

"This is Amanda," Joe said, turning so Cassie could get a better view.

Cassie stuck her finger in the baby's open fist, marveling at the tiny perfect fingers, the almost transparent nails.

Joe spoke to the baby. "This is your aunt

Cassie—the one your mommy is always talking about."

Cassie's head jerked up, her eyes meeting Joe's for the first time. Before she could call the words back, she asked, "Does she really?"

Joe nodded, almost shyly. "Every day, just about. Pictures of you and her are all over our house—even in the kids' rooms. She wanted to make sure they knew who you were." He paused for a moment, then said, "We sent you letters, at first. But . . . but they kept coming back unopened, so we stopped. But that didn't mean we stopped thinking about you or caring for you."

She swallowed, trying to think of what to say. She wanted to tell him that it was okay now, that the anger she had felt each time she marked "return to sender" on the letters no longer mattered or even existed. But the memory of her humiliation made the words stick in her throat. They'd been there for fifteen years, and would not be dislodged so easily.

The baby burped, spitting up over Joe's shirt and creating a needed diversion. Sam stood, holding a chair out for her, and she sat down heavily. Aunt Lucinda came and put a plate in front of her filled with bacon, eggs, grits, and her famous buttermilk biscuits. She felt Aunt Lucinda kiss the top of her head.

"I want you to eat all of it, you hear? You're much too thin."

Cassie stabbed a slice of bacon, eyeing it speculatively. As she was about to put it in her mouth, Joe said, "You've lost weight, Cassie. A lot of weight."

She dropped the bacon back on her plate and picked up her coffee. She stared at him through the steam. "It's been fifteen years since you last saw me. Plenty of time to change."

He sat down again, putting Amanda over his shoulder, and began to pat her back. "Things change slowly here, Cassie. You won't find anything a whole lot different. Even Mr. Purdy's still the high school principal. He's probably older than dirt by now, too."

Cassie's lips turned up at the mention of Principal Purdy. "It's a good thing I left, then. Because I happen to think that change is good."

Sam scraped his chair back as he stood and picked up his plate. "Not necessarily. Especially when it means picking up strange new customs."

She knew he was referring to the incident in the upstairs hallway, and she scowled at the creases in his cheeks as he walked toward the sink with his dishes. Cassie opened her mouth to say something, but stopped when she spotted Harriet in the doorway. Her sister wore a peculiar expression, like a person who'd just seen a plane fall out of the sky. Cassie put down her cup quickly, the hot coffee spilling over the sides.

Cassie's fingers grabbed at the gold chain

around her neck as the air seemed to still around her, and her gaze roamed the kitchen, searching out objects, people, anything to help her remember things the way they used to be before her life changed once again. Her eyes took in the stack of newspapers in the corner, her father's gardening shoes dumped inside the back door, his glasses on the counter next to the jar of frying grease. She looked down at her feet briefly, willing herself not to cry. There would be time to cry alone later.

"Is Daddy . . . ?"

Harriet's voice was thick, full of unshed tears. "Oh, Cassie . . ." She looked at her sister, but Cassie broke the connection by looking away, not yet wanting to share her grief with this woman who hadn't shared her life for so long.

Harriet didn't move. "It was . . . peaceful. And quick. I would have called you, except that it was over so fast. He just said good-bye, and . . . and went to sleep."

Joe stood and went to his wife, putting his free arm around her narrow shoulders, and kissed her on the cheek.

Cassie stood, her knees shaky. Sam watched her closely as she grabbed the back of her chair. "I want to see him."

Harriet looked at Joe, and then back at Cassie. "Wait a minute. There's something else."

Cassie swayed, wishing she had somebody to hold her with compassion and understanding, to kiss her cheek. And for some reason she couldn't imagine Andrew doing either. "What is it?"

Harriet tilted her head to the side, as if trying to make her news less off-kilter. "He told me . . . he told me . . ." She looked at Joe again, as if for strength, then back at Cassie, still wearing the same odd expression.

Cassie just stared at her sister, her nerves tight. "What?"

Harriet's eyes met Cassie's, and Cassie knew. Her father would do whatever he could to make her stay in Walton. Maddie opened the back door, creating a gust of warm air, bringing in the heavy scent of the boxwoods that lined the back walk. Cassie sucked in her breath, the scent suffocating, intoxicating, painful. She wanted to put her hand over Harriet's mouth, to stop the inevitable words from coming out, but found she couldn't move. The screen door slammed shut.

Softly, Harriet said, "He's left the house to you. And everything in it."

CHAPTER 5

Cassie stepped outside, carefully closing the screen door behind her so as not to attract attention. She had seen enough deviled eggs, sweet potato pie, and corn casserole to last an entire year, yet people were still arriving at the house with even more food. She wasn't sure whether everybody was there to pay their respects for her father, or if they were there to gawk at her and see if she had grown horns in the time she had spent away. She looked down at her black suit and saw fingerprints of powdered sugar and grease from the fried drumsticks old Mrs. Crandall brought. Through the screen door, she spotted the woman in question hovering over the kitchen counter, arranging a tall vase of flowers. Cassie studied the pudgy fingers as they straightened long stems of gladiolas, the same fingers she remembered clutching a stick of chalk and stabbing out long-division problems in fifth grade. All of Mrs. Crandall's contemporaries called her Sweet Pea, but to Cassie's generation, she would always be Mrs. Crandall.

Cassie sighed, tired of being poked, prodded, hugged, and squeezed. Trying to brush off some of the fingerprints, she stepped off the back porch and her high heel immediately sank into the soft red clay edging the walk. She yanked it back and began hobbling down the cement walkway, trying to dislodge the chunk of red earth clinging to her shoe. Without really knowing where she was going, she headed in the direction of the gazebo, slipping off both shoes before crossing the wide backyard. Too late, she remembered the prickers hiding in the grass, and did a combination of hops, hobbles, and leaps before making it to the sanctuary of the gazebo.

She sank down on one of the built-in bench seats and lifted a foot. Dozens of miniature double-pronged hooks clung to the sole, creating small holes in her panty hose and hurting like hell. How could she have forgotten so easily the stern warnings from her father not to go barefoot in the backyard? Cassie and Harriet had even taken turns giving each other piggyback rides to the gazebo just so only one of them had to don shoes. Shoes didn't exist in the summer world of Walton's children, and Cassie had made sure she'd never gone barefoot again once she'd left her father's house for good. Until now.

Staring at the bottom of her foot, Cassie felt stubborn tears fill her eyes. She hadn't cried when Mr. Murphy had come from the funeral home to discuss arrangements. Nor had she cried at the wake as the black-clad citizens of Walton had filed past the coffin like ants at a picnic. And she hadn't cried earlier that morning at the funeral. But now, staring at her ruined hose, and the tiny prickers sticking out of her foot, she sobbed. She sobbed for the loss of her father, for his words of wisdom, for his constancy, and for the little girl at his knee she could never be again.

A heel scraped against wood, and Cassie jerked her head up. Sam Parker, wearing yet another pair of cowboy boots—these were black—stood on the top step of the gazebo, looking at her with a curious expression.

She turned away. "I'd like to be left alone right now, if you don't mind."

Ignoring her words, he sat down on the bench next to her. "Those prickers must hurt something awful, with the way you're crying. Didn't your daddy ever tell you not to go barefoot back here?" He reached for her foot and held it in his lap.

She resisted at first, and then relaxed as he bent over her foot and began removing the prickers with his fingers one by one.

Cassie gave an unladylike sniff. "What is it about you that you're always there to see me do something humiliating?"

Without looking up, he said, "Crying's not humiliating—it just lets others know you're human."

Cassie wiped a drip off the end of her nose with the back of her wrist. "Do you mean there's been some discussion?"

He put one foot down and reached for the other one. "Not yet."

His gaze met hers, and she quickly looked away, not sure why blood rushed to her face.

To distract herself, she leaned back on her hands and stared up at the gazebo ceiling, painted blue to prevent bees and birds from building their nests in what they assumed to be sky. She remembered Joe telling her that on their first summer. The summer Harriet was away at cheerleading camp and Joe was all hers.

Cassie glanced back at Sam, realizing that he had stopped, and was now just resting his hands on her legs in a casual manner, her feet draped on his lap. It felt so normal and comfortable, and definitely disconcerting. She thought of Andrew, something she'd done with an alarming infrequency since arriving in Walton, and couldn't think of the last time they'd just sat together in companionable silence, without the bustle of their lives interfering. Quickly, she sat up and moved her feet to the floor.

Sam reached into his back pocket, pulled out a neatly pressed linen handkerchief, and handed it to her.

She stared at it for a moment but didn't touch it.

He shook it. "Your nose is dripping."

"Thank you," she said, sniffing again. She took it, dabbed her eyes, then blew her nose into the clean square of cloth.

Sam spoke softly. "I'm going to miss him, too. He was a great man."

Cassie began to sob again, and it seemed the natural thing for Sam to put his arm around her and pull her closer. She held the handkerchief to her face, smashing it between her nose and his chest.

Sam rubbed her shoulder as he spoke. "The whole town will miss him, Cassie. But one thing you should always carry with you is the fact that he believed you and Harriet were his greatest accomplishments. Everything else he did paled in comparison to you two—and he was never ashamed to admit it."

Cassie sniffled into the handkerchief, feeling like a failure for the first time in many years. She had failed as a daughter, for not allowing her own father into her life for so long, and pretending that monthly phone calls and yearly meetings in Atlanta were enough.

Her voice was muffled against his shirt. "He must have been a very forgiving man, too."

She felt him nod. "That he was. He hired me every summer to do his lawn, even though he could have hired somebody better and cheaper, because he knew I was saving up for college. Even wrote my letter of recommendation. And that was after I accidentally mowed over your mother's rose garden."

Cassie lifted her head for a moment. "I always thought you worked here so you could catch a glimpse of Harriet."

He looked down at her from the corner of his eye. "No. That's not the reason I came over every week to slaughter your father's lawn."

Something in his gaze made her shift and move her head off his shoulder. She slid away, embarrassed suddenly to be sitting so close to a man who wasn't her fiancé—or anything like him, thank God—and let her gaze drift over to the house and beyond. Bulldozers rumbled in the

71

distance where the old cotton field used to be. Her father had told her he had finally given in to a local developer and sold the land the previous year, and a small neighborhood of executive homes was being raised on the site. Gone, too, was the old stand of trees Cassie and Harriet had once called their enchanted forest, concocting visions of their future princes, and the exotic lives they once expected to have.

A dark cloud hovered on the horizon, blocking the sun and dimming the light. The heavy scent of rain filled the air, making the grass smell sweeter. A crisp breeze stirred the linens Aunt Lucinda had forgotten on the back line, making them dance like ghostly apparitions tethered to the earth.

Cassie rested her elbows in her lap, her hands cradling her chin. "I ran away once—when I was thirteen. I only made it as far as the little cluster of trees that used to stand over there. I was chasing a rainbow, and it disappeared from the sky as I walked across the lawn. I sat down on a rock and waited until my father came and got me." She paused for a moment to wipe her nose, then crumpled the handkerchief in her hand. "He said it was okay to be chasing the rainbow's end, as long as I always remembered where the rainbow started."

Sam leaned back on the bench, his elbows resting on the seat back. "I ran away once, too."

Cassie raised an eyebrow, trying to imagine the perpetually relaxed and casual Sam caring enough about anything to make him run away. "You? Whatever for?"

He slid her a narrow glance. "Guilt. And unrequited love."

Cassie sat back. "Guilt, huh? There's certainly plenty of that to go around. What did you do? Break some country girl's heart?"

Sam didn't smile, and stared over Cassie's head. "No. Guilty because my brother, Tom, died at the age of twelve trying to save my sorry butt from drowning."

Cassie frowned, remembering the stories. She had been about four or five when it happened. Something about Sam's being told not to go swimming in the creek by himself, and sneaking out to do it anyway.

Cassie looked down at her feet. "I'm sorry."

Sam picked up a small pebble from the bench and threw it off the side of the gazebo. "Yeah, me, too. I guess if guilt can drive a man, it had hold of me with both reins. It's what made me push myself—all through grade school, high school, and college. Then medical school." He sat back again, his forehead creased. "It never made me feel any better, but at least my parents had a child they could be proud of. It was my fault I was an only child, and I was damned determined not to be a disappointment to them."

"Is that why you came back to Walton? You could be doing so much more with your life."

He turned to face her, his eyes dark. "It's one of the reasons."

Their gazes met for a long moment before Cassie looked away and sat back against the bench. She stared up at the darkening sky, the scent of rain heavy in the air, wondering what those reasons might have been and just starting to realize that she might even know the answer.

MADDIE STARED OUT AT THE GAZEBO from behind the screen door, Knoxie jumping up and down next to her. They'd been looking for Aunt Cassie to tell her that their mama needed her back inside.

Aunt Cassie and Dr. Parker were sitting really close together, for some reason reminding Maddie about what she'd overheard about her daddy and Aunt Cassie. It was bad enough knowing that your parents kissed even when nobody else was around, but to think about her daddy and Aunt Cassie kissing made her feel a little sick in the stomach. As much as she liked her aunt, Maddie was glad she wasn't her mother. Mothers baked things, and fixed skinned knees and elbows, and sent you to your room when you talked sassy. Maddie just couldn't picture Aunt Cassie doing any of that. Besides, Mama would never have just picked up and moved to New York, and Aunt Cassie could never have done that if she'd had five kids and a husband tagging along.

Studying the two adults again, Maddie said, "I think Aunt Cassie thinks Dr. Parker is hot."

A distant rumbling shook the clouds, making her look at the sky again before glancing down at her little sister. "Where are your shoes?"

Knoxie shrugged. "Joey wanted to know if they were small enough to flush down the toilet."

Maddie just stared at her for a moment, not sure if she should find her mama now and tell her or if it could wait. She looked up at the darkening clouds and decided it had to wait. Squatting down, she said, "Get up on my back and I'll run to the gazebo before it starts raining."

With Knoxie on her back, Maddie galloped toward the gazebo.

"Prickers!" Knoxie shouted, her words hard to hear because the clouds seemed to open like a door, sending down rain in sheets.

Maddie raced across the yard and up the steps. Aunt Cassie took the dripping Knoxie, and the four of them huddled in the center of the gazebo, their backs turned to the spraying rain sneaking in through the arched openings. Sam wrapped his arms over their shoulders, his forehead nearly pressed against Cassie's. The spray of rain chilled Maddie's skin, but she was too busy watching her aunt and Dr. Parker to really notice.

Knoxie dug her head into Cassie's chest, looking

up only when the rain finally sputtered to a light drizzle. Her wide green eyes moved to the two adults. "Dr. Parker—is Aunt Cassie your girlfriend?"

Aunt Cassie plopped Knoxie on the ground like she was a hot potato, and patted her head absently. "Of course not, Knoxie. I'm getting married—to somebody else."

Knoxie's mouth opened a little bit as her gaze continued to jump between Aunt Cassie and Dr. Parker.

"Maddie says that you think Dr. Parker is—"

Maddie quickly clamped her hand across her little sister's mouth. With a small smile, she hoisted Knoxie in her arms. "Never mind that. We came to tell you that people are starting to leave and Mama wanted us to come and get you."

The sound of the rain lessened, allowing everyone to step back. Maddie frowned up at the sky as she weighed how wet and muddy she'd get running back to the house now against staying a little longer and having Knoxie say something else embarrassing.

Knoxie, now sitting on the edge of one of the bench seats between Dr. Parker and Cassie, turned to her aunt and asked, "Are you gonna need a flower girl?"

Aunt Cassie bit her lip. "I haven't gotten quite that far with the arrangements. But if I decide that I do, you'll be the first person I call, okay?"

Maddie rolled her eyes as she sat down and tucked her knees under her chin. Aunt Cassie was acting weird around Dr. Parker, and this could be interesting to watch.

Dr. Parker put his arm around Knoxie so he could nudge Aunt Cassie. "How come your fiancé isn't here?"

"What's a fiancé?" Maddie asked.

"The man I'm going to marry. Andrew Wallace." Aunt Cassie turned back to Dr. Parker. "He's very busy—especially with me not there. But I'm sure he would have been here if he could have."

Trying to be helpful, Maddie added, "He's called three different times today and left messages with Aunt Lucinda. She was wondering why you hadn't called him back yet."

Dr. Parker had a weird smile on his face. "Are you just planning on showing up again in your apartment and office, and resuming life as usual without any questions as to what all happened here?"

Aunt Cassie looked at him as if that was exactly what she'd planned on doing.

He continued. "I imagine you'll need to let him know you'll be here a lot longer than expected. I mean, you own this house now—you can't just leave."

Cassie shrugged, shaking her head. "I can't keep it. I've got no use for it in New York." She picked up her shoes, then stepped down onto the first step. "I need to get back now. Harriet's expecting me."

Maddie watched as her aunt stared down into the mud, then at her shoes—the kind of shoes that Carrie Bradshaw wore in that television show Maddie's mama had forbidden her to watch—and hesitated for a moment.

"There's prickers in the grass, Aunt Cassie," Knoxie shouted.

Standing behind her aunt, Sam said, "I don't think that's what your father intended, Cassie."

Cassie didn't turn around, but from where Maddie was sitting it looked like she was trying not to cry. "He's not here anymore. But I know he'd respect my decision."

"But what about the rest of your family?"

Maddie sat up, knowing he was talking about her and her brother and sisters. And her mama and daddy. She knew that her granddaddy had left his house to Aunt Cassie. It just hadn't occurred to her until now that her aunt might not want it. That being away from Walton for so long hadn't been long enough.

Aunt Cassie's shoulders drooped. "I'm not as coldhearted as you think. I'll offer it to Lucinda, and if she doesn't want it then to Harriet and Joe. But if they don't want it, I'll have to sell it."

His voice sounded like her daddy's after he'd caught Maddie in a lie. "You just can't sell it. It's been in your family for over a hundred and fifty years. It would be like selling your own child."

"Aunt Cassie has a child?" Knoxie shrieked.

"No, stupid. It was just an expression." Maddie stood and picked up her little sister and dumped her on her lap, making sure her hand was readily available in case it needed to cover Knoxie's mouth again.

Cassie continued to stare down into the mud. "Trust me—it's not my first choice. But unless you're offering to buy it, you really don't have any say in the matter."

"I can't afford it right now." He moved to stand next to her as they both watched the rainwater sliding off the gazebo's roof and splattering in the mud. The rain was only spluttering now, making it safe to return to the house. When he spoke again, he no longer sounded like friendly Dr. Parker. "Need some help?"

Before Aunt Cassie could answer, he scooped her up in his arms and began carrying her back to the house. Maddie tried not to laugh as Aunt Cassie started arguing for him to put her down, until her aunt looked at the mud and figured out she was better off where she was. Besides, despite all of Aunt Cassie's caterwauling, it seemed to Maddie that her aunt didn't mind being carried by Dr. Parker all that much anyway.

Maddie sat Knoxie on the bench and squatted in front of her so her little sister could climb on her back before Maddie stumbled down the steps and splashed away through the soaked grass and mud. She walked slowly, thinking about what her aunt had said about selling the house—the house that Cassie and Maddie's mama had grown up in. What Aunt Cassie had said about not needing it made sense, but in the place around Maddie's heart it just didn't seem right.

When she and Knoxie reached the middle of the yard, Maddie looked up and stopped. "Look, Knoxie," she said, pointing upward. Arcing across the dark purple sky, a multihued rainbow floated over the big white house, its end disappearing into the spot where the old cotton fields had once been. They stared at it for a long moment before Maddie moved onto the front porch, wanting to avoid the crowd in the kitchen and needing to think about how she felt about somebody else living in her grandfather's house.

HARRIET WATCHED AS SAM SET CASSIE DOWN hard on the back porch steps, then disappeared inside. By the grim line of Sam's mouth, Harriet thought they might have been arguing, but it was hard to tell from Cassie's face. She'd once been able to read every emotion on her sister's face, but the years in between had taught Cassie how to keep her feelings tucked neatly away where nobody could easily find them.

Cassie spent a few moments straightening her

hair and wiping away any mascara that might be smeared under her eyes. Slowly, she pulled open the screen door, her other hand reaching to her neck, and entered the kitchen, where she spotted Harriet.

"Maddie found me. Thanks."

Harriet nodded, feeling dowdy and old-fashioned in her Sunday-best black dress that she'd worn to every funeral for the last ten years. Cassie wore a black suit, overnighted from New York along with a bunch of other outfits by her fiancé, that fit her like it had been tailor-made for her, with tucks and seaming in all the right places and with a little surprise pleated fan in the back. Her shoes were just as elegant, their height making Cassie tower over Harriet even more in her own well-worn flats. "Everybody's congregating at the front door."

Harriet followed Cassie as she moved forward through the house and listened to the low buzz of voices, the ebb and flow of the sound like a swarm of bees. Small groups of people stood around the front parlor, while others hovered over the mahogany pedestal table in the dining room, its surface brimming over with food. The old Sedgewick twins, Thelma and Selma, in their late seventies and still wearing matching outfits, took turns hugging the breath out of Cassie.

Selma's brittle hands clutched Cassie's forearm.

"Your daddy wanted a clipping of our Red Radiance rosebush for your mother's rose garden. If it's all right with you, I'd like to plant it myself, as a sort of tribute to him."

Cassie blinked, as if she'd forgotten what roses were, or now thought of roses as something she received by the dozen from the florist on the corner, and then stuck in a vase on her desk, where she could watch them slowly wither.

Harriet prodded her gently in the back. "That would be lovely. Both of our parents surely loved that rose garden."

Cassie nodded quickly. "Thank you, Miss Selma. I'd like that very much." Then, without any further prodding from Harriet, Cassie bent and kissed the old lady's soft cheek, carefully avoiding scratching her cheek on Selma's straw hat.

Harriet kissed both ladies, enjoying the scent of baby powder, then thanked them both for coming and the ham they'd brought.

Harriet watched Cassie flush as she spied Mr. Purdy taking his hat off the rack by the front door, making Harriet wonder whether Cassie was reliving the pink-porch incident all over again. He approached Cassie with a smile and outstretched arms, and embraced her.

"It's so good to see you again, Cassie. You've been sorely missed around these parts. I understand your education at Walton High has served you well in the big city."

"Yes, sir," she said, a shaky grin crossing her face.

"I'm sorry about your father. He will be missed greatly." He paused for a moment, then smiled softly. "Though I must say that the best thing to come of this is that it's brought you home. I hope you're giving some serious thought to staying here permanently. I know it was your father's wish."

Cassie swallowed audibly, and Harriet found herself holding her breath, waiting for her reply. "I'm sure I'll think about it, but I really don't—"

Mr. Purdy cut her off. "No need to rush to any hasty decisions right now. There're a lot of other things going on in your life that will take your mental energies, so take your time." He put his hat on his head. "Just try to stay out of mischief while you're here."

Cassie's eyes widened, but Mr. Purdy only smiled as he turned away before kissing Harriet good-bye and letting himself out the front door.

Slowly, the crowd thinned, all of them patting, kissing, or hugging both Cassie and Harriet on their way out. Harriet felt exhausted. Between caring for a baby and four other children, planning the funeral, and walking on eggshells with Cassie, she should be tired. But this exhaustion seemed different somehow, as if she'd finally depleted all her resources.

Cassie frowned as yet another person asked her if she'd be staying in Walton, and Harriet did her best to deflect the question and usher them outside with lots of thanks. When she turned back to her sister, Cassie was still frowning.

"You know they're not being nosy just for the sake of it. They're curious about you because they care for you." Harriet touched her sister on the arm. "We've all been worried about you these past years. We feel that . . . well, that it's our duty to check on you—to make sure you're all right. And that you haven't changed too much."

Cassie turned to face her sister, her fingers finding the necklace Harriet was surprised to see she still wore. "Well, one thing that's changed is my knowing how to dress. What is it with all these wide lace collars and big hair? Don't they sell *Vogue* here?"

Harriet regarded her calmly. "You always did turn mean when you were scared. I guess some things never change."

Cassie stared back. "What do I have to be afraid of?"

Harriet continued to look at her without speaking for a moment, as if they both knew the answer to the question. Finally, she said, "Everybody's just about gone. Come on. Let's go find Aunt Lucinda to see if she needs any help."

She flung open the swinging door that led to the kitchen, quickly stepping inside to the welcome silence, the only noise the soft ticking of the fisherman clock above the stove. She and Cassie had given it to their father one year for Father's Day, loving the way the small fish ticked around the face of the clock, marking off the minutes.

Aunt Lucinda stood at the back door, her face pressed against the screen. Cassie called her name, and they began to walk toward her. But something in the way Aunt Lucinda stood, with her shoulders rounded and her hands, for once empty and still, by her sides made them stop.

"Aunt Lucinda," Cassie said again, and her aunt turned around.

"Oh, Cassie," she cried, and stumbled toward her.

Cassie snapped open her arms and gathered her aunt to her as sobs shook Lucinda's shoulders. Cassie's hand seemed to automatically pat the black polyester of Lucinda's dress, softly at first, and then more firmly.

Harriet watched, unsure of what she was feeling. She knew it wasn't jealousy; Harriet had known that for all the years of Cassie's absence, she had been only a stand-in. But Lucinda's sobbing brought something else: a reminder that she and Cassie were the old guard now; that their childhoods were officially over and the wisdom and guidance from their father were gone forever. It was like they were standing on a fault line, with no choice but to step over the widening crack.

"There, there, Aunt Lu. You'll see—things will be all right." Cassie's expression was doubtful.

Aunt Lucinda lifted her head, blinking her eyes, her smile wobbly. "They will be, won't they? Things always manage to work out in the end, don't they?" She grabbed Cassie's hand. "I've got wonderful friends, and you, and Harriet, and Joe, and the kids. Things will be okay." Her smile faltered. "But I'm going to miss him. I've been taking care of him for so long, I hardly know what to do with myself now."

Cassie put her arm across Lucinda's shoulders. "There are lots of things you can do. Don't worry about a thing. I'll make sure you're settled before I go back to New York."

Aunt Lucinda's eyes widened. "Go back? You can't go back! What about the house? And your family? You can't just leave us. We need you."

The unexpected rush of hurt at being so overlooked was deadened somewhat by Harriet's exhaustion. Her knees seemed about to give way, and she quickly seated herself at the kitchen table. She made a mental note to talk with Sam about vitamins, or whatever she needed to deal with her lack of energy. And all the emotions Cassie's return had brought.

Cassie continued to console Aunt Lucinda. "You've all managed very well without me for a long time; I think you'll survive again. But I promise I'll visit often, all right? I won't be a stranger anymore."

"But what about the house?"

Cassie shook her head. "I don't want it." She paused for a moment. "Actually, I was thinking of giving it to you. You've lived here for so long, you might as well own it."

Cassie stopped, alarmed by the change in her aunt. Lucinda glared at her with narrowed eyes, mascara trails running down her rouged cheeks. "Your father wanted you to have this house. I will not be the one responsible for thwarting his plans. Besides—what would an old woman like me do with a big house like this? Just keeping it up all by myself would be the death of me."

Cassie sighed heavily. "But I could pay for help. You wouldn't have to do anything."

Her aunt turned to her. "Your father wanted you to have the house, Cassie, and that's that. I'm sure he had his reasons—and I learned a long time ago that my brother was usually right." She dabbed at her nose with a crumpled tissue. "Besides, maybe it's time I find my own place. Your daddy left me a nice little nest egg—more than enough to buy a house. A small one, of course, but mine. It's been a long time since I was on my own."

Cassie opened her mouth to argue, then closed it as Sam entered the room and leaned against the counter, crossing one booted foot over the other. Cassie averted her eyes, making Harriet wonder again about that undercurrent between her sister and Sam.

Cassie seemed to catch sight of something

sticking out from the top of the chair rail behind the kitchen table. She walked over to where Harriet sat and plucked it out of the woodwork behind her.

She held the tiny pine needle in her palm, the smell of Christmas suddenly seeming to fill the room. Cassie faced Harriet, and her open expression of surprise made her look like the sister Harriet had once known and loved.

"Remember how Mama loved Christmas? How she used to practically drape the whole house with pine boughs?"

Harriet nodded, smiling. "Aunt Lucinda still does. Every year she'd threaten to send miles of the stuff up to you in New York, but we talked her out of it, saying you probably had your own traditions."

Cassie sighed, crushing the pine needle in her hand. "Andrew's allergic. We have a little artificial tree we stick in the corner of the bedroom." She looked up, her expression almost defiant and all remnants of the young girl she'd been gone again. "At least we have real snow. And Rockefeller Center."

Sam cleared his throat. "I'm leaving now. But I wanted to make a suggestion before I left. This house will be pretty lonely tonight with just you and Lucinda. Why don't the two of you go sleep at Harriet's?"

She shook her head. "No. I want to stay here. It makes me feel closer to Daddy."

Aunt Lucinda gave him a weak smile. "I'd just as soon stay, Sam. Staying here will feel almost like nothing's changed."

Sam nodded before addressing Cassie. "Then you might consider asking Harriet and her family to stay with you. It will make you both feel better." He glanced over at Harriet, who nodded. "And I'm sure she wouldn't mind."

A scream from Sarah Frances made them start, and then Sam stepped back at the sound of running feet. The young girl flew past them, a loose hair ribbon dangling in her hair, followed closely by Joey. Lucinda pressed herself against the wall, and Cassie flew back against Sam when she spied what the boy was chasing his sister with: a small garter snake, its skin reflecting the light from the chandelier over the table, and its red tongue flicking in and out.

Harriet struggled to stand until she spotted Joe following on their heels, shouting at Joey to stop, but not quite succeeding in getting the laughter out of his voice.

Cassie disengaged herself from Sam's hold. "Yeah. Great suggestion, Sam. I'll feel a lot better having them in the house with me tonight." She rolled her eyes. "Besides, it's a lot of trouble for all of them to bring their stuff over here."

"Not at all," Harriet said, preferring to stay right where she was, because she wasn't exactly sure she could find the energy to move.

"Well, then, that's settled." He said good-bye and winked at Harriet before leaving through the swinging doors.

Cassie called out, not quite hiding her smile, "Don't let the door hit you in the butt on the way out."

His only reply was the front door slamming shut.

Aunt Lucinda regarded her with still eyes. "You must be scared, honey. You're acting mean."

Cassie looked at Harriet to disagree, to re-create the old team of "us vs. them." But Harriet could only smile and nod, since Lucinda was completely right.

Lucinda took Cassie's elbow. "Let's let Harriet rest her feet a bit longer while you and I grab the food that's on the dining room table and bring it into the kitchen."

Harriet watched as Cassie allowed herself to be led away, her expression thoughtful, as if she were wondering why everybody seemed to think there was anything she could possibly be scared of.

CHAPTER 6

The sound of a crying baby startled Cassie awake. Sitting up, she stared at the dark outline of the pink canopy, and wondered how she had gone to sleep so easily. She still wore her black suit, having just flopped onto the bed right after dinner, not thinking sleep would find her. She didn't want to admit that Sam was right, but she had felt strangely comforted knowing that the bedrooms around her would be filled with the sleeping members of her family.

The wailing got louder as Cassie heard a door open and footsteps come up the stairs, cross the hall, and head back down the stairs. She slid out of bed and opened her door, not wanting to go back to sleep and needing somebody to talk to.

The front door closed quietly as Cassie descended the stairs, then let herself outside. The full moon shone brightly, illuminating the porch and columns in a milky blue light. She spied Joe on the swing, a small twitching bundle in his arms.

Joe held a finger to his lips before bending his head to look at the baby's face. He motioned for Cassie to join him on the swing. She sat down softly, trying not to jolt it.

They swung in the stillness for a while, listening to the unseen insects in the grass humming their ceaseless nighttime lullaby. A bullfrog croaked nearby, its lonely call the only percussion to the crickets' string section. Cassie was thankful that Joey wasn't there to add the unfortunate amphibian to his collection. The baby let out a few more cries, each one softer than the last, until she settled down to the rhythm of the swing.

The baby sighed softly in her sleep, a light breeze carrying with it the scent of jasmine and honeysuckle, and a host of forgotten memories of many summer evenings spent on the same porch. She pictured her mother sitting on the steps and singing to her and Harriet, the cotton twill of her mother's skirt soft under her cheek, while her father read the paper, the discarded pages fluttering like moths on the wooden planks of the porch floor.

Joe spoke first. "Aunt Lucinda says you're wanting to sell the house."

Cassie nodded. "I don't need it. What would I do with a big old house in Georgia? I don't live here anymore." She looked over at Joe. "But, if at all possible, I'd like to keep it in the family." She stilled the swing by putting her feet flat on the floor. "Aunt Lucinda doesn't want it or need it, but if you want it, it's yours. I'll give it to you."

Joe absently patted the baby's back, and Cassie tried not to look at his hands, the old hands of her memory. "No, Cassie. We couldn't afford it. Even if you gave it to us, we could never afford the upkeep. I don't make much as a high school teacher, and Harriet's boutique barely provides for a few extras. Your father was very generous to us in his will, but we've got five college educations to consider."

Cassie sat up straighter. "But I could help! I could send—"

"No." Joe's voice was firm, causing the baby to stir. He waited a moment, then continued. He eased back against the swing again. "That's not what the judge wanted. I vote you hang on to it. You never know when you might need it."

She shook her head in the darkness. "This house was so much a part of me a long time ago—but that life is gone forever and there's no need for me to hang on to it. Clinging to the past isn't the healthiest thing." She looked away for a moment. "Like clinging to old hurts. It hampers the growing process."

Joe looked at her as the baby sighed in her sleep, his eyes glittering in the moonlight. "So, what are you going to do?"

She shrugged, jostling the swing slightly. "I guess I could sell it. I noticed the under-contract signs on the Haneys' and Duffys' yards. Somebody's buying property in Walton."

With a snort, Joe carefully moved the baby to his other shoulder. "Yeah, but it's not somebody you want to sell this house to."

"What do you mean?"

"A developer bought those lots—gave the families a really sweet deal. Not that your daddy ever gave them the time of day. Wants to put a high-end retail mall right here." He scratched his chin furiously. "Ever since they put that exit in off the interstate, we've had Atlanta commuters moving in, and all sorts of builders wanting to change Walton. It's been like a damned circus around here."

Cassie let her gaze wander out over the moonlit

expanse of lawn, the nighttime quiet like a gentle song to her soul. "Is it the same developer Daddy sold the cotton field to?"

"Nah. And you're never going to believe who bought that." He looked at Cassie expectantly.

She tried to hide her impatience. "Just tell me— who?"

"Ed Farrell."

"Ed Farrell? You're kidding, right?"

The swing squeaked as Joe moved. "Nope. He's got his own realty business now—and he's actively recruiting all those suburbanites to move into this new neighborhood down there below your house. He even had the gall to call it Farrellsford."

Cassie's eyes widened as she pictured the tall, gangly Ed from high school, and the pants he wore that were always a size too small or too large—just whatever his mom could find at the thrift shop. If he was buying up property and building neighborhoods, he'd come a long way since she'd known him. "Wow," was all she could manage.

Joe sat up straighter. "You wouldn't consider selling this house to a developer, now, would you?"

She stood abruptly, the swing rocking in her wake. "I honestly don't know. If nobody wants it, I'll have to sell it. And that's that."

"Would you do that to punish us? To get back for what happened fifteen years ago?"

She leaned back against the railing that stretched between the columns, nudging aside a paint can, the smell of fresh paint heavy in the humid air. "No. Of course not. I'm . . ." She closed her eyes for a moment. "It's funny, but none of that old stuff seems to matter anymore. It did for so long, when I stayed away, but now that I'm here, I realize how inconsequential it all seems to my life right now. Right before Daddy died, I told him that staying away was just a habit I'd gotten used to. I think I was right."

"We didn't do it to hurt you, you know. We loved each other—and we loved you, too. But every time we tried to tell you, you'd change the subject or run away. It was like you knew what we were going to say, but didn't want to hear it. I guess you're just the type of person who has to be hit over the head with something before you believe it."

She smiled at him across the darkened porch. "Maybe. Not that any of that matters anymore. I have a new life. I've got to do what I need to so I can get back to New York and resume the life I've worked so hard to build."

Joe's voice was quiet, almost completely obliterated by the squeak of the swing. "Are you happy?"

His words surprised her, reminding her of what her dad had asked. *Do you still laugh?* "Well, yes. Of course. Of course I am. I have a great job, making a great living. I live in one of the most exciting cities in the world. A highly intelligent man is crazy about me and we're going to be married. How could I not be happy?"

He nodded in the darkness. "I see. Well, all I can wish for you is that you find the kind of happiness Harriet and I have."

Cassie looked away, out across the front lawn to the lane of oaks. "I wish you would reconsider about the house. It has all the room you need for the kids. I would really rather not have to sell it."

He swiped a hand through the air at a flying insect that seemed intent on dive-bombing his sleeping daughter. "You do what you want, Cassie. It's your house. And when you're finished burning all your bridges, we'll still be here, waiting to help you back across."

The baby began to whimper as Joe stood and walked toward the front door. Before he shut it behind him, he called over his shoulder, "And don't lean on the railing. I couldn't get to sleep so I entertained myself by painting it." The door shut softly behind him.

She twisted around to see the seat of her black suit, a telltale white stripe glowing in the dim light. She moved back to the swing and sat down with a thump, the night around her alive with sounds and movement slithering in the grass and twinkling in the sky. Fingering the charms around her neck, she thought of her dead father, and his house, and the paint on her suit, and didn't know whether to laugh or cry. So she sat on the swing and listened as the night sounds gave way to morning, and the sun cracked the sky.

MADDIE ROLLED OVER IN BED and slammed down the button on her alarm clock before it woke anybody else. Sarah Frances sighed in her sleep in the bed next to hers and then settled back down as Maddie let out a breath she hadn't realized she'd been holding. Quietly, she tiptoed to the door and let herself out, closing it softly behind her. She made her way to the other side of the hallway and sat down cross-legged on the floor outside her aunt's room to wait.

Maddie and her family had stayed in her grandfather's house for two nights now and Maddie knew her aunt went running at six o'clock every morning. This was Maddie's opportunity to get to know her aunt better—and maybe get a few steps ahead of Lucy Spafford in learning the secrets of how to look sophisticated. Aunt Cassie obviously knew about that sort of stuff. She lived in New York, after all.

She heard her aunt's alarm clock go off, followed by a muffled curse and the alarm clock hitting the floor. Within seconds, her aunt had stumbled to the door and opened it.

"Good morning, Aunt Cassie." Maddie beamed her brightest smile.

Cassie blinked as if trying to focus, her lips moving but not quite succeeding in forming a smile. "Morning, Madison. Going for a run. See you later."

Madison scrambled up, pulling down the elastic on the bottom of her baby-doll pajamas. "Can I go with you?"

Her aunt tried to hide a yawn. "Do you run regularly?"

Maddie looked down, her big toe stabbing the carpet runner, unsure whether she should out-and-out lie or just try to bend the truth. "Well, kinda. In PE we run laps around the football field." She glanced up, trying not to sound too eager. "But it would be fun with you. Would you wait a minute while I change?"

Aunt Cassie blinked again, as if still unsure that she was actually awake. "Sure. But hurry, okay? I want to be done before the heat gets any worse. I'm not used to it."

Madison darted back to her room and slipped on a shirt, shorts, and sneakers. By the time she made it back to Cassie's room, her aunt was standing by the bed with her shorts in one hand and a single shoe dangling in the other, as if she were trying to figure out what to do with them.

"Do you want me to make you some coffee, Aunt Cassie?"

"No, thanks. Not before I run." Cassie slipped into the walk-in closet to change.

Madison sat down on the floor, then drew her legs up in front of her, resting her elbows on her knees and cupping her chin in her palms. "Is your fiancé handsome?"

Her aunt's voice sounded muffled coming from the closet. "Well, yes. He is. Very, as a matter of fact."

Maddie peered over at the open suitcase on the floor with curiosity, wondering what the scrap of black lace was attached to. "Do you spend lots of time walking in Central Park and holding hands?"

There was a long pause, then, "Probably not, since the only time we ever walk anywhere together is home from work, when our hands are full of briefcases and take-out bags."

Maddie frowned, realizing the lace was actually a really small pair of underwear. Certainly not bought from the same JCPenney catalog from which her mother ordered her own white cotton briefs. "What do you do for fun?"

Cassie stepped out of the closet, pulling her hair back with a black elastic band. "We're very busy at the advertising agency that Andrew owns. We have plans for a romantic getaway once things settle down a bit, but there just doesn't seem to be the time right now."

Madison pictured her aunt in a great outfit with another pair of those high-heeled shoes, sitting in a glass-walled office with a phone to each ear and ten people standing around her, waiting for her signature. Or approval. Or whatever it was that Aunt Cassie did. "When do we get to meet him?"

Cassie pushed against the edge of the dresser, stretching her hamstrings. "Oh, um. I don't know. He's so busy at the agency—especially with me being gone—that it's just about impossible for him to come down here. . . ."

Maddie scooted herself into the middle of the floor and sat with her legs spread in a wide "V." Stretching her fingertips to her toes, she gasped out, "Mama said something about throwing you a wedding shower. Maybe he'll come down for that."

She glanced up in time to see her aunt's eyebrows shoot up. "A shower? Oh, I don't think I'll be here long enough for that. . . ."

Madison ignored her and continued to stretch. "Mama's real excited—but I think it's supposed to be a surprise, so don't go and say anything to her." She stood and began to stretch her hamstrings, not yet ready to drop their earlier conversation. "So what do you and Mr. Handsome do for fun in New York City when you do get the chance?"

"Oh, we, um, well, we went to a musical once—*Wicked.* I'm sure we'll do more of that once we can hire some more people at the agency, but right now we're just so overwhelmed, it's kind of hard to find leisure time." Cassie switched legs and began to stretch the other hamstring. "We do go out to eat at nice restaurants quite often—but we're always with clients, so I don't think you'd count that as being fun."

Madison bent to tighten her shoelaces. "Do you think it's fun?" She tilted her head to the side.

Cassie raised her hands over her head and leaned to the left. "Well, sure. It's fun. I mean, what could be better than mixing great food with business?"

Maddie stood still for a moment, thinking of drive-in movies and swimming in the creek with her friends. "Oh."

Cassie looked at the clock on the bedside table. "Give me a few minutes, okay? It's almost six thirty, so I'm going to try to reach Andrew at the office before anybody else gets there."

With a nod, Maddie headed toward the bathroom to brush her teeth and splash water on her face, thinking the whole time about ways to adjust her perception of what having fun meant. Obviously, she had a lot to learn.

When she was finished, she shut the bathroom door and quietly crept down the stairs. She was surprised to hear a man's voice before she reached the doorway to the study and realized that her aunt was listening to the speakerphone while using her hands to sort through papers on her grandfather's desk. Not wanting to interrupt, Maddie slid down the wall in the doorway, hidden from view by her grandfather's desk, and prepared to wait.

Her mama always told her it was rude to listen in on other people's phone conversations, so she did her best to ignore Aunt Cassie and the man on the speakerphone. She focused instead on the table near where she sat where her granddaddy had all of the family pictures in frames.

There were lots of pictures of Maddie and her brother and sisters since they were babies, the picture of the whole family they'd had done last Christmas, an old black-and-white photo of her granddaddy and her grandma—the one who'd died before she was born—standing next to a really cool antique-looking sports car. But most of the pictures were of Aunt Cassie and Maddie's mama when they were little. Maddie sat up to better see the pictures of her aunt starting in what looked like kindergarten and ending with her senior high school photo.

Maddie stared hard at the pictures and tried very hard to find her aunt in the face of the girl with winged bangs framing a much rounder face with thick glasses and braces. Even her shirt didn't match the aunt sitting now behind her granddaddy's desk. It had a wide collar and whales swimming all over it, something Maddie was pretty sure her aunt wouldn't be caught dead in now. She glanced briefly at her mama's senior photo, taken of her in her cheerleading outfit, with her blond hair spilling over her shoulders, and realized that while her aunt Cassie looked like she'd been redone by *What Not to Wear*, her mother looked exactly the same.

Her aunt's tone of voice changed, bringing Maddie's attention back to the phone conversation.

"I have not. You're kidding, right?"

"No, really. You've, um, sort of picked up an accent, I think."

Maddie heard a frown in her aunt's voice. "Don't worry. I'm sure it's temporary."

"So, how are you? I've been trying to reach you. Your cell phone goes right to voice mail and every time I call the house phone I've left a message with somebody called Lucinda. Man! Talk about somebody who needs speech therapy. I could hardly grasp what she was saying. Might as well have been speaking Russian, for all I understood."

The tapping sound of fingers on a computer keyboard shot through the phone line while Maddie sat up a bit to see her aunt's expression. "That's my father's sister. The one who raised me and Harriet when our mom died and has been a sort of surrogate mother ever since."

There was a short pause, filled with the clacking noise. "Oh. Well, I'm sure she's very nice. Did she give you the message that I called?"

"Yes. I, um, just haven't really had a chance to call you. It's been crazy since Daddy died. There've been some, um, developments, which is why I didn't call you back right away. I wanted to make sure that I had explored all my options first."

The key tapping stopped. "I see. What kind of developments?"

Aunt Cassie leaned back in Granddaddy's chair as Maddie tried to curl up as small as she could so she wouldn't be noticed, having long since given up trying to pretend she wasn't listening.

"Well, it seems I've inherited this house and just about everything in it. Neither Lucinda nor Harriet wants it, so I'm kind of stuck for the time being."

"Sell it."

Maddie sat up to see her aunt's expression, then followed her aunt's gaze as it traveled through the large doorway and up the stairwell, then stopped on the old paintings of all the long-dead Madisons. For a moment, Maddie wondered if she might have seen a frown from Great-great-great-great-grandfather Madison.

Aunt Cassie continued. "Well, sure, I could sell it. Which is what I'll probably have to do. But this house has been owned by my family since the 1840s. It'll be a major decision. Not to mention the fact that I'll need to go through everything in the house—especially the attic, which I don't think has been touched in over fifty years."

Maddie relaxed against the wall, not liking the person attached to the voice coming through the speakerphone. She couldn't place it—it didn't sound Southern or Northern, as if the owner of the voice was trying to hide who he was.

A phone rang in the background before the man's voice spoke again. "Why don't you just call a Realtor, and then hire one of those companies that goes in and gets rid of clutter for you? Then you can be back here within a week."

Cassie dumped a pile of papers in the top drawer and opened another. "Andrew, I don't know. I . . . I don't think I can do that."

Andrew sighed into the phone. "Why not? Our clients need you up here. *I* need you up here. I miss you."

Quietly, but not too quietly, so Maddie could still hear if she stopped breathing for a second, Cassie leaned closer to the speaker. "I know. I miss you, too. Just give me a week and I'll have a better idea. I'm sure I'll have things sorted out by then."

"I hope so. I don't like it when you're gone. The bed seems too big."

Cassie stood, noticing Maddie for the first time as Maddie quickly began to study her fingernails. "I bet. Maybe you should move to the twin bed in the guest room."

Cassie picked up the phone and turned off the speakerphone button so Maddie missed Andrew's reply. But from the frown on Cassie's face, Maddie was pretty sure it wasn't what she'd wanted to hear.

"I'll try," Cassie whispered before hanging up. She continued to stare at the phone until Maddie stood and moved next to the desk.

"You ready?" Without waiting for an answer, Aunt Cassie moved from behind the desk and into the foyer, then held open the front door while she waited for Maddie to go first. With a giant leap, Cassie was off and running down the driveway at a pretty fast pace. It didn't take Maddie long to catch up, although it seemed that her aunt was struggling a bit to keep up the pace. Maddie deliberately slowed up so she wouldn't have to remember how to do CPR if her aunt passed out.

They ran in silence for a while, jumping over the large cracks in the sidewalks, dodging out into the street to avoid the fat fists of crape myrtles and hydrangea blossoms dangling over the pathway. Maddie waved to every car they passed, recognizing friends, neighbors, and schoolmates she'd known all her life. Aunt Cassie seemed more focused on breathing, so after at first trying to identify everyone Maddie waved at, she remained silent.

When they reached the large Victorian house on the corner, Maddie paused, jogging in place as she spoke to the old woman in the rocking chair on the porch. Cassie stopped beside her, breathing hard.

Maddie waved. "Good morning, Miss Lena. Read any good books lately?"

The old lady grinned a toothless grin, her bespectacled eyes reflecting the blue sky. She held up a paperback novel with one of those naked-people covers Maddie's mama would never allow into her house. "I'm just getting to the juicy part. She just saw his wicked manhood for the first time."

106

Cassie shot a shocked glance at Maddie.

"Don't tell Mama she said that, okay?" Maddie asked as she waved to Miss Lena and took off again.

Cassie shook her head, but Maddie could see that she was trying hard not to laugh, and trying very hard to breathe. Through pants of breath, her aunt said, "Holy shit!"

Maddie looked sideways at her aunt, whose face was even redder than it had been the last time she'd checked.

"Sorry. I don't know where that came from—I don't usually swear. It's just that Miss Lena taught my Sunday school in tenth grade—and her daddy used to be the preacher at Walton First Baptist. What happened?"

Madison scrunched up her nose. "Her sister in Mobile runs her church library. She sends Miss Lena all the donated books she can't use. She reads the same ones over and over because she doesn't remember them."

"Is she still teaching Sunday school?"

Madison nodded, and wiped a drip of sweat off her cheek. "Never misses a Sunday. But she's only an assistant teacher now. She mostly just stands in the front of the class and smiles. Her mind wanders in and out of reality, but she doesn't want to go into a home. We all pretty much take care of her now." Maddie paused for a moment, taking deep breaths as their sneakers pounded the sidewalk. "Mama takes turns with the other ladies to bring her dinner and stuff."

They ran down Madison Lane and crossed Orchard, with the ancient oak towering over the intersection from the Hardens' front lawn and blocking the stop sign. A rope swing hung from a high branch, and a small child stood under it, trying to jump high enough to grab hold. The little girl waved to them as they passed, and Maddie waved back.

Cassie, struggling to breathe, forced out a question. "Do the Hardens still live there? I remember . . . swinging on the same . . . swing."

Madison shook her head. "Mr. and Mrs. Harden sold their house to their daughter, Mary Jane, and moved to Florida. Did you know her?"

Cassie nodded. "I remember Mary Jane Harden. We were best friends from kindergarten all the way through our second year at the junior college." She paused for a moment, and Maddie wasn't sure if it was because she was out of breath or just thinking of how much she should say. Finally she said, "And then I moved away and didn't really keep in touch with anybody. It seems kind of stupid now to have lost contact with Mary Jane." Cassie shook her head, sweat dripping off her face. "Maybe I'll look her up while I'm in Walton. I doubt we'll have anything in common, but it would be nice to see her."

They continued down Madison Lane until they

reached Walnut, and headed east toward Main Street and the town square. No matter how many times Maddie saw it, or how many times she said she hated it and couldn't wait to leave it, the downtown area looked like something you'd see on a postcard: a town that other people might want to visit. The tall brick storefronts with window boxes, bright awnings, and large picture windows weren't too bad to look at, and Maddie always felt a sense of pride knowing that it was her mother and her gardening society that planted all the beautiful flowers along the sidewalks each fall and spring.

Diagonal parking spaces jutted out from the sides of the wide sidewalk like legs on a centipede crawling up Main Street. The courthouse towered over the square at the intersection of Main and Monroe Avenue, the grass always kept trimmed around the Confederate monument and another statue on the opposite end.

Cassie jogged toward the other statue before stopping completely, her face red and looking like she might need that CPR sooner rather than later. She slumped over, her hands on her slippery knees, and looked up at the statue. "Oh. My. God," she panted out.

Madison slowed to a stop beside her, and stared up at the scaled-down replica of the Statue of Liberty. "Does it look like the real thing?"

Cassie straightened, adjusting her sweatband on

her forehead. "Not . . . quite." She examined the wooden head of the thing. "I think that part was carved with a chain saw from a stump pulled out of a nearby swamp."

Maddie followed Cassie's critical eye as it traveled from the upraised arm that looked like it had been made of Styrofoam, to the hand holding the torch that was definitely an oversize electrician lineman's glove. The whole thing had been painted a softly glowing green.

Aunt Cassie had a small smile on her face as she shook her head. "I remember the parade, the flag-waving, and all the convertibles carrying veterans through the streets of downtown the day this statue was dedicated by the proud men of the Lions Club. But I somehow don't remember thinking it was so hideous when I was seven."

Madison squinted in the sun, staring at the statue as if seeing it for the first time—as if seeing it through the eyes of somebody not from Walton. She suddenly felt as if she'd just discovered her daddy stuffing her stocking instead of Santa Claus. "It's really pretty stupid-looking, isn't it?"

Cassie sat down on the small ledge at the base of Miss Liberty, her mouth opening and then closing several times before she actually said something. "You know what, Madison? What those men who erected this statue lacked in sophistication, they certainly made up for in enthusiasm." Cassie stared out over the town square toward the courthouse. "I remember an old army veteran on the steps of the courthouse giving a speech about what this statue represented and how proud they all were to have a small piece of it here in Walton." She squinted up at Maddie. "You don't really see much of that anymore."

A familiar truck pulled into a parking space on the square and Cassie stood. "Hey, at least it's not that statue over in Plains. You know—the world's largest peanut in the shape of Jimmy Carter. Now *that's* embarrassing."

Maddie grinned, then shrugged her shoulders. "Yeah. I guess it could be worse."

They both turned their attention to the truck as two people climbed out. Cassie squinted, holding her hand over her forehead to block the sun as Dr. Parker and a woman pulled long garlands of something green out from the bed of the truck. The couple then approached Maddie and Aunt Cassie, their arms wrapped around the greenery.

As they got closer, the woman smiled at Cassie. "Bet you don't remember me."

Aunt Cassie seemed unsure at first, and then she smiled back. "Mary Jane Harden—of course I recognize you. I think it must be the dimple, although your hair seems shorter. And blonder."

Miss Harden moved to hug Cassie, but Maddie's aunt held up her hand. "You don't want to do that—I'm pretty sweaty. We just ran past your parents' house and saw a little girl swinging on the tree swing. Is she yours?"

Mary Jane shot a quick glance at Dr. Parker, and shook her head. "No. Don't have any kids. Not married—yet. That was my brother's girl. He and his wife are visiting for a couple of weeks."

"Stinky got married? You're kidding!"

Mary Jane nodded. "Yep. But we don't call him Stinky anymore. He's changed a lot. Reads more than just action-hero comic books, and actually takes baths now."

They all laughed as Mary Jane and Dr. Parker dropped the stuff in their hands. Looking serious, Miss Harden said, "I'm sorry about your father, Cassie. I wanted to come to the funeral, but one of us had to stay at the clinic."

Cassie tilted her head in question, and Miss Harden smiled. "I'm Sam's nurse and general office gofer. We run the clinic together—along with a few rotating doctors and nurses from Providence Hospital in Monroe."

"Oh. I see." Aunt Cassie pulled her soaking shirt away from her stomach, and Maddie wondered if she felt as yucky as she did, standing with sweat-soaked clothes in front of two people who looked like they'd not only had a shower but had recently stepped out of air-conditioning. Aunt Cassie continued, "It's great seeing you. I hope we'll have time to talk before I leave."

The other woman frowned. "You're not planning on leaving soon, are you?"

Dr. Parker shifted, but Aunt Cassie didn't look at him. "Not today, anyway. But as soon as I get everything settled."

"Are you staying at your father's house?"

Aunt Cassie nodded.

"Good. I'll call you, and we'll go have lunch at the Dixie Diner—just like old times. We'll do some catching up."

"Great. That'll be fun."

For the first time, Maddie realized with a sinking feeling what it was that Dr. Parker and Miss Harden had hauled out of the truck. She reached down and picked up a section of kudzu vine.

Aunt Cassie stepped back. "Madison—is that what I think that is?"

Sam reached down and picked up an end, his long fingers fiddling with an oversize heart-shaped leaf. "It's kudzu. Surely you haven't forgotten what it looks like?"

She stuck out her chin. "I know what it is; I just wanted to know why it's here."

Miss Harden chipped in. "It's for the Kudzu Festival. It's coming up, and Sam and I are on the decorating committee." She smiled up at Dr. Parker and touched his arm, and Maddie wondered if Aunt Cassie knew she was frowning at Miss Harden as she studied the plain khaki shorts, sandals, and cotton button-down shirt the other woman wore. Sort of like mom clothes without the mom part.

Miss Harden turned her attention to Maddie. "And I'm sure that now you're in high school, you'll be in the running each year for kudzu queen. You are your mama's daughter, after all."

Maddie wanted to throw up, but managed a smile instead. Queen of kudzu went to girls like Lucy Spafford, with blond hair and petite figures, not to Amazon-tall brunettes like Maddie.

Aunt Cassie pointed to a green strand. "Since you've picked it, won't it be dead in two weeks?"

Dr. Parker snorted. "If it were only that easy. We'll stick an end in the dirt, and it will start growing as if it's always been here. Our only problem will be pulling it down after the festival before it has time to take over the town."

Miss Harden laughed out loud, as if what Dr. Parker had said was the funniest thing she'd ever heard. Still smiling, and with her hand on Dr. Parker's arm, she looked at Madison. "Your mom's supposed to be here in a minute to help. All the former kudzu queens are supposed to help out, and Harriet's so good with decorating and things that Dr. Parker and I just grabbed her to work on our committee." She sent another sickening look at the doctor, and this time Maddie did almost puke.

Miss Harden turned to Aunt Cassie. "We felt bad about your father's funeral being so recent and everything, and we even told Harriet she didn't have to come, but she said she wanted to. I guess it helps to keep her mind off of things." Her hazel eyes regarded Aunt Cassie casually. "Sort of what running must do for you."

Dr. Parker looped several long strands of kudzu around his neck, then rubbed his hands together. "We'd better get started. I'm supposed to be at the clinic at one, and we've got lots of this leafy stuff to drape. Madison, why don't you and your aunt stay and give us a hand?"

Maddie, who'd rather lick a cockroach than have anything to do with decorating for the Kudzu Festival, looked at her aunt for help. Instead, Aunt Cassie glanced at her bare arm. "Sorry—I'd love to but I can't. I've got an appointment with a Realtor at eleven thirty. Plus I desperately need a shower."

While Maddie tried to come up with a good excuse herself, Dr. Parker paused with the kudzu around his neck and a small pucker between his eyebrows. He looked for a moment as if he were going to question Aunt Cassie about her appointment, but then changed his mind. "Yeah, you're right. You could use a good hosing down with soap and water."

Cassie stuck her hands on her hips. "You should try running yourself sometime—it'll keep some of that fried food you eat off of your stomach."

Maddie glanced at her aunt to make sure the heat hadn't fried her brain. Even though Dr. Parker was way old, even she could tell that he was pretty cut. And if she was as old as her aunt Cassie, she might even call him hot. Without his cowboy boots, of course.

Dr. Parker smiled. "But I do. Five miles a day. I just go at night when it's cooler and I won't be running into anybody who might catch a whiff of me. You should go with me sometime."

Maddie watched as her mama pulled the van into a space across the square and began to unload the double stroller.

Aunt Cassie smirked. "No, thanks. I like to run with somebody who can challenge me. Or alone. I like to be alone."

Dr. Parker didn't reply as he picked up more kudzu from the ground and handed it with a smile to Miss Harden. Without looking at Cassie, he said, "That's another bad habit she's learned up north. We'll have to do our best to break her of them while she's here."

"Don't bother," Aunt Cassie said, waving a dismissive hand in the air. "I won't be here long enough for anything to stick."

Miss Harden cleared her throat. "Is your meeting with Ed Farrell?"

Cassie nodded. "I was surprised to hear he had a respectable job. You'd think he'd be scratching out a living on the old dirt farm he grew up on." An evil grin split her face. "Hey, Sam, weren't you Ed's favorite punching bag in high school?"

Dr. Parker smiled, but it wasn't a real smile. "I was skinny as a stick and wore thick glasses. I was everyone's punching bag. But yeah, mostly Ed's."

Miss Harden nodded. "And those two are still at it—but in a more civilized way now. As a matter of fact, they're both running for the vacant town council seat."

Aunt Cassie wiped a bead of sweat off her nose that was threatening to drip. "Gosh, Sam. Do you ever have time to do any doctoring? With all your other activities, it's a surprise that you have any time left at all."

"Actually I do. That's one of the main reasons I left Boston to practice medicine here. I can have a life and a career."

Aunt Cassie's hands went to her hips so that she looked so much like Aunt Lucinda that Maddie almost laughed. "I have a life!"

Dr. Parker turned back to his kudzu. "I'm sure you do, Cassie. A very exciting and glamorous one."

Aunt Cassie dropped her hands, then faced Miss Harden. "I'll talk to you later. Tell Stinky I said hello." Without looking at Sam, she waved in his direction, then turned to jog across the square and join her sister. She called over her shoulder, "Come on, Maddie. Let's go see if your mama needs anything."

As they reached the van, Amanda started to whimper inside in her car seat.

Her mama smiled, but her eyes seemed to be only half-awake, reminding Maddie of what she'd looked like right after the births of all the siblings she was old enough to remember. But the baby was already on formula and had been sleeping through the night for months, so it made no sense why her mama would be so wiped out.

"I'm so glad I found you. My babysitter canceled last-minute, and I can't get a thing done here with Knoxie and the baby. At least Joey and Sarah Frances have vacation Bible school this week. Otherwise I might as well just duct-tape myself to the kitchen sink, since I wouldn't be moving from there anyway."

Mama handed Knoxie to Cassie. "Just stick her in the back of the stroller. I learned not to put her in front because Amanda grabs hold of Knoxie's pigtails and it really puts her in a state."

Knoxie smiled at her aunt as Cassie took her, holding her suspended over the double stroller like a person would hold a stinking garbage bag. Cassie saw the two feet holes and began lowering the toddler, kicking legs and all. Knoxie ended up with her right leg in the left foot hole and her left foot somehow in the front seat, and began to whimper.

"Here," said Harriet, handing Amanda to Maddie. She scooped up Knoxie and had her seated properly in the stroller without breaking a sweat. Calmly, she took the baby and set her in the front seat. "See? It's easy with just a little bit of practice. You won't have any problems."

Aunt Cassie's eyes opened with realization. "Wait a minute. I don't know anything about taking care of children. Besides, I have an appointment at eleven thirty and I need to shower." The baby gurgled and Cassie stared at her with a really scared look on her face.

Mama waved her hands through the air. "Don't be silly. You took care of me when I was little— it's just like riding a bike: you never forget how."

Maddie stepped forward. "I'll help. I've got a tennis lesson at eleven, but I can help until then."

Mama reached into the van and pulled out the enormous diaper bag and looped the shoulder strap over the handle of the stroller. "Everything you need is in here—and there're a few bottles already made in the refrigerator at your house. She'll probably be hungry in about an hour."

"But what about my appointment?"

Harriet slid the large heavy door of the van shut. "I'll try to be back by then, but if I'm not, just bring them with you. Everybody in town knows them, and they'll be glad to keep an eye on the girls while you do your business." She waved and took off at a brisk walk toward Dr. Parker and Miss Harden.

"But . . ." Aunt Cassie's objections faded as a little hand pulled on her fingers. She looked down at the stroller and Knoxie beamed up at her.

"See—it's easy." Maddie smiled. "And thank God I don't have to put up kudzu vines. If I hear one more thing about my mama being kudzu queen or how I'll have my chance to be queen, too, I will definitely throw up."

Aunt Cassie tugged on the stroller, but it didn't budge. Maddie leaned down and unhooked the lock, and began walking next to her aunt.

"When I get old like you, I'm not going to have any babies either. Mama had me nine months after she was married, and she's been stuck here ever since." Maddie lifted her ponytail off the back of her neck and wiped off the sweat. "I'm going to live in New York, or London, or Paris, and have an exciting career and be just like you. I don't want to have anything to do with diapers and bottles. I've had enough of that to last me a lifetime."

Cassie raised an eyebrow. "I never said I didn't want babies—" She stopped. "I mean I've never really discussed it with Andrew, but that doesn't mean . . ." She waved her hand. "My apartment's not baby-proof; let's put it that way."

Knoxie had been singing tunelessly to herself but stopped suddenly. She twisted her head around, her red hair almost gold in the morning sunlight. "I'm not a baby. Do you like me?"

Cassie poked her head around the top of the stroller. "Of course I do. You're pretty darned cute."

Suddenly, and at the top of her lungs, Knoxie shouted, "I need to go potty. Right now!"

Amanda, jerked out of a doze, began to cry.

"Uh-oh. When she says now, she means now." Maddie picked up the baby and handed her to Cassie, then yanked Knoxie from the stroller. "I'll be right back."

Madison ran with her little sister up to the front door of the nearest house. She knew one of the daughters from Sunday-school class. When a woman answered, Madison explained the situation, then went inside with Knoxie. After they were finished, they emerged from the house, each with a freshly baked chocolate-chip cookie.

Amanda's cries had now turned into yelps, until Cassie figured out that Amanda liked to be cradled. By the time Knoxie and Maddie reached them, Amanda had quieted down and was cuddled in Cassie's arms.

Maddie put Knoxie in the stroller while Cassie continued the rest of the walk with the baby tucked in her arms, apparently not too grossed out about the drool sliding onto her arm.

When they reached the house, Madison held the door open for her aunt. Knoxie ran back to the kitchen to get a drink of water while Maddie and Cassie walked slowly up the stairs with the now-sleeping Amanda. Aunt Cassie nudged open Mama's old bedroom door with her foot, and spied the portable crib in the corner. Slowly, she lowered the baby into the crib and they watched her rumpled bottom wriggle until she settled down again.

They stood in the hushed room for a long time, as Aunt Cassie's eyes took in the old wallpaper and white furniture.

"Has anything changed?" Maddie whispered.

Aunt Cassie shook her head. "It seems like yesterday that your mama and I were sitting cross-legged on that bedspread talking about crushes, dances, and fights with friends. Of course, I did most of the listening, since Harriet was the one with a social life."

The baby sighed in her sleep, and Cassie's eyes widened. She looked frantically at her arm. "What time is it? Oh, my gosh, I can't believe I forgot my watch. I never forget my watch."

She headed out of the room and was halfway down the hallway before she turned back to Maddie. "Thanks for your help. And thanks for the run, too. We'll do it again sometime, okay?"

"Sure." Maddie smiled, then waited for her aunt to return to her own room and close the door. She stared down at her own naked wrist. She'd never had a watch, had never even wanted one. But maybe it was time she got one.

Maddie headed for the stairs and took them two at a time, avoiding all the creaks and grunts she'd memorized since she was small, feeling, as she always did, the watchful eyes of all of her Madison ancestors.

CHAPTER 7

The stroller bumped into the curb, then rolled back onto Cassie's foot. She winced at the pain, then winced again as she noticed the scuff mark on the toe of her shoe. She pushed it harder this time, bringing it successfully over the curb, then strolled the children down the sidewalk to where Ed Farrell had told her his office stood. The building had once housed Hal's Heavenly Bakery, and as she stood before the large storefront window, she had a brief memory of herself on her father's shoulders, eating a doughnut on the way home from church. She saw her mother holding Harriet, a wide smile on her face as she reached up to stroke Cassie's cheek.

Cassie stared at the brick three-story building, sandwiched between Bitsy's House of Beauty and Walton's Drug Emporium, and blinked hard, erasing the memories along with the pang of nostalgia in the pit of her stomach. Propping the door open with her foot, she maneuvered the double stroller into the office. The strong odor of new carpet and the feel of crisp air-conditioning hit her hard.

She paused for a moment inside the door while she took off her sunglasses and tried to stick them in her purse. Her smart leather bag was now crammed with two pacifiers, a small squeaky toy, and a container of Cheerios, leaving little room for anything else. With a sigh, she stuck the glasses on top of her head. She lifted her gaze and caught a glimpse of a richly furnished waiting room, with dark polished wood floors, Oriental carpets, overstuffed leather sofas, and real oil paintings on the walls. Nothing remained of Hal's bakery, not even a lingering aroma of baking bread. Cassie's first thought was to step outside and make sure she was in the right place.

A squeal from a corner erupted from a woman pulling herself to a stand behind an elaborate mahogany desk. A wide pink headband cut through a near-bouffant hairdo, sitting on the white-blond hair like a lipsticked smile.

"Cassie Madison! I can hardly believe you're standing here in front of me." The woman enveloped her in an embrace of downy arms and bosom, then held her at arm's length as if to get a good look at her.

Cassie stared at the woman in her soft pink knit suit, more cleavage showing than was necessary for a receptionist in a Realtor's office, and tried not to smile as she thought how much this woman resembled a dish sponge.

The woman spoke again, small white teeth peering through the brightly hued lips. "You don't remember me, do you?"

"Um, sure I do. You're . . ." Cassie leaned over

the baby to tuck a blanket around her, racking her brain for the identity of this stranger.

"I'm Laura-Louise Whittaker." She paused, seemingly waiting for a glimmer of recognition. "You probably remember me as Lou-Lou—I was on the cheerleading squad with Harriet all through high school."

Cassie's eyes widened with recognition. "Of course. I didn't recognize you with, um, your hair. It's, ah . . . You're doing something different with it, aren't you?"

Lou-Lou patted it gently with the palm of her hand. "I'm a blonde now." She leaned forward with a conspiring air. "And it's true—we really do have more fun." She let out a shrill giggle—the same giggle that had made Cassie's skin crawl in high school. Some things never changed.

Lou-Lou straightened and smoothed her skirt. "My. Where's my professionalism? I'll tell Ed, um, Mr. Farrell, that you're here. But we'll have to chat later—I'm just dying to hear all about New York."

She slid behind her desk and pushed a long pink nail on an intercom button. She winked at Cassie. "Mr. Farrell. Your eleven thirty is here."

Cassie gave Lou-Lou the warmest smile she could find. "Lou-Lou, I hope you don't mind, but I was wondering if you could watch my two nieces while I meet with Ed?"

Lou-Lou threw her hands up in a picture of

apparent delight. "Why, I'd love to. Me and Harriet are practically sisters and I love her kids— all five of them!—like they were my own. Just leave that stroller right there, and Aunt Lou-Lou will take care of these little dumplings while you attend to business."

At that moment, a door at the back of the office opened, and a man appeared in the doorway. Cassie noticed the man's height first. His dark slicked-back hair, parted in the middle, almost skimmed the top of the doorway. She remembered that Ed Farrell had played on the junior varsity basketball team his freshman year before quitting for a reason she couldn't quite recall.

He approached her with an outstretched hand, his broad smile traversing most of his slender face. She looked again at his hair. She remembered that it had been the same mousy brown as her own, and wondered absently if he dyed it. His double-breasted suit made a slight swishing noise as he walked, and the sheen of it under the fluorescent lights convinced Cassie it wasn't made with natural fibers. She chided herself silently for being such a snob. Ed Farrell had apparently done very well for himself, and she should be admiring him for his success instead of belittling him for an unfortunate choice in suits.

He shook her hand while cupping the back of it with his other hand. His skin was rough, a cold reminder of his years pulling a hoe. As if reading

126

her thoughts, Ed slipped his hands from hers a little too quickly.

"You look wonderful, Cassie. Long time no see, huh?"

His deep voice was a smoker's voice: like hot tar over gravel. She smelled nicotine mixed with mint as he spoke.

"Thank you, Ed. And, yes, it has been a long time. But it wouldn't be gentlemanly of you to make me remember exactly how long it's been." Cassie stopped herself from saying anything else, wondering why she was talking like Scarlett O'Hara all of a sudden.

He winked, then touched her on the elbow. "Let's go back to my office, where we can sit down and chat."

Cassie glanced over at Lou-Lou, who seemed to be having a marvelous time shaking a rattle and making funny faces at the girls. She watched as Lou-Lou sent a luminescent gaze to Ed. "I'll bring you some coffee in just a minute, Mr. Farrell."

He nodded with a wink, then ushered Cassie into his office.

The office decor was even more elaborate than the reception area. Built-in bookcases with recessed lighting illuminated small *objets d'art*. An oversize crystal chandelier dangled from the ceiling, each pendant tipped with gold. A blueprint, almost the size of the huge mahogany desktop, hung in a gilt frame over the fireplace.

Cassie was about to sit down on a sofa when the blueprint caught her gaze.

Slowly she walked over to it, staring closely, and pointed at a small rectangle in the lower right of the paper. "That's my house."

Ed approached her with a small smile. He spread his blunt fingers, a gold signet ring circling his pinkie, over the northwest quadrant of the paper that was covered with about two hundred blue squares.

"Yep. That's my development. That used to be your cotton fields, now quickly becoming Farrellsford swim and tennis community. Bought it from your daddy."

Cassie could only nod. After a moment, she said, "I didn't realize how big it was—and how close to the house."

Ed led her back to the sofa and motioned for her to sit. He joined her on the opposite end of the cushion. "Don't worry about your privacy. We've plans to plant pine trees at the boundary line that will eventually block the view from your house entirely." He smiled and she noticed how incredibly white his teeth were.

Cassie waited a moment for him to continue, and when he didn't, she said, "Looks like you've done pretty well for yourself, Ed."

He shrugged. "Yep. Well, there really wasn't anywhere for me to go but up, you know what I mean?"

She looked down at the hands in her lap, unsure how to respond.

He spoke first. "So. You want to sell your house. You've certainly come to the right place."

She smiled up at him, grateful for the change in conversation. "Yes. I'd like to put it on the market as soon as possible. I have some cleanup to do—like the attic and all the closets need to be gone through—but I have a job and a fiancé waiting for me in New York and I'm really eager to get back."

"A fiancé, hm? You marryin' a Yankee?" He winked at her, but gave the impression that he really wanted to hear an answer.

Cassie flattened her hands on her lap. "He's not from New York originally. He was born and raised in California, but he's been in New York since college. He owns an advertising agency there, and I work for him."

Ed nodded. "Yes. Well. I hope you're both patient people, because it could take a while to unload an old house like yours. People these days wanting to spend that kind of money want something new—like what I'm offering them in Farrellsford. Sure, an old house is nice to look at and all, but it lacks a lot of modern conveniences that today's sophisticated buyers want." He stood, his brows furrowed as if he were in deep thought.

"If you don't have a spa tub in the master bath or granite and stainless steel in a superlarge kitchen . . ." He paused, pursing his lips together.

"Let's just say it'll be a hard sell. Even if you add all those things, you'll still be competing with new homes in the same price range."

Cassie's face fell. "I've never sold a house before, and I just had no idea. How long do you think it could take?"

He lifted his shoulders. "A month. Two months. A year. Who knows?" He smiled warmly. "Now, don't get me wrong. It's a beautiful house—and I'm sure there's a buyer for it out there somewhere. It could just take a while. Unless you're willing to look at other options."

Cassie sat back on the sofa. "Like what?"

Ed leaned against the edge of his desk, concentrating on a brass globe on its surface.

"Well, you could always sell the land. It's a lot more valuable than the house. Or convert the house to apartments, or just start all over with retail space. Or, if you sold to a developer, they could always use the house as a clubhouse for a housing development."

Her eyes widened, and dread settled in her stomach area. "A clubhouse?"

The suit rustled again as Ed folded his arms across his chest. With a compassionate smile, he said, "I know. It's not what we want, but I wanted to mention that you had options. With local zoning the way it is, you could pretty much do anything." His brows furrowed. "And I wanted to thank you for coming to me first instead of Roust

Development. They're the ones who've already bought the property on either side of yours. They want to put up a mall—can you believe? Imagine the noise and traffic—and all in our backyards." His tongue clucked. "That's what happens when outsiders move in. They don't care about what was here first." He shook his head solemnly. "So I'm glad you came to me. I'll make sure that whatever happens to your property, it's for the benefit of both you and the town of Walton."

He walked back over to her and sat down. "I'm here to help you make the right decision for you." Cassie stood, needing to move. "I'd like to start with trying to find a family to buy the house. If that doesn't work, then we can discuss plan B. And, of course, everything with the understanding that I won't be staying here to oversee the sale. I really need to get back to New York."

He nodded, his face solemn. "I understand. And I will do my very best to find a nice little family for your house." He stood, too, and moved to the chair on the other side of his desk, looking up as Lou-Lou walked in with a silver tray and coffee service.

Ed grinned again and his perfect white teeth, definitely a new acquisition since high school, beamed at her. "Let's just fill out some paperwork now, and schedule a time for me to come out for an appraisal." He looked up expectantly. "And I'll need a spare key to put in a lockbox on the front door. I'm assuming I won't need to call each time I come to show a client the house. You get more traffic that way."

Cassie agreed, then moved her chair closer to the desk, trying not to stare at the light brown roots cropping up under the slicked-back dark hair of her newly hired Realtor.

CASSIE SLUMPED OVER her father's desk, the drawers open and their innards stacked all around the floor, like an old teddy bear with its stuffing pulled out. The hall clock struck six times and she rubbed her eyes. She had accomplished virtually nothing. There had been a steady stream of visitors, friends and neighbors of her father's, calling to give their condolences and bring food. Lucinda had made enough trips out to the huge icebox inside the detached garage that a well-worn path now marked her way. There was enough macaroni mousse ring, lemon-parsley chicken casserole, and scalloped eggplant to feed an entire city block and then some.

Most of the visitors were familiar faces, and all had stayed for a long social call to catch up on what Cassie had been doing in her extended absence. Her throat was parched from telling them the same thing over and over: yes, she lived and worked in Manhattan, and yes, the taxi drivers did drive like maniacs, and, no, she had not yet been to the Statue of Liberty, although she had seen a

Gay Pride parade, but only because it marched on the street in front of a client's building where she'd happened to be at the time.

The desk chair squeaked as Cassie sat back and stretched. She found some comfort sitting in her father's chair, the wide, well-worn feel of it behind her a gentle reminder of her father's never-ending love and support—even when she least deserved it. Especially the last fifteen years. The familiar sting of tears threatened again and she rubbed her eyes harshly with the heels of her hands.

Almost without thinking, Cassie reached out to the plate carrying old Aunt Millie's famous nut cake. She stared in horror, realizing she had eaten nearly half of it, pinching off a bite at a time. Her thighs seemed to stick to the leather chair as it occurred to her that it had probably been made with real eggs and butter. She just couldn't imagine Aunt Millie, with her jowly arms and double chin, thinking egg or butter substitutes had any business being in her kitchen. Cassie pinched another small bite off the side of the cake. She had to admit nothing tasted better than the real thing.

With a sigh, Cassie slammed the drawer shut. The drawers had been a jumbled mess consisting of old letters, paid bills, canceled checks, and an assortment of school papers and report cards from when she and Harriet were in elementary school. There was no rhyme or reason to their organization. They had seemingly just been tossed into whatever drawer had the most room, and forgotten. Until now. Now they lay in separate piles, ready to be distributed as Cassie saw fit. The largest pile, with her high school graduation photo on top, had a date with the garbage can.

She stood, grabbing a large bite of cake, and shoved it in her mouth. As she crossed the foyer, the doorbell rang. Her eyes widened in horror as she realized Sam Parker had already spied her through the lead glass sidelights next to the door. She tried to swallow the nut cake, but such a large amount had been stuffed in that it couldn't be budged without a tall glass of milk. Resignedly, she pulled open the door, her cheeks puffed out like a chipmunk's. As an afterthought, she swiped the back of her hand across her mouth.

Sam raised his eyebrows. "You missed some."

"Hrumphmm?" She dared not open her mouth.

"Crumbs. You've got crumbs all over your chin."

She left the door standing open with Sam in the threshold and quickly ran into the powder room off the hall. When she was done, she came out and found, to her irritation, that Sam had let himself in, closed the front door, and was seated comfortably in a chair in the front parlor. He was staring up at the crown molding on the fourteen-foot ceilings, but stood when she entered the room. "The woodwork in this house never ceases to amaze me. They just don't make anything like it anymore."

"Is there something you need?" she asked, wondering whether she should have checked her teeth for more crumbs.

"Just you."

It was her turn to raise an eyebrow. "Excuse me?"

"Harriet and Joe have requested the honor of your presence at dinner tonight. They know Lucinda's gone to Atlanta to visit her cousin, and didn't want you left alone. They think you'll starve if nobody's here to feed you." She could tell he was trying to hide a smile. "As if the fine folks of Walton would let that happen."

Self-consciously, Cassie brought her hand to her mouth to search for crumbs, then dropped it with annoyance.

Sam smiled brightly. "So they've been trying to reach you for most of the day to invite you for dinner, but the house phone's been busy and nobody knows your cell number."

Cassie shrugged. "Cell number won't work because I forgot my charger for my BlackBerry and the battery's dead. And I took the house phone off the hook. Everybody and their mother was calling to find out how I was, and I just couldn't get anything done. So I took it off the hook." She didn't know why, but she felt embarrassed to admit it.

He crossed his arms, revealing well-muscled forearms that protruded from rolled-up sleeves. He wore the ubiquitous jeans and cowboy boots, and Cassie had to silently admit that he looked good in his choice of clothing—even if it wasn't her style. He stared at her in a silent question.

"What?" she asked, wondering if something was still clinging to her chin.

"I'm ready when you are. Unless you've spoiled your dinner with too much nut cake." He pointed his head in the direction of her father's desk and the half-eaten cake. "I peeked."

"Of course not. I didn't have that much. I offered some to the visiting hordes today." She didn't feel guilty because it wasn't a complete lie. She had offered some to her visitors, just hadn't had any takers.

"Then let's go."

Cassie tried to think of an excuse, but she was tired of going through her father's things, and maybe some real food would settle her stomach. She also found she wanted to talk to Harriet—to reminisce about their father, to bring him to mind and to reassure each other that he still lived in their hearts. After discarding so much of his life in piles lined up against the study wall, she needed reminders of his existence.

"All right—hang on. I need to get my shoes." She ran up the stairs, feeling his gaze on her backside, and wishing again that all her skirts weren't so short. Everybody was wearing them in Manhattan, but she'd yet to see anything above the knee since she'd been in Walton.

She flicked on the closet light in her bedroom and eyed the various shoes, finally deciding on the beige pumps. Sliding her feet into them, she closed the closet and went back to the stairs. She found it hard to resist galloping down the wood steps as she had as a child, but instead walked sedately down to where Sam stood in the foyer.

His gaze slowly swept down the length of her legs, finally resting on her feet. "Heels?"

She looked down. "What's wrong with heels?"

"Nothing at all. In fact, they look real fine on your feet. But wouldn't you be more comfortable in something else?"

She lifted her chin and walked past him, opening the screen door before he could reach it and open it for her. "No, I wouldn't. I'm used to them. Besides, I don't own anything else except for my running shoes and I wouldn't be caught dead wearing those with a skirt."

He followed behind her, his boot heels clumping on the wood floor of the hall, then out onto the porch. Cassie stopped and used her key to dead-bolt the door, then pulled on the knob to make sure it was locked tight.

Sam leaned one arm on one of the tall columns of the porch. "That's not necessary, you know. Nobody's going to take anything while you're gone. Unless you're trying to stop people from bringing more food, of course; then by all means you should lock up."

Ignoring him, she turned and walked down the porch steps, spotting Andrew's Mercedes in the circular driveway.

"Finally! I was wondering when I'd see it again."

Sam didn't answer, but instead rapped his bare knuckles against the solid wood column. "This house is amazing. You don't know how lucky you are."

"You think so? Ed Farrell thinks I might have a hell of a time trying to unload it." She dropped her keys in her purse and hoisted it onto her shoulder.

He paused for a moment, looking as if he wanted to say something, then continued across the yard in the opposite direction.

Cassie called after him, "Where are you going?"

"I'm getting into my truck."

"I can see that—but we've got my car back."

He turned the ignition, and a blast of country music danced out of the open window. "*You've* got your car back. I'd rather not be seen in it. People 'round here might think I've been hit on the head."

"Don't tempt me," she muttered. Sticking her hands on her hips, she asked, "Then how'd you get it over here?"

Sam slammed his door, then leaned over to push open the passenger door. "My dad and Mr. Anderson. Looked like a couple of fools going through their midlife crisis two decades late. Now get in or we'll be late for dinner."

Cassie didn't budge. "This is a very nice car, I'll have you know. I could blow the doors off your truck without even trying."

"Can't haul anything in it, and the third passenger has to lie down horizontally in the back. I think they should halve the price, since they're only giving you half the car. Now climb in." He patted the seat next to him. "I even had my truck customized with a bench seat with a lady's comfort in mind. It'll give you the chance to scooch up next to me if you like."

Ignoring him, Cassie asked, "Where are my keys? We could waste gas and take two separate vehicles." She shifted her feet, already feeling the sticky perspiration under her arms, and not wanting to be standing in the heat one second longer. She wondered why she was being so stubborn about something so stupid. Yes, she wasn't particularly fond of trucks, bench seat or not, and dreaded stepping up into them in a short skirt. But it was more than that. Maybe it was his attitude that she'd grown too big for her britches. Which wasn't true. Not really.

He raised an eyebrow. "In my pocket."

A drip of sweat crept down her back between her shoulder blades. "May I have them? Please?"

Grinning broadly, he said, "You'll have to get them yourself."

She pulled the front of her blouse away from her chest where it had begun to stick. The air-conditioning blew Sam's hair off his forehead, and she could almost feel its chilling breeze.

She looked again at the Mercedes, sitting in the hot sun, then back at Sam's truck. Without another word she climbed in and sat down, regardless of whom she flashed.

Sam moved the vents to blow in her direction as Cassie donned her sunglasses.

"I can only hope that nobody recognizes me." She knew that was mean, but he'd asked for it with his snide comments about Andrew's car. Maybe now he'd call it even.

Sam slid the truck into gear. "There are worse things than to be recognized as a small-town country girl, you know. Like being thought of as a big-city snob."

That did it. Cassie's sunglasses had moved down her nose with sweat, and she pushed them up with a well-manicured index finger. "At least I don't think 'genitalia' is an Italian airline."

Sam snorted as he pulled the truck down the gravel drive to the main road. "I think you've been listening to too many Jeff Foxworthy jokes."

As Sam drove slowly down the block, Cassie tried to ignore the driver, but her gaze kept straying to his side of the bench seat. Even the way he sat, his left knee drawn up casually, his right elbow resting on the back of the seat, and his hand light on the wheel, screamed confident self-assurance. This man, with his pickup truck, cowboy boots, and drawling accent, seemed more sure of himself than anyone she had ever met. And it irked her no end.

"Did you really go to Harvard?"

He glanced at her briefly. "Yep. But only for med school. Went to Yale for undergrad. I transferred there from the junior college after you left."

She studied him for a moment. "Then why on earth did you come back here?"

He kept his gaze straight ahead, the light from the windshield brightening his eyes. "Because this is home. I figured life had to be about more than just work and making money. I wanted a place to grow roots. Become part of a community. Raise a family in a familiar environment." He stole a glance at Cassie.

"You forgot guilt. Your parents must have pulled on you at every chance. At least I wasn't an only child, so I had the option."

Sam looked at her hard. "Guilt over my brother, you mean? That had nothing to do with it. My parents never once asked me to come back. I did it on my own."

Cassie was surprised by his vehemence, wondering whom he was really trying to convince.

"But didn't you like Boston? There's so much excitement there. So much to do."

Sam shrugged. "It's fine—to visit. But I never really fit in."

She gave him a sardonic smile. "Gee, I wonder why? Could it be the way you talk or the way you dress?"

He caught her with a withering glance. "And what's wrong with the way I dress?"

Unobtrusively, Cassie eyed the plaid shirt rolled up on his strong forearms, the jeans hugging his well-muscled thighs, and the cowboy boots. She opened her mouth to say something, then swallowed thickly. "Oh, never mind."

He shrugged. "I found out later from a friend of mine that a lot of people at school thought I was gay. Could never figure that one out."

"Really? Did you have a truck?"

He shook his head. "Nope. Couldn't afford to park one up there."

She laughed out loud. "Then it's the boots. In Manhattan, that's a dead giveaway."

"Humph." Sam pulled to a stop at a light, and rested his wrist on the steering wheel. "I guess I didn't date much either, which probably fueled the fire. Not much time with all that studying, plus those city girls just seemed too, I don't know, glittery for my taste. I guess I prefer something less shiny." He reached up and adjusted his rearview mirror. "You know, someone who doesn't reveal all her feminine secrets in the first fifteen minutes."

Cassie stared out the window with studied nonchalance. How dumb were those girls, anyway? One didn't have to know Sam Parker to know there wasn't a gay bone in his body. He practically reeked of masculinity, and sitting this close to him in his truck made her squirm. She shifted closer to the door.

"Too bad you didn't have this truck with you. The bench seat would have made them swoon." She gave an inelegant snort. "You must have a lot of confidence in the lady's department if you really had your truck custom done with their comfort in mind."

"Actually, I was making that up. I needed a bench seat because sometimes I have to transport people to the hospital or boxes of handouts and stuff for various conferences I go to. Practical reasons, I suppose, but you can't fault me for hoping it'll appeal to the ladies, too."

Remembering the high step she had to take just to get inside, she said, "Don't go holding your breath on that one."

They drove in silence for a few moments before Sam spoke. "How did your meeting with Ed Farrell go today?"

Cassie raised her eyebrows. "I'm surprised you haven't already read the minutes from the meeting. News sure travels fast in a small town."

Sam nodded, but didn't smile. "That's certainly one thing you can bank on here. That and plenty of contestants for the watermelon-seed spitting at the Kudzu Festival. It just is. And that Lou-Lou

Whittaker is the biggest gossip this side of the Mississippi."

He turned onto Harriet's street. "What did he have to say besides that it will take a long time to sell your house?"

"Why do you want to know?"

Sam pulled into the driveway of a neat two-story brick colonial. Bikes, bike helmets, and Roller-blades decorated the neatly clipped yard. He shifted the truck into park and switched off the ignition before turning to her. "There are lots of people in this town who believe Ed Farrell is in the developers' pockets. The old farm his parents worked was the first thing to be bulldozed. They're building a poultry processing plant on it now. That's all well and good, but now he's focusing on other chunks of land throughout the community."

The front screen door opened and Sarah Frances and Joey tumbled out and ran down the stairs toward the truck.

Sam continued. "One by one they're selling out, and Ed's pocketing lots of cash brokering these deals. They all know him as one of them, and they trust him. All I know for sure is that if we're not careful, we'll be a commercial wasteland in a few years. Nothing but plants and industrial parks. And big neighborhoods with cookie-cutter houses. No character, no history. Nothing left of what makes this town so great." He yanked the keys out of the ignition. "And don't believe him when he tells you he's one of us and not one of those other developers who want to tear apart our town. He's still cut from the same cloth."

Sarah Frances tapped on the window and Cassie reached for the door handle. "I think I understand your point, but it's got nothing to do with me. Ed's merely going to help me find somebody to buy my house—he even mentioned a family he already had in mind." She pushed the door open, angry at him for lecturing her on something that was none of his business. "But even if I were to sell it to a developer, that would be my own decision. Ed's opinion wouldn't sway me one way or the other."

Sam held her forearm for a moment, preventing her from leaving the truck. "You're wrong, Cassie. It's not just your decision. Your house is part of Walton's history. There're a lot of people here who would care very much what happens to your house. Including me."

She yanked her arm out of his grasp and stepped out of the truck. Four small arms encircled her waist. A warm glow started somewhere deep inside, surprising her. Even more surprising was the fact that she hardly gave a second thought to the dirty handprints that were bound to be smudged on her skirt.

Cassie hugged them both, and rumpled their hair, then reached for their hands. But they pulled out of her grasp and raced to Sam.

"Dr. Parker!" they shouted in unison, running

and jumping on him. He eagerly caught them, then adjusted them easily on each hip before sauntering toward Cassie.

She turned her back on him and walked up the three brick steps to the front door, where Harriet now stood in the doorway. As Cassie neared, Harriet's cheerleader smile faded. She stuck out her hand and gingerly touched the necklace around Cassie's neck, letting the charms slip silently through her fingers.

With a soft voice, Harriet said, "I remember this. Keeper of hearts, right?"

The memory of her mother's voice uttering those same words stilled Cassie's breath. She felt, rather than saw, Sam slipping by with the two children. She reached up to the charms and touched her sister's fingers.

"Keeper of hearts." The words barely made it past her lips. Before she realized what she was doing, she hugged her sister, holding on tightly.

"Mama! Sarah Frances won't help me set the table." Maddie's voice came from back in the house, amidst shouting and the clatter of small feet on wood floors.

Cassie smiled, then awkwardly pulled away, the silence of fifteen years still heavy between them, but the bond of a father's death bringing them together by a degree. Then she followed Harriet back into the kitchen, her hand still clutching the gold charms around her neck.

CHAPTER 8

Harriet found Sam in the kitchen, leaning over a steaming pot on the stove.

He smiled as she approached. "Something sure smells good. If you're not careful, Harriet, you're going to find me hanging around your doorstep every night around suppertime."

She tapped him gently on his flat abdomen. "That's what I like about you, Sam. You're so easy to please."

Cassie shook her head; then they all turned toward the table.

Maddie was busy throwing place mats, napkins, and silverware on the table with a heavy scowl on her face. A tall stack of dishes awaited her attack on the corner of the table. When she spotted her aunt, she beamed. "Hey, Aunt Cassie."

Harriet watched as the two faces, so eerily similar, grinned at each other. She and Maddie had always been on different wavelengths—especially now that her daughter had reached adolescence. Harriet leaned back against the counter, closing her eyes and feeling suddenly overwhelmed with exhaustion. Maybe it was the constant battles with Maddie that were consuming all her energy. She opened her eyes and smiled at her sister, glad to have found a translator to help her communicate with her eldest child. With a small stab of guilt, she couldn't help but hope that the growing closeness she could see between the two might be yet another incentive for Cassie to become a part of their lives.

Cassie reached over and flicked Maddie's hair. "I like what you're doing with your hair."

Madison slid a spoon and fork across the table's surface, sending them almost careening off the table. "I've pinned it up to see if I like the shorter look. Then I think I might get it cut"—she made a chopping motion with her hands, indicating a blunt bob—"like this." She slapped a place mat down in front of her before dumping silverware on it. "I've been trying to find a picture to show Miss Bitsy so she can do it right."

Harriet's gaze caught Cassie's and they shared a smile, realizing that Maddie's new hairstyle closely resembled her aunt's.

With studied nonchalance, Cassie grabbed a stack of plates and began placing them around the table, picking up the disarrayed silverware and placing it neatly next to the plates. "Maybe I could come to Bitsy's with you."

Harriet recognized the expression on her daughter's face—the expression that said, *I'm listening intently but I have to pretend I don't care*—and turned away for a moment to hide her own smile.

Maddie began studiously placing glasses at each table setting. Without looking up, she said, "Sure.

Whatever." Then she looked away, but not before Harriet saw a pleased flush cover her daughter's cheeks.

Cassie shook her head. "I can't believe Bitsy is still cutting hair. She gave me my first real haircut."

With a mock look of horror, Sam said, "It was a hideous bowl cut, if I recall correctly. And you wore a handkerchief over your head for a week."

Cassie paused for a moment with a fork in midair, her expression a mixture of surprise and annoyance. "Yeah. I did. And you have my permission to forget about that, too."

The sliding glass door opened, letting in Joe and the smell of barbecue. Harriet smiled, wondering if she would still have that heart jolt every time she saw her husband even after she became an old woman.

Cassie looked up and froze, her gaze centered somewhere between the tip of Joe's nose and his left ear, as if she were unable to look him in the eye. They still seemed unsure how to behave around each other, acting like neighborhood dogs sniffing about to mark their territory and state their rules of engagement. Harriet knew it would take time for them to settle into a friendship, and there was nothing she could do but let them sniff until they were comfortable.

"Hi, Cassie." Joe nodded in her direction. "Hey, Sam. Why don't you grab a couple of beers and come outside with me? I want to show you my new gas grill. Does just about everything but pluck the chicken and wash dishes."

Sam whistled. "Now that's an offer a man can't refuse."

Sam pulled two beer cans from the refrigerator, then left the room with Joe, sliding the door shut behind them as Harriet gave an exasperated sigh.

"Men and their toys. They never really grow up, do they?" She turned toward the counter and started tearing lettuce into a salad bowl, knowing there was nothing she would want to change. Over her shoulder she said, "Please hurry up with setting the table, Maddie. You're moving slower than a herd of turtles through molasses. I need you to finish this salad so I can see to the rest of dinner."

Cassie spoke up. "I'm not that handy in a kitchen anymore, but I can help chop stuff for the salad." She stood next to Harriet and grabbed a cucumber and a sharp knife. Their arms brushed, and they looked at each other, as if simultaneously remembering the same image of them helping Lucinda prepare dinner in their father's house.

Harriet grinned. "Remember when Aunt Lucinda went on that health food kick?"

"How could I forget? That's when Daddy almost set the house on fire trying to fry chicken in the middle of the night so he could get a decent meal." Cassie shook her head. "He said it was his

150

God-given right as a Southerner to eat fried food." She diced a few chunks off the cucumber, her voice quieting. "He still had those grease-fire scars on his hand, didn't he? Don't think he minded, though. Man, how he loved fried chicken."

They were silent for a moment as tears sprang to Harriet's eyes and Cassie looked away. Harriet wasn't sure if the tears were for her father, or for all the lost years that had separated her from her sister. She leaned heavily on the counter, the overwhelming exhaustion overtaking her again, and made a vow to herself to go to bed early.

Cassie stared down at the cucumber. "Don't you dare start with those tears—or I'll start, too, and not be able to stop. Then dinner will never be ready."

Harriet sniffled and nodded, tearing another leaf of lettuce into small bits, and taking comfort in the presence of her sister working nearby.

They were eventually rejoined by the men, and when Amanda's fretting sounded from the baby monitor, Joe went upstairs to get her. He settled her in the baby swing in the corner of the kitchen, then joined Harriet in the dinner preparations, accompanied by the usual mayhem of a large family. Children ran in and out, the door swinging open and shut in a rapid procession, while all sorts of conversations were shouted across the room and to the backs of departing children.

"Supper's almost ready. Don't go too far, you hear?"

"Don't pick your nose, Joey. Now go wash your hands and get ready to eat."

"Go practice your scales, Sarah Frances, until it's time for supper."

Harriet realized how strange and noisy it must seem to Cassie, but when she looked at her sister, Cassie was smiling.

As they worked side by side, Harriet felt Joe come up behind her and kiss her cheek. When he stepped away, Harriet found Cassie watching them, an expression of loss mixed with wonder and hope clear and readable on her face. And at the same time, Harriet couldn't help but notice that Sam was watching Cassie with the same expression.

The whole crew, with the exception of baby Amanda, who was busily gnawing on a rattle in her swing, sat elbow-to-elbow around the large pine table in the kitchen, and it made Harriet's heart swell just a little to see them all together for the first time. She had deliberately seated Sam to Cassie's direct right, and felt some satisfaction every time she noticed Sam's arm rubbing against Cassie's. Harriet sent a disapproving glare to her sister when Cassie moved her chair as far away from Sam's as she could get it without leaving the table entirely.

Harriet said the blessing, encouraging everyone

152

to join hands. Cassie reached tentatively toward Sam's fingers, and his hand quickly swallowed hers. As soon as the blessing was finished, she pulled her hand away and reached for the collard greens.

To Harriet's eternal relief, the children were amazingly civilized at the table, with no arguing and remembering their "no, ma'ams" and "yes, sirs" when they were spoken to by their parents and other adults.

Harriet watched Cassie and Sam closely, how they each tried to pretend that they were unaware of the other, but how quickly each movement of one was followed by a furtive glance from the other.

Flattening her napkin in her lap, Harriet smiled to herself. She'd been aware of Sam's interest in her sister since grade school. But Cassie had always been so busy trying to attract attention that she had failed to notice she already had a fan. Now that Cassie was back, it would be interesting to see how this all played out. Harriet didn't know anything about this Andrew fellow back in New York, but she'd place her bet that he didn't come close to Sam Parker in any category, and wondered how long it would take Cassie to realize it. Leaning back in her chair, Harriet prepared to watch the show.

Cassie had just taken a bite out of a piece of barbecue brisket when Sam brought up the subject of Ed Farrell and Harriet groaned inside.

Turning to Cassie, he asked, "Did you give Ed the key to your house?"

Cassie washed down her food with a quick swallow of sweet tea. "Yes, I did. How can he show the house if he can't get in?"

Sam didn't answer right away. Instead, he got involved in a conversation with Joey about the best time to go fishing in Senator Thompkins's creek, and then everybody's attention was diverted by a request from Knoxie for another glass of milk. Cassie motioned for Harriet to stay seated while she went to the refrigerator and retrieved the carton of milk, placing it in the middle of the table after refilling four glasses.

The family continued to eat in relative peace, and Harriet hoped the entire subject of Ed Farrell had been dropped. She tried to engage everyone in conversation by mentioning old friends they had all once known, but all topics seemed to lead to Joe and Harriet running off, or to Ed Farrell. As the conversation lulled, Sam turned to Cassie again.

"I don't think it's a good idea to give Ed access to your house." He began buttering a large piece of corn bread.

Putting down her fork, Cassie stared at him. "Excuse me?"

He placed his knife carefully on the edge of his plate. "I don't think somebody like Ed should have free access to your house."

"Really. And you call me a snob. You're no better. Just because the guy was poor as a child, you think he's out to rob us blind. Let me tell you something, Dr. Parker: if his office is any indication of how well he's doing, he doesn't need anything from me or you or anybody."

Sam slid his chair back slightly so he could turn to face her. Harriet watched as a tic began in his left cheek. "He wasn't the only one born poor, Cassie, if you'll remember. But he sure as hell . . ." With a guilty expression, he looked across the table at the youngest three children staring at him with large eyes. "Um, heck . . . has not reached his current level of affluence by playing by the book.

"And I'm not just saying this because of the way he used to bully me in school. I'm referring to the way he's allowing the most god-awful businesses and buildings to go up just anywhere. The town council doesn't want to oppose him because they think he's all civic-minded because of all the money he throws at the high school booster club and the Beautify Walton campaign. He even planted about one thousand petunias on his own in the town square just to convince people of his sincerity." Sam shook his head, then took a long drink of tea.

Harriet knew better than to interrupt him when he was talking about a subject so near his heart. She let him finish. "The next day, he sold the Northcutts' house over on Willow, and now the new owners are selling used car parts from the front yard. Now, you tell me how he got that zoning changed."

Cassie opened her mouth to speak but was quelled by a harsh look from Sam. "And now Ed's running for that town council seat, saying he's got Walton's best interests at heart." He forced air out of his lips. "He doesn't care about anything except lining his own pockets."

Cassie took advantage of the opportunity to speak when Sam took another drink. "So what does this have to do with my giving him my house key? I've hired him to sell my house, and I trust him to get the job done to the best of his abilities. Obviously, he knows a lot about the market."

Sam dropped the corn bread onto his plate. "I'm sorry, but I just don't trust the man. There's always the question that lingers in my mind of how he found the money to not only go to college but to start his own business. There's something there, and I don't like it. He's the last person in the world you should be giving your house key to."

Cassie picked up her fork again, and Harriet saw her clenching her jaw, an old sign that meant she was trying to keep her anger in check. "All I want is for him to sell my house as quickly as possible. Whatever he wants me to do to facilitate that, I'll do. Even if it ends up that I need to convert it to apartments to sell."

Sam rested his hands on the table for a moment and stared down at his plate. The throbbing in his cheek beat faster. Finally, after wiping his mouth with a napkin, he pushed his chair back.

"Thank you, Harriet, Joe. It was delicious. But if you will excuse me for a bit, I need to go out to my truck and check my messages and return a few calls."

Without looking at Cassie, he slid his chair out farther and left. Harriet and Joe switched their gazes from Sam's retreating back to Cassie.

"What crawled into his boots?" Cassie asked, taking a heaping forkful of collard greens.

Joe spoke quietly. "I think it's the stress about the election. He's always hated to lose at anything, but especially this time, since he believes so much is at stake."

Reaching for her glass, Cassie asked, "Election? What election?"

Harriet dabbed at her mouth with a napkin. "Sam and Ed are both running for a town council seat. Sam's under the impression that Ed will have Walton looking like Trenton, New Jersey, within a matter of years if he wins." She sent Cassie a wry smile. "I don't know. I know Sam's heart is in the right place, but I also think a little bit of progress is good. Sam would like everything to stay the same, but if we don't have any businesses to attract people from Atlanta to move here, then this town will just wither."

157

Joe leaned back in his chair, lifting the front legs off the floor. "I dunno. I pretty much agree with Sam. Sure, Ed's certainly come up in the world, and he does contribute financially to the town, but there's something not right there. Where did he get all that money to start his business? His parents died a few years after he graduated from high school, but I know they didn't have two coins to rub together. It's a mystery, all right, and I'm inclined to agree with Sam about maybe that money coming from something not quite on the up-and-up."

Cassie shook her head. "Haven't you ever heard of a bank loan? People do it all the time. I didn't get any bad feelings from him at all. He seems to be a pretty serious businessman who wants to make money, and the last time I checked there was nothing wrong with that."

Harriet and Joe looked at each other with shared bewilderment, but Cassie missed their expressions when she bent to retrieve a rattle Amanda threw on the floor.

Harriet cupped her chin in her hands. "I have to say I'm surprised Ed has done so well for himself. Remember how all the other kids used to tease him about the dirt under his fingernails?"

Cassie chewed thoughtfully for a moment. "Yeah, and I also remember you defending him, too. I never teased him, but I never had the guts you had to stand up in front of everybody, either."

She took a sip of tea. "Do you think he still remembers all that?"

Joe leaned back, rubbing his stomach with one hand. "I don't think Ed Farrell's the kind of man who forgets anything. Like the time his father traipsed across the basketball court in the middle of the game to haul Ed back home. Said he needed help with the plowing, and that was that, basketball game or not. I don't think Ed ever came back to school after that."

"Pass the corn bread, please," shouted Joey, his lips, chin, and cheeks covered with the remnants of his first piece.

Madison stretched her arm toward the breadbasket.

Harriet nodded. "Remember how he used to cuss? I still don't know what some of those words meant. You'd think he'd grown up in the city or something."

Madison's fingers nudged the edge of the basket, shifting it in the opposite direction.

Joe sat up. "Now, really, Harriet. People in the city don't cuss any more than they do out here. I don't know where you get all these stereotypical ideas about city people."

Maddie, still reaching for the corn bread, managed to flop her elbow on the table at the precise spot where a glass casserole lid lay. The force propelled it into the air in a perfect somersault before it crashed to the floor and split in half.

"Holy shit!" she yelled, effectively silencing all and sundry at the table, with the exception of the cooing baby and Knoxie, who had the sudden impulse to imitate her older sister.

"Bowly shit!" she shouted with glee.

Harriet stood quickly, feeling like she would faint. "Madison Cassandra Warner! Get to your room this instant. You've never heard that kind of language in this house, and I certainly don't expect to hear it coming out of your mouth. I've a good mind to wash it out with soap."

Cassie looked down at her plate, the color deepening in her cheeks.

Madison slowly slid out of her chair. "I didn't mean anything by it. It just sorta slipped out. . . ."

Harriet leaned toward her, her anger barely held in check. "Where have you heard that before?"

Madison glanced over at her aunt, and Cassie swallowed before speaking. "I . . . I must have said it without thinking, Harriet. I'm sorry. I didn't realize—"

Harriet shook her head, cutting her off. "It doesn't matter. Maddie is old enough to know what's inappropriate language for a young girl." She turned back to her daughter. "We'll discuss this later. Up to your room, please. And no peach ice cream for you tonight."

"Mama . . ." Madison's whole demeanor whined along with her voice, and for a moment Harriet remembered Maddie as a chubby-cheeked two-year-old and it suddenly didn't seem all that long ago.

Joe spoke, his words soft but strong. "Do as your mama tells you, and do it without complaining or there'll be a worse punishment than being sent to your room."

Madison banged her chair up against the table and ran out of the room. Each stomping foot as she climbed the stairs reverberated in Harriet's heart, causing a pain that was almost as bad as childbirth. She held her breath, listening as the end of the stomping was punctuated by the slamming of Maddie's bedroom door.

The front door shut quietly and Sam returned to the kitchen. "Was that an adolescent girl or a tornado I saw flinging its way up the stairs?"

Joe shook his head, then stood. "Don't go there, Sam. Don't even go there. I can only question God as to why he gave me four hormonal girls and just one levelheaded boy." He reached across the table and started stacking dishes.

Harriet stood, too, and tried to look stern. "Watch it, buddy. The couch in the living room isn't all that comfortable."

Joey dropped his fork on his plate with a clatter. "Let's go catch lightning bugs!"

His pronouncement was followed by the sound of three chairs being scraped back from the table.

Harriet waved her hands in the air. "Don't think this excuses any of you from your after-dinner

161

chores. They'll be waiting for you when you get back."

She walked to a cabinet and pulled out four empty peanut butter jars, all with lids that had small holes poked in them, and a different initial painted on the front.

Sarah Frances grabbed two, then took Knoxie's hand and followed Joey out the door. Harriet squatted and reached into the far back of the cabinet and pulled out two more jars. These were older, the bright yellow lids pale and faded. She approached the table again, holding the jars out so Cassie could read the "C" and "H" on the sides.

"Remember these?" she asked, handing Cassie the one with the "C" initial on it.

"I can't believe you kept them," Cassie said as she ran her thumbnail against the ridged side of the lid.

"How could I throw them away?" Harriet watched Cassie examining the jar closely, as if remembering all the things of her childhood she'd discarded fifteen years before without a second thought.

Finally, Cassie looked up. "Thanks. Thanks for keeping them." She even sounded like she meant it.

Madison lingered in the doorway. "Can I come down now?"

Harriet turned toward her. "Are you ready to apologize?"

Madison nodded, and mumbled, "I'm sorry. I won't say it again."

Harriet just stood, looking at her eldest child with a mixture of love and incredulity, trying to remember the sweet baby she'd once rocked to sleep. Then she walked over and handed Madison a jar with an "M" on it.

A small smile tugged at the corner of Madison's mouth. "Thanks, Mama. Can I have peach ice cream, too?"

Harriet frowned so she wouldn't smile. Even as a baby, Maddie had always prodded her limits. "Don't push it, young lady. Now go outside and keep your sisters out of the mud puddles."

The screen door banged open and Joey poked his head into the kitchen. "Dr. Parker—c'mon. It's us boys against the girls to see who can catch more."

Sam looked up at Harriet and winked before turning back to the small boy. "Hold on a minute. I'm going to need another jar, and I need your permission to appropriate a female for our team."

Joey wrinkled his nose. "Huh?"

Sam laughed. "Okay. How 'bout your aunt Cassie joining us on our team? It would make it more even."

A chair slid back from the table as Cassie stood. "Sorry—can't. Not only am I woefully out of practice, but somebody's got to help your mother clean up this mess." Cassie drained the last of her sweet tea, making the ice cubes tinkle against the glass.

Harriet gave her sister a playful shove. "Oh, you go on, Cassie. Joe and I can handle this, and the kids will finish up when they come back in. I insist."

Cassie scanned the faces of the people around her like a caged animal. "But I've got loads of work to do back at the house, and I should really be getting back."

Sam sent her a level gaze. "How are you going to get there?"

"I'll drive, of co—" She stopped. "Oh. Right. And I guess I can't walk with these shoes."

"I promise to drive you home just as soon as we can catch us more fireflies than the girls' team."

"I'm really not dressed for running around outside." Cassie looked down at her short skirt and heels. "How about if I just stay inside and root for your team?"

Madison plopped down at the table next to her aunt. "We're too old for kid games like that. We'll stay here."

Harriet's heart squeezed a little, but Cassie spoke up before Harriet could say something.

"Now, Maddie—" Cassie stopped, as if wondering why it was so important to her that Madison go outside and have fun instead of staying inside. "Look, it's not because I'm too old; it's just that it's hard to run in heels."

"I'll help." Sam leaned over and picked up the bug jar with the big yellow "C" on the outside.

"And anybody who stays behind has to scrub the pots." Harriet smiled brightly.

Maddie stood, making the chair wobble in her haste. "Come on, Aunt Cassie. Please?"

Amused by her niece, and looking only halfway reluctant, Cassie followed Sam and Madison out into the humid night.

"Have fun," Harriet said quietly before turning back to the sink, where Joe had already begun to fill the pots with hot soapy water.

He winked at her and held out his hand. "Come on, Har. Let's show 'em how it's done."

She melted into his arms and allowed herself to close her eyes, just for a moment.

A CHORUS FROM hundreds of tree frogs hummed and burbled in the tall pines on the far side of the property. Bright lights from the houses at Farrellsford could be seen clearly through large gaps in the trees. Cassie stepped tentatively off the path, feeling her heel grip solid ground. So far, so good.

"Over there—look! By the trees." Madison ran, her hair swinging loose behind her. Joey ran after her, shouting, "Don't get all of them, Maddie. Save some for me!"

A cluster of blinking lights pulsed underneath a giant magnolia, and Cassie ran toward them, her feet crunching on the ground cover of faded magnolia leaves. Quickly, she unscrewed the lid and swiped the jar through the air.

"I got two! I got two!" She put the lid back on, then held the jar up proudly to show Sam. As she began walking toward him, her heel held fast to a hole in the ground, twisting Cassie's ankle and sending her sprawling, facedown, in the bed of leaves. Her bug jar rolled a few feet away, coming to rest on its side by the magnolia. The fireflies inside winked at her.

"Dangnabit!" she shouted, struggling to a sitting position.

"Don't try to stand." Sam's voice was full of concern as he lifted her under her arms and slid her gently to rest against the trunk of the tree.

"I'm fine. Really." Mortified by her clumsiness, she put her foot under her to try to stand, but was rewarded with only shooting pain from her right ankle.

"Umph," she groaned.

"I told you not to stand." Sam knelt in the grass in front of her and picked up her foot. With studied concentration, he let his fingers gently probe her ankle, foot, and calf. His hand slid up the back of her calf, and she bit her lip hard enough to make it bleed. Anything to distract herself, and it had nothing to do with her ankle. He asked her to rotate her foot as he supported her leg, his fingers brushing her thigh, and she forced herself to think

166

of fireflies, and prickers in the grass, and the shouting children running around in the dark. She picked up her jar and clutched it tightly, thinking she could feel the thrumming of the energy inside, causing the little bodies to light up with an inner heat.

She needed to talk or she'd go crazy. "This tree reminds me of that large magnolia in the yard back at my daddy's house. Did you know my mother planted it as a sapling when I was born? I can't believe it's still there. And it's just huge now."

Sam's movements paused for a moment as he regarded her. "Its roots go pretty deep. It's not going anywhere for a long time."

She looked away, not able to meet his eyes. Prickly grass tickled the heel of her foot and she realized he had set her foot down.

"It's not broken. Most likely you've got a little sprain. I'll bring you inside and wrap it with ice."

Cassie nodded, knowing an ice-cold shower would be even more therapeutic for what ailed her. She found she still couldn't look at him, and instead stared intently at the jar. "Why do they do that?"

"Blink?" Sam shifted in the grass, pulling himself up on his haunches. "It's a mating thing. The lady fireflies do that to catch a suitor. The guy fireflies find those glowing butts real attractive, then light up their own rear ends to show they're interested." He looked up at her with a smile. "It's the bug world's equivalent to short skirts and high heels."

She tossed the jar at him, causing him to lose his balance and fall back as he caught it. "That's not why I wear what I wear. It's called *fashion*—a word I'm sure you're not familiar with."

Hoisting herself up using the trunk for support, she resisted his offer of help. "It just goes to show how similar males are in every species. They only want one thing, and they rely on superficialities to find a mate."

Sam grabbed her elbow, his tight grip making it clear he wasn't letting go. He stood near enough that she could smell him—a faint whiff of cologne and outdoor air. His breath brushed her cheek as he spoke.

"Not all males are alike, Cassie. Some actually make a point of peeling through all that outside stuff to see the real woman underneath. It's hard-won, but what a prize. A man just has to be patient."

Cassie leaned into him, taking the pressure off her ankle. "And are you a patient man, Dr. Parker?"

His eyes glittered from the porch light, reminding her of the fireflies. "Call me Job."

Suppressing a grin, she allowed herself to be lifted and carried inside.

THE RIDE HOME WITH SAM was silent except for the soft twangings of a Dwight Yoakam CD on the stereo. Cassie didn't remember to be nauseated by it until they were almost at her father's house.

Sam came to her side of the truck and lifted her out, closing the door with the heel of his boot. Effortlessly, he carried her across the drive and up the front steps to the porch. A full moon crept through the trees, dappling the porch and front door with mottled light and illuminating the bandaging around Cassie's ankle. She tried her best to keep her head away from Sam, but the sturdy wall of his chest under the soft cotton shirt was the natural spot to rest her cheek. With seemingly reluctant hands, Sam set her down, but didn't release his hold.

He stared at her neck. "I remember that necklace."

Her hand instinctively went to the four small charms.

A brief flash of white appeared on his face as he smiled. "I remember you always clutched at it when you felt nervous. It's a dead giveaway, but I think it's endearing."

Her defensive hackles had been raised with his remark about her habit, recalling Andrew's negative comments about it, but now she warmed toward him, smiling softly.

"My mother gave it to me."

She moved her hand away and he touched the charms tentatively, his fingers brushing the tender skin under her chin.

"What do they mean?"

An unseen insect hummed, teasing the air between them. Cassie took a deep breath. "The three hearts are for me, my father, and Harriet." She brushed at the air, listening to the humming fade away. "The key is for me—the keeper of the hearts." Swallowing, she continued. "My mother gave this to me right before she died."

He stared at her openly, not blinking. She looked down, not wanting him to see the shame in her eyes. He lifted her chin with his finger, forcing her to meet his gaze. "Keeper of the hearts."

She blinked rapidly. "Yeah. It's kind of silly. And I would laugh if I hadn't been such a failure at the one thing my mother wanted me to do."

He let go of her chin and stroked her cheek softly before dropping his hand. A humid breeze, full of the summer smells of grass, jasmine, and wisteria, lifted her hair. "I don't think so. You may have taken a detour, but you're not a failure."

This man, with his cowboy boots and bright eyes, was standing too close. Way too close. She dropped her gaze and began fumbling for her keys. "I've got to call Andrew."

Sam didn't say anything, but continued to regard her evenly.

"My fiancé."

His expression didn't waver. "Give me your key. I don't want you falling over and hurting yourself opening the door." He took the key and turned, stopping abruptly. A lockbox hung from the door handle.

"My, my. Our Ed Farrell does move fast, doesn't he?" He frowned at the heavy metal combination box hiding a house key inside.

She hopped over to him and leaned against the sidelight. "Where I'm from, that's called not wasting time. I'm glad to see he's taken the initiative."

Sam raised an eyebrow but didn't say anything. He stuck the key in the lock and turned it, pushing the door and letting it swing open.

"Would you like me to carry you upstairs to your bedroom?"

His expression was so innocent, she couldn't understand why his suggestion made her heart flutter like the fireflies in her jar.

"No. Thanks. I can manage."

He handed her the key and a small rectangular card. "All right. But call me on my cell if you need me. Anytime—day or night. Here's the number."

She held up his business card. "Right. I got it. Thanks."

"Well, then. I'd better let you call Andy."

"Andrew."

"Yeah. Whatever. Good night."

"Good night. Thanks for the doctoring. You can bill me, if you like."

He waved a hand at her before turning away and walking toward the steps. "It's on the house."

He waved again as she called out good night and shut the door. The dead bolt slid home with a solid, final sound. She dropped her purse on the hall table but brought the bug jar upstairs with her. She'd let the fireflies out of the jar in the morning, but she felt the need to keep them close tonight.

She took off her clothes and left them on the floor, too tired to hang them up. After sliding on a long T-shirt, she collapsed into bed and turned out the light. Andrew would be mad, but he'd have to wait until the morning to talk to her.

The flickering light from the jar on her nightstand illuminated the room briefly before casting it into darkness again. She thought of her father, and she strained to hear his footsteps walk up the wooden stairs, just as she'd done all those years ago as a child. But the house remained quiet, her father's tread forever silenced.

Outside, the sounds of the tree frogs and crickets crept into her room, singing to her like a forgotten lullaby. It was as if this place had frozen in time, and she was a little girl again, safe in the cocoon of this house and her family's love. She snuggled deeply into her pillow, the pulsing light from the jar growing dimmer and dimmer as her eyes closed, and fell asleep.

CHAPTER 9

Something thumped downstairs, bringing Cassie out of bed in one leap. Sun streamed through the open blinds, illuminating the mantel clock in her bedroom. Ten o'clock. She never slept late. Never. Even on weekends she was in the office by eight.

A thump followed by a scrape emerged again from downstairs. Bleary-eyed, she searched for a weapon. Lucinda was gone all week visiting a cousin recuperating from surgery, and Cassie was supposed to be alone in the house. She grabbed a fireplace poker, then cracked the door open and waited. Her blood pounded in her ears as she stood with the poker poised over her shoulder. The stealthy sound of a key turning in the latch and the front door opening came from downstairs. Cassie moved quietly to the top of the steps and peered down into the foyer. The two-toned hair, viewed clearly from her vantage point, was unmistakable.

"Ed? What are you doing here?"

He glanced up, his eyes wide. A broad smile quickly replaced his look of surprise. "Cassie, darlin'. I'm so sorry. I knocked, and when no one answered, I thought nobody was home." His gaze swept Cassie's T-shirt; then he looked away as if he were embarrassed. "I, uh, was here to do the appraisal."

"But you were supposed to call me this afternoon to let me know when you'd be over."

His gaze bounced from the newel post to the light fixture and back, as if he were studiously avoiding looking at her. Sensing it was her state of undress that was bothering him, she ducked into her room and grabbed her bathrobe. It came only to midthigh, but it was better than the almost sheer T-shirt. She dropped the poker on the floor, feeling foolish.

Her bare feet slapped the wooden risers of the stairs as she jogged down to the foyer. Her ankle, still wrapped, felt stiff but no longer painful. "Why didn't you call first?"

His smile didn't falter. "I wanted to get down to business as soon as possible. I know how eager you are to sell."

Mollified, Cassie relaxed. "I guess since you're here, then, we might as well get started." She yawned. "But I've got to have some coffee first. May I make some for you?"

Ed seemed absorbed in studying his surroundings, and made no indication that he had heard.

"Ed?"

He jerked, and faced her. "I'm sorry. Did you say something?"

"Yes. I asked you if you wanted coffee."

He blinked, as if wondering why she was there. "Ah, yes. Coffee. That would be fine. And if you

174

don't mind, while you're doing that I want to go ahead and get started."

Cassie turned toward the kitchen, wondering where he had learned his get-up-and-go attitude. From what she could recall of his family and childhood, he certainly hadn't been born with it.

When she returned with two steaming mugs of coffee, she couldn't find him. She called his name twice before he responded. She found him in her father's study, sitting at his desk and staring at the photos of her and Harriet.

"What are you doing?" Her voice still held an early-morning scratchiness.

He seemed to be trying to pull himself together, and quickly began gathering his notepad and pen off the top of the desk. "I was just trying to get a feel for the ambience of this house. Buying a house is rarely based on something you can touch. If I can give potential buyers the feeling of the house, I'll have a better chance of selling it, even with all of its problems."

She handed him his mug. "Problems? Like what?"

The question seemed to take him by surprise. "Oh, well, ah . . . ." His eyes brightened. "There's no central air-conditioning. That's a big no-no in this market. Especially with these tall ceilings—I bet it's hotter'n a fire ant's rear end in the middle of July." He chuckled at his own joke.

Cassie recalled the days before they had even the

window units, the days when her daddy would take her and Harriet for a ride in the car with the windows open just to catch a breeze. But she didn't think of it as a problem. It was one of those recollections that brought back a pleasant feeling in the pit of her stomach, a happy, albeit long-forgotten memory.

Cassie frowned. "It's not so bad, Ed. Yesterday it was ninety-eight degrees and ninety percent humidity, and I was completely comfortable inside." That wasn't entirely true, but she was quite certain that any stickiness she had felt simply from moving from one room to another was due to the fact that she wasn't acclimated yet. She pushed aside the childhood memory of Aunt Lucinda walking about doing her household chores wearing a wet washcloth right out of the freezer around her neck.

"Hmmm." Ed walked toward the velvet draperies and touched one reverently. "Are you leaving any of the furnishings?"

She took another sip of her coffee. "I hadn't really thought about it. I don't have room in my apartment, but I'm assuming Harriet and Lucinda would want at least a few pieces. Maybe I could auction off the rest."

He clutched the curtain tightly in his fist, then let it go. "That's a good idea, Cassie. I'm sure you don't want to be saddled with any of this old stuff."

Her gaze skipped around the room, taking in all the highly polished mahogany and cherry antiques. She felt a proprietary surge creep into her veins. "It's not just old stuff, Ed. This furniture has been in my family for generations."

He nodded, his eyes filled with a knowing compassion. "Well, family heirlooms to you, just old stuff to other people. Personally, I love it. Just like I love everything about this house. But a prospective buyer might not have the same sense of history that you and I share."

She took another sip of coffee and found herself eyeing his suit—a double-breasted number with a tie that had reached its fashion zenith about five years previously. Feelings of doubt assailed her. Even though he was the only Realtor in town, did she have to use him? Sure, they both wanted to keep the house intact, but was he savvy enough to attract a prospective buyer? She looked down at her bare feet on the wood floor. She would give him a try, if only because she thought everyone deserved a chance to prove themselves. If it didn't work out, she'd find another Realtor in a different town if she had to.

"Do you need me to show you around?"

Ed shook his head. "Nope—I've been here before. You just go on about your business and don't mind me. I'll be fine."

She looked at him with a perplexed frown. "When . . . ?"

"Your father showed me around. When I was here to talk to him about selling that land."

"Ah, yes. Well, I'm going to be in the study. If you need me just holler." *Holler?* Why on earth did she use that word? "Um, yell. I'll be in here." Raising her mug to him in a salute, she headed for the desk.

As she sat down, the scents of leather and pipe smoke settled on her, making her feel her father's presence, if only for a moment. She looked behind her, half expecting to see him standing there, his expression of quiet support and patient understanding crossing his face. She had the strongest urge to call Harriet and see if she felt their father still, too, but instead dialed Andrew's number.

It took a few moments for the receptionist to patch her into Andrew's office. Hitching her feet under her in the desk chair, she waited.

"Andrew Wallace here."

"Hi, Andrew. It's Cassie—Cassandra. Sorry I didn't call you last night—"

He cut her off. "I'm glad you called. I've been trying to reach you. Where's your BlackBerry? I've been strict about nobody bothering you while you're gone, but a return phone call to me or even an e-mail would have been appreciated. And what's with the home phone ringing and ringing? Please tell me you at least have an answering machine."

She bit her lip, wondering if she should tell him that not only did her father not have an answering machine, but that the phones in the house still had cords. Her father had called himself a "traditionalist," but Cassie had always had the feeling that he just didn't have the patience to learn new technology.

"I'm sorry, Andrew. My battery's dead and I forgot my charger and I just haven't had a chance to go pick up a new one."

Cassie could almost sense him frowning into the phone. "Well, I've got Joan Dorfman from BankNorth here in my office right now. We've got a problem."

She closed her eyes, her heart sinking with disappointment. This wasn't what she wanted right now. She wanted soft words of warmth and love, not the frigid words of market share and the cost of full-page four-color print ads in *Time* magazine. She almost felt the need to remind him that she'd just buried her father. Instead, she pulled open a desk drawer and slid out a pad of paper and a pen. "Okay, Andrew. What's the problem?"

Pushing aside the feelings of disappointment, she allowed the comforting, familiar lull of work to fall over her, obliterating all bothersome thoughts of her family, the house, and Sam. The pen scratched over the yellow paper: one page, then two. The back of the third page was covered in price-per-share calculations. Finally, she sat back in the chair and let go with what she did best: the negotiation. Her voice soothed and cajoled the client on the other end of the line. Cassie was so engrossed in what she was doing that she didn't even look up at the brief knocking at the door. She ignored it, and swiveled her chair so that her back was to the entranceway.

Cassie continued on the phone. "Joan, I'm sorry you didn't like the sixty-second spot. We had our best people working on it, and we were pleased. We just weren't aware of your negative feelings regarding Ryan Seacrest. It will take some juggling to replace him, but it can be done."

She turned the chair around so she could rest her elbows on the desk. As the client talked, Cassie doodled on the pad in front of her, not paying attention to what she was drawing. The Sedgewick twins, in matching sundresses, appeared in front of the desk, making her jump in surprise.

"We brought those Red Radiance clippings for your mother's rose garden, and a few clumps of violas for that front bed. We were thinning ours out this morning and thought you could use them."

Cassie stared at them in horror, her finger to her lips to get them to be quiet. The older women managed to look like chastised two-year-olds.

Holding her hand over the receiver, Cassie whispered, "I'm sorry—but I'm on an important phone call."

Selma smiled. "Is that Lucinda? Please tell her that we said hello—and that the bridge club meeting has been moved from Wednesday to Friday."

Thelma broke in. "And please remind her that we need her black-currant jam recipe. We're going to serve it on Tuesday at the Women's Guild meeting."

Keeping her hand on the receiver, Cassie vigorously shook her head at the two women.

Thelma stepped closer to the desk, reaching for the phone. "Well, I never! It's only a silly jam recipe. Please tell her that I would like to speak with her."

Cassie shook her head again, and clutched the receiver closer to her chest. Thelma reached over to take the phone.

"No!"

Joan Dorfman, marketing director for one of the nation's biggest banks, stopped her diatribe. "Excuse me?"

The front door opened again and Harriet and Sam appeared in the foyer carrying an assortment of large packing boxes. Sam set his boxes down to prop open the doors, then reached for Harriet's. He nodded toward the two women. "Thelma. Selma. How are y'all doing today?"

Cassie was mortified to find Selma had tears in her eyes. "Joan, I'm sorry. That wasn't meant for you. I've got to call you back."

Joan kept talking, ignoring Cassie's request.

Ed Farrell came down the stairs and joined the fray in the study. Sam, with his arm around Selma's shoulders, looked at him oddly. Cassie ducked her head in an effort to hear Joan better, and her gaze rested on her doodlings. Sam's name, in big block letters, danced across the page in thick black ink while hearts, doodled in all different sizes, covered the rest of the paper.

She jerked her head up to see if anybody else had noticed, and her eyes met Sam's widened ones. She didn't know if he was surprised at what she had drawn, or just wondering why she was making Selma Sedgewick cry.

"Yes, Joan. I'm still here. Yes. I'll talk it over with Andrew, but I've really got to go right now—"

Her voice was cut off by the movement of a large animal—she wasn't sure if it was a dog or a pony—as it bounded into the house and into the study. It leaped on top of the desk, then onto Cassie's lap, toppling over her and the chair, and yanking the phone cord out of the wall.

"George—sit!"

At Sam's command, the beast trotted away from Cassie and sat down. Cassie struggled to get her T-shirt and robe over her thighs as she stood. Sam reached her side in one long stride.

"Are you all right?"

Furious, the disconnected phone still in her

hand, she shouted, "What in the hell was that thing? And why are all you people in here? Doesn't a closed door mean anything to you?"

Selma and Thelma, their chins waggling like a pair of twin turkeys, pulled their shoulders back and left the room. The genteel ladies didn't slam the front door as they left, as if to show Cassie that even if she lacked breeding, they certainly didn't.

Sam scowled at her. "I hope you know you've just insulted two of the finest people I have ever met. Your father would be ashamed."

His words stung. It was one thing to feel ashamed, and that she did in spades. It was another thing to have it pointed out to her. That only made her angrier. She met his gaze head-on.

"You didn't answer my question—what in the hell are you doing here?"

A throbbing tic had begun in Sam's cheek and was going wilder now. Harriet stepped between them.

"We came to help with the attic. Remember? We talked about it last night while Sam was patching your ankle. Sam mentioned he had some boxes at the clinic and offered to bring them here for me."

As if in response to Cassie's ungratefulness, the box at the top of the stack slid off and landed with a soft thud on the wood floor. The hairy beast gave one loud, sharp bark, then thumped its fat tail against the rug for an added effect.

Deflated, all Cassie could think to say was,

"Oh." She placed the telephone receiver on the desktop, but stopped herself in time from sitting down on empty air. She caught sight of the hairy mutt.

"What is that thing?"

Sam didn't answer, but seemed intent on staring at her scantily clad body. The scowl reappeared on his face. "And why is Ed Farrell coming down your stairs at ten thirty in the morning when you're wearing next to nothing?"

Ed's eyes widened, accompanied by a smirk. "Come on, Sam. We aren't in high school anymore. Whatever Cassie chooses to do—whether to herself or her house—is none of your business."

Sam folded his arms across his chest, clenching his hands into fists. His cheek thrummed wildly. "Oh, really. And since when did Cassie give you permission to speak for her?"

"Enough!" Cassie moved to stand between the two men. "Sam Parker. You have some nerve. How dare you question Ed's or anyone's presence in my own house. It's none of your damned business. And besides, he wasn't the one ogling me in my nightshirt and robe." She waved her hand between them to stop him from speaking. "Look, I'm going to go take my shower, then make a phone call to hopefully repair a badly damaged client relationship." She took a deep, cleansing breath. "While I'm gone, Ed, I'd like you to finish up with the appraisal." Turning to Sam, she said, "And I would like you to bring those boxes up to the attic." He frowned at her, prompting her to add, "Please," as an afterthought.

Rubbing her hands over her face, she turned to her sister. "Thanks for your help, Harriet, but I really think I can do all this myself. If you want to go up to the attic and see if there's anything you want, go ahead. Feel free to take everything—I don't think there's anything I'll want. My apartment has absolutely no storage space as it is."

Mustering all the dignity she could, considering she wore next to nothing and hadn't even brushed her teeth yet, she stepped over the hairy beast named George and headed for the stairs. "When y'all leave, please lock the door behind you. And don't forget to take that . . . that . . . him"—she pointed at the animal calmly appraising her from the floor—"with you."

As she climbed the steps, a stunned expression came over her face. *Y'all?* Had she really said that? *Oh, Lord.* She'd already been in Kansas way too long.

HARRIET SAT ON her knees in front of the trunk, her bare feet tucked under her, ignoring the attic's dust. It had been too many years since she'd last been there for a visit with her past. The large space with the sloping ceiling and porthole window had been her sanctuary—hers and Cassie's. At first it

185

had been their playroom, and then, as the girls got older and Lucinda had decided she was too old to be climbing so many stairs, it had become their refuge. The attic walls held all the confidences of adolescence and the tears of frustration, disappointment, and loss as only a young girl could express them. Sitting in the attic now was like opening the cover on a dusty and cobwebbed scrapbook album. With a deep breath, she pushed at the lid of the trunk.

Sam leaned over her shoulder. "Here—it looks heavy. Let me do that."

Without argument, Harriet scooted out of the way and let Sam hoist open the lid, its unused hinges squealing in protest. "Thanks, Sam. I don't know where all my strength has gone these days."

He looked at her with warm blue eyes. "Joe said you're still nursing Amanda. Maybe it's time to wean her so you can build back your strength."

Harriet sat back, forcing an energetic smile she didn't quite feel. "I think I will. I'm only nursing her at night now, but she takes a bottle with just as much enthusiasm, so I might as well."

Sam continued to regard her closely. "Is there anything else you're not telling me? Are you getting enough sleep?"

She gave a small laugh. "Sam, I'm the mother of five, the youngest still in diapers. Of course I don't get enough sleep. It comes with the territory."

Sam moved aside a layer of tissue from the

trunk. "Yeah, well, you should still try to take care of yourself."

Harriet scanned the inside of the trunk, her gaze riveted on two white and familiar-looking objects. "I know, and I promise I'll try. But right now I'm more interested in finding out how you're feeling."

He reached into the trunk and lifted out the two soft white balls. "Me? I'm fine. What makes you ask?"

She touched his hand, forcing him to look at her. "It's your heart I'm concerned about, and your feelings for Cassie."

He studied the lock on the trunk for a long moment. "My feelings for Cassie should have been locked up here in the attic with the rest of this stuff years ago. They're just no longer relevant. She's engaged, she's got a big career going in New York, and people think that I'm practically engaged to Mary Jane. Cassie and I are from two different worlds and we want different things in life. I think I'll just continue to admire her from afar and get on with my life."

He squatted down on his haunches but Harriet tugged on his sleeve to get his attention again. "For somebody who went to Yale and Harvard, you can be pretty stupid. From what I can see, you and Cassie have a lot more in common than either one of you thinks. Just give her time. I think she's still going through culture shock."

She squinted at the two items in his hand, her memory tugging hard at her brain. "And there's a reason why you've dated Mary Jane all these years but have never gotten engaged. Think about it."

"Cassie never even knew I existed. And now I'm left wondering if the Cassie I knew still exists. She goes to a lot of trouble to make us believe she doesn't."

"But she made you laugh when you didn't have many things to laugh about."

Sam let out a deep breath, the years of longing letting go in a single sigh. "She was always doing crazy things to get attention, thinking that was the only way to get people to notice her. And her fierce loyalty to you and those she loved. You don't find that in too many people, and I guess I found the combination pretty irresistible."

"We were her biggest fans, but I think we did a lousy job of showing our appreciation."

Sam opened his mouth to respond but was cut short when Harriet let out a shriek of laughter when she realized what he held in his hands. "I remember what those are!"

He stared down at his hands and his eyes lit with recognition. Throwing his head back, he let his laughter join Harriet's.

A loud sneeze from the direction of the stairs brought both their heads around. "God bless you," they said in unison. Harriet sent a guilty look toward Sam, then quickly stuffed the white padded balls back inside the trunk.

Cassie stood at the top of the attic steps in her high heels, staring at them with curiosity, her hands on her hips.

Sam stood. "I don't think you should be wearing heels with your ankle, Cassie."

"My ankle's fine." She took a few steps closer. "What are you looking at?" Cassie tap-tapped her way across the attic floor.

"Oh, nothing. Just some old high school stuff."

Cassie peered into the trunk. "What was so funny?" She looked at where Harriet's hand covered up the evidence. "What's this?" she asked, as she reached under Harriet's fingers and pried the two soft white balls out of the trunk.

"Oh . . . my . . ." The bra inserts she held were still in pretty good condition—still white, fluffy, and perfectly round, like oversize tennis balls. "I can't believe somebody saved these."

Harriet wasn't being completely successful about hiding her laughter. "I think Aunt Lucinda is responsible. She doesn't like to throw away anything."

Sam didn't even try to hide his mirth. "We were just both remembering how you went from an A cup to a double-D cup overnight your freshman year. Like nobody would notice."

They both gave up all pretense of hiding their merriment and let out big roars of laughter.

Cassie stood with the inserts still clutched in her hands, her outrage apparent on her face. She looked down at the white pads for a long moment, and her lips twitched. "Oh, damn," she managed, before tossing them back into the trunk and then starting to laugh until the tears rolled down her face.

When Cassie found her composure again, she nudged Harriet. "It was all your fault, you know. It was embarrassing having a younger sister with bigger boobs. I was only trying to even the playing field."

Sam looked up at her, his eyes sparkling. "Instead it looked like you took something off the playing field and stuck it in your shirt."

All three of them buckled with laughter again, and Harriet felt some of her bone-dead weariness lift slightly. Maybe all the years of missing her sister had congealed in her veins, crowding out some of her spirit. Harriet watched as Cassie punched Sam on the shoulder, then leaned over the trunk and pulled something out. It rustled like taffeta, but whatever the fabric, it had been covered with green plastic kudzu leaves all sewn closely together. The only things that verified that it was actually a dress were the neck and armholes.

"My queen of kudzu gown!" Harriet reached for it, and Cassie dropped it into her waiting arms.

As Cassie rooted around the trunk she said, "I wouldn't go modeling that to Maddie, if I were you. I think she's pretty much Kudzu Festivaled out."

Harriet was standing now, holding the dress in front of her and remembering. "I know—but it's not all my doing. Lucy Spafford is mostly to blame."

Cassie examined a bundle of Barbie dolls, all roped together with rubber bands at the neck, and dropped them on the floor outside the trunk. "You can have those." She wiped her hands on her skirt. "Who's Lucy Spafford?"

Harriet sighed, frowning. "The bane of Maddie's existence. Since the beginning of middle school Lucy's made the cheerleading squad and Maddie hasn't. It wouldn't be so bad if she were a nice girl, but she's real snotty about it to Maddie. Drives Maddie out of her mind to see Lucy in her cheerleading skirt. Maddie swears it's because Lucy's mom—do you remember Doreen Cagle?— is the squad leader." She placed the green dress over her arm and reached for the Barbies.

Cassie and Sam looked at each other with eyebrows raised. "So what does that have to do with your kudzu dress?"

Harriet knelt in front of the trunk next to Cassie. "Lucy's the kudzu queen this year. I think Maddie's planning on coming down with pneumonia on the day of the festival so she doesn't have to go and see Lucy on her parade float." Not that she thought Maddie really would. Maddie was made of the same tough stuff as

191

Cassie, and Harriet knew with deep feelings of trepidation that Maddie would find a way to not only be there, but to enjoy the proceedings.

Sam stood, brushing dust off his jeans. "I remember the year you were queen, Harriet. That was when somebody dressed the Statue of Liberty in a woman's bra and panties and filled the fountain with bubble bath. I thought I'd bust a gut laughing. But then when Cassie showed up behind your float walking a pig dressed in kudzu, I just about died." He shook his head, smiling broadly. "They never did find out who did that to the statue and the fountain."

Both Harriet and Sam looked at Cassie, but she remained silent, pointedly studying the inside lid of the trunk. She kicked off her shoes and tucked her feet under her as she rooted under a pile of stuffed animals. With a small frown, Harriet watched as she pulled out something small and wooden. Moving closer, she looked at the object in Cassie's hands. The old pipe still hinted of the aroma of tobacco, and Cassie closed her eyes, as if remembering the man who had once smoked it. Harriet closed her eyes, too, sure she could feel his presence there in the attic.

Harriet's voice cracked when she spoke. "It's Daddy's old pipe. Remember when you hid it in here when you were trying to get him to stop smoking?" She smiled gently, taking the pipe from Cassie and running her finger slowly down the smooth stem. "I think he tried to quit for a week or something, but he ended up just buying a new one." She handed it back to Cassie, trying once more to make a connection with her. "You can keep it if you like."

Cassie nodded, her eyes heavy with unshed tears. She took the pipe and held it closely to her chest. "Thanks," she managed, and Harriet was relieved to see the old Cassie, if only for a moment. At least it meant that she hadn't disappeared completely. She only hoped that Sam had noticed it, too.

"Hey, what's this?" Sam had walked past the area illuminated by the bare bulbs overhead and pulled out a wooden box from the dark corner of the attic. "It looks like an antique writing desk."

He walked over to Harriet and Cassie and placed it on the floor in front of them, a billow of dust rising in its wake. It was made of a dark wood, probably cherry or mahogany, with tarnished brass hinges and a nameplate on the front. It was sloped on top with a ledge at the bottom, as if to hold reading material. Sam pointed to a key sticking in the keyhole. "That's certainly not much of a challenge, is it?"

Cassie moved to get a better look at the nameplate. " 'HRM.' That certainly narrows it down to about fifty people. There's been a Harrison Robert Madison in our family in every generation—except for ours. Daddy didn't have a son to leave the name to."

Harriet interrupted. "So I got stuck with it. I always wanted a pretty girl's name like you, Cassie, and instead I got stuck with Harriet. Please give me credit for not inflicting such torture on my own children."

Absently, Cassie rubbed the nameplate. "I guess he was waiting for one of us to use it."

She looked up at Harriet. "Well, this could be Daddy's, although I don't ever remember seeing it before. Do you want to open it?"

Harriet shook her head. "No. You're the oldest; you do it."

Kneeling in front, Cassie gingerly turned the key, a small click sounding in the quiet attic. She paused before opening it. "I kind of wish there were more of a mystery to us finding a locked letter box in the attic. It's a little too easy. Almost as if Daddy wanted us to find it."

With one last glance at Sam and Harriet, she opened the lid. The smell of old wood and stain wafted out of the box as the three of them peered inside. Scattered around the bottom of the box were stamped envelopes with elegant handwriting on the front. The capital letters in the words were enormous, with swirled tails and large loops. It could only have been written by a woman. On top of the envelope lay an old black-and-white photograph of a man and a woman standing in front of a small two-door sports car.

Gingerly, Cassie lifted the picture and held it up

to Harriet. "Look, it's Daddy and his old car, but I'm pretty sure that's not Mama." They both peered closely at the woman, her head swathed in a chiffon scarf and knotted under her chin, and pointy cat's-eye sunglasses blocking her eyes.

Harriet took the picture and stared at it for a moment. "That's definitely not Mama." Her gaze met Cassie's, an unspoken question between them.

Harriet reached inside and sifted some of the envelopes off the top, only to find more of the same underneath. All were addressed to her father, in this house. She checked the postmarks. All she could see were postmarked in Walton, except for one that came from Atlanta. The dates on all of them were from 1973 or 1974. She did a mental calculation, then looked up excitedly.

"These might be from Mama!"

She watched as Cassie picked up the one with the Atlanta postmark, her brows furrowed, and gingerly opened the neatly slit top, then pulled out a letter. Leaning over Cassie's shoulder, she and her sister read the letter silently.

April 10, 1974

My dearest Harry,
Our child was born this morning at two thirty-eight. The baby weighed only three pounds and I knew without the doctor telling me that our child was not long for this world. The baby

died at four ten in my arms, having known only love and security in its brief two hours of life. That thought gave me some comfort, and I have every hope that it will bring the same to you. My father will see that the baby is given a Christian burial, and perhaps one day I'll have the strength to go visit the grave.

I have decided it would be best if you didn't know whether you had a son or daughter. This way your dreams of our child will end in babyhood, and you won't see it grow into a young man or woman in your mind. Still, I hope you will always hold this child in your heart, as I will, and remember the love that we shared that created a human life.

I have accepted that your heart belongs to another, and even though your intentions were good in offering to make an honest woman out of me and be a father to our child, I knew I could not stand in your way of happiness. The bitterness would find its way into our home, and destroy whatever love there might be. I would rather see it die now, while in its youth and passion, than see it wither and fade. This way, I can live with my beautiful memories and never have to face the loss. Perhaps I am a coward, or maybe I'm too prideful, but this is the way it has to be for both our sakes.

As much as I wish our child had lived, I can't help but have faith that things happen as they are meant to be. You will go on with your life, and I with mine, on separate paths. And I will be content knowing that I loved you once, and those days were the happiest of my life. I will treasure them always.

Please do not try to find me. My parents are sending me to visit family in Atlanta for two months, and then to Europe for an extended tour. When I return this will be behind us. You don't even have to acknowledge me when we pass on the street. I'll understand.

I wish you nothing but happiness and joy the rest of your days. I love you.

Always, E

Harriet stared at the letter, her throat dry. "Our mother's name was Catherine Anne. If these aren't from her, then . . . ?" Her gaze strayed to the woman in the picture.

Sam spoke, and both women looked startled, as if they'd forgotten he was still there. "What is it?"

Harriet held the letter, the paper smooth under her fingers. "Do you think he should see it? He might . . . know something."

Cassie looked at Sam, her expression unreadable. "Will you keep it confidential?"

"Of course." He took the letter from her and read it.

Cassie collapsed against the large trunk. "I just can't believe this."

Sam squatted in front of Harriet and handed

back the letter. Feeling as if she had invaded somebody's privacy, she quickly tucked the letter and picture back on top of the stack and closed the lid of the letter box.

Harriet sat down hard next to her sister. "It's so sad about the baby dying—but not as sad as that poor woman's story."

Cassie lifted the box to her lap and clutched it fiercely, her face hard. "That woman slept with our father and had a baby at the same time he must have been dating our mother. I just can't feel sorry for her."

Sam smoothed his hand over the letter box, brushing Cassie's fingers. "It was before your parents were married, so it would appear your father was faithful to your mother. If anything, I think this letter is a testament to how much he really loved her. This 'E,' whoever she is, knew that what was between your parents was the real thing, and bravely stepped out of the picture."

Harriet smiled wanly. "It's kind of romantic, really."

Cassie turned to her with a harsh look. "I guess you would find it romantic to read about a love triangle and being jilted. Believe me when I say it's not romantic when you're the one left behind."

Harriet felt as if the breath had been stolen from her lungs. "You're right. I'm sorry."

With a contrite look on her face, Cassie placed her hand on Harriet's arm. "No—I'm sorry. I shouldn't have said that. I didn't mean it. I just think this has been a bit of a shock. . . ."

Sam stood, brushing his hands on his pants. With a reproachful look at Cassie, he turned to Harriet, offering his hand to help her up. "I agree—you girls have just been handed a whopper of a surprise. It will take some getting used to. Do you think you'll read the rest of the letters?"

Cassie frowned. "Why?"

"Well, this Miss E talked about passing him on the street. She must have lived in Walton then. Maybe she still does. I don't think you'd be able to walk away not knowing. You used to be like a dog with a bone whenever you had a problem or something to solve."

She stared at him for a moment, then shook her head slowly. "Someone should read them, I guess." She glanced up at Harriet. "Would you like to do the honors?"

Harriet shook her head. "No. I think you should do it first—and then share them with me. Sort of like how you used to do—always protecting me from something that might hurt."

With a lopsided grin, Cassie struggled to stand, still clutching the worn box. "I knew better than to come up to the attic. I really did. This house—it's like quicksand. The more I struggle to extricate myself, the harder it is to get free."

Sam's voice was even, carefully measured. "Feeling scared, Cassie?"

Cassie turned away, but not before her sister saw the stricken look on her face, and it hurt Harriet to see it. What was Cassie so afraid of? That she'd forget who she'd become or realize that she really hadn't changed that much? Or maybe she was afraid that the tugs she was feeling weren't on her feet but on her heart.

Cassie brushed by Sam without looking at him and headed toward the stairwell. "No, I'm not. But I am upset. How would you like to find out that your father had a lover before he married your mother?" She shook her head, blowing out a heavy breath. "I wish I'd never come up here."

Sam held her back with his hand. "Maybe this is a chance to get to know your father better. Even now, after he's gone."

She pulled away. "This isn't a part of him that I want to know about." Straightening her shoulders, she faced Harriet. "Stay up here as long as you like. I've got some business I need to take care of."

Harriet leaned against the trunk, feeling completely depleted. "I'll probably go through a few more boxes before calling it quits. I know how eager you are to get through with this." She waved weakly and Cassie nodded.

Harriet watched her sister begin her descent, the letter box snugly under her arm, and Cassie's free hand fingering the gold hearts dangling from the frail chain around her neck.

CHAPTER 10

S nake in the grass!"
The children of Walton had congregated on Madison Lane and were now standing in two opposing lines on opposite curbs. The snake was a blindfolded Sarah Frances, who stood in the middle of the street as the children tried to cross the space between the lines without being caught.

The shrill calls of the children in the dusky air slowed Cassie's pace. Running at night was certainly cooler, if not less humid, and at least she didn't have to bump into anybody she knew while sweating like a horse. Or "glowing," as Aunt Lucinda referred to it.

She stopped completely to watch the children, a smile tugging at her mouth. It was so much like the summers of her youth. The summers when all she had to worry about was saving enough of her allowance for the Friday-night movie and running faster than the snake in the middle. Cassie breathed deeply, smelling the fresh-cut grass and her own sweat. Things didn't change much in Walton, but somehow, at that moment, it didn't seem like such a bad thing.

Heavy footsteps pounded behind her, and she turned to see Sam approaching at a slow run. He stopped, panting heavily, his hands on his hips.

Her heart seemed to skip a beat, and she turned

back to the children. Sarah Frances had latched hold onto somebody's pigtail and the girl was shrieking for her to let go.

"I see you took my advice about running at night. It's a lot better, huh?"

Cassie refused to argue with him. She tilted her head into the warm breeze, remembering the same sights and smells that had drifted into her bedroom through the screened window all those years ago. Her breathing slowed, reaching a harmonious rhythm with the cicadas and crickets.

"As your doctor, I don't remember telling you it's all right to run on that ankle so soon. You should give it at least a week."

Reluctantly, she turned her attention toward Sam. "Right. And I'd be as big as a house if I didn't run off some of that food everybody's been shoving at me. The town's conspiring to make me fat, I swear. Either that or they want to send me into cardiac arrest. I've never seen so many fried foods in my life. They seem to know just what to tempt me with." She shifted her feet, watching the children once more. "Besides, the ankle feels fine. Good as new."

Sam watched with her, laughing softly as Joey pinched Sarah Frances on her bottom as he sped by his blindfolded sister. He cleared his throat. "Since you asked, I'll be happy to tell you firsthand that I won today's election. I'm the newest member of the town council."

"Hmm?" Cassie murmured, mesmerized by the padding of bare feet on the asphalt as children scurried back and forth across the lines. Offhandedly, she said, "Oh. Congratulations."

She continued to watch the children, a wistful smile on her face. "Remember playing that when we were younger? I don't think I was ever caught. I must have been too fast for everybody."

Sam looked at her from the corner of his eye. "You think so, huh? I remember that people were afraid to catch you because when they did, you would hit them. Really hard."

Cassie turned to face him. "How would you know? I don't remember you ever being there."

His smile faded slightly. When he spoke, his voice was low, almost a drawl. "Oh, I was there. You were just too busy chasing Joe Warner to notice anybody else."

She glared at him in the fading light. "That's ancient history. Everybody else seems to have forgotten it, so why don't you? You seem to remember an awful lot of bad things about me. I hope your memory is as good with important stuff."

He moved closer to her, making wild thoughts of whether or not she'd used enough deodorant run rampant in her head. She tried to turn her attention back to the game, but his nearness unnerved her. Bending over, she began stretching her hamstrings, looking for an excuse to move away.

"After casting my vote, I went over to the town hall to see who was ahead and Mr. Harmon said you'd already been there."

Cassie shrugged. "Yeah, I figured I'd check on birth and death records from the early seventies. I figured that an illegitimate birth might have easily escaped public records—especially if the child died. And I doubt they gave the baby my father's last name. But I figured I should try anyway." She glanced up at him, crossing her arms across her chest. "I'm just like a dog with a bone, I guess."

Laughter spilled from the street as a mother called her children in for supper, the sound safe and comforting to Cassie. She turned her head back to Sam. "I think my next step will be to go to the library and check old newspapers for birth records from April of 1973. It's a long shot, but I have no idea where else to go. The letter was postmarked Atlanta, so I'll check the Atlanta papers, too. But I have a feeling that whoever this woman was, her priority was keeping her privacy a secret."

"That's a good idea. Have you had a chance to look through the rest of the box yet?"

Cassie shook her head, feeling chastised. "No. Not yet. I've been busy. But I'll get to it."

He nodded, watching her closely for a moment. "If you don't find anything between the letters and the library, I'm going to Atlanta at the end of next month for a medical conference. I can check hospital records while I'm there if you'd like me to. I should have a little downtime."

Two frown lines formed between Cassie's eyebrows. "Why are you helping me out? What do you want from me?"

Sweat beaded on his forehead and dripped down his face, but he didn't wipe it away. "It's called helping out a friend. And no, I don't expect payment. I enjoy challenges." He sent her a pointed look.

"Good. Because I happen to be engaged." Why did she say that? He had said nothing that might be construed as an interest in a more intimate relationship, and she had gone and blurted that out. Mercifully, he only raised his eyebrows, giving him that wizened look she had come to admire from afar.

With a final glance at the dispersing children, she started to walk away. "I've got to get back. Harriet wants to talk about plans for a wedding shower. She can't seem to take no for an answer."

Sam began to walk with her. "But you could say thank you. Assuming you remember how."

She halted, putting her hands on her hips. She stopped so suddenly that Sam bumped into her, grabbing her upper arms to stop them both from falling over. He didn't let go.

"Thank you, Sam. For taking the trouble on my account. I do appreciate it." Gently she pulled away and resumed walking.

Sam fell into step beside her. "It's a great story. I know—that's easy to say because it's not about my parents. But even I'm curious to find out what happened to 'E'."

Cassie looked down at her feet, concentrating on not stepping on the sidewalk cracks, recalling the little verse she and Harriet would sing as they walked to school: *Step on a crack and break your mama's back.* Purposefully, she stepped on the space between two squares, silencing the singsong voices in her head. "Well, you and Harriet both. She thinks it's this wonderfully romantic story. And I can't decide if I should be angry at my father, or angry at this woman—or neither. This horrible thing has happened to this woman—she's lost both the man she loves and the child they created—yet she wishes him joy and happiness for the rest of his life. And then tells him she'll love him always." Her voice caught, and she coughed to hide it. "I can't help but wonder if she ever found somebody else. Had more children."

She stopped in front of the house and looked up at the sky, the same sky from her childhood, with the fading ribbons of pink and red strewn on the horizon and framed by the graceful limbs of the oak trees. It was as comforting to her as a mother's kiss. "Even the cynic in me wants to believe that she did."

Sam stood close, and she could feel the heat from his body. When he spoke, his breath brushed her hair. "Maybe there's only one love for everyone out there. And if you miss it—that's it. You don't get another chance. You can hang around waiting for them to be free, and then hope they'll love you back, but it's all pretty much chance."

Cassie tilted her head to look him in the face. "You don't really believe that, do you? That out of the millions and millions of people out there, there's only one for each of us?"

An air conditioner whirred to life from the bedroom window above them. Sam's face stilled in the near darkness as he spoke. "Angelfish mate for life. When one of them dies, the other one simply sinks to the bottom of the ocean and dies, too."

Cassie tried to add levity to her voice, but only half succeeded. "And black widows eat their mates." She tried to laugh but couldn't. "I'm glad I'm not an angelfish, then. Or maybe I would have crawled up into a ball and died after Joe." She regretted saying that, but Sam seemed to bring out the confessor in her. None of the psychiatrists she had seen in New York had ever had that effect on her. And they charged her money.

Sam sat on the bottom step, crossing his long legs at the ankles, and Cassie joined him as if it were the most natural thing in the world. "Maybe you did. There're lots of ways to die that don't involve physical death."

She stretched out her legs, leaning over her toes to stretch the hamstrings. "Well, you're wrong about that. I'm very much alive and kicking."

Sam remained silent, watching her.

She waved her hands in front of his face. "See? I'm here. And I'm just fine. And I'm engaged to be married."

Finally, he spoke. "I see." His tone was unconvincing. "So maybe Joe wasn't your one and only."

Leaning back, Cassie rested her elbows on the next step. Serious now, she angled her head back and watched the evening stars poke holes in the growing darkness. "I know that now. All anyone has to do is watch Harriet and Joe together to know that they have something really special. But try telling that to a twenty-year-old." A fine sigh escaped her, the sadness of it surprising even Cassie. "Oh, to have the wisdom of thirty-five at the age of twenty."

Sam leaned back, too. "But why all this time? Why did it take you so long to forgive and forget?"

Cassie straightened, facing him. "It's none of your business, Sam. You have a nasty habit of sticking your nose into things that have nothing to do with you." Free therapy was one thing, but his knowing her most private thoughts was quite another.

Sam remained where he was, casually studying her. "It wasn't so much Joe, was it? It was more your loss of pride. And you Madisons have enough pride to fertilize a field."

She leaped off the step and stood in front of Sam, her hands on her hips. "You have a lot of nerve. You don't know anything about me—anything about the kind of life I live now. I'm very happy with the way things have worked out."

She began marching up the stairs, but he blocked her way with an arm stretched out to the opposite railing. "The truth hurts, doesn't it? And I know a lot more about you than you think."

"Excuse me, please." Her voice thickened with sarcasm.

He stood slowly, but without moving out of her way. Their faces were only inches apart.

"I have a question—and this is one I asked your father but never got an answer. Why did he never visit you in New York for all those years?"

Surprised by the question, Cassie took a step back. "It's not because I never asked him to—because I did in every letter and every phone call. But he wanted *me* to come home and visit, and I wouldn't. So we just talked on the phone and met once a year in Atlanta. It was a neutral enough place for both of us, I guess."

"I guess that means you come by your stubborn streak honestly."

She ignored his jibe. "Can I get by now, please?"

As he stepped out of the way he said, "Oh, just one thing before I leave that I thought you should know. One of my first acts as town council member will be to find support for an ordinance to protect more than twenty historical buildings in this town, as well as initiating a moratorium on any further development until we can get a land-use plan into effect. I'm also preparing the groundwork to have large chunks of the town, including your house, placed on the National Register. It shouldn't affect you at all—unless you decide to do something with this house that would affect its architectural integrity. Like bulldozing it. Or converting it into apartments."

She stared at him in disbelief. "You've got to be kidding. This is *my* house and it's nobody else's business what I decide to do with it. Now please get off of my property and don't come back. Or speak to me. Nobody"—she wagged her finger at him—"not you or any of your small-town, small-minded people, are going to tell me what I can or cannot do with my own house."

He paused for a moment, chewing on the corner of his mouth. Slowly, he turned around, speaking in a drawl as he walked away. "Good night, Cassie. Was a pleasure, as always."

Her only answer was the slamming of the door.

MADDIE TURNED THE HANDLE on the front door of her granddaddy's house, although she supposed she should be thinking of it as her aunt Cassie's house—something that would definitely take some getting used to. She'd been coming to this house every week for Sunday supper since she was born, and it was hard to picture her aunt Cassie having everybody over to eat on a weekly basis. In fact, when she pictured her aunt, she just saw high heels and designer dresses—definitely not something a person wore when frying chicken or burping babies.

Maddie turned the handle again and realized with some surprise that it was locked. Nobody locked their doors in Walton. Her daddy sometimes joked that people in Walton put things *in* your house if you left the doors unlocked. She rapped hard with her knuckles and waited for a minute before stepping back onto the porch. Aunt Cassie had said to come over after school and see if there was anything she wanted from the attic. Her aunt had also said to call first in case she was running an errand, but Maddie hadn't paid any attention to that, because she figured the stupid door would be unlocked.

There was some kind of box dangling from the handle, but it was locked, too, and the key wasn't under the mat where it should have been. It felt disloyal, but even Maddie thought her aunt was a little out of touch.

Her eyebrows lifted as she remembered the window in the laundry room in the back that never closed all the way and was impossible to lock. Jumping off the porch steps, she ran around the back. After pulling a chair from the back porch, she managed to shimmy the window open and crawl inside, her landing made easier by the washing machine.

"Hello?" she called as she walked out into the kitchen. It felt weird being in the house all alone, but mostly, she thought, because the house seemed lonely. Maddie always imagined how great it would be to live in an apartment without all of the noise and commotion of her family, but she found herself listening for footsteps or even her name being called out. But the house was quiet, and as Maddie made her way up the stairs to the second floor, past all the paintings of her ancestors, she could almost imagine that she could feel it waiting, too, for the sounds of running feet.

She made her way to the attic, where piles had been started by her mother and Aunt Cassie. There were the save, throwaway, and giveaway piles—as explained by her aunt—and two very small piles of items that had been claimed by her mama and Aunt Cassie. One pile held only a stack of very old books and a picture frame that had been placed facedown, and Maddie imagined those were her aunt's. But as she paused by the second, much larger pile, she spotted a green satin dress covered in kudzu vines.

Not really knowing why she was doing it, Maddie leaned over and picked up the long gown, apparently made for someone who wore a size two or smaller. Maddie held it up against her body and wanted to laugh but couldn't. It was so tiny it would maybe cover one thigh but definitely not both, and there was no way she was getting it over her hips. Maybe it was a good thing she'd never be kudzu queen, because she could imagine her mother's disappointment that she couldn't fit into the same dress her mother had worn.

She let the dress drop back into the pile and returned to her aunt's stack of books and lifted the picture frame. It was an old color photograph, the colors faded so that the reds looked orange and the greens yellow. But there was no mistaking what it was.

The tail end of the kudzu queen's float that included the queen's throne showed up in brilliant flash photography. Maddie could barely recognize her mother under the sparkling crown draped with vines and all the heavy makeup and wearing the green dress. But it was obvious the photographer hadn't been focusing on the queen at all, because centered in the photograph was a picture of a tall girl wearing a lime green jumpsuit, walking behind the float and holding a leash. The girl was looking away so Maddie couldn't see her face, but she knew without a doubt it was her aunt Cassie, and pulling on the other end of the leash was a fat sow wearing a kudzu dress that looked just like the one the kudzu queen wore.

This time Maddie did laugh, and not just

because it was pretty darned funny seeing a pig in an evening gown. But it was so clear to her that her mother thought it was funny, too, and that she was okay with Aunt Cassie marching in the parade in whatever way she wanted.

Maddie sat down on the closed lid of a trunk, still holding the framed photograph. It was sad to think that all that had changed because of a stupid boy—even if the stupid boy turned out to be Maddie's father. Still, Aunt Cassie had ended up with the better deal, so maybe her mama was right whenever she said that things always worked out in the end.

She was about to put the picture down again when she stopped, the frame in midair. She wasn't kudzu queen this year and not likely to be for the next three. But her aunt and her mama had shown her that there was more than one way to shine in a parade and to make your mark in the world.

With a smile, she slid off the trunk and opened it, barely seeing what was inside because of how hard she was thinking. It was probably too late to make a dress for a pig, but there were so many other possibilities. She looked at the photograph again, knowing in her heart which girl she'd rather be, and giving her aunt a silent thank-you for teaching her that it was okay to not be the kudzu queen, no matter how badly you wanted the crown.

• • •

CASSIE SAT UNDER the large circular window at the library, trying to shade the screen of the ancient microfiche machine from the full sun streaming in. Her back ached, and the beginnings of a headache began to throb in her temples from squinting her eyes at the blurry words on the screen. Computerized records at the Walton Public Library were still a thing of the future, and Cassie cursed under her breath again at the ignominy of having to use something so archaic as microfiche. The damned thing belonged in a museum.

She had checked every birth and death record for the month of April 1973 in not only the *Walton Sentinel*, but also the *Atlanta Journal-Constitution*. She had jotted down all the pertinent information for mothers whose first names started with the letter "E," but realized she'd need help to follow up on all of them. Not that she expected anything to turn up from these voluntary announcements; she just had no other ideas. Sighing, she slid out the tray holding the film and began winding it back into the cartridge. What a waste of time. She should have just hired a private investigator to begin with. Andrew and her life were waiting in New York. She had no business allowing her feet to get mired in the thick Georgia clay, but she couldn't seem to help herself. She wasn't stalling, of course. It was just that so many things, like involving herself in the lives o

Harriet's children, going through years of accumulated junk, and searching for her father's old lover, just seemed to be interfering in her progress in getting everything settled and returning to New York. It just couldn't be helped.

Clutching her notebook, Cassie jogged down the library steps and toward the curb where the Mercedes was parked. That was one thing good about this town—one never had to hunt for a parking space. Or pay for it, either.

Sliding into the driver's seat, she stuck the key into the ignition and turned. Instead of the soft hum of the engine, she heard the car choke, then do a fine impression of a dry heave. Successive tries yielded the same result, the only addition being Cassie's cussing, which grew exponentially worse with each key turn.

A familiar truck pulled alongside her car. With a wave and a honk, Sam guided his vehicle into the parking space in front of hers. Cassie ignored him, turning the key once more. Grind, cough, splutter, splutter.

Sam came to stand next to the passenger side of her car, speculatively eyeing the thick cloud of smoke billowing out of her exhaust. "Cassie, I'm afraid that dog won't hunt."

Ignoring him, she tried the ignition one more time. A hideous clunk banged under the hood, followed by a thick cloud of smoke from the exhaust pipe.

"I'll call my father to have him tow it into the station and have a look at it." Before she could protest, he had flipped open his cell phone and was speaking to his father's service station. Sam wore an Atlanta Braves baseball cap, the front brim casting his face in shadow as he talked. She had always hated baseball caps on men, wondering what the appeal was. Until now. There was something oddly attractive about the way Sam Parker looked in a stupid baseball hat.

Cassie swung herself out from the car and slammed the door. "What's wrong with it?" Her voice sounded high and panicked. She'd have to remember to lower it when she told Andrew about his ailing baby.

Sam closed his phone, then tipped up the brim of his hat. "Dunno. These foreign cars can be mighty temperamental and will throw fits to show you who's boss. Don't know why people buy them." A lopsided grin lit his face. "Hey, I thought you weren't talking to me."

"I'm not. I'll stay here and wait for the tow truck. You may leave."

He looked at her as if he found something vastly amusing. His smile faded as he spotted Ed Farrell approaching them on the sidewalk.

Ed's drawl almost hid the animosity in his voice. "So, it's Walton's own king of antiprogress. Forgive me if I don't congratulate you, Sam. But I can only see your winning as the beginning of

217

Walton's untimely death. Tell me when the funeral is, and I'll be sure to come."

Sam's face closed, all signs of humor quickly erased. "I'll do that." Without another word, he turned his back on Ed to face Cassie. "I guess you'll be needing a ride. Where can I take you?"

Ed stepped around the car to stand beside Cassie. "Car trouble, sugar? I've got my nice air-conditioned Cadillac parked right on the corner if you need a ride. It's the least I could do for a client." His smile broadened. "And a beautiful one at that."

She was too old and wise to fall for that kind of flattery, but it couldn't be helped. She felt hot and sweaty and overly annoyed at the car and at Sam. Smiling up at Ed, she said, "Thank you, Ed. I'm on the way home, if you wouldn't mind." As she turned to catch Sam's expression, her satisfied smile faded. He wasn't even watching her. Instead, his attention was focused on Mary Jane Harden walking down the sidewalk, her hands clutching bags from Walton's Drug Emporium.

"Hey, y'all." She beamed at everyone, but her warmest smile was for Sam.

Sam took her packages and stored them in the back of his truck. "I'll give you a lift back to the clinic."

"Thanks, Sam." She faced Cassie. "Do y'all have your tickets yet for the Kudzu Festival? We're selling them quickly, so you'd better hurry.

Don't forget—this year we're having a prize for the cutest couple." She indicated Ed and Cassie with her index finger. "Are y'all going together?"

Ed put a hand on Cassie's elbow. "Well, I hadn't quite gotten around to asking, but now's as good a time as any. Would you do me the honor, Cassie?"

Flustered, all she could do was stammer, "Um, well, uh, I probably won't be here. When is it again?"

Mary Jane stepped closer. "It's this weekend. Surely you won't be leaving before then?"

"Uh, no—unless the attic miraculously empties itself."

"Great! Then I'd love for you to do me the honor of being my date."

Cornered, she could do nothing but agree. She watched as Mary Jane completed her web.

"Sam—you don't have a date, yet, do you? Seeing as how we both have to leave right from work, why don't we just go together?" She reached her hands around Sam's forearm and squeezed.

Sam's face was closed, his thoughts unreadable. He smiled gently. "Sure. That's a great idea."

Cassie reached for Ed's elbow. "Come on, Ed. Let's go. I'll call you, Mary Jane, and we'll do lunch." As an afterthought, she called over her shoulder, "Sam, tell your dad I'll call him about the car."

They walked to Ed's car, where a large white Fleetwood monopolized the corner like a hulking polar bear. Ed opened the door for her and she slid onto dark red leather upholstery. All it needed was a crystal chandelier hanging from the ceiling to complete the look of a bordello.

Ed crawled in behind the steering wheel and pulled out onto the street. "Like it, huh?"

Cassie was busy staring at the large gold pinkie ring on his finger. "Uh, the ring? Yeah. Sure. It's very nice."

He lifted a finger, the gold catching the light. "It sure is nice, but I was talking about the car. Never thought Ed Farrell would be driving one of these, did you?"

His smile was wide enough that Cassie could see the gold fillings in his back teeth. "You've certainly come far, Ed. You're a real tribute to this town." Her sentiments were genuine. He had come far from the dirt farm where he'd grown up. She looked down at her hands in her lap, remembering the boy with soiled clothes and dirty fingernails, remembering how he'd been mercilessly teased because of circumstances he couldn't control. "I'm real proud of you."

Under his dark skin, she could have sworn she saw him flush. She assumed it was from pleasure, but couldn't tell because he turned his face toward the side window.

After a few moments of silence, he said, "Just ran into Lou-Lou walking past the library. Said you were doing some research."

Cassie sat back against the cushy seat. "Now that was something I never expected to see: Lou-Lou Whittaker in a library. She told me she was there to check out books for you on American antiques." She stopped before adding what an additional surprise that had been.

Ed shrugged, turning left on Oak Street. "Yeah, well, I'm trying to educate myself on things they don't teach you in community college. I want to be able to furnish my house the way rich folks do—and I have a feeling going to the furniture section at Sears isn't going to cut it."

Cassie smiled to herself, wondering yet again where he'd gathered his get-up-and-go.

He turned onto Madison Lane. "So, what were you researching?"

Her fingers found their way to the necklace around her neck. If "E" still lived in Walton, Cassie needed to be very careful about protecting her identity. At least for now. "I'm doing some genealogy research on my family. It's all the rage now, and I thought that while I was here I might as well try to be productive."

Ed nodded as he pulled the car into the circular driveway in front of her house. Harriet's minivan was parked farther down the drive. He got out of the car and walked around to let Cassie out. "Just give me a call if you need a lift anywhere. I'd be happy to do it for my prettiest client."

Obviously the waves of political correctness had

bypassed his neck of the woods. "Thanks, Ed. Oh, and by the way, just to let you know. You've probably already heard, but Sam told me that he's petitioning the town council for a moratorium on any further development. Not that I think it will affect the sale of my house, but it might in the long run if we decide to exercise another option for the property besides keeping it residential. Is there anything we can do now to keep our options open?"

Ed's face turned an unhealthy shade of red. "That son of a . . . Damn! No, I didn't know." He reached for the cell phone clipped to his belt. "I'm sorry, Cassie, but I've gotta make some phone calls. I'll get back to you."

Without a good-bye, he flung open his car door and left in a hasty gust of red dust.

Cassie stared after him for a long moment before turning and mounting the porch steps, an odd feeling of sanctuary possessing her as she approached the front door. It had been a long time since she'd felt that old feeling. The familiar pace of work had been a fine substitute. She stepped onto the top step, then stopped. The squeak of the floorboard, or maybe the scent of the boxwoods, brought the memory flash so clearly it made her skin tighten. She could almost hear the snatches of old conversations coming through the screened windows, reminding her of the many nights she had lain in bed, listening to the comforting voices of her parents downstairs, and then, later, of her father and Aunt Lucinda. The memory was like food to her soul, and she paused her breath, trying to hold on to it.

The front door opened, and Harriet stood in the threshold, holding the phone from the study, its cord stretching as far as it would go. Placing her hand over the receiver, she said, "It's a guy from *Preservation* magazine. He's doing an article on endangered historical structures and wants to know when it would be a good time to come out and take pictures of the house. Says Sam Parker gave him your name and number."

Cassie's eyes widened, all peaceful thoughts deserting her completely. "He what?" She took the phone from her sister, pushing the "off" button without speaking to the person on the other end, then dropping it on a hall table. She could almost feel the accusing stares of her ancestors from the portraits on the wall. Her MBA training and years of working in New York had taught her to ignore that twinge of conscience. "That no-good damned redneck son of a bitch. He's going to regret messing with me." She stomped into her room and began rummaging in her garbage can for the business card Sam had given her. It was time to show Dr. Parker that she could play dirty, too. She punched the numbers on the phone with a shaking finger, trying to erase the image of Great-great-great-grandfather Madison's accusing glare.

CHAPTER 11

The older woman's voice on the other end of the phone surprised Cassie. She sat down on the small bench in front of her dressing table.

"Hello? I'm trying to reach Sam . . . uh, Dr. Parker. I might have reached the wrong number."

"Oh, no. This is his mother. He forwards his calls here when he comes to visit—and I'm expecting him soon. Who's calling?"

Cassie caught sight of her reflection in the mirror. Her geometric bob was in dire need of a trim, and her roots were no longer exactly matching the chestnut brown of the rest of her hair. "This is Cassandra Madison. Perhaps I should try at the clinic. . . ."

"Cassie Madison! Why, this is a pleasure. So sorry to hear about your daddy. What a fine man. This town will certainly miss him."

"Thank you, Mrs. Parker." She vaguely remembered Sam's mother. Mrs. Parker had worked in the lunchroom at the high school. She was round, with gray hair even then, fixed tightly in a bun on top of her head, with lines crisscrossing her cheeks from being in the sun too much. But her smile brightened her plain face and warmed the room around her. What Cassie remembered most was the way Mrs. Parker would give her second helpings of dessert without an admonishing stare or a pointed glance at her thighs. She pictured her now wearing a sleeveless apron with lace frills on the edge.

Cassie sat up straighter, pulling her shoulders back. "Thank you so much for the sweet potato pie. That was so kind of you. I've put it in the freezer for when Aunt Lucinda comes back. I remember it was her favorite. I must get your recipe before I go back home." Recipe? She didn't even think she could remember how to turn on an oven. "I've been meaning to write you a thank-you note, but it's been so busy. . . ."

Mrs. Parker cut her off. "Oh, no need for that. Take all your time to grieve, and don't worry about no thank-yous. Just know you're in our thoughts and prayers."

Tears parked themselves in Cassie's eyes. God—where was that coming from? If all it took to set her off these days were kind words, she needed to get back to New York as soon as possible, before she softened too much. She couldn't even imagine Andrew's reaction if she burst into tears every time a client said he didn't like her idea.

"Thank you, Mrs. Parker. I appreciate that. Um, could you have Sam call me when he gets in?"

"He's at the clinic right now. Would you like the number?"

Cassie glanced back down at the business card. "Ah, let's see . . . no. It looks like I have it—I meant to dial it to begin with, but my eyes switched lines on me."

Mrs. Parker laughed. "Happens to all of us as we grow older. I wish my arms would grow longer so I could hold a book at a distance I can read it."

Older? Thirty-five wasn't old. Well, maybe here, where most of the girls from her graduating class were not only married but had several children by now. "I guess so. Well, sorry to have bothered you. . . ."

"No bother at all. And I'm glad you called. I'd like more of a chance to chat. Why don't you come by for supper tonight?"

A flood of panic rushed over her. "Ah, tonight? No, I really couldn't impose. . . ."

"It's no trouble at all. When I cook fried chicken, I make a whole mess of it, so there will be plenty to go around. Sam will be here, too." She made it sound like Sam would be the icing on the cake.

Cassie stared at her reflection again in the mirror, her eyes looking like those of a condemned woman. "Well, thank you. What time would you like me to be there?"

She finished the conversation, then dialed the clinic while trying to revive her anger. Mary Jane picked up the phone.

"Cassie, hi. Are you calling to make lunch plans?"

"Uh, yes, actually. Are you free tomorrow? Thought we'd do that lunch at the diner we talked about."

"Great. I normally take lunch at about one o'clock. I'll check with Sam and let you know."

Cassie swallowed. "Speaking of Sam, is he there? I need to speak with him."

There was a brief pause. "Actually, no. He just left. Shall I leave a message?"

Another pause as Cassie chewed her lip, wondering how much she should tell Mary Jane. "Um, no, thanks. I'll just see him tonight."

She didn't realize how insinuating those words were until after she'd already said them. With some perverse pleasure, she didn't elaborate.

"Okay, then. I'll let you know about tomorrow. Bye, Cassie."

Hanging up the phone, Cassie let her shoulders slump. She needed to go back and take a refresher course in assertiveness training. If she kept it up, Andrew would never recognize her when she got back. She looked at her reflection. Her cheeks were softer, rounder, more pink. The perpetual circles under her eyes had faded, making her brown eyes brighter. She leaned forward on her elbows and sighed. Perhaps that would be a good thing.

Her gaze caught on the letter box on the dressing table behind her, and she swiveled to stare at it. She hadn't opened it once since it was brought down from the attic, a part of her feeling that in reading the letters she was trespassing on her father's secret. But he hadn't exactly hidden the box, and she thought again that maybe he'd wanted them found.

With slow steps, she approached and opened the lid. Her father was dead now, and if he'd had a life before he'd met her mother, she wanted to know about it. Her fingers gently rifled through the small stack of letters, feeling the brittle feel of old paper brush against her skin, and she studied the beautiful handwriting of the unknown woman once again.

A glossy corner stuck out of the stack and Cassie pinched it between her fingernails to pull it out. She looked at the photograph in surprise, recognizing her sixth-grade school picture. There she was, standing next to Mrs. Browning, her knee socks drooping around her ankles and her hair part looking like a fault line. Harriet stood nearby in the front row, looking perfect and wearing a hair bow that matched her outfit. Joe and Sam stood next to each other in the back row, making horns over each other's heads. Sam's eyes were invisible, the sunlight reflecting brightly off the wide frames of his glasses. Cassie squinted, trying to recall knowing Sam in sixth grade, but the memory eluded her.

She was about to slip the photo back in the box when she noticed the tall figure in the back row, standing slightly apart from the other children. Ed Farrell. He had been held back two different years, and sixth was the first time they had been in the same grade. His face was smudged with dirt, his eyes downcast as if he wanted to remain invisible to the camera. She could see the top of his stained overalls, and remembered with abject shame how the boys in school had teased him mercilessly for being a bona fide redneck.

She dropped the picture back in the box, wondering why it had been put there instead of downstairs in her father's desk with the rest of their school pictures.

Tentatively, her hand floated over the stack of letters like a curious butterfly before settling down and pulling out the first yellowed envelope. Bringing it over to the bed, she sat down and opened it.

September 25, 1972

My dearest Harry,
My daddy said he spotted you waiting for me after church last Sunday. When he asked me why you hadn't been to hear the sermon, I said it was because you were Episcopalian. I thought his head would explode, it turned so red.

I always knew this would be a problem, which is why I insisted we be quiet about us. But it seems now we are found out. Daddy says he doesn't want me to see you anymore, which is quite silly seeing as how I'm a grown

woman way past her prime and what many
would have called an "old maid" back in the
day. I think things between us are too far gone
for us to stay apart, don't you? I've never
disobeyed him before, but what I feel for you
makes me forget everything else.

I wear the beautiful necklace you gave me
every day—but I'm careful to keep it under my
blouse. I like feeling it so near my heart, and it
keeps you in my mind until I can see you again.

Love,

E

Cassie sat for a long time with the letter opened
on her lap, her emotions moving rapidly between
guilt, disgust, and a strong dose of romance.
Eventually, she got up and put it back in the letter
box, then gently closed the lid.

HARRIET WAS LEANING OVER an antique sewing
table, trying to reach a small box on a shelf behind
it, when Cassie entered the attic.

"You're going to hurt yourself, Har. Let me get
it. There are advantages to being big and bulky,
you know."

Harriet stepped aside to let Cassie grab the box.
"You're not big and bulky. I always thought of you
as Wonder Woman from TV. You were so tall and
strong. I wanted to be like you." She plopped
down on an old steamer trunk.

A frown puckered Cassie's brow. "I don't believe that for a minute, Har. All of the boys at Walton High went for the blond, petite type—not the Amazon brunette. Considering how tall I am, I was pretty invisible."

Harriet shook her head slowly, her head tilted to the side, and wished she could pretend that Cassie were one of her children and she could kiss the hurt away. But she knew Cassie's hurt went deeper than that. Sometimes she thought Cassie had been born with all that hurt buried deep inside her. "You're supposed to be the smart one, but sometimes I'm not so sure." A small smile formed on her lips. "So, are you still mad at me?"

Reaching into an old appliance box, Cassie looked up. "About what?"

"About me thinking that daddy and his lady friend had a terrific romance."

Cassie shrugged, burying her head in the box again. "No, I'm not angry. Even I have to admit there's something terribly romantic about it all. I read a letter today. I'll show it to you later." She scratched her nose as dust motes rose from the box. "I didn't see any letters dated after that one we read up here—the one about the baby. I have to admit I'm pretty relieved about that. Maybe the love affair really was over before Daddy married Mama."

Harriet turned to look out the small window. "I

hope we find her. I'd like to know that everything worked out for her."

Cassie offered a gentle smile. "Things usually do, I think. I lived, after all." She ducked her head back in the box and pulled out a past-its-prime naked baby doll. It had been neatly decapitated at some point. She dug back in the box to find the errant head.

Harriet spoke softly. "Yes, you sure did, didn't you? They say that living well is the best revenge."

Cassie held up the doll head.

"Baby Betsy!" Harriet reached out her hands for it, but didn't stand, unable to find the energy that would require. She took the proffered doll from her sister and stuck the head on top of the neck. "Remember when Cousin Nathan cut her head off with his daddy's hunting knife?" She laughed at the memory. "You went after him with the knife until Aunt Lucinda caught up with you. Then you glued the head back on, but it never would stay." She eyed the doll wistfully, then gave it a soft hug. "You were always trying to fix things for me. It made you mad when you couldn't fix everything."

Cassie stopped her rummaging for a moment and turned to her sister. Her gaze roamed around the dusty attic, touching on the piles of boxes, clothes, and trunks: all the reminders of their shared past. She faced her sister again. "I guess I didn't want you to know what it was like not to have a mother. It was bad enough that one of us did, but we both didn't have to."

"Keeper of hearts, right?" Harriet's gaze fell to the necklace Cassie wore, the flash of gold somehow reassuring.

"Yeah. Right." Cassie turned back to the box she'd been digging in.

"Do you still miss her?"

Cassie sat back on her heels. "Yes. I do. Not every day, like I used to. Just sometimes. Like when I get a whiff of that perfume she used to wear." She threw her head back and laughed. "Or when I walk around my apartment in my slip. I swear I'm the only woman under sixty in New York who wears a slip. Mama had such beautiful ones—all silk and all sorts of colors. She used to call it her 'secret femininity.' I just remember her running around before church, wearing her slip and jewelry and trying to get us ready. I remember how soft they felt on my cheek when I hugged her."

Harriet dipped her head. "I don't even remember that much. But I've missed her—especially at those times when a girl needs her mother." She closed her eyes, the loss close to her skin. "I missed her on my wedding day. I wanted her to help me pick a dress and put her pearls around my neck." She shook her head slightly. "Not that I ended up having those things, but I couldn't even ever dream about them. But most of all I missed her during all my pregnancies—especially the first. I needed her guidance." She looked directly at Cassie. "And I missed you, too. I wanted you to experience it with me. I will always regret that you weren't here with me when they were born." She felt her eyes misting, and she dabbed at them with the corner of her dress.

Cassie remained silent, but Harriet understood. Cassie had always been more comfortable doing something to show her feelings instead of talking about them.

"You know, Har, I can clean up this attic myself. Just give me an idea of the things you want me to save for you, and I'll add them to your pile."

Harriet wanted to respond, but a sharp pain somewhere in her abdomen took the words from her mouth. She sat on the trunk, not moving, with her eyes closed as if that would make the pain go away.

"Are you all right?"

Harriet opened her eyes slowly and forced a smile to take away the look of concern on her sister's face. "Yes. I'm fine. I'm just so . . . fatigued. I don't seem to be snapping back so fast after Amanda's birth like I did with the others." She gave a feeble laugh. "Guess I must be getting older."

Cassie reached deep inside the box. "I'm sure owning your own boutique and raising five children has nothing to do with it." Her brittle smile dimmed as they both noticed what her hand had latched hold of. Purple taffeta. After fifteen years the vibrant hue had hardly faded. She held it up, the small arc of light bouncing off of it and making it sparkle. She tried to tuck the dress, unnoticed, back into the trunk, but Harriet stopped her.

"Wait, Cassie. Knoxie or Sarah Frances might want to play dress-up with it."

With a resigned sigh, Cassie dredged up the dress again. "Here. You can have it. I certainly have no use for it."

She turned her face away, but not before Harriet saw the old hurt in Cassie's eyes. It was the dress Cassie had worn to the sophomore formal, the dress she'd been wearing when Sam had told her about Harriet and Joe.

Harriet stood and walked over to Cassie who'd sat down on a small wooden rocking horse. "I'm sorry, Cassie. I've always wanted to tell you that. I really am. Not about me and Joe, but about the way you found out. And you leaving. We never meant that to happen."

Her voice broke, but Cassie didn't look up. Instead, she shrugged. "Yeah, well . . ."

There was nothing either of them could think of to say. Harriet wanted to bury all of the old ugliness away in the old trunk, along with the dress. If only Cassie would let her. To Cassie, just looking at the dress must be like pushing on a bruise: tender to the touch, but easily ignored if one didn't get too close.

Harriet knelt next to Cassie on the dusty floor, wanting more than anything for Cassie to understand. To forgive the unforgivable. "We've wanted you to come back ever since you left. It just isn't the same without you here. We want you to be part of our lives, part of our children's lives." She touched Cassie's arm. "We were hoping this visit would make you forget all the bad feelings, and remember all the good that came before them. And maybe make you want to come back."

Turning, Cassie looked at Harriet, and Harriet saw all that had changed in her sister in the last fifteen years. So much of it—the confidence, the more sophisticated look—was so good to see. But at such a cost. The funny, silly, carefree girl who had once been Cassie Madison had been buried under all of that hurt so that a newly minted woman could emerge from the wreckage. Somehow in those fifteen years Harriet had lost the sister who had once loved and protected Harriet as if it had been her mission in life—the same sister Harriet had loved back with all her heart. The sister Harriet had hurt in an almost unimaginable way.

Cassie looked down at her fingers, studying her chipped and faded French manicure. "It doesn't matter anymore, Har. I have a new life—I'm engaged. Moving back just isn't an option for me."

She looked up, meeting Harriet's gaze. "I'd always wanted to get out of this town, and you gave me a reason to leave." With a stilted laugh, she added, "Maybe I should thank you."

Harriet stared hard at her sister. "Do you still have feelings for Joe?"

Cassie shook her head slowly. "No, definitely not. I can see him as a friend—or a brother-in-law—but he's most definitely not the type I would marry."

Harriet tweaked her lips into a little smile, still looking for the old Cassie. "Well, then. Maybe you should be thanking me."

Cassie threw a velvet hat with three peacock feathers at her sister. "Don't hold your breath for that one, okay?" Sobering, she looked at Harriet with clear eyes, as if seeing a truth for the first time. "Small hurts that are allowed to fester sometimes seem to grow out of all proportion."

"It wasn't a small hurt."

"Yeah, well." Cassie took a pair of moth-eaten woolen long johns out of the trunk, looking at them closely, but her focus somewhere else. "But I shouldn't have punished Daddy and Aunt Lucinda, too. I was just so busy trying to prove to myself and everybody else that I didn't care."

Harriet stroked the smooth velvet of the hat, her fingers gently moving over the feathers. "No—I think you were too busy trying to prove to everybody that you didn't belong here."

Cassie stood, brushing off her knees. "Well, I don't. It's nice to visit. . . ."

The pain shot through her again, and Harriet leaned back against a box, her eyes closed.

"Are you all right? You're as white as a ghost."

"I'm fine. I'm fine. Just tired." Harriet waved a pale hand in front of her. "I think I just need some rest. But I need to get ready for inventory at the boutique. . . ."

Dropping the long underwear onto the growing pile of things to be discarded, Cassie crouched in front of Harriet. "Don't be ridiculous. You're obviously unwell. Go lie down, and I'll see if I can get hold of Sam."

"No, really. This has happened before. I just need a quick twenty-minute catnap and I'll be as good as new. I'll go to my old room and lie down—just promise me you won't let me sleep longer than twenty minutes."

Cassie looked at her doubtfully. "Are you sure . . . ?"

Trying not to struggle too much, Harriet hauled herself to her feet. "I'm sure." Unsteadily, she walked toward the stairs, then grabbed the banister tightly. "Twenty minutes, okay?"

Still frowning, Cassie nodded. "But only if you let me go to the boutique with you and help you out."

Harriet hoped her relief wasn't too obvious. "All right. But only if you really want to."

"I do." Cassie gave her a reassuring smile.

"Thanks." Harriet made her way down the stairs and to the room she'd grown up in. And as she lay down on the pillow, already half-asleep, she hoped that Cassie would let her sleep a little bit longer than twenty minutes, and knew, somehow, that she would.

CASSIE STOOD IN FRONT of the pink Chevrolet Malibu, thinking it even smelled like face powder. Aunt Lucinda had returned from her trip just in time to loan out her car to Cassie, who otherwise would have to walk in the heat the ten blocks to the Parkers'. She pondered whether walking wasn't a better alternative to being seen in the pink car.

She lifted her arms, already feeling the stickiness, and decided that, pink or not, it had air-conditioning. With one last look at the license plate that read LIPSTICK, she climbed in behind the wheel. As she flipped on the radio, she casually wondered how many skin lotions, clarifying masks, and mascaras Aunt Lucinda had to sell to the fine ladies of Walton to win this car. She turned a quick corner and listened to the boxes and bags filled with beauty potions shift and titter on the backseat like giddy children.

The small ranch-style house on Orchard remained much as she remembered. She'd never been inside the Parker house before, but had passed it every day to and from high school. The most memorable thing about it was its porch: almost as deep as it was wide, with plenty of hiding space behind large wicker rocking chairs. She had learned this firsthand the night she'd painted Principal Purdy's porch across the street.

After locking the car door, and flipping the handle to make sure it was locked, she headed down the front walk. She recognized the tall form standing behind the screen door, and immediately felt her anger rise.

"I know it sounds unnatural to you, Cassie, but you don't need to lock your car doors here. Especially not in our driveway." He held the door open for her, an insouciant smile crossing his face.

Cassie stopped, looking nervously around. "Is that animal of yours here?"

"No, ma'am. On account of your skittishness, I left George at my place. He was mighty upset, though. Seems he's taken quite a liking to you."

Ignoring him, she stomped up the porch steps. "You've got some nerve, Sam Parker. How dare you call that magaz—" Her foot caught on the doormat, sending her straight into Sam's chest.

Their arms were wrapped around each other when Mrs. Parker emerged from the kitchen. She caught sight of them, and her wide gray eyes beamed with what appeared to be surprise, quickly shifting to satisfaction.

Cassie quickly extricated herself from Sam, and

allowed herself to be enveloped in the soft pillow of Mrs. Parker's hug. The woman hadn't changed one bit. Everything was the same—all the way down to the little apron with frilly lace sleeves.

"You're just as pretty as your mama, aren't you? Just the picture of her." She bent toward Cassie's hair and sniffed loudly. "That's Saucy, ain't it? Just bought some of that perfume from your Aunt Lucinda last month. Drives my Walter wild."

She gave a throaty laugh just as Mr. Parker stomped down the stairs, rolling down sleeves over still-wet forearms where the wet hairs curled themselves up like small tufts of cotton. "Yep— that's me. A wild man."

He reached his wife and gave her a big kiss on the cheek. His hand did something behind her, making her squeal like a schoolgirl. She slapped his arm. "Walter! Mind your manners, now. We've got company."

The same dark blue eyes she remembered from the gas station peered at her from under bushy white eyebrows. The ubiquitous overalls covered his rounded abdomen, and he smelled faintly of soap. The thought of this man being wild with a woman made Cassie want to laugh outright.

"So I see. It's good to see you again, Cassie." He bent forward and kissed her loudly on the cheek. "I'll hardly be able to eat my supper tonight—I'll be too busy staring at the two lovely visions sitting at my table."

241

Mrs. Parker giggled again, and slapped him on his arm. "Be careful, Walter. Flattery will get you everywhere."

He winked at his wife, and Cassie had the oddest compulsion to hug them both. There was something so refreshing and authentic about them. She tried to picture her and Andrew as old marrieds and the picture just wouldn't focus.

"Come help me in the kitchen, Walter. Sam, why not show Cassie to the parlor and get her something to drink."

Cassie caught the sly wink Mrs. Parker sent her husband, and immediately offered her services. "I'll help!"

Mrs. Parker waved a pudgy hand. "Oh, no, darlin'. You just go sit and chat with Sam. Won't have our guest workin' in the kitchen."

The overalled Mr. Parker followed his wife with a few lighthearted remarks about women's work and disappeared into the kitchen.

Cassie faced Sam, her hands hugging her elbows. "Why does your mother think that I would rather talk to you than chop lettuce?"

He led her into a room off the small foyer, and motioned her to sit on a green velvet love seat. "Because I'm her son and she thinks I'm the neatest thing since sliced bread and can't imagine everybody else not thinking the same thing."

He took a seat in a well-worn recliner, the remote control perched on the armrest. She rested

242

her head against a homemade quilt on the back of the love seat and gazed at the angel figurines sitting on a lace table mat on the coffee table. Her fury over the magazine shoot lingered under the surface, but she was loath to unleash it here, within earshot of his parents. Their opinion of her suddenly mattered, and she didn't want to be interrupted before letting Sam get an earful.

Standing abruptly, Cassie approached the fireplace to examine framed pictures set among old sailing boat models and bronzed baby shoes on the mantel. The brick fireplace had been swept clean, but the smell of old ash still lingered. Cassie bent forward to look at a color photograph of two boys, one about eleven and the other a mere toddler. Both wore cowboy hats and were grinning goofily into the camera. The younger boy also wore cowboy boots and a strategically placed holster—and nothing else.

"Nice outfit," Cassie said.

"That's me and Tom."

Cassie whirled around, surprised to find Sam standing so close to her. His eyes burned with a gentle blue light, making her temporarily forget her anger at him. She took a step back and looked down at the picture.

"Your brother?"

Sam nodded. "That was taken the year before he died. We'd gone to the state fair and gotten those hats. Thought we were two tough customers."

Cassie ran her finger over the glass. "I'm sorry. You must miss him very much."

He said nothing, but continued to regard her closely. She stepped back, her fingers toying with the charms around her neck. "I guess there are worse reasons than guilt over something that wasn't really your fault to give up everything you've worked so hard for."

Sam made a hissing noise as he sucked in his breath, and Cassie knew she'd touched a sore spot. But she couldn't back down.

Gingerly, she placed the picture back in its place, staring at the picture so she wouldn't have to see his face.

"Is that why you're trying to make it difficult for me to leave? Because you're jealous that I have a choice—and you felt that you didn't?"

Long, tanned fingers moved to the mantel within her field of vision, and she turned to find herself blocked in by his arm and his body. His voice was calm. "Maybe it's the other way around. Maybe you're jealous of me because I had a reason to stay."

His words stung but she would be damned if she'd let him know it. "I have more reasons to return to New York than you could count. As soon as I've finished going through everything at the house and divvying it all up any way I can, I'm leaving."

He raised an eyebrow, then slowly withdrew his

arm from the mantel. He turned away, but not before Cassie spied his furiously working jaw.

Mrs. Parker bustled in at that moment carrying a steaming platter of fried chicken to the adjacent dining room. She was followed closely by Mr. Parker with a bowl full of mashed potatoes and a gravy boat shaped like a football. It had the University of Georgia bulldog painted on the side.

Cassie plastered a polite smile on her face and sat down at the table. One glance around at the dishes told her there was more cholesterol and fat on that table than her body had been allowed near in over fifteen years. She closed her eyes and sniffed deeply, rationalizing that she could run an extra mile the next day. When Mrs. Parker came around the table with the platter of chicken, Cassie held her plate up with an eager smile.

After everyone was served, Mr. Parker cleared his throat as he tucked his napkin into the bib of his overalls. "Let's say grace." Everyone bowed his head, and Cassie was relieved she didn't have to hold anybody's hand.

Afterward, Mr. Parker turned to Cassie. "I sure hope you don't need your car before the end of the week. Seems that engine part I need to get it running again has to come all the way from Germany. I saved some time ordering it off the Internet, but it will still take a while to get here."

Cassie swallowed a mouthful of potatoes before nodding. "That's fine. I've still got stuff to clean up at the house. I haven't even gone through half the attic yet. I don't think anything's been thrown away since the house was built."

Mrs. Parker reached over and touched Cassie's hand. "More stuff to treasure, dear. Enjoy going through all those memories."

Cassie nodded, and went to open her mouth in agreement. But she felt Sam's gaze on her, and fell back, silent, not wanting to give him the satisfaction.

After dinner, Mrs. Parker all but ordered Cassie and Sam out to the front porch, pushing aside protestations that Cassie wanted to help with the dishes.

"You two young people go out and enjoy that gorgeous night. It's going to be a full moon and you can watch it rise over the magnolias. The sight will just break your heart." With a pat on Cassie's shoulder, pushing her in the direction of the door, Mrs. Parker turned to take the pitcher of iced tea off the table. "I'll bring y'all some lemonade and apple pie in just a minute."

Cassie walked on ahead of Sam, knowing that if anything was going to break this evening, it would be his head. The cool blue light startled her, making her stop and gaze out at the sparkling night. She never noticed the moon anymore. If she ever thought to look for it, it had already drifted behind a tall building, hiding it from her sight. She stood still for a moment, bathing in its ethereal light, listening to the night sounds all around her.

The squeak of a porch swing made her turn. Sam patted the seat next to him. Turning her back to the moon, she ignored Sam and found a comfortable spot in a large rocking chair.

She didn't allow herself to rock, but steeled her feet on the floor.

"I want you to call that stupid magazine and inform them that if they show up on my doorstep, I'll have them sued for trespassing. And then I'll sue you for harassment just for fun."

He didn't even shift in his seat; just the slow, comfortable squeak of the swing answered her.

Annoyed, she asked, "Did you hear me? I'm serious. You're interfering with my life and it's none of your damned business."

Sam continued the slow swinging motion. "How come you didn't change the color of your eyes when you got contacts?"

Her eyes widened, her fingers flying to her face. "What's wrong with the color of my eyes?"

The blue light made his smile glow. "Nothing. I always liked them. Sort of reminded me of a fine glass of whiskey backlit by a fire."

Cassie sat back, her arms folded in front of her, feeling flattered but unwilling to let him know. "My, my. So we're a poet, too."

He shrugged and the swing groaned. "I guess I'm just a man of many talents."

Self-conscious now, she asked, "Then why do you think I should have changed them?"

"Changed what?"

She stamped her foot. "The color of my eyes. Are you sure your medical license is legit?"

He stood, the swing swaying drunkenly behind him. "You changed everything else that didn't need changing, and it just surprised me that you didn't change your eye color, too."

His words caught her by surprise. Her voice softened a degree. "They're the same color as my mother's, and I thought hers were beautiful."

"So are yours."

Blood rushed to her cheeks and she was glad for the cover of darkness. Then sane realization hit her. This man was trying to ruin her life. "Don't try to sweet-talk me—I'm furious with you. And if you don't stop this harassment right now, you'll be hearing from my lawyer."

Cassie stood, trying not to notice how the moonlight lit his eyes. She focused on a spot above his head. "Please send my apologies to your mother—tell her I couldn't stay. It was a wonderful dinner." Cassie walked purposefully toward the pink car now resembling a brilliant marshmallow in the moon glow.

"And, yes, it's legit," he called after her.

Facing him again, she put her hands on her hips. "What is?"

"My degree. When you come to visit, I'll show it to you. It's hanging on the wall in my living room."

"Don't hold your breath, Sam. On second thought, please do. That'll be one less irritation in my life I'll need to deal with."

She opened the car door.

"Cassie?"

"What?"

"Moonlight becomes you."

She slammed the door shut and started the engine, feeling blood again rush to her cheeks. She caught sight of herself in the rearview mirror, and paused with her hand on the steering wheel. Her skin appeared pale and smooth, unmarred by freckles, like a lake in early morning before the first fishing line was lowered. Her eyes smoldered, and her hand touched her cheek. It had been so long since someone had said something so . . . so frivolous to her. It made her feel . . . like a woman. Not a businesswoman but a woman. Feminine. She put the car in reverse and looked at herself again and saw her mother's eyes, but the look in them was harder, warier.

Pulling the car out onto the street, Cassie put it into drive and drove home slowly, one hand turning the steering wheel, and the other hand trailing outside the window. Her pale fingers opened wide as if to capture some of the milky night air and some of the wistfulness that seemed to stir up from the dark road and push at her temples.

CHAPTER 12

Maddie stood next to her aunt Cassie behind the counter at Harriet's Skirts 'n' Such, and watched her aunt cringe. The Sedgewick twins, with bright peacock feathers perched on identical straw hats, were approaching the shop.

It was only ten o'clock in the morning, but it was obvious that Aunt Cassie's day was already turning from bad to worse. Maddie had been at her aunt's house early in the morning to help load old clothing headed for the Salvation Army into Aunt Lucinda's pink car. The phone had rung while she was lugging a large bag filled with the contents of one of the trunks from the attic down the stairs, and she paused when Aunt Cassie answered it and said the name Andrew. Her aunt was going through the stuff in the desk again and had flicked on the speakerphone.

Her aunt's voice sounded higher than usual. "Why didn't you call me on my cell?"

"Does that mean you've finally gotten around to buying a charger?" He didn't wait for an answer. "When are you coming back? I can't run this whole company on my own—things are getting out of control. I need you to come home. Now. Just jump in the car and leave."

For a moment, Maddie had been afraid that Aunt Cassie would agree. Not that she didn't think her aunt had far more important things to do than sorting through her granddaddy's old papers and old junk in the attic, but there was something about what this Andrew said that made Maddie a little angry. Because through all of his reasons why he thought Aunt Cassie should come back, not one of them had anything to do with missing *Cassie.*

"No, Andrew. I can't come now. I've got responsibilities here, too. You can't just tell me what to do."

"The hell I can't. I *am* your boss."

There had been a short pause and Maddie leaned over the banister to see her aunt's mouth freeze in a hard line. "As a matter of fact, Andrew, I think I need to ask for a formal leave of absence. I'll still be available to handle client problems long-distance and answer questions if you need me. But I'm sure Carolyn Moore would be more than happy to take my place in my absence—she's really good at brownnosing." She paused, and Maddie looked at her face again to see who was more surprised by her words. It was apparent even to Maddie that this was the first time her aunt had thought about staying, much less said it out loud.

Aunt Cassie continued, "I won't be gone much longer—maybe a month or so—but you're going to need somebody there to fill in."

"A month? Are you kidding me?"

Cassie's hands stopped moving papers on the desk

and she sat up straighter. "Yes," she said, taking a deep breath. "I think so. I can't just . . . leave."

"Why not? It's not like you ever wanted to spend time there before."

Maddie breathed quietly, waiting for Aunt Cassie to answer.

"Yes, well. I'd never met my nieces and nephew before. And I guess it's been nice getting to know my sister again. Fifteen years is a long time. Surely you can understand that."

There was complete silence on the other end of the line. Then: "What about my car? How am I supposed to get that back?"

Cassie had simply hung up the phone without answering. The house phone, then Aunt Cassie's cell phone had rung again and again, and Maddie knew he'd texted her aunt several more times because she'd heard her cussing up a storm every time she checked her BlackBerry, but Aunt Cassie kept deleting them.

Her aunt had been in a bad mood on the way over to her mama's store, and now, as Aunt Cassie watched the Sedgewicks approach, it didn't look like her mood was going to get any better. Maddie turned to her aunt to ask her why she seemed so afraid of two little old ladies, when her aunt ducked behind the counter, hunched into a tight ball, and stayed there as the bells above the door chimed and the twins entered the store and exchanged a greeting with Maddie.

Aunt Lucinda, who worked at the boutique three days a week, stepped out of the stockroom and stopped as she spied Aunt Cassie cowering beside the hangers and panty hose boxes. Cassie held her finger to her mouth and Maddie turned away so she wouldn't laugh.

"Did you drop something, dear?"

Startled, Cassie jerked her head around to stare at the sweet face of Thelma (or was it Selma?) Sedgewick, the peacock feather bobbing up and down as if nodding a greeting.

"Um, yeah. Got it." Aunt Cassie grabbed a handful of tissue paper and stood, knocking over a stack of hangers. She gave the twins a big smile. "What a pleasure to see you two again. How can I help you?"

The two sisters glanced at each other, then back at Cassie. "We've come to apologize. We saw Harriet at Bitsy's and she told us you were here, and we just couldn't start our day without clearing the air, so to speak."

Cassie blinked. "Apologize? To me? But I think I'm the one . . ."

Selma waved her hand. "No, dear. The misunderstanding was all our fault. We simply neglected to recall that you've lived without a mother's guidance for so long." She placed a gloved hand on her chest and rolled her eyes heavenward. "And that you've lived in a big city where nobody knows you or who your people are.

It's bound to have an adverse affect on a girl."
She patted Cassie's arm. "But we're quite sure
that now that you're back home, your good
breeding and upbringing will soon blossom
again."

Speechless, Aunt Cassie merely blinked her eyes
as Selma plopped a plastic lawn bag on the
counter. It reeked of moist earth and hot plastic.
"So we're asking your forgiveness and bringing
this as a token of our sincerity."

Cassie met Maddie's gaze for a moment before
moving the top of the bag back to see better.
There, nestled in a ball of dirt, was a plant.

"What is it?"

Two pairs of identical eyes stared back at Cassie,
as if amazed she couldn't identify the species of
whatever it was that sat on the counter.

"It looks like a gardenia," said Maddie, trying to
help wipe the confused expression off of her aunt's
face.

"That's right, sweetie. And it's a clipping from
our garden. Our great-grandmother planted the
first one, and we've been giving clippings ever
since we can remember. I would say that most of
the gardenias in the county are related to ours."

Cassie lifted the bag carefully. "What, um, what
do I do with it?"

Again, incredulous eyes stared at her. "Why, you
plant it, you goose. Here, anyway. Don't think you
could take it to New York. That's too far from its

natural habitat. It would just shrink up and wither, I'm afraid."

She clucked her tongue as if talking about a distant relative. She reached two gnarled hands up to the bag and knotted it closed. Sliding it over to Cassie, she said, "Just take this home and plant it. If you need help or advice, you know where to find us."

"I can help, Aunt Cassie. I help Mama in her garden all the time."

Aunt Cassie held the bag like it was a dirty diaper. "Thanks, Maddie. I'll be sure to hold you to that offer."

The bell over the door chimed again, and Mary Jane Harden stepped inside. It was Maddie's turn to want to duck behind the counter. Miss Harden was in charge of the float decorations and Maddie could think of only one reason why she'd be in the store.

Aunt Lucinda was the first to greet her. "Mary Jane—what a pleasure. What can I help you with this morning?"

Mary Jane looked around the room as Maddie held her breath, taking in the Sedgewick twins, her gaze coming back to rest on Aunt Cassie. She smiled and gave a quick greeting before turning her attention to Lucinda. "I was looking for something, uh, well, special. Maybe something eye-catching?"

It was Maddie's turn to blink.

Lucinda winked like she was in on some big joke. "Eye-catching? That would depend on whose eye you're trying to catch. If it's for Ed Farrell, we don't do T-shirts and hot pants. But if it's for that nice manager over at the bank, well, we just might be able to—"

Miss Harden spoke so low it was hard to hear. "No. It's for tonight." She glanced briefly at Aunt Cassie, who was pretending to study the stitching on a push-up bra. "I'm going with, um, Sam."

Maddie let the breath slowly ease out from between her teeth.

Aunt Lucinda nodded, a smile widening her reddened lips. "I thought so. And I know just the thing." She walked to a wall of blouses and pulled out a low-cut silk tank top in flamingo red. Miss Harden's eyes brightened. "I'll take it."

Aunt Lucinda fumbled with the hanger, trying to unhitch the shirt, and Maddie took it from her to help her out. "Don't you want to try it on?"

"I can't—I've got to get back to work. If it doesn't fit, I'll return it."

Aunt Cassie stepped away from the counter to allow Lucinda to ring up the purchase and Maddie to wrap and box it.

As Miss Harden fumbled with the money in her wallet, she said, "I'm sorry about canceling lunch today—I just got swamped at the clinic. We'll do it another time, okay?"

"Sure." Aunt Cassie said good-bye, and Lucinda

256

returned to the stockroom, taking the gardenia and its bag with her.

The twins left with busy feather bobbings and bell chimings, and Cassie opened up the inventory book.

"Aunt Cassie?"

She looked up. "Yes, Maddie?"

"I found a picture in the attic—the picture of mama on the parade float and you pulling a pig in a dress."

A corner of her aunt's mouth turned up. "Yes?"

"Did anybody know you were going to do that?"

Her smile got bigger. "Nope. Not even the pig. I borrowed her from the Adlers' farm and returned her before they even knew she was missing. Well, they wouldn't have known if I'd thought to take off the dress first."

Maddie snorted. "Did you get into a lot of trouble?"

Cassie nodded. "Yep. I sure did. No friends, no movies, no Dixie Diner, no anything for a really long time."

Maddie nodded, considering. "Was it worth it?"

Aunt Cassie didn't even pause before she answered. "Yes. Every minute of it. I figured nobody got hurt and I made a lot of people laugh—even Harriet—so it couldn't have been that bad." Her eyes narrowed. "Why do you ask?"

Maddie picked something off the counter and pretended to study it. "Just curious." She realized that she was holding a pair of really large granny panties and quickly dropped them. Putting her hands behind her back she said, "So you're going to the Kudzu Festival with Mr. Farrell."

Aunt Cassie frowned. "We're not going *together* together—we're just driving in the same vehicle. Not like a date."

Maddie laughed. "Yeah, I get it." She met her aunt's gaze, admiring her perfect eyebrows and how her makeup covered her freckles. She'd have to ask Aunt Cassie to show her how she did that before she left. She remembered what she'd heard Dr. Parker and Aunt Cassie talking about in the gazebo on the day of her granddaddy's funeral and she decided to go ahead and blurt out the question that had been bugging her ever since. "Are you glad you left Walton and never came back?"

The door chimed and they both looked up and greeted two young women who'd entered the store. Aunt Cassie looked back at Maddie and smiled, but her eyes seemed sad. "I'm not glad that I've never gotten to know you or your brother and sisters. And I'm not glad that I didn't have your mama and daddy in my life for so long. But I like where I am now; I'm proud of all that I've accomplished, and I don't think any of that would have happened if I'd stayed here."

Maddie nodded, studying her aunt's hands and the sparkling diamond on her left ring finger. "So are you happy?"

Her aunt looked at her for a long time, as if she didn't understand the question. Finally, she said, "I have a great life, a career that I love, and I'm going to get married soon. It's all good." She looked away quickly, then tapped her pen against the inventory book. "Well, then, if you'll wait on our customers, I need to get started with this."

"Sure," Maddie said as she moved away and began straightening the hanging racks of half and full slips, and wondered if her aunt knew that she hadn't really answered her question.

ED PULLED UP in his mobile bordello precisely at five thirty. He'd called at lunchtime to tell Cassie he wanted to get to the festival early to make sure he got first pickings at the food tables.

He blew the car horn outside, causing Aunt Lucinda to march out to the porch and insist he come to the front door. With grave apologies to Lucinda, he flicked his gaze over Cassie's slim black capri pants and emerald green linen crop top. He held the door open for her and she could feel him staring at the low vee in the back of her blouse.

"That sure is some outfit, Cassie. You get that in New York?"

"Actually, I did. And thank you."

He opened her car door, then settled himself behind the wheel. "You're always dressed so nice. Like one of them models from those fashion

259

magazines you see at Bitsy's House of Beauty. Maybe I need to go to New York, too, to learn how to dress."

He smiled at her, but she could tell he was waiting for her response, maybe even a reassurance. She recalled the tall kid in the back row of her sixth-grade picture, and her heart went out to that friendless boy who still seemed to lurk beneath the surface of Ed Farrell.

"You know, looking at those pictures is a great way to learn what's new and what works with what. I mean, I'd even be happy to go shopping with you sometime, if you'd like."

His eyes lit, and he seemed to struggle for the right words, his eyebrows jerking up and down. Finally he started the engine, his face now a mask of studied concentration. "Well, thanks. Maybe sometime. But clothes are pretty expensive. I mean, your outfit must have cost you a pretty penny. Bet your daddy sent you lots of money, huh?"

Cassie stared at his profile, wondering if he really expected an answer. He looked at her with raised eyebrows, showing her he did.

"Actually, no. He offered, but I didn't need it. I make a pretty decent living myself." Her hand reached up to touch the gold charm necklace around her throat.

He narrowed his eyes in a look that made it seem as if he didn't believe her, then turned his attention back to the road.

Cassie situated herself in the seat, the leather sticking to her bare arms, and changed the subject. "Guess who called me today? Jim Roust himself, from Roust Development. Wanted to talk to me about my house."

Ed's eyes widened. "And what did you tell him?"

"That you were handling the property for me and that we had no immediate plans for anything other than to keep it residential. He kept pressing for a meeting, but I was pretty firm. I remembered what you told me about them, and I'd really rather have somebody local take care of this deal for me. I told him that and he seemed pretty mad."

Ed nodded, redirecting an air-conditioning vent that was blowing on his hair. "Well, I certainly appreciate the business. I'm actually surprised it took Jim this long to call you. He or one of his people is usually out on your front porch before the For Sale sign is even in the ground. Did I tell you that your old neighbor is working for Roust now? That Richard Haney fellow—the one with the three teenage boys who are always up to something. After Haney sold his property he decided to stick around and see what other kind of damage he could do to Walton. Like selling his house to Roust and creating those three boys wasn't enough. Unbelievable." He scuffed the toe of his shoe in the dirt. " 'Course, I've got to take some of the blame. I sold him a house in Farrellsford after he sold this one."

Cassie shook her head. "I've known the Haneys all my life and practically grew up with Richard, even though he was a couple of years older than me. I can't believe he's working with Roust. Maybe with the boys heading toward college he needed the money."

Ed shrugged, his eyes focused on the road ahead. They crunched over gravel, stirring up clouds of red dust as Ed maneuvered the car into a spot in the field behind the high school stadium. The sun lay low on the horizon, spilling yellow onto the grass like a giant cracked egg.

Thick, dark clouds mottled the sky off in the distance, hinting at foul weather to come. Cassie lifted the hair off the back of her neck, already sticky from the thick layer of humid air that seemed to congeal on everything and everyone during the July days of a Walton summer.

A familiar truck pulled past them, kicking up a red dirt cloud. It drifted over their heads for a brief moment before collapsing and adhering to sweat-dampened skin.

Ed crossed his arms over his chest. "Well, well, well, if it ain't Walton's antiprogress police."

Sam stepped out of his truck, gave a brief nod in their direction, then opened the passenger door to help out Mary Jane. The red tank top skimmed over well-rounded breasts and was tucked into a pair of skinny black jeans. She hadn't looked like that in high school, Cassie recalled. They

262

approached Cassie and Ed, Sam and Mary Jane standing close together but not touching. The sky rumbled in the distance.

Sam smiled congenially. "Sure am glad to run into you. I was afraid we'd be the only people here over eighteen and under sixty."

Finding his expression contagious, Cassie smiled back. "There will be at least six of us—Harriet and Joe and their brood are already here. They didn't want to miss the parade. Even Maddie seemed pretty eager to see it. Probably wanted to see if Lucy fell off and broke her nose."

Sam looked at his watch. "The midpoint of the parade is the town square. My guess is they'll be there in the next twenty minutes or so. If we hurry, we'll see it."

Ignoring Sam, Ed pulled on Cassie's arm, leading her away in the opposite direction. "I'm gonna get me some of those fried dumplings first. We'll catch up."

Annoyed, Cassie pulled her arm back. "Come on, Ed. I don't want to miss the parade. I promise as soon as it's over, we'll get you something to eat." She sent him a smile he couldn't refuse, and he relented.

She wasn't sure why it was so important to her. It had been years since she'd been to a parade like this. The last time was the summer before her sophomore year in junior college, and she had gone to the Kudzu Festival with Joe. They'd held

263

hands, their palms slick with sweat, and shared a cotton candy. He'd won her an enormous stuffed pink elephant by biting an apple out of a barrel full of water. His shirt was soaked and plastered to his skin, defining the word "lust" to Cassie for the first time.

It had been just one of many shining moments of her girlhood, unmarred by all the things that had happened since. Their reminders decorated her bedroom in her father's house like a museum—the pennants, dried corsages, faded invitations. Even the pink elephant. Many times since her return, she had gone to her room with an empty garbage bag to clean it out, but hadn't yet succeeded in removing one frayed streamer. The old Cassie might be gone, but she wasn't ready to be swept up, boxed away, and forgotten.

The four of them raced across the open field, past the stadium, and through several backyards before coming up behind the town hall. Cassie's shirt now clung to her skin with sweat, and she dared not think about what state her hair was in. She looked at Mary Jane and saw that her old friend had fared no better.

They spotted Knoxie's bright red hair right away. She was perched on her father's shoulders, her head a veritable beacon in the fading sunlight.

Mary Jane waved to catch their attention and Harriet waved back. They pushed through the crowd as they made their way to Joe and Harriet, who had claimed a spot on the curb in front of the square—a perfect vantage point for the parade. Joey and Sarah Frances sat on the curb eating ice-cream cones, with most of it dripping down their chins and forearms. Baby Amanda slept peacefully in her stroller, her lips pursed in a perfect bow. Cassie looked over at Madison, expecting her to be wearing a glum expression, but was surprised to see the young girl fairly bouncing with excitement.

Knoxie wore the remnants of her ice-cream cone on the front of her dress and her face, along with something that looked like congealed ketchup and mustard. When she spotted Sam, she stretched toward him. "Hold me, Dr. Parker!"

Heedless of the artistic arrangement of food on the child, he held out his arms and the little girl fell into them.

His smile slowly dipped as he stared into Knoxie's face. "Are you feeling all right, peanut?"

She shook her head. "My tummy hurts a little bit."

The trill of a cell phone sounded behind them. Everybody in the vicinity turned to stare. Sam pulled his phone off his belt, then shook his head. "Not me."

Ed yanked his out of the pocket of his denim shirt as Cassie noticed the wide lapels for the first time. Either Ed was getting a jump start on a new fashion trend, or he'd hung on to that shirt for at least a couple of decades.

He put the phone to his ear. "Ed Farrell."

Cassie watched as his color deepened on his cheeks.

"Well, you just tell them that I had it surveyed and that's the damned property line. Show them the papers, for Pete's sake."

He stayed on the line for a few more moments, shaking his head and muttering expletives. Finally, he ended the call and shoved the phone back in his pocket.

"I gotta go. Those idiots by the old MacLaren farm are threatening my guys with shotguns, telling them it's private property. I'm goin' to get the sheriff and then we'll decide who's right."

He glared at Sam. "And if I find you're responsible for this, I'm hauling you to jail, too."

Sam didn't notice. He was too busy watching Knoxie. Mary Jane had moved to stand next to them and was smoothing the sticky strands of flaming hair off of Knoxie's face. A distinct green tinge covered the little girl's pale cheeks.

"I don't feel so good." Without warning, she leaned over Mary Jane and vomited up what food had escaped her face and clothes and actually made it down to her stomach. The glorious red silk tank top now closely resembled an elementary school art project.

Miraculously, no one else had sustained any damage. Sam set Knoxie on the ground as the rest of the adults stood in shocked silence and the younger children added the requisite potty-humor remarks. Only Harriet, her skills honed by years of motherhood, flew into action.

Delving deep into the diaper bag that hung suspended on Amanda's stroller, she pulled out a box of diaper wipes and a handful of cloth diapers. She handed several wipes to Sam for Knoxie's forehead, then set to work on Mary Jane's blouse.

Sam sent a wry grin to Cassie. "Guess it kinda runs in the family."

Cassie blinked, trying to understand what he meant, then remembered the humiliating scene on her father's porch the night of the fall formal. Patently ignoring him, she turned her attention to Mary Jane, who appeared near tears as Cassie moved closer to help.

"Don't worry. If you take it to the dry cleaner's tomorrow morning, I'm sure they'll be able to get it all out." The stench of throw-up mixed with scented diaper wipes made her throat constrict. She swallowed thickly and closed her eyes.

Harriet bit her lip. "And please send me the bill. I feel just awful."

"Don't worry about it. It couldn't be helped." Mary Jane shook her head. "I need to go home—I reek to high heaven."

Cassie turned to her friend. "But you just got here. Why don't you at least stay and see the parade and then see how you feel."

"No. I'm . . . I'm not in the mood anymore. I want to go home."

Sam looked up from a quickly recovered Knoxie, who was asking for more ice cream.

"I'll take you home, if that's what you want. Harriet—I'll take you and Knoxie home, too, but I think she's back to form now. Just needed to empty her stomach. Maybe not so much cotton candy next time."

Harriet cast a glance at her husband. "Yeah—I knew better than to let her eat all that stuff but her father had other ideas. I'll let her stay if she promises not to eat anything else."

Knoxie frowned at her mother, but Harriet turned her attention back to Sam. "But it's silly for you to leave. It looks like Ed has to go, too, so why don't we have him drive Mary Jane back?"

Ed shifted impatiently, then eyed Mary Jane closely, his eyes focused on her shirt. "Sure, I'll do it. Just hope you don't mind if I drive real fast—I got business to attend to." He cleared his throat. "And by the time I'm done, I'll swing by your place to bring you back. That will give you plenty of time to get all prettied up again." He cast a quick glance at Cassie. "That all right with you, sugar?"

Cassie nodded, anxiously eyeing Mary Jane, who looked like she might burst into tears.

Sam stepped forward. "Really, Mary Jane. Let me bring you home."

Mary Jane shook her head. "You just got here. It would be silly for you to miss the parade and everything." She forced a smile. "I'll just go home and get cleaned up and then Ed can bring me right back." Straightening her shoulders, she moved toward Ed. With a stoic expression she said, "I'll see you all later. Come on, Ed, let's go," then followed Ed into the crowd. Cassie felt a nudging in her ribs, and turned to see Harriet winking at her.

"What . . . ?" Cassie's eyes widened as she realized what Harriet was trying to tell her.

She started to give her sister a piece of her mind when a large roar went up from the crowd lining the main square. The tinny sounds of a marching band could be heard coming down the street. Everyone sitting on the curbs now stood and stepped back onto the grass, pressing the crowd backward. Cassie found herself wedged against Sam Parker but couldn't extricate herself.

A convertible came first, carrying the retired state senator and his wife, perched incongruously on the rear of the backseat and waving stiffly. Cassie recognized Senator Billy Thompkins. He lived in an old Victorian on the edge of town and raised chickens in his yard. She remembered being chased by the man as a child when she'd been caught trying to mix dish soap into their feed. She'd wanted to see them cackle up bubbles. Senator Thompkins hadn't been amused. She

269

laughed at the memory and found herself waving back.

Young girls in leotards of red and white stripes, the high school colors, marched by, their skinny legs off step but their silver batons flashing in unison as they tossed and twirled them over their heads and across their bodies. One baton fell and rolled to the curb nearby. The girl rushed over to retrieve it and caught Maddie's eye. With a wink and a smile, she ran back to her position.

Next came the marching bands, the members sweating under their tall hats and pom-poms, their capes rising limply in the humid air. The perennial disco favorite "Celebration" bounced around the crowd, encouraging not a few people to start singing.

Finally, the float carrying the kudzu queen ambled by, pulled by an old bright red pickup, the driver looking to be of the same vintage as the truck. Lucy Spafford, wearing a sparkling crown, stood on a tall platform, waving proudly, her chiffon-and-feather dress floating dreamily around her. Cassie smiled to herself, thinking how much she resembled cotton candy. Kudzu vines and bunches of plastic flowers and balloons clustered around Lucy like clouds, and her celestial expression added to the effect. Out of sight of the float's occupants, cream-colored balloons edged the rear of the float, jiggling up and down with every bump in the road. They seemed stiff and oddly shaped, making Cassie do a double take. She nearly choked when she realized what they were.

She turned to Harriet, who was squinting at the back of the float, where a whole line of the peculiar balloons were strung together like a tail. "What on earth . . . ?"

Cassie caught Sam's gaze over Harriet's head. Together, they turned to focus on Madison, who was now doubled over in an apparent coughing fit.

Harriet gave firm pats to the middle of Madison's back. "You okay, honey? What's the matter?"

Cassie leaned down to her niece and spoke quietly. "Do I take it that you were in charge of the decorations on the float?"

Madison managed only a nod.

Sam's hand gripped Madison's shoulder. "Come on, Maddie—let's go get you some water." He steered her away from her mother just as Harriet's eyes widened in comprehension.

"Were those"—she lowered her voice to a mere whisper—"condoms?"

Cassie quickly turned and began to walk away. "I'm going to go check on Maddie to make sure she's okay. I'll be back." She followed Sam and her niece into the crowd, trying her best to keep a straight face.

She found them standing by the drink stand, Sam holding a cup of water out for Madison. Her face was deep red, tears rolling down her cheeks.

Cassie fought the urge to congratulate her niece on a prank well-done. Sam's stern expression stopped her from giving Maddie a high five.

Sam's expression didn't change as he spoke to the young girl. "When Lucy sees those, uh, balloons, she's going to be mighty embarrassed. And I don't think she'll need to look far to figure out who's behind it."

Madison looked up at Sam, her face now a fading pink, and took a deep swallow of water. "No, sir."

"How do you think your mother's going to like getting that call from Lucy's mother?"

For the first time, Maddie looked chagrined. "I only meant to embarrass Lucy—she deserved it. But my mom doesn't need to get involved."

Sam straightened. "I think it's a little late for that."

They all turned to see Joe and Harriet marching toward them, pushing the stroller like a weapon, their faces grim. Joey and Sarah Frances ran behind them as Knoxie clung tight to her daddy's shoulders. They all came to a stop in front of Madison. Sam and Cassie took their cue to leave, but not before Cassie gave her niece a reassuring squeeze on her shoulder. Sam grabbed Cassie's hand and led her into the thick of the crowd.

"Where are we going?"

He didn't answer, but kept his hand firmly gripping Cassie's.

She asked again, "Where are we going?"

When he didn't answer, she dug in her heels. As he faced her, she realized that he was laughing— hard. His eyes sparkled with merriment. When he caught his breath, he gasped out, "That was about damned near the funniest thing I've ever seen. Almost as funny as that pig you got for Harriet's float when she was kudzu queen."

Cassie's lips twitched in an effort not to smile. "You mean you're not really mad at Maddie? I think you had her about ready to cry."

He swiped his hand over his face as if trying to sober himself up, but didn't completely wipe off his grin. "Well, I had to at least pretend to be a grown-up with no sense of humor. I've got a reputation to keep in this town."

At that, Cassie finally lost the last of her control, and she burst out laughing, not able to stop. She clutched Sam's arms for support, and looked up into his face. Breathless, she asked, "What are you staring at?"

His smile softened, but his eyes never dimmed. "You. Your laugh. I've always loved the sound of it."

The smile dipped on her face as she watched something flicker in Sam's eyes. Lou-Lou Whittaker walked by, her bleached hair teased out into perfect roundness, a bright red headband bisecting it and making it look like a beach ball. Her arm was tucked into the crook of the arm of a tall cowboy Cassie didn't recognize, but she practically purred as she passed Cassie and gave her a knowing look.

Cassie swallowed her laughter when she realized there were about another dozen sets of eyes staring at her and Sam and probably coming to the same conclusion Lou-Lou had. She dropped her hand from Sam's arm.

"I need a drink." She headed for a concession stand.

Sam moved in front of her. "Allow me. What would you like?"

She smacked her lips. "I want some of that kudzu punch. I was never allowed to have it when I was a kid, so I think it's about time."

"One kudzu and one water, please."

While waiting for their drinks, Sam turned around and leaned both elbows on the counter. "I'd join you, but I'm on call tonight. You do realize that there's mostly grain alcohol in the punch, right?"

Cassie looked at him with a practiced smirk on her face. "I can handle alcohol. We have that in New York." She took the Styrofoam cup and stared inside at the bright green liquid. "Perhaps not exactly any in this particular hue, but we do have alcohol." She took a small sip and smiled. "It tastes like lemonade. I doubt there's very much alcohol in it." With that, she took a large gulp, ignoring Sam's protests. She slapped her empty cup on the counter. "May I have another one, please?"

Raising an eyebrow, Sam leaned against the counter while another cup was slid over to Cassie. "Guess you hadn't heard the rumors about this punch, then."

Cassie took a big gulp. "What rumors?"

He winked. "That it's what they call an aphrodisiac. More babies are born in Walton nine months after the Kudzu Festival than at any other time. I know never to schedule vacations or conferences in the month of April."

Cassie plopped her half-filled cup up on the counter. "April? Oh, Lord—I was born in April."

Sam straightened and winked. "So was I."

"Ew. I'd rather not think about that." She shook her head, wondering why things appeared to be swimming in front of her. The rumbling and shouts from the roller coaster caught her attention. "Let's go on that."

Sam held her back. "You might want to rethink that. Aren't you feeling a bit woozy right now?"

"I'm perfectly fine." She stumbled over a piece of trash on the ground. "I want to go on the roller coaster. It's just a kiddie ride, anyway."

He studied her for a moment. "All right. I know better than to get in the way of a determined woman. Come on—we should go now, before it starts to rain." He grabbed her hand and led her across the field to the roller coaster.

The first tremors of nausea didn't hit her until they had clack-clacked up the rickety track to the first plunge. By the time they had reached the second plunge, Cassie had her face buried in the side of Sam's shoulder. At the third one, she was holding her hand over her mouth and begging to get off.

When the ride was over, Sam had to help her out of the car and almost carry her away from the roller coaster and to the open field behind the festival buildings. Without warning, she stopped abruptly and knelt on the grass. Unable to stop herself, she bent over and threw up.

With gentle hands, Sam pulled her hair away from her face and placed his fingers on the back of her neck. When she had finished, she sat back but kept her face down.

Sam rubbed her neck. "Just like old times, huh?"

She threw out a halfhearted punch that barely brushed his shoulder.

He dug into his back pocket and handed her a handkerchief.

Cassie took it and wiped her face. "Thanks. I'm starting quite a collection of these."

Sam said nothing but continued to rub her neck and her back.

Cassie sighed. "You know, if you weren't such a burr under my saddle, I'd say you were a pretty nice guy, Sam Parker."

"Thanks. I think."

A few sprinkles began to fall on them from the darkening sky, the moon all but obliterated by the hulking clouds.

Sam sat back on his heels. "Guess we're not going to make it to the watermelon-seed spitting contest."

Cassie looked at him sharply. "I don't spit, and I have no intention of being seen anywhere near it." She clutched her head, her skin slick and clammy under her fingers.

"Hmmmm. I seem to recall you winning it one year in high school—our senior year, right? You should have that trophy somewhere in your room."

She did. The faux-brass trophy, an enlarged replica of a watermelon seed, was indeed still displayed proudly on her dresser. Whenever she got around to cleaning out her room that would be the first thing in the garbage. For a brief moment, she pictured bringing it back to her apartment in New York and placing it on the black lacquer of their bedroom dresser and explaining its significance to Andrew. The thought made her laugh out loud.

Sam quirked an eyebrow. "What's so funny?"

She studied him for a moment before answering. Damn, he was good-looking—better-looking than such an annoying man had any right to be. He was comfortable in his skin, in the way he moved and talked. And in the way he dressed. Not like the carefully orchestrated persona Andrew constantly worked at portraying. Sam was cotton flannel to Andrew's linen, and she couldn't help but think that flannel was a heck of a lot nicer to cuddle up to.

Cassie shook her head. She needed to get away from this man. Now. "I need to brush my teeth. Where're the bathrooms?"

Sam threw his head back and laughed. "Let me guess. You carry a toothbrush and toothpaste in your purse at all times—just in case you get caught at a client dinner with spinach between your teeth."

Her mouth fell open. Those had been Andrew's exact words to her when he'd given her the little dental hygiene travel set. "Just show me where the bathrooms are."

Sam stood in one fluid motion and helped her up. The ground tilted a bit, then leveled out.

"I'll take you up to the high school. I know the night security guard and he'll let you in."

As they crossed the field, the sky opened up and dumped water on them, drenching them to the skin. She turned her face to the sky, welcoming the cool rain on her face. By the time they reached the high school, their clothes were plastered to their bodies. Sam waited outside the building while she tried to make herself presentable.

She scrubbed her teeth with the toothbrush and paste, gargling twice, then splashed her face with water from the tap. After looking in the mirror, she realized she resembled a drowned rat, and improving on the situation would be hopeless. She was more than ready to go home, but had no idea how to find Joe and Harriet in the crowd. And she hadn't seen Ed since he'd left with Mary Jane.

She found Sam outside leaning against the brick building in the shelter of an overhang and chewing on a long strand of grass. She hated asking him for anything, but her options were limited. "Would you mind taking me home? You could still come back for a chance to win the cutest-couple contest with Mary Jane, assuming the rain lets up."

He studied her for a moment, as if weighing her request, then simply nodded his head and pushed off from the building. "Let's go." The rain had slowed to a light drizzle as they found their way through the sodden grass and to the muddy parking area.

His truck still smelled like Mary Jane's perfume. Despite the rain, Cassie cracked open her window, then leaned against the seat back. She closed her eyes and promptly fell asleep for the duration of the short ride home.

Cassie awoke to the feel of Sam touching her cheek. She opened her eyes as he helped her slide her soggy bottom off the seat. He closed the door, but Cassie didn't move forward. She remained where she was, groggy and light-headed, but feeling that all was right in her world. The wet grass tickled the exposed part of her foot in the

279

high-heeled sandals, but still she remained rooted to the spot.

Flashes of light echoed in the sky as the trees dropped their watery burden onto the already soaked ground. All around them in the hushed night the water dripped, a heady background beat to the resumed chorus of the crickets. Steam rose off the gravel drive, floating like apparitions in the glare of the porch light.

Cassie stared at the way Sam's rain-soaked hair fell over his face. She lifted her hand and pushed it back, her fingers reluctant to leave the smooth skin of his forehead. The backs of her fingers swept over the bristles on his cheek, then slid along his jawbone.

His hand wrapped around her wrist and pulled it away.

Embarrassed, she said, "I'm sorry." Her words tumbled and tossed against each other, making her feel like an awkward teenager. "I'm . . . I'm sorry for getting sick. I should have known better about that kudzu punch. I mean, it's not like I've never been to a fraternity party." She attempted a smile.

He stood so close she could feel his breath on her cheek. She almost expected to see the steam rise from his shirt. She should step back.

"We all make mistakes." There was no smile in his voice, and his jaw seemed to tighten with tension.

She should go inside now. "Some mistakes are more permanent than others."

His eyes brightened in the dim light. "Nothing's permanent, Cassie. Things change."

The sky exploded with light, illuminating Sam, the house, the truck, this place. It made things so clear for a moment, like she was staring at a photograph. His head bent closer to hers, and she closed her eyes, swaying in his direction. A rippling wave of thunder rent the sky, but he made no move to kiss her. She forced her eyes open, and found herself staring into probing blue eyes. She placed both hands behind his neck and pulled him forward, closing the gap between them.

His lips were warm, soft, responsive, making her knees soften like butter in a frying pan. His hand fell to her waist while the fingers of his other hand crept through her hair at the base of her skull, cradling her head. The move was so unexpected, so different, she almost pulled back. It made her feel . . . cherished.

Rain pelted down now with renewed force. Cassie opened her mouth, tasting warm rain and skin. She sucked on his lower lip until he took control and opened his mouth, touching her tongue with his.

Light flashed under her eyelids, but it wasn't the lightning. Burned ions from the electrified air popped and fizzled between them, creating a storm of their own. He moved her against the truck and she welcomed the solid feel of him against her.

The rain beat steadily on them, dripping down her neck and into her blouse, thudding gently on the hood of the truck. Her hands clutched the back of his shirt, and she pulled on it, releasing the shirttails.

He pulled back, and she found herself gasping for air. He didn't say anything, but stood staring at her, rivulets of water running down his face.

Cassie blinked the rain out of her eyes. His chest rose and fell as his gaze dropped to the ground. The rain plopped and splashed on the wet gravel between them.

He shook his head before looking back at her. "Do you want me to come inside?"

She swallowed thickly, wondering why her New York cool had suddenly deserted her. In a small voice she said, "Sure."

Sam reached behind him and began tucking in his shirt. "No."

She stared at him, growing humiliation quickly extinguishing the fire in her blood. "No?" She swallowed again. "You practically toss me over the hood of your truck to ravage me, and then you just stop cold?"

She knew she was being unreasonable, but humiliation was never a feeling she could live with.

Sam merely raised an eyebrow, then turned to

rest his hands against the truck, trapping Cassie neatly between them. "Believe me. It's not because I don't want to."

Cassie ducked under his arms to escape him, her feet squelching in the mud as she made her way to the porch steps.

"I want more from you than a one-night stand, Cassie. It's all or nothing with me."

She pulled open the door. "Better get used to that 'nothing' part then, Sam Parker." Stepping inside, she was about to shut the door when she heard him laughing.

" 'Ravage,' huh? I don't think I've ever heard anybody use that word in a sentence before. That's too funny. You haven't changed a bit."

She slammed the door and leaned against it, a small smile forcing itself onto her face. She wanted to be mad at him and she had every right to feel humiliated. But somehow, she didn't. He'd acted like . . . well, like a gentleman. So different from most of the men she knew. So different from Andrew.

Andrew. The keys fell from her hand, falling with a thunk on the wood floor. She'd barely even thought about her fiancé since their disagreeable phone call that morning. Out of sight, out of mind, indeed. She wore the man's ring on her finger, yet she'd been pawing at the body of the first available candidate. She was humiliated, all right, alcohol or not. And it was all her doing.

Slipping out of her shoes, she ran up the stairs as fast as she could to call Andrew. He needed to come down to Walton for a visit. As soon as possible.

CHAPTER 13

Cassie stared at the ceiling in her bedroom, the flashes of lightning creating odd shadows on the plaster. She turned on her side and listened to the steady fall of rain, a sound she usually found sleep-inducing. But not tonight.

Finally, she dragged herself out of bed, threw on her robe, and went downstairs hoping a midnight snack might help her sleep. She was surprised to see a light under Aunt Lucinda's bedroom door. Without hesitating, she knocked.

"Come in."

Aunt Lucinda sat propped in a chaise longue in the corner of the room, her feet resting on a pink chiffon pillow. Each toe shone with crimson brilliance, the smell of fresh nail polish hovering about the bedroom. A fluffy cotton ball was wadded between each digit like punctuation marks. Bristly pink curlers covered her head, and Cassie would have laughed if it weren't for the tears glistening on Lucinda's cheek.

Cassie stood in the threshold. "What's wrong, Aunt Lu? Do you want me to leave?"

Lucinda shook her head. "Oh, no, honey. I just

finished up one of Miss Lena's books. Those happy endings always make me cry." She moved her feet and patted the chaise. "Come sit, sweetie, and tell me what's wrong."

Cassie did as she was told. "Nothing's wrong. I just couldn't sleep."

Lucinda bent over and started removing the cotton balls. "Who were you talking to on the phone?"

"Sorry—didn't know I was talking so loud. That was Andrew. I had to convince him that he needed to come down here."

Her aunt clapped her hands together. "Why, that's wonderful. I'll tell Harriet and we can get those bridal shower invitations out. We'll make it one of those couples showers—maybe an outdoor barbecue. Let him meet the whole town."

"Like a sort of 'Donald Trump Meets the Clampetts.' Yeah—sounds like fun." She had meant it to be a flippant comment but realized too late how it must have sounded to her aunt.

Lucinda used one of those looks Cassie remembered from childhood, the look that was reserved for times when she was due a spanking but managed to elude her aunt's grasp.

"There's no need to be scared, Cassie. We'll behave ourselves."

Cassie's eyes widened. "Scared? Why would I be scared?"

"Well, you're acting mean, and that's always

meant just one thing. But, sugar, if this is the man you're going to marry, you've got to let him meet us sometime. You can't go hidin' us forever."

"I wasn't trying to hide you." Cassie looked down to her lap, wondering whom she was trying to hide from whom. She stood. "He says he'll be here this coming Friday. He doesn't know what flight he'll be on, so he'll call from the airport to let us know when to pick him up. That's probably not enough time for Harriet to organize a shower."

Lucinda adjusted one of the curlers that had drooped precariously over her forehead. "Nonsense. She's got it half planned already. Even has the invitations addressed. Just didn't know the date or time. I guess we do now!"

Cassie leaned against the dressing table, her arms folded over her chest. "Wonderful."

Lucinda sent Cassie that look again but didn't say anything. She took out an emery board and began filing her fingernails. "I think we should both help her out. Harriet just hasn't been herself lately. She's so tired all the time. And did you notice how pale she looks?"

"I just figured that's what a mother of five should look like. She's probably exhausted. Sure, I'll help. Maybe I can work on damage control— you know, warn everybody on the invitations about making 'damn Yankee' remarks."

"Cassie, really, what are you so afraid of? That he'll be so appalled by all of us that he won't want to marry you? Because if that's the type of person he is, maybe you shouldn't be marrying him anyway."

Cassie sent her aunt a sharp look, but Lucinda was studiously filing her thumbnail. "It's not that. It's just that Andrew is so . . . different from everybody here. I'm afraid he'll feel out of place."

Lucinda smiled. "Honey, we all have something in common—we love you. And if he loves you like we do, then he'll fit right in."

Cassie pushed away from the dresser. "Yeah, well. I guess I should turn in—you've always told me to make sure I got my beauty sleep." She paused for a minute. "Aunt Lu?"

The older woman looked up, her thin eyebrows raised expectantly. "Yes, sweet pea?"

"Do you remember any of Daddy's old girlfriends—girls he met before Mama?"

Lucinda thought for a moment, then shook her head. "I really don't. But remember, I was living in Mobile back then, so I really wouldn't know." She smiled softly. "The first woman I ever remember him mentioning in a letter was your mama, though. That's when I knew he was really in love." She bent back to her filing. "Why are you asking?"

Cassie pursed her lips thoughtfully for a moment before deciding that trespassing into her father's life had gone far enough without sharing the letters with his sister. "No reason. Just curious, I guess."

Lucinda sniffed, the file stilling against her thumbnail. "I miss him so much. I wasn't . . . ready . . . for him to go yet. It's hard losing a sibling—it's like losing a part of my past."

Blinking back her own tears, Cassie gave her aunt a hug. "I know. I miss him, too." Kissing her on the cheek, she said softly, "Good night, Aunt Lu."

The older woman didn't look up. "Good night, honey." When Cassie reached the door, Lucinda sniffed loudly, then said, "Was that Sam Parker's truck bringin' you home tonight?"

Cassie's face colored, and she wondered how much her aunt had seen. She tried to sound nonchalant. "Um, yes. It was. We couldn't find Ed to bring me home. . . ."

"He's a nice boy. And so good-lookin'."

Cassie kept her face blank. "You mean Ed?"

Aunt Lu lowered her head, raising her eyebrows and piercing Cassie with a look that said she wasn't fooled. "No. That's not who I meant. I was talkin' about that delectable Dr. Parker."

Cassie sent her a sidelong glance, but Lucinda had returned to her nails. "Really? I hadn't noticed."

"Uh-huh. Sugar, would you mind bringing over my Brunswick stew to Miss Lena tomorrow? It's my turn to bring her supper and visit for a spell, but Harriet's so tired, I thought I might just spend the day with her and help her out with the kids and the party plannin'." She handed her the book she had just put down. "Would you please bring this back to Miss Lena, too? Be careful, though. She might want to discuss it with you. And you, being a single lady, wouldn't have any idea about some of the stuff that goes on in these books."

Cassie colored again, realizing she had probably blushed more in the last day than she had in fifteen years. "Sure, I'll do it first thing." She took the book, said good night again, and left the room.

THE STORM CONTINUED through the night and into the next morning. Cassie stood on her front porch, balancing the stew pot with one arm while she wrestled the umbrella with her other hand. A car door shut and she glanced up to see Sam's dog, George, bounding toward her. Sam caught the pot just in time as Cassie moved the umbrella between her and the large animal.

"Afraid he's going to ravage you?"

Cassie heard the smile in his voice, but she refused to smile back. "Could you call off your dog, please?"

The animal lay down on top of Cassie's feet, exposing his underbelly.

"He likes you. He wants you to scratch him."

Cassie was about to step over the large dog, but something soft and sweet in the dog's expression made her pause. It reminded her of her father's faithful companion, Hunter. Her earliest memories included the mixed-breed bloodhound: memories of her pulling on his tail, and putting Harriet on his back to ride like a horse. Hunter had died after she left home, and, looking at George's face, she suddenly missed him terribly.

She bent down and rubbed the sable hair on George's belly, the fur soft and damp from the rain. The dog went limp in an attitude of supreme satisfaction.

"Why are you darkening my doorstep, Dr. Parker? Anybody sick that I should know about?"

"Lucinda called me last night and asked me to drive you to Miss Lena's, seeing as how I needed to visit her today anyway."

Cassie raised her eyebrow, wondering what Lucinda had really been thinking, especially to call the doctor so late at night. She wished for Lucinda's pink car. Anything would have been preferable to being in close proximity to Sam Parker. But Lucinda and her car had already left for Harriet's. It was either Sam and his truck or a walk in the pelting rain with a stew pot and an umbrella balanced precariously in her arms.

"I'm only going to say yes because I don't want to dump Brunswick stew all over Madison Lane. And because I need to get out of the house. Ed's bringing a couple by today to look at it, and I'd rather not be here."

"Let's go, then." As George raced to the back of the truck and leaped in, Sam took the umbrella

290

from Cassie and held it over their heads. Sending her a warm look, he said, "Unless you're afraid that I'm going to try to ravage you again."

She wished she had her hands free to throttle him. "Look. About last night . . ." She paused, hoping Sam would wave a dismissive hand in the air and relieve her of the need to continue. Instead, he looked at her expectantly.

She found she couldn't look directly into his eyes. "I must have had too much of that kudzu punch. I wasn't in my right mind, and I apologize for acting like that."

"Like what?" Sam opened her door and took the stew pot from her while she settled herself inside.

Cassie studied the dash in front of her. "Like a sex-starved maniac. I'm not like that at all."

Sam leaned in close enough that she could feel his breath on her cheek. "I never thought you were. Besides, I'm not complaining." The door closed with a solid thunk.

When Sam drove his truck to the end of the drive in front of the property, Cassie noticed that the For Sale sign in front of the house was lying prone on the ground, conspicuous tire tracks marring the red-and-white logo of Farrell Realty.

"Stop!" she yelled.

She shoved the stew pot into Sam's lap and clambered out of the truck and into the teeming rain. She ignored the squelching sound of the clinging mud that sucked at her shoes as she stomped over to the sign and righted it.

After hoisting herself into the truck again, she glared at Sam as she took back the pot. "That was pretty juvenile. How about next time you just hang a bucket of water over the front door?"

Sam put the truck into gear. "Or maybe I'll just attach inflated condoms to the sign."

Cassie coughed to stifle her laughter, then turned her head toward the window so he couldn't see any sign of amusement in her face.

Leaning an elbow on the doorjamb, Sam glanced over at Cassie. "Have you made any headway yet on finding your father's girlfriend?"

"No. But I put a classified ad in the *Sentinel*'s Sunday edition. It's pretty discreet, not mentioning any names or anything—just asking anybody who had a stillborn baby in 1973 to call Harriet's cell phone number. Thought the New York area code or the home number would be a dead giveaway alerting people that it's probably me looking. I didn't want to scare her off." She sighed, slapping her hands on her thighs. "Well, it's a start anyway. I'd like to think I can do this on my own. I mean, if whoever it is has kept her secret this long, then she doesn't want to be found. I might just have to leave it at that."

Sam glanced at her for a hard moment. "You mean you'd walk away with that secret because you respected her privacy? Or because it would be one more thing to tie you down in the quicksand?"

She stuck her chin out, but didn't respond. Instead, she rode the rest of the way watching the town of Walton flash by outside the car window, aimlessly fingering the gold charms around her neck.

Despite the weather, Miss Lena sat on her front porch, stockings rolled down around her swollen ankles, the ever-present romance novel clutched in her hands. She waved wildly, her smile showing perfect white dentures.

Her smile softened as Cassie walked up the porch steps. "Catherine Anne," she said, reaching for Cassie's hand. Cassie put the pot down on the floor and placed her hand inside the old woman's.

Sam's voice was gentle. "No, Miss Lena, this is Cassandra. Catherine Anne's oldest."

The woman gripped Cassie's hand tighter. "She was such a pretty young thing—no one knew why she wanted to marry the judge. She could have had any of the young men in the county, but instead she chose a man old enough to be her father." She studied Cassie's face closely.

"Nobody would have ever thought he'd outlive her." She stroked Cassie's cheek with her other hand. "You're the spittin' image of her, too." She glanced up at Sam. "Is she just as sweet?"

"Sweet as vinegar." He reached for Miss Lena's elbow. "Come on, let me help you inside." The old lady giggled as Sam gently pulled her from the chair.

Cassie was left to bring in the pot, and she resisted the impulse to dump the contents on Sam's sandy brown head. She walked inside the small but immaculate house, making her way to the kitchen in back. The wood floors gleamed with polish and the stainless sink shone. As Cassie opened the refrigerator door to deposit the stew, she noticed a large color-coded chart on the door. Curious, she looked at it closely.

Days of the week and familiar names filled out the chart's headers. On closer inspection, she realized it was a food and cleaning schedule. Apparently, most of the women in the town contributed to Miss Lena's daily upkeep. Every day somebody was scheduled to come by and clean and keep her company, while somebody else brought breakfast, lunch, and dinner.

As Cassie made room for the stew pot in the tidy and clean refrigerator, she thought briefly of the old homeless woman who appeared frequently on the corner of the street in New York where Cassie worked. She was dirty, her hair unkempt, her clothes tattered. The crowd on the sidewalk swayed in unison, like a great big roiling wave, to avoid her. It was doubtful anybody had ever brought her a covered casserole.

She shut the refrigerator door with a thoughtful thud and returned to the living room, where Miss Lena sat comfortably in a worn recliner as Sam took her blood pressure. The older woman smiled.

"Come over here so I can see you better. I don't think I've seen you in a very long time. Where have you been, child?"

Cassie sat on a stuffed vinyl ottoman next to the chair. "I live in New York now."

A frown shadowed Miss Lena's face. "I'm so sorry. Will they let you come home soon?"

Cassie bit her lip as she looked up at the older woman. "I like it there, actually. I'll be going back before too long." She reached up and placed Lena's soft and gnarled hand in her own. A confused frown covered Lena's face for a moment; then she smiled. "Do you read? I've just finished the best book and I'd love for you to borrow it."

Sam took the blood pressure cuff off her arm and she leaned to a nearby table. "Here—take it, and when you're done, we'll discuss it."

She handed Cassie the same book that Lucinda had given her to return. The same book that was still in her purse waiting to be given back to Miss Lena.

Cassie stared at the cover, a picture of half-naked people. "Thank you, Miss Lena. I'll look forward to it."

As Cassie opened her purse to put it next to the other book, Miss Lena sat up and leaned forward so Sam could place his stethoscope on her back.

"I know you'll love it, too. It has the best love scenes. His swollen manhood is supposed to be just absolutely enormous, and he's quite adept at pleasuring his women." She chortled gleefully. "My favorite scene is when they're riding bareback—naked. Oh, my—it just about gives me heart palpitations every time I read it."

Cassie swallowed, then smiled, nodding agreeably. "I see. Why, aren't they lucky!"

She could see Sam valiantly trying not to laugh as he spoke to his patient. "Miss Lena, I need you to lean back now and unbutton the top button of your dress so I can hear your heartbeat."

Miss Lena's eyes clouded and she looked up at Sam as if she'd never seen him before. "Young man—I hope you're not taking liberties with me. I might have to tell your mama."

Sam calmly took a step back. "No, ma'am, I wouldn't think of it. I just need to put this on your chest to hear your heartbeat—like I do every week. It will just take a second."

The older woman pressed her lips tightly together. "No, sir. I'm an unmarried woman."

Cassie looked at Sam. His expression remained calm, his arms relaxed against his sides. He seemed to be weighing different tactics to get Miss Lena to cooperate. The patient sat indignantly in her chair, bright spots of color suffusing her cheeks. Her eyes remained cloudy, momentarily confused at what was happening around her.

Cassie leaned forward and placed the woman's hands in her own. "Miss Lena—I'm here. How about if I stay next to you and hold your hands while Dr. Parker listens to your heart? I'll make sure that he treats you with the utmost respect."

Miss Lena blinked, as if trying to focus. "Doctor?"

Cassie nodded. "Yes, this is Dr. Parker, and he needs to listen to your heartbeat. Will you let him?"

The older woman gripped Cassie's hands tightly, then nodded her head.

Gently, Sam undid her top button, then slid his stethoscope to her chest. The room was in complete silence, the only sound that of the clock ticking away life's moments on the mantel. As Sam put the stethoscope back into his black bag, Cassie buttoned up the collar. When she moved her hand away, Miss Lena held it. "Thank you, dear." Her gray eyes were suddenly clear and moist with unshed tears. The look of gratitude in them made Cassie's heart feel as if it had swelled just a bit.

She leaned forward and kissed the older woman's cheek, surprised at the softness of it. "You're very welcome," she said, and meant it.

When they were ready to leave, Sam leaned over Miss Lena with a smile. "You're still healthy as an ox. We'll see you next week, all right?" He, too, planted a kiss on her cheek.

She beamed up at him, her early reticence apparently forgotten. "I'll look forward to it." She pushed herself up to whisper in a conspiratorial tone, "And don't forget to bring Catherine Anne's daughter. Although I'm sure I won't need to ask you twice." She elbowed Sam in the ribs, making him grunt.

"I'll try, ma'am. But that woman is like a pig in grease to pin down."

They winked at each other, looking like conspirators in a great plot, making Cassie want to laugh out loud.

The clouds had scattered along with the rain, leaving no obstacles to the sun's direct rays. George barked in greeting from the truck as Sam and Cassie walked down the porch steps toward him. "If I'm not mistaken, Sam Parker, you just called me a greased pig."

"Not exactly . . ."

Cassie stopped, holding up her hand. "That's all right. I'll forgive you because you were so sweet to Miss Lena. And I guess I don't need to ask if you ever bill her."

Sam opened the truck door and threw his bag on the backseat. "It's one of the perks of being old— you get a lot of things for free. Which reminds me, I gotta ask Ed if he can trade mowing days with me at the end of the month. I hate even talking to the man, but we're the only two on the schedule and I've got to switch. I'm going down to Atlanta for that conference. And if you still want me to, I could check through the hospital birth records while I'm there."

Cassie looked up into those infernal blue eyes, trying to read them. "Why are you being so nice to me? It's not like I've gone out of my way to ever be nice to you."

Sam studied her for a moment, his eyes unreadable. "Because . . ." He looked away for a moment. "Because you used to make me laugh. After Tom died, I didn't find much to laugh about, and you put that giant cockroach in Susan Benedict's lunch box because she'd said something mean about Harriet. I laughed till I almost wet my pants. I was hooked after that—you changed my life. You showed me that there's nothing in life that can't be laughed about, and what real loyalty was. Remember how Harriet used to stand up for Ed? She learned it from you, you know." His eyes turned somber. "I guess you could say I'm still a fan."

He was standing so close, reminding her of the night before. She stepped back, her hand flying to the necklace around her neck.

"And I appreciate what you did for me in there with Miss Lena. You were a big help."

Cassie shrugged and scrambled into the truck. "Glad I could help," she said, staring out the windshield as Sam shut the door.

After Sam climbed in, Cassie turned to him. "Do you have any plans right now?"

Something flickered in his eyes, but his expression remained neutral. "I don't have office hours until one o'clock, and I have my cell in case anybody needs me sooner. Why?"

"Could you drive to Harriet's? She's been complaining of being fatigued and out of sorts lately, and she is looking a little peaked. I asked her if she'd been to see you, but she said she hadn't seen you for an appointment since her postpartum checkup after Amanda was born. I thought that since she wouldn't go to you, I could bring you to her. Maybe you can prescribe her some vitamins or something."

Sam cranked the engine, but didn't answer right away. He looked oddly distracted.

"Sam?"

"Um, yeah. Sure." With a slight grin, he said, "Still taking care of your little sister, huh?"

Cassie stuck out her chin. "Old habits die hard, I guess."

He pulled out onto the street. "Careful, Cassie. People might start thinking that you care."

Cassie didn't answer and remained silent for the short ride to her sister's.

HARRIET SAT UP IN BED, hearing screaming and laughter coming from the backyard. She looked at the bedside clock and blinked, wondering if she really could have slept that long. Sitting up, she slid off the side of the bed and moved to the window, sliding it up so she could see better.

Sam, his dog, and Cassie were just entering the

backyard from the driveway. Aunt Lucinda stood in her red heels leaning over the patio table and cranking the old-fashioned ice-cream machine. Maddie stood next to her trying to hold the table steady so it wouldn't rock in response to Lucinda's exertions.

Sarah Frances, Joey, and Knoxie were running around with what looked like the majority of the neighborhood kids, telltale signs of peach ice cream dripping down their chins. Another bin of homemade ice cream stood open, the frost on the outside quickly dissipating in the heat, anything inside undoubtedly turned into a puddle of peach-colored liquid swimming at the bottom.

A card table stood nearby with large wedges of watermelon decorating a red-and-white-checked tablecloth. Two boys stood next to it, globs of the pink fruit staining their faces and shirts, large chunks of watermelon gripped in grimy hands as they spit out the seeds to see who could spit the farthest. For a moment, Harriet thought she might still be dreaming, seeing the world as it had once been when she and Cassie were small and their whole world had been another backyard with a gazebo and a tall magnolia tree.

Lucinda greeted Sam and Cassie with a wide smile, and she momentarily lifted her hand from the crank to wave. "Hi, y'all. Come join the party. I should have known that the sound of this here machine would bring people out of the woodwork."

Homemade peach ice cream. The words alone brought back memories of long summer days spent in the gazebo with Cassie. The cones would drip down their forearms in the ever-losing battle of trying to lick the drips before they fell. They'd spend hours out there during summer vacation talking about everything—especially boys. And the summer when Harriet was away at camp, Cassie had sat in the gazebo eating her ice cream alone, watching Joe slap coats of blue paint on the ceiling, and falling in love in the process. Harriet had always wondered how different things might have been if she'd stayed home that summer—if she'd been the one to fall in love with Joe first.

Cassie scanned the crowd of children. "Where's Harriet?"

For some reason, Harriet fell back, unwilling to be noticed yet, wanting just to watch life play out below her window.

Lucinda straightened, putting a hand on her hip. "That girl was just about to give out. I had to force her to go inside and take a rest. She said she'd only go in for a minute, but last I checked on her, she was sound asleep."

Sam stowed his bag underneath the table. "In that case, we'll let her rest awhile longer. That'll give me a chance to dig into this ice cream." At Lucinda's direction, he went inside to the large freezer and brought out another bin.

Cassie held out two cones while Sam dropped

generous portions on top. When Cassie bent her head to get a bite, her nose bumped into the large mound of ice cream, leaving a dollop of the peach stuff on the tip.

Harriet watched Sam as he looked at Cassie, and finally knew for sure what she'd suspected all along. She wondered if Cassie had seen it, too, or if she'd just been pretending to be oblivious.

"That's cute, Cassie," Sam said after taking a small bite from the side of his ice-cream cone.

"Here, then." With her index finger, she scooped up some ice cream from her own cone and gently placed it on the tip of Sam's nose.

Knoxie, who had come to stand by her aunt, giggled uproariously and stuck her nose in her own cone.

Harriet started to lean out of the window, to call down to Knoxie to stop, when she saw Sam take a step toward Cassie. "You think that's funny, sweetheart? Watch this." He stuck three fingers into his cone and deposited a large chunk onto Cassie's cheek.

With that, Cassie squeezed her hand over her cone, then carefully wiped it through Sam's hair. Harriet brought her hand to her mouth, not knowing whether she should be appalled or laugh out loud.

Most of the children had now stopped to stare at the two adults making spectacles of themselves.

Lucinda stopped cranking and came and stood

between them. "All right, you two, that's enough. It's going to take forever to get all that sugar out of his hair. . . ."

"Excuse me, Lucinda." Gently, Sam guided Harriet's aunt to the side. Then he calmly plopped his cone upside down on Cassie's head.

Cassie stood still for a moment, her expression showing more shock and surprise than anger. And then she began to laugh: great gasping howls of laughter that were so familiar to Harriet that it made her want to cry. Of all the things she'd missed the most about her sister's absence, it had been her laughter.

A movement by the driveway brought Harriet's attention to a man standing on the edge of the cement, as if he were unwilling to get his shoes dirty in the grass. Harriet turned her head back to Cassie and Sam, wanting to warn them, but wanting Cassie's laughter to last longer and knowing, somehow, that this man's appearance was about to make it stop.

"Cassandra?"

Cassie immediately quieted, turning on her heel toward the sound of the voice. "Andrew?"

Harriet studied her future brother-in-law closely, realizing she was trying to find fault with his appearance. His double-breasted suit jacket hung open, the front of his shirt saturated with sweat. His blond hair appeared streaked with brown, and perspiration dripped down his forehead. He was good-looking, Harriet supposed, but she couldn't imagine him looking quite as handsome as Sam did with peach ice cream dripping down his head. In fact, she couldn't imagine this man eating ice cream, much less wearing it.

Cassie stared at him a moment as the ice-cream cone on her head slipped to the side and then splattered on the ground beside her. Harriet watched her sister, her breath held, and waited for what she would say.

Without seeming to think about it, Cassie opened her mouth and said, "Well, butter my butt and call me a biscuit."

Harriet stepped back from the window and fell on the bed, her hand held tightly over her mouth so they couldn't hear her laughing, feeling better than she had in a long while, and finally knowing that Cassie, despite all the outward changes, hadn't changed a bit.

CHAPTER 14

Cassie grabbed a couple of napkins off the red-and-white-checked tablecloth and handed one to Sam. She wiped the other one over her face, pieces of the paper sticking to her nose and cheek. Forcing a smile, she approached her fiancé, trying to ignore his look of shock. "Andrew. This is a . . . surprise. We weren't expecting you until Friday."

He dropped his suitcase on the ground and

loosened his tie. "After our last phone conversation, I decided I'd better come earlier. What the hell's going on, and who's that guy?"

Before she could answer, Sam swaggered forward. She blinked, wondering why he was walking like he spent most of his days straddling a horse. He stuck out his hand toward Andrew. "Hey! Now, ain't this a pleasure. You must be Cassie's beau. I'm Sam Parker."

Cassie didn't know whether to laugh, cry, or just run away screaming. The ice cream in Sam's hair had started to melt and drip down the side of his face, while pieces of yellow napkin stuck to his beard stubble and fluttered as he moved. He looked utterly ridiculous but amazingly, completely appealing.

Andrew looked down at the outstretched hand for a moment before shaking it. "Nice to meet you. Andrew Wallace."

"Nice to meet you, Andy. Our Cassie's just been talkin' up a storm about you, and finally gettin' to meet you is just about gooder'n grits."

It was Andrew's turn to blink. "Um, it's *Andrew*."

Not able to stand looking at the yellow scrap of napkin stuck on Sam's nose, Cassie reached over and pulled it off, Andrew scrutinizing her movements. He stepped toward her and pulled her close in an intimate embrace. When she looked up to protest, he kissed her, sliding his tongue against her lips. She stiffened, but he didn't let go of her. He smiled as he lifted his head. "I've missed you."

She put her hands on his chest and tried gently to push away. "I've missed you, too."

When he bent his head toward her again, she raised her hand between them to wipe sweat off her forehead. "Gosh, it's so hot. Let's get you home so you can change into something more comfortable."

He dropped his arms from around her, his lips smiling but his eyes cool.

Cassie looked at the large suitcase in the grass. "I'm assuming you had a taxi drop you off at Daddy's house and nobody was there. Why didn't you leave your suitcase on the porch?"

Andrew sent Cassie a curious glance. "That's expensive luggage. I wasn't about to just leave it on a porch." He glanced around at the children running around the backyard. "Some old guy wearing overalls in a pickup truck even offered me a lift. Hard to believe. But he at least told me where I could find you."

Sam leaned down and scooped up the suitcase. "Heck, Andy, people here in Walton are so honest, they'd put stuff *in* your suitcase." He gave them both a wink. "Now, seein' as how you're without transportation, let's all just pile into my truck and I'll take you home."

Andrew's face blanched. "You mean my car's not here? Is there anything wrong?"

Cassie smiled brightly. "Nothing that can't be fixed. I'll fill you in later."

Sam waved to Lucinda and led the way to the front of the house. Cassie did a brief introduction between Andrew and Lucinda, then rushed to follow Sam. George gave them all a welcoming bark, making Andrew take a step back, but he held on to any complaints he might have had as he saw his suitcase lifted into the bed of the truck with the dog.

Sam pulled open the driver's-side door. "We'll all have to squeeze into the front seat. Got all my huntin' gear back there and there's just no room."

Narrowing her eyes, Cassie regarded him closely. She knew the backseat was full of presentation materials and handouts for the following week's medical conference in Atlanta. Before she could protest, he threw an old flannel blanket from the truck bed onto the pile, hiding all of it.

Cassie slid into the middle, then tried not to laugh as she watched Andrew negotiate his way into the truck. Sam flipped on the air-conditioning full force. "Man. It's hotter'n a goat's butt in a pepper patch."

Cassie elbowed him in the ribs, then focused her attention on the dashboard as she tried to enjoy Andrew's proprietary hand on her thigh and remember that he was the man she loved and was planning to marry. As soon as Sam put the truck in drive, his hand snaked its way over the back of the seat, coming to rest on her right shoulder. The ride home was the longest five minutes of her entire life.

The truck stopped in front of the old house and they all climbed out. Cassie stared up at the familiar facade with its stately columns and felt an odd surge of pride. Turning to Andrew, she waited for his reaction.

"So. This is the old pile of lumber." He put his hands on his hips and walked back behind the truck as if to get a better view. He turned in a circle, surveying the property. "I didn't get a good chance to look at it before, but now I see why you're having such a problem selling it."

Sam slammed the truck door a little louder than necessary.

Cassie tugged on Andrew's arm. "How can you say that? You haven't even seen the inside."

He turned toward the house again, squinting into the sun. "It's old. I don't like old. But really, the land it's sitting on could be a real gold mine."

Cassie bit down hard on her lip, wanting to defend her house and the place she had called home throughout the many happy years of her childhood. But she kept quiet instead, catching sight of Sam watching her closely.

Sam hoisted the suitcase out of the truck bed and slung it solidly onto the ground and right in the middle of a small puddle.

"Sorry 'bout that, Andy. Didn't see the puddle."

Andrew yanked on the handle and lifted it up. Cassie recognized the belligerent jut of his chin and knew she had to separate the two men before things came to blows. She pulled on his coat sleeve. "Andrew, let's go inside and get you cleaned up. Thanks for the ride, Sam." She tugged on Andrew's elbow and led him toward the steps. Andrew moved ahead and stopped at the front door. Cassie hung back, turning toward Sam. "Sam? Please don't forget—"

"I won't forget." The foolish grin disappeared as he spoke, the country hayseed gone.

A small grin crept across her face. "How did you know what I was going to say?"

He didn't return her smile. "I've known you for a long time." He turned and opened the door to his truck. "Don't worry. I'll go check on Harriet now. But you're probably going to have to be a real pain in the butt to get her to make an appointment for a complete office checkup." He climbed behind the steering wheel, slammed the door shut, then leaned one muscular forearm out of the window. "I know you can be real good at that." He started the engine and pulled away before she could think of a response.

When she approached the waiting Andrew, his scowl turned into a smile. "Alone at last." She allowed herself to be pulled into his embrace, her face plastered against his custom-made Egyptian cotton shirt. She sniffed, smelling the familiar expensive cologne, the starch of his shirt, and tried to nestle into his arms until she found a comfortable spot. She sniffed again, wondering what was missing. Jerking her head up, she met his gaze.

"What's wrong?" His voice deepened as he pressed her closer to him.

She closed her eyes for a moment, trying to figure it out. Her eyes widened with realization. There wasn't anything wrong. There was just something missing. The smell of outdoors, Dial soap, and the rough feel of denim.

"Nothing. It's just so hot, that's all." She broke away and opened the door. "See? It was unlocked. You could have just put your stuff inside."

He followed her into the foyer, plopping down his dirty suitcase on the Oriental rug and gazing about the room. "It's like a museum in here. Who are all those goofy-looking people in the portraits?"

Cassie crossed her arms in front of her. "Your future in-laws. So be nice."

"Oops. Sorry." He faced her, not looking at all repentant. "Are we alone?"

Her fingers strayed to the charms around her neck. "Ah, yes. But Aunt Lucinda should be back soon. . . ."

He approached her with a purposeful look. "Where's our bedroom?"

Something akin to panic rippled through her. What had gotten into her? This was the man she was supposed to marry. "Our bedroom? Oh, you mean mine?" She tried to picture Andrew in the pink canopied bed, taking the place of the giant stuffed elephant that had been keeping her company of late. "It's upstairs, but—"

"Come on then." He pulled on her hand, dragging her toward the steps. There was no mistaking the look in his eyes. It occurred to her to wonder why she felt nothing at his touch. Before she could think of an excuse, she heard a car door slam outside. She pulled away. "That's Aunt Lucinda." She almost skipped to the front door and flung it open.

"Hey, Aunt Lu." Even to her own ears her voice sounded as country as collard greens. She didn't bother to turn around to catch Andrew's expression.

Lucinda fairly ran up the stairs and into the house, breathing heavily as she teetered in her four-inch heels. She wore freshly applied Bingo Night Red lipstick and smelled of baby powder. Cassie spied lines of the white stuff in the elbow crease of her aunt's arm. The older woman tottered toward Andrew and smothered him in an embrace, leaving powder smudges on his jacket and a look of alarm on his face.

Lucinda smiled brightly. "I didn't get the chance before over at Harriet's house, but I just had to give you a hug and welcome you to the family, Andy. It's so good to finally meet you."

A small smile plastered itself on Andrew's face. "That would be Andrew. And, yes, it's nice to meet you, too. You're exactly how I pictured you."

The wattage on Lucinda's smile didn't dim. "Why, thank you. And you're exactly what I pictured, too." She looked down at the muddy suitcase. "Here, why don't I take that and let you get settled in your room. I'm putting you down here in my room. It just wouldn't be fittin' to leave you and Cassie alone upstairs. I'll sleep in Harriet's old room instead." With a wink at Cassie, Lucinda hoisted the suitcase and sashayed out of the foyer and to the back of the house.

Cassie ignored the stunned expression on Andrew's face and silently thanked her aunt. She wasn't sure why she should be so relieved to be rescued by Lucinda. But there was something about seeing Andrew here, in this town, in her house, that illuminated him in a strange new light. He stuck out like snow in July, and as she stared at him with new eyes, she realized for the first time in their relationship how very different they were. She couldn't remember ever thinking that before, but maybe he had changed in the short time they'd been apart.

Cassie gave him a quick peck on the check before escaping past him and up the first couple of stairs. "I've got to shower and get this sticky ice cream off of me before I start attracting ants. When I'm done, I'll show you the house."

"Oh, boy," he said, looking entirely unenthusiastic. "Can't wait."

As Cassie turned to run up the rest of the stairs, she could have sworn the eyes of Great-great-great-grandfather Madison sent her a scolding look.

CASSIE SAT ON THE PORCH SWING, her bare feet skimming the surface of the floorboards, her eyes closed and head tilted back to catch the breeze from the ceiling fan. The door shut with a bang and she jerked up.

Andrew's hair was still damp from his shower. With the high humidity in the air, it wasn't going to dry by itself anytime soon. Splotches of perspiration already marred his pale green silk shirt, and wet streaks snaked down under the waistband of a pair of mocha-colored linen trousers.

"Damn, it's hot! How can they stand it?"

She eyed his outfit with amusement. "Well, for one thing, they dress appropriately."

His gaze traveled from her bare feet up to the denim shorts and cotton tank top with spaghetti straps she had bought, along with a bathing suit and a bunch of T-shirts, on the spur of the moment during a trip to the local Wal-Mart. "I have my standards."

She moved over to make room for him on the swing. "Then stop complaining about being hot."

He eyed the swing speculatively, awkwardly maneuvering himself next to her. He slid back on the seat, then rested his arm around her shoulders, his fingers caressing her collarbone. They swung in silence for a moment before Andrew spoke.

"So, Cassandra. What's going on here?"

She looked down at her hands, noticing her peeling fingernails. She hadn't bothered to get a manicure since she'd been in Walton. "What do you mean?"

"Well, for starters—who's that guy? Sam something-or-other."

Cassie swallowed in an effort to make her voice sound nonchalant. "Sam Parker. He's the town doctor. An old family friend."

Andrew shook his head. "Oh, great. I guess everybody here spends a lot of time praying they won't get sick. What a clown."

Cassie pulled away. "You don't even know him. You can't always tell who a person is by the way he looks." Cassie pushed at the floorboard with a dig of her heel, sending the swing into an odd rocking pattern.

Andrew snorted. "He reminds me of that Goober guy on *The Andy Griffith Show*. Hell, he's so perfect, we might be able to use him in one of our commercials as a redneck gas station attendant. He'd be a natural."

She almost mentioned Sam's Ivy League degrees, but kept silent, figuring it would be a lot more amusing to have Andrew find out for himself.

They turned their heads in unison at the sound of tires on gravel. Ed Farrell's Cadillac, its whitewalls sparkling, pulled into the drive and parked. Slowly, Ed slid out of the car and sauntered toward them, his pin-striped suit reflecting the sunlight.

Cassie stopped the swing and stood. "Hey, Ed." There was that word again. When had the word "hello" fallen from her vocabulary?

"Hey, Cassie." He approached Andrew with an outstretched hand and a smile. "And you must be Cassie's fiancé. It's a real pleasure to meet you."

Andrew stood and shook hands. "Andrew Wallace. Nice to meet you." He studied Ed's face closely. "Have we met before? You look vaguely familiar."

"Nope. Don't think so. Can't imagine there being somebody looking just like me, though. Pretty scary, huh?"

He chuckled as Andrew simply nodded. Cassie noted Andrew's smirk as his gaze took in Ed's suit, and she had the oddest desire to go stand in front of Ed as a protective shield.

Seemingly oblivious to Andrew's expression, Ed hitched up his pants. "So. What do you think of the property? Cassie's got a nice thing here. Have you

316

had a chance to check out my new neighborhood, Farrellsford?"

Andrew's eyebrows rose with interest. "You're a builder?"

Ed's gaze shifted to Cassie for a moment. "Not exactly. I'm a Realtor who just dabbles in land development, and improving the town of Walton. It's been pretty lucrative these last few years."

"Really?" Andrew's attention had been aroused. "How lucrative?"

"Follow me." Ed led Cassie and Andrew off the porch and around the side of the house, where the backs and chimneys of some of the houses in Farrellsford could be seen. Ed pointed. "I bought that piece of property for a song not three years ago. Now I've got close to a hundred and fifty houses on it, each going for around a quarter million." He grinned widely at Andrew. "Now, that's what I call lucrative."

Cassie narrowed her eyes at the slate gray hip roofs of the houses in Farrellsford. "But Ed also believes in keeping the integrity of Walton. Which is why he's not pressuring me to do anything with the house besides sell it to another family for residential use. Right, Ed?"

"Well, yes, Cassie. As long as that solution remains feasible." He hitched up his pants again, looking uncomfortable in the stifling sun. "But I told you it would be hard, since everybody wants new construction these days. I've shown it to four families so far, and every single one of them has decided on one of the newer homes. That's why I came over today. To start talking about our plan B."

Cassie looked beyond his shoulder to the white house behind him. Every brick, every shingle, every floorboard was as familiar to her as her own skin. The squeaks and sounds of the old house had been her nightly lullaby as a child. Her gaze strayed to the front lawn as a small breeze blew toward them, carrying on it the scent of her mother's roses. Beyond the house, towering over the driveway, the magnolia her mother had planted as a sapling when Cassie was born fluttered its leaves in the breeze.

Ed continued. "And the good news is I think I've got part of the town council on my side to end that moratorium to halt further development. The police chief and Judge Moore have sworn to oppose, and I'm working on the others. Sam can't pass it without a majority and I don't think he's going to get it." He smiled gently at her. "I'm not talking about bulldozing the house, Cassie. You know I'd hate that as much as you would. I'm just talking about finding some other uses for the existing structure with only minimal changes."

Cassie's gaze fell to the backyard, where she saw the ghosts of her childhood friends playing hide-and-seek in the twilight of a long-gone day. She smelled her mother's roses again and turned back to the men. "I don't know if there is going to be a plan B, Ed. I know that's not what we originally talked about, but the more I think about it, the more I'm pretty sure I'd never be able to see this property used for anything else except for a family who wants to live in the house." She looked at Ed. "I'm willing to rent it until we find a buyer, and have you manage it."

Andrew gave her a contentious look. "I beg to differ, Cassandra. First, you have a job in dire need of your attention back in New York and you can't really afford to be diverted. Second, there's an awful lot of money to be gained here."

Cassie stared at her fiancé, waiting for him to say something about how much he needed her and loved her. Then she realized what she wanted most was for him to turn around and look at the house, to see it through her eyes, and to know that the brick, mortar, and wood were worth far more to her than money. He did neither. Instead, he frowned as he tilted his head back. "This old place looks like a fire hazard."

Cassie looked at Andrew in disbelief, then turned at the sound of her aunt's voice.

Lucinda stood on the edge of the porch, waving at them. "Hey, y'all, I brought out some sweet tea. Thought you could sure use it on such a hot day."

Without waiting for the men, Cassie charged forward toward the steps. Her hand shook as she poured herself a glass. She paused for a moment, looking intently at the fuchsia aluminum cup. She held the frosty metal up to her cheek and closed her eyes, remembering going to the Green Stamps store with her mother to buy them. With her mother's help, Cassie had licked and pasted all those stamps into their little book until they had enough to get those silly aluminum cups. They were as much a part of her childhood as church picnics and swimming in the creek behind Senator Thompkins's house.

The two men walked up the steps, deep in conversation. Cassie handed Andrew a fluorescent blue cup and watched with amusement as he raised an eyebrow before placing his lips on the curved edge to drink.

Ed took a bright yellow cup and took a sip before addressing Andrew again. "If you like, I'd be happy to show you around Farrellsford and some other projects I've got going on around town. I'm always looking for investors." He winked.

To Cassie's surprise, Andrew nodded. "I'd like that."

"Aunt Cassie!" They all turned to see Maddie walking up the drive, Knoxie on her hip and Joey and Sarah Frances following close behind. "Dr. Parker said Mama needed to rest, so he sent us over here."

The children clattered up onto the porch and stopped, staring at Andrew. Cassie made the introductions and was proud of the children as they each held out a small hand to Andrew.

Knoxie slid down from Maddie's arms and wailed, "I need to go potty."

Maddie grabbed her hand and led her into the house. Quickly the screen door popped open again and Maddie stuck her head out. "Before I forget—are batteries made of metal? Like, would they set off a metal detector?"

Cassie puckered her eyebrows as she regarded her niece. "Yes, I believe they are. Why do you need to know?"

Knoxie wailed again from inside the house. "*Now,* Maddie. I don't wanna wet my pants."

Maddie smiled. "Oh, no reason." She let the screen door slam behind her as she disappeared inside.

Andrew stared at Joey and Sarah Frances, who were now sprawled in the porch swing. "Oh, my God! You mean your sister has four children?"

Cassie put her cup down and poured more sweet tea. "Actually, five. Baby Amanda must be home with Harriet."

Sarah Frances's small voice piped up. "Mama says we shouldn't use the Lord's name in vain, Mr. Wallace."

Andrew's eyes widened with a look of horror before he turned to Ed. "You know, I'm not doing anything right now. If you've got a few minutes, I'd love to take that tour now."

Ed put his cup down on a railing. "Nope. Got nothin' planned at all. It would be my pleasure."

Andrew turned back to Cassie. "Assuming that's all right with you."

Cassie waved her hand in dismissal. "It's fine with me. I'll stay here and play with the children."

With a curious glance in her direction, Andrew kissed her quickly on the cheek, then left to get into Ed's Cadillac. Ed faced her for a moment with a sympathetic smile. "We'll talk later, all right? And if you just want to wait it out by renting until we find the right family for your house, then that's fine with me."

He winked and began walking toward the Cadillac with the same lanky gait he didn't seem to have outgrown. Cassie paused for a moment, recalling the memory of going with her mother to deliver a bucket of apples and old clothes to Ed's mother. Ed had walked away from them without a word as soon as they reached the bottom broken step of the front porch. His bare feet stirred up clouds of red dust as he strode across the parched and bare yard in front of the dilapidated house, as if the embarrassment of facing charity was more than he could stand.

Cassie turned and opened the screen door. "Maddie. When you come out, grab some apples and meet us under the magnolia out front."

She reached for the hands of the two children and the three went running across the lawn, the freshly cut grass tickling her bare toes, reminding her again of the old summers of her childhood that no longer seemed so far away.

MADDIE AND KNOXIE found everyone sitting under the old magnolia tree. They handed out apples, then sat in the shade made by the thick branches, crunching noisily. Maddie sat cross-legged on the grass in front of her aunt. "So that's the guy you're gonna marry?"

Aunt Cassie nodded, her mouth full of apple.

Knoxie and Sarah Frances squealed and giggled and Joey blurted, "Ew, they're gonna kiss!"

Maddie gave her brother a shove and he quieted. "Why does he dress so funny?"

Her aunt seemed to choke on her apple. "It's not 'funny.' Just different from what you're used to. That's how many of the professional men dress in New York. It's more fashionable."

Maddie munched thoughtfully, then said, "It doesn't look very comfortable, but I suppose I could get used to it."

Aunt Cassie raised both eyebrows as she took another bite.

Maddie leaned her head back against the trunk, figuring it couldn't get that hot in New York or people wouldn't be dressing like that Andrew guy. She spotted a large bug close to her head and started. Turning her face to examine it more closely, she realized it was the shell of a cicada stuck in the tree trunk, the bug itself long since gone. Glad she'd spotted it before Joey, who would have spent the rest of the afternoon with it chasing a screaming Sarah Frances around the yard, she plucked it from its prison, holding it gently between two fingers. She brought it close to her face to study it.

"What did you find, Maddie?" Her aunt leaned closer to see better.

"A cicada shell. Wanna hold it?"

Without hesitating, Aunt Cassie held out her hand and Maddie gently rolled the shell into her open palm. They sat very close, examining it. The shell was nearly see-through, the wings gone. Maddie squinted, staring hard, and saw something she'd never seen before. It seemed to her that the body of the insect had taken flight, leaving its soul in the place it called home under the shade of the magnolia leaves.

Digging her bare toes into the cool summer grass, Aunt Cassie cupped it in both hands, then blew hard, letting the delicate shell drift slowly to the ground.

Maddie looked up and spotted Dr. Parker's truck pulling up the driveway. Aunt Cassie looked up, too, and they both watched as he got out and walked toward them.

Maddie faced her aunt again. "Dr. Parker's much cuter than Mr. Wallace, don't you think?"

Her aunt turned a funny shade of pink. "I, um,

well, I think they're both good-looking. Just in, um, very different ways."

As Dr. Parker approached, Maddie sent her aunt a sidelong glance, wondering if she needed glasses or something.

He said hello to everyone, giving Joey a high five. Then he turned to Aunt Cassie and reached for her hand. "We need to talk."

Surprising Maddie by not arguing, Aunt Cassie dropped her apple core and grabbed hold of his hand. He didn't let go until they'd reached the front porch steps. Maddie swallowed her last bite of apple and didn't take another one, wanting to hear every word.

Dr. Parker spoke first. "I need you to do me a favor."

Aunt Cassie tilted her head. "Depends. What do you need?"

He lowered his head for a moment. "I've scheduled an office appointment for Harriet next Wednesday morning at eight o'clock. I need to make sure she doesn't forget or postpone it. Can you make sure she gets there?"

Maddie felt cold all of a sudden, as if fall had come suddenly while they'd been sitting under the giant magnolia.

Aunt Cassie said, "Yes. Of course. Why?" Her hand moved up to the chain she always wore around her neck, touching the small gold hearts first, then sliding down to the key that hung lower than the other charms. "Is she . . . is she sick?"

He didn't look away. "It's too soon to say anything. Her fatigue has me worried, but I'm not here to jump to conclusions. We'll know more after her appointment."

Cassie looked over at Maddie, and Maddie looked down at the cicada's shell lying in the grass, trying to pretend she wasn't listening.

Aunt Cassie spoke again. "What do you think is wrong with her?"

"I won't know until I can give her a thorough exam. There're lots of reasons for fatigue, and four of them are sitting right over there under that tree."

Maddie watched as Dr. Parker rubbed his knuckles gently over Aunt Cassie's jaw. "It'll be all right, Cassie. I'll be right here with you, okay? You can count on it."

Maddie looked away, wanting very much to believe Dr. Parker, but not able to shake the cold feeling that seemed to have settled in her bones. She stared back at the cicada shell, then watched as the afternoon breeze lifted it in the air and rolled it over the wide front lawn until it disappeared as if it had never even existed at all.

CHAPTER 15

Cassie sat on the swing in the cool shade of the porch, the letter box settled next to her. The breeze from the fan above rustled the pages of the yellowed letter in her hand, whispering its secrets.

December 1, 1972

Dear Harry,

I was nearly caught last night. The window jamb slammed shut after I had crawled inside, and I think it woke Daddy. I threw myself under the covers just in time. It was so hard to make myself breathe slowly—but I think I had him fooled. I don't like this sneaking around— I'm much too old for this. I'd like to shout our love from the town square, on top of that soldier's horse, but until Daddy's heart is feeling stronger, it's just something we need to keep to ourselves.

I have a little favor to ask of you. There's a new girl in town, Catherine Anne Abbott. I know you've heard me talk about her, because she's my best friend in the whole world. She's moving here from Columbus and will be living with her aunt, old Miss Shrewster. Catherine Anne's parents died recently in a horrible car wreck, and her aunt is the only living soul in her family. I know her because our parents were friends and we've been spending summers together ever since I can remember. She's quite a few years younger than me, and just as sweet as can be. But she's come here to live now with that old shrunken, prune-faced aunt of hers, and I'm afraid she'll become just like Miss Shrewster if she isn't brought out at all. If you do happen to run into her in town, introduce yourself. Don't mention you know me—I don't want to force her to keep our secret—but do say hello and make her feel comfortable. And please tell all your single friends about her. Maybe, when we're free of our secrets, we can double-date or something.

Daddy has just come home, so I'll close this letter. I don't know if I can stand waiting a whole week to see you again. Think of me kissing the locket and thinking of you.

Love,

E

A car door slammed in the driveway, making Cassie look up. Harriet approached, a crisp yellow linen sundress hanging loosely on her small frame. "I thought you might like a ride over to Bitsy's." She held up something in her hand. "And I brought you one of the shower invitations—for your scrapbook. I had napkins printed, too, and I'll save you one from the party."

328

Cassie nodded, feeling a little shell-shocked. She moved the letter box to her lap, and allowed Harriet to sit next to her. "How are you feeling?"

Harriet sighed. "Oh, the same, I guess. I suppose I'll find out what kinds of vitamins I need to be taking when I see Sam on Wednesday." She indicated the letter with a nod of her head. "Anything interesting?"

"I'd say so." Cassie handed her the letter.

The moving air from the ceiling fan played with the fine blond hairs that had strayed out of Harriet's headband as she bent over to read. She finished and handed the letter back, her green eyes wide. "So. That's how it happened. Sort of like it was meant to be."

Cassie stuck the letter back in the box, slamming the lid a little too hard. "Meant to be? She practically threw Mama at Daddy. Imagine how she must have felt." Cassie turned away and stuck out her chin. "No, never mind. You couldn't. But trust me, it feels awful."

Harriet ducked her face. "I guess I deserved that. But we're not talking about you and me and Joe. We're talking about Mama and Daddy. I know they were the loves of each other's lives, and nothing will ever change that. Unfortunately, Daddy was also the love of Miss E's life."

Cassie stood abruptly, clutching the box to her chest. "How can you say that? She left him. She went away to have their baby, as if she didn't want Daddy to be a part of her life anymore. How could she have done that if she really loved him?"

Harriet twisted the gold wedding band around on her finger, her gaze focused far beyond the front porch and green grass. "She loved him so much that she sacrificed everything she loved so he could be happy." Her eyes met her sister's, her expression somber.

Cassie shook her head. "Love isn't about sacrifice. It's about meeting each other's needs— it's about companionship. Not to mention the fact that Miss E's sacrifice makes Daddy sound incredibly selfish."

"I don't think Daddy was being selfish— because that's not like him at all. I don't think he was given a choice. I read that letter up in the attic, too. It seemed that Miss E was doing everything she could to make sure Daddy didn't find her." She pushed hair out of her eyes, her gold band catching the sunlight. "And I think you're wrong about the sacrifice part. Love is all about sacrifices—big and small ones. It's only when you know how much you could give up for somebody that you know what true love really is."

The whirring fan spun above them, the only sound on the silent porch, the unspoken words of what lay behind their fifteen-year estrangement lying scattered about them. Yes, Cassie knew all about being sacrificed in the name of love, and it didn't seem right that so much pain could walk so easily with love.

Finally, Cassie hoisted the box under one arm. "We're going to be late if we don't get a move on. Let me go put this inside and I'll be right out."

Without waiting for a response, she disappeared inside the house, the screen door banging shut behind her.

THE LADIES SAT UNDER DOMED DRYERS at Bitsy's House of Beauty, their hair wrapped in scraps of foil. Harriet sent a crooked smile at her sister, feeling like she could pick up the local radio station with the contraptions on her head. She glanced around at the other women in various stages of beautification, knowing she'd see most of them at the shower that evening.

She watched as Cassie warily eyed the comb and scissors in Bitsy's hand. "I just want a sleek bob— nothing fancy. Just what I have now, but trimmed up a bit." She chewed on her lip. "I don't want big hair—no need to tease it at all, okay?"

Bitsy nodded, a patient expression on her face. "Don't worry about a thing, sugar. I'll have you fixed up, sleek and pretty, in no time."

Harriet handed another foil to Ovella, Bitsy's sister and co-owner of the salon, and forced her eyelids to stay open as she stifled yet another yawn.

Ovella's words were muffled by the bobby pins

in her mouth. "You look wore out, Harriet. If I didn't know you had a baby at home, I'd swear you were pregnant." She paused, a tissue held in midair. "You aren't, are you?"

Harriet laughed. "It sure feels like it, but not likely. And I wish people would stop saying that." She slid a glance toward Cassie. "I'm not saying no to another baby in the future, but just not so soon."

Ovella nodded, visibly relieved. "Why don't you leave those little ones with me for a bit so you can get some rest?"

Harriet smiled. "It's just a busy spell for me right now, that's all. But you watch out. I just might take you up on your offer." Eager to change the subject, she caught Cassie's reflection in the mirror. "Miss Lena stopped by this morning. She wants to give you a copy of *Sweet Wicked Love* for a shower present. Before she earmarked all the juicy parts to use on your honeymoon, she wanted to make sure you hadn't read it yet."

Cassie waited for Bitsy to raise her chair before responding. "For an unmarried older woman, one would wonder about her fascination with sex. Do you think she's ever done 'it'?"

Harriet closed her eyes for a moment, trying to shake the unbidden mental image. "Really, Cassie. Do we need to go there?"

Cassie turned to Bitsy. "Do you ever remember Miss Lena having a boyfriend?"

Bitsy's forehead creased. "She's a good bit older than me, you know. She used to babysit for me and Ovella and our five brothers. We were monsters, really. She used to tell me she only did it for the money, because we were truly terrible. Climbing out windows after she put us to bed and that sort of thing." Long red nails combed through Cassie's wet hair, preceded by the snip of the shiny metal scissors. "She was working as the church secretary back then, right before her parents decided to send her to Europe to get 'cultured,' whatever that means. I'm pretty sure she had a boyfriend, though. Sometimes she'd be dropped off at our house by a boy and she'd be all dreamy and googly-eyed. Don't know who it was, though. Too young to care, I guess."

Her fingers straightened Cassie's jaw, then she clipped off more hair with the scissors. "Couldn't have been very serious. Once she got back from Europe, she started back at work at the church again, and that was it. Never got married, which was a shame. She was so good with us kids and would have been a wonderful mother. She was always volunteering at the nursery at the church, and those kids just loved her." She sighed heavily. "Even me and Ovella and our brothers. Oh, well. I guess not everybody can find their true love, like me and my Henry. Course, I had to go to another county to find him, but I think it was destiny. We would have found each other no matter what."

Harriet glanced over at her sister, whose gaze seemed focused on her diamond engagement ring. And if she'd been the betting sort, Harriet would bet that she and Cassie were both trying to reconcile the words "true love" and "destiny" with Cassie and Andrew's relationship and drawing the same blank.

Maddie walked in from the back of the shop, her gait stiff as she hobbled on her heels, her toes separated by cotton balls, the nails painted a bright, fluorescent green.

Harriet only half succeeded in looking shocked. "Are your toes radioactive, Maddie? I don't want them changing the taste of my cheese straws at the shower."

"Very funny, Mama. This color is very fashionable. I just saw it in *Seventeen*. All the girls are wearing it."

"Not in Walton, they're not." Not having the energy to argue, Harriet closed her eyes.

As if wanting to defuse any mother-daughter tensions, Cassie suggested, "Why don't we go for the works, too, Har? We can have a manicure and pedicure—maybe even a facial. My treat."

Without opening her eyes, Harriet smiled. "I'd like that. Maybe Aunt Lucinda can do our makeup, too. I don't think I have the energy to even put on mascara."

Maddie stood by her mother. "And why don't you borrow something with a waist out of my closet to wear tonight. I'm tired of seeing you in those muumuus. It's all you seem to wear anymore."

Before Harriet could respond, the bells over the door jangled and Harriet looked through the strands of wet hair combed over her forehead. The two women who walked into the salon could have been a matching pair of bookends, but one generation apart. They both were pale blondes with slender builds and creamy skin, and were wearing matching pink sweaters with pearls.

Harriet tried to shrink back in her chair. Of all times to run into Doreen Spafford; with her wet hair, in her yellow shapeless dress, and wearing an unattractive orange vinyl cape, Harriet looked like something the cat dragged in. In her younger days, Doreen had been Harriet's rival for everything—class president, cheerleading captain, prom queen, and kudzu queen, with the winnings evenly split between each of them. But now the cards seemed decidedly stacked in Doreen's favor.

Harriet watched as Maddie eyed her nemesis.

"Hey, Lucy."

Lucy was much shorter and finer-boned than Maddie, giving her a delicate look. She eyed Madison's toenail polish with a raised blond brow and without comment before answering. "Hello, Maddie. What are you doing here?"

The question sounded innocent enough, but Harriet could see Madison pulling her shoulders back. "What does it look like I'm doing?"

Lucy rolled her eyes. "Well, it's just that I've never seen you here before." She regarded Maddie casually with clear gray eyes. "I mean, you're on the girls' basketball team. They'd probably have you kicked off if they found out you were here."

Harriet was still struggling to find enough energy reserves to stand and give Lucy a proper set-down, but Cassie held up her hand, making Bitsy step away. Flinging her hair out of her eyes, she approached the two women with a smile. "Doreen, it's so nice to see you again. What's it been—fifteen years? Gosh—is that the same hairstyle you wore in high school? I haven't seen that look in New York, but it suits you. How have you been?"

Without giving the other woman a chance to speak, Cassie gushed on. "And those cute matching sweaters—how sweet! I just don't think those stores on Fifth Avenue know what they're doing when they ignore the homey styles that so many small-town girls cling to. It's just so, well, quaint. And I for one miss it terribly."

Doreen and Lucy gave her identical plastered smiles. Cassie grabbed Maddie's arm and brought her closer. "Now, just look at this gorgeous girl. I can hardly believe that she's my own flesh and blood. She's got that height and that dark look that all those New York modeling agencies are going for these days. I can't believe y'all have been keeping her hidden here in Walton all this time."

She reached her hand around her niece and squeezed.

All six women wore stunned expressions while Harriet gave her sister a mental high five.

Doreen put her arm around her daughter. "Yes, well. It's good to see you again, Cassie. You, too, Harriet." She smiled, adjusting her purse on her shoulder. "And you're right, Cassie. Most of Walton hasn't changed a bit. Did I tell you that Lucy was kudzu queen this year? Guess we're lucky that the petite blonde is still in style here in Walton."

Suddenly struck dumb, Cassie gave them a plastic smile.

Doreen, leading her daughter away, said, "Bye, y'all. Lucy's got a big date tonight with Kevin O'Neal, so we'd better let Bitsy get started working her magic. See y'all later."

Maddie looked as if she'd been struck. Harriet waved Ovella away, then walked over to Cassie. Speaking softly into her sister's ear, she said, "You can't fix everything for everyone all the time, you know. But thanks for trying."

Cassie grimaced. "She may have won this battle, but the war ain't over yet."

Harriet laughed, then spoke loud enough for Maddie to hear. "Come on, let's get finished here so we can go get our toenails painted neon green."

Maddie smiled one of her old smiles, the ones Harriet was seeing less and less of. "And I've decided to get my hair cut." She pointed at Cassie. "I think shorter hair would look good on me."

Harriet lifted the brown hair from Maddie's shoulders, remembering how many times she'd stuck rollers and curling irons in it in a vain attempt for some kind of curl. She folded it under and turned Maddie's face toward the mirror. "I think you're right, Maddie. And if that's what you want, then that's what we'll do."

Maddie sent her a grateful look and Harriet squeezed her daughter around the shoulders, knowing not to press her luck by planting a kiss on her cheek.

Cassie came to stand next to them and the three of them stared at their reflections before Cassie said, "Well, come on, y'all—let's get that neon color on our nails now. And if it curdles the cream or changes the flavor of your famous cheese straws, Harriet, then that's a chance I'm willing to take."

They smiled at each other in the mirror, and Harriet sighed to herself, wondering how she'd lived so long apart from this woman she called sister.

AS THEY LEFT BITSY'S, Cassie heard her name being called and squinted into the sun toward the sound of the voice.

"Whooeee! Be still, my heart. I must be in heaven with all this beauty."

She couldn't stop the grin that spread across her

face as Sam slid his truck into a parking space and joined them on the sidewalk.

He studied Maddie and Harriet closely. "My. A vision of loveliness. It's a good thing I don't have a weak heart. And, Maddie—I like the new hairstyle. Just like a runway model." As Maddie blushed, he turned to Cassie and eyed her hair judiciously. "Hmmm. Not as big as I usually like a lady's hair, but simply stunning just the same."

Sam dodged Cassie's hand as she reached to slap his arm. "I'm heading to the Dixie Diner for lunch. It would do me proud to have you beautiful ladies join me."

Harriet squeezed his arm playfully. "You're such a flirt, Sam. Don't ever stop." She pushed Cassie toward Sam. "You two go on. Me and Maddie need to head home and get ready for the shower. I hope you're planning on attending, Sam. Joe's doing his famous barbecue." She winked. "And lots of beer, too. That should guarantee your presence."

Sam squeezed her arm. "Sure, Harriet. I'll be there. Wouldn't want to miss Senator Thompkins's clogging routine. He likes to save that for special occasions, so I don't get to see it as often as I like."

Harriet started to move off, Madison in her wake. "Yeah, I bet." She stepped off the curb, wobbling a bit until her daughter took her elbow. She faced Sam and Cassie with a wide smile. "We'll see you two at six, then."

Cassie stepped toward her. "I can help, Har. It's really silly for you to do all that work."

With a dismissive wave, Harriet stepped away. "I've got Lucinda and Maddie and a ton of other helpers. You're the guest of honor and I wouldn't dream of putting you to work. I'll just see you later."

Cassie watched as Harriet and Madison walked toward the van parked on the town square.

"I need to take her away for a week at a spa. She has got way too much on her plate and she needs to take a break."

Sam touched her arm. "If you want me to prescribe some R and R for her, let me know and I'll do it. If it comes from me, it will make it more official and maybe even make her listen."

Her face puckered as she regarded him. "You know what, Sam? Every time I see you, I either want to slap you or give you a hug. Why is that?"

She allowed him to lead her toward the diner. "It's because you've never tried any of the in-between stuff. You just give me a time and place, and we can get started."

Facing him to give him a retort, Cassie let the words die on her tongue.

"Where have you been, Cassandra? I've been waiting for over half an hour."

Andrew stood outside the door of the diner wearing olive linen pants and a dark yellow silk shirt with sweat stains showing under the arms.

His annoyed gaze flickered over Sam as he gave him a terse greeting before turning his full attention back on Cassie.

She'd completely forgotten she was supposed to meet Andrew at the diner for lunch. "Oh, Andrew. Sorry. Took a little longer at Bitsy's than I thought."

He bent to kiss her lips, but she tilted her head so that his lips merely slid across her cheek. Cassie smiled at him while a sickening picture of her squeezed between Sam and Andrew on one side of a booth flickered in her mind.

The bell over the door tingled as they pushed it open and went inside. Andrew put his arm around Cassie. "Does this place have sushi? I could really go for some sugata."

A cell phone rang and both Sam and Andrew patted their pockets. It was for Sam. "It's the clinic. Sorry I won't be able to join y'all for lunch. Guess I'll see you tonight." He pushed open the glass door. With a slack grin and an accent as thick as lard, he said, "And, Andy, only place you'll get sushi around here is at the bait shop." With a wink, he let the door close behind him.

CHAPTER 16

Cassie stood in the doorway of Andrew's room, watching him in the mirror as he knotted his tie. She recognized it as the Hermès she had given him for his last birthday, and wondered if he had ulterior motives for wearing it.

Lunch together had not gone well. He had insisted on sitting on the same side of the booth as her, and then rubbing her thigh throughout the meal. She remembered how she'd once found that arousing, but now couldn't figure out why. She was sure the other customers noticed and it embarrassed her. These people had known her parents and knew that she had been raised better than that.

Things had further deteriorated when even Burnelle Thompkins, the senator's wife and longtime waitress at the diner, had her perpetually chipper demeanor darkened by Andrew's carping on fat grams and ingredients as he scrutinized the menu. At first she had simply stood by the side of their booth, pad and pencil poised, as she suggested the chicken-fried steak with cheese fries. After ascertaining that the cook didn't use low-fat vegetable oil for frying, Andrew had eliminated half the items from the menu. Eventually, Cassie took over and ordered them both house salads, minus the fried chicken and bacon bits.

The final straw had come after they'd left the diner and were walking across the town square. Andrew had spied Miss Liberty, glowing particularly green in the direct light of the midday sun, her Styrofoam arm and lineman's glove proudly holding the torch aloft.

"Good Lord—what is that?"

Cassie drew herself up tall. "It's a replica of the Statue of Liberty. We're very proud of it."

Andrew's only response was to laugh until tears sprang to his eyes. When he could finally speak, he gasped out, "That's the stupidest thing I have ever seen in my life. Are you sure it's not a joke?"

Cassie's lower lip quivered. She felt as if her family pride, her honor, her whatever had been gravely insulted. She wanted to do something with that torch that would make it so Andrew would think twice about voicing any negative opinions about it again.

Instead, she said, "I'm going home," then turned on her heel, walking quickly in the opposite direction.

He had to jog to catch up with her, placing his hand on her arm to make her stop. "Damn it, Cassandra. It's not like it means anything to you. It's just a stupid statue."

She took a deep breath, wondering where her deep-felt indignation was coming from. It hadn't been that long ago that she had thought the same things that he'd just said out loud. "No, it's not.

343

It's much more than that. It's about recognizing the gentler things in life. But even if I explained it to you, you still wouldn't understand, so I'm just not going to waste my breath." She could tell from his blank expression that nothing she said was sinking in. "Never mind. I need to go home and change for the bridal shower. Just try not to embarrass me in front of my friends and family tonight, all right?"

He snorted. "Right. Like you have to worry about that. Isn't it the other way around?"

She shook her head at him. "You're so stuck-up you'd drown in a rainstorm. Maybe you should try harder to fit in; then we won't have to worry about anybody embarrassing anybody else."

Before he could make her any madder, she pulled away and began walking home, Andrew following doggedly at her heels.

That had been two hours earlier, and she still felt the sting of anger despite his apologies and his insistence that it was the heat that was making him so difficult. Pushing her feelings aside, she took a moment longer to scrutinize him without his being aware she was there. His long, tapered fingers—artist's fingers, that was what she'd always called them—jutted in and out of the silk tie as he adjusted it to perfection. Leaning her head against the doorframe, she studied those fingers, wondering if they knew her body better than he knew her mind and soul. And how well did she know him? She knew he had been born and raised in Southern California, the only child of a dentist and a salesclerk at Neiman Marcus. She had never met them, and Andrew had been to see them only once in the years she had known him.

Andrew loved the ad agency and his work there, and their relationship had evolved around the rise of the agency's success, feeding off it like a parasite. They lived the agency, breathed it morning, noon, and night. There was never any time for anything else. His affection and admiration coupled with their success had seemed to be enough. But what had any of that to do with marriage? She realized with a start that she didn't know his favorite color, or whether he had once caught fireflies in a jar, or what his grandparents were like. She didn't know the color of the house he had grown up in, or the name of his first-grade teacher, or his first serious crush. She blinked hard, moving away from the threshold before he could see her.

She had reached the first step before his voice called out.

"Cassandra? Are you ready for the big hoedown?"

He stuck his head out of the room and Cassie looked at him and his carefully groomed hair. "Better stay away from the barbecue pit. That stuff on your hair looks flammable." She gritted her teeth. *Oh, Lord. I must be scared, because I'm sure as hell acting mean.*

He looked hurt and Cassie felt a stab of remorse. With great effort, she smiled and offered her hand. "Come on. Lucinda's driving." She didn't have to force her smile this time, anticipating his reaction to Aunt Lucinda's car.

"I hope my car's fixed soon, and that Mr. Overalls knows what he's doing. I'd hate to make him pay for any damages."

Cassie's smile faded as she led him to the door.

CARS LINED BOTH SIDES of the street approaching her sister's house. Lucinda pulled into the one open spot in the driveway, claiming it was reserved for the guests of honor. Her gaze met Cassie's in the rearview mirror and she winked. "Well, y'all. This is it." She didn't drop her gaze, and Cassie couldn't help but wonder if there was double meaning to her words.

They stepped out of the car and headed toward the squeal of children and the hum of adult voices from the backyard.

Andrew swiped at his forehead, his skin already glistening with sweat. "I hope this thing is inside, because if I have to spend another minute in this heat I'll melt."

"Have you ever been to an indoor barbecue, Andrew?" Cassie grabbed his hand and led him to the gate in the fence surrounding the backyard.

Her first stop would be at the drinks table. Hopefully, there would be kudzu punch. She had a feeling she was going to need it.

Lucinda walked past them and into the milieu of people, but Andrew and Cassie stopped. Small children, dressed in their Sunday best, ran around chasing one another, playing a wild game of tag. Cassie recognized the shrieks of one child, and turned to see Sarah Frances, a ribbon hanging precariously onto the end of a long braid, chasing a boy her age.

Old Mr. Crandall, the husband of Cassie's fifth-grade math teacher, sat on a stool, a large vat of lemonade in front of him, stirring the lemon-dotted liquid with a broken oar. He tipped the brim of his straw hat as he spotted the couple.

The spicy aroma of barbecue on an open pit teased Cassie's taste buds as she spotted Joe, beer in hand, basting the chicken parts with his secret sauce. Nearby, Joey and several of his friends stood, spitting watermelon seeds at one another while little girls hung behind them, squealing as each small dart hit its target.

Thelma and Selma Sedgewick, in matching Hawaiian-print sundresses and large straw hats, spied Cassie and Andrew and headed toward them, brims nodding, like a couple of parakeets on a mission. It appeared the whole town was there, standing or sitting around the deck, patio, and backyard. Old people sat in lawn chairs with grandchildren, or even great-grandchildren, perched on creaky knees or cradled in wrinkled arms. Miss Lena, the tops of her knee-high stockings peeking out under the hem of her polka-dotted dress, sat next to the senator's wife, and Cassie watched in amusement as she took a paperback novel out of her large purse and handed it to the baffled Mrs. Thompkins.

Cassie smiled. It was like looking at an old movie from her childhood. She had been to many such parties as a child. Nothing had changed, not really. Perhaps some of the older folks were no longer here, and some of the town's matrons had progressed to the lawn chairs, the altering faces changing the individual threads of the fabric that made up her hometown. Today, Harriet played hostess instead of their mother, and the young boys Cassie and her sister used to chase now had receding hairlines, thicker waists, and families of their own. Yes, the threads were different, but the richly woven fabric remained strong. These were her people. No matter how far she would ever roam, that fact would never change.

Sam leaned against a tree and said something that made Joe laugh. Cassie's gaze caught Sam's long enough for him to dip his head in greeting and raise his beer bottle. His blue eyes seemed to sparkle in the sun, and she found herself winking at him. She turned her head to see Reverend Beasley do his inside-out-eyelid trick in front of an enraptured crowd of children. They were probably the third generation of Walton children lucky enough to be privy to such an experience. Cassie breathed in deeply, feeling for the first time in a long while that perhaps lack of change might not be such a bad thing.

She glanced over at Andrew, her smile fading. A bemused frown sat on his face, as if he couldn't quite make out what he was seeing. He shook his head as he looked back at her. "How long do you think we have to stay?"

It was as if a large spotlight had suddenly turned on above, illuminating just the two of them. Her first instinct was to flee in the face of the harsh reality, to run away from this huge problem looming on her doorstep. She'd done that once before, after all. Looking away for a moment, she let her gaze wander back to the yard's edge. Sam's parents and Harriet, with baby Amanda on her hip, had joined Sam and Joe. Mr. Parker said something with a laugh, making his gray-haired wife nuzzle into his shoulder like a young girl. Cassie watched as Mrs. Parker's hand snaked behind her husband and pinched him through his overalls.

She caught Sam watching her with a questioning look, and realized with surprise that she wore a silly grin. He winked at her, and she wanted nothing more at that moment than to go over to that group and be enveloped in the gentle comfort of people who really knew her, and loved her anyway.

Instead, with a deep breath, she faced Andrew again.

"Come on, Andy. We need to talk."

She yanked on his arm and pulled him back through the gate, letting it slam hard behind them.

Cassie didn't stop walking until she had reached the cool respite of her own porch. Perspiration poured down her face and body from the short walk, making the cotton of her dress stick to her skin. Ignoring Andrew, she kicked off her shoes, then reached under her dress and pulled off her panty hose, throwing them to the ground. She plopped down on the porch swing, breathing heavily. She hadn't said a word, and Andrew hadn't asked any questions. But it was plain on his face that he was annoyed, and very, very hot.

She frowned at him. "You know, you'd be a lot cooler if you wore something that doesn't stick to your skin. Like a nice cotton knit. Or a T-shirt."

He gave her a disdainful look, then wiped off the sweat from his forehead. "Cut the bull, Cassandra. What's going on here?"

She tugged at the fourth finger of her left hand, pulling off her ring and grasping it tightly for one last moment. Slowly, she opened her palm, watching as the light played on the large diamond in her hand. "I can't marry you, Andrew."

He blinked. "Why not?"

"Isn't it obvious? We don't belong together. We work well together, but that's not enough to base a marriage on." She looked down at the ring, at its flawless perfection, but saw only a piece of jewelry. It meant nothing to her, and the thought surprised her. She looked up again and met his gaze. "I don't love you, Andrew. At least, not enough to marry you."

He took a step toward her, his eyes narrowed. "What? You're walking out on me now? In the middle of the BankNorth campaign?"

She stared at him, incredulous. "I'm not talking about work here, Andrew. I'm talking about you and me and how a marriage between us would never work. Our backgrounds are miles apart. I don't even think I realized that until today. Did you know that we have never even talked about having children? Or where we want to live when we retire? Gosh, Andrew—we never take a vacation because we never find the time to discuss whether we want to go to the beach or go skiing." Her voice shook. This was probably the most honest conversation she had ever had with him, and she wanted to make sure she got her point across. "There's more to life than work, Andrew. And that's all we've got between us."

She stood, the swing swaying behind her. Her voice quieted. "I've never even met your parents. And that's probably the saddest testament as to why I can't marry you."

She stopped talking, her breath coming hard and deep. Wide-eyed, she waited for his response, half hoping he'd defend himself and call to mind why she had agreed to marry him in the first place.

He leaned closer. "It's that Sam guy, isn't it? Are you sleeping with him?"

Cassie blinked once. Then, without a word, she pulled her arm back and threw the ring at him, hitting him right between the eyes. It landed on the floorboards, bounced once, then came to rest near the welcome mat.

Andrew stared down at it, but didn't make a move to pick it up.

Cassie's anger bubbled up into her head to a point where she thought smoke might emerge from her ears. "You think this has to do with Sam? After everything I've just said, you think I'm breaking our engagement because I'm sleeping with another man?" She shook her head. "You're cracked, Andrew. You're just completely clueless. Seek help—but I won't be there to hold your hand during therapy. Maybe Carolyn Moore would be happy to do it instead."

He looked at her like she had just sprouted horns. Almost under his breath, he said, "I knew better than to let you come down here. These people have changed you."

She felt the reassuring pressure of the porch railing against her back. "It's taken me fifteen years to realize it, but they're *my* people, and I

352

love them. If I've had to change to see that, then so be it." She reached up with her right hand to grasp the gold charms on her necklace.

"Does that mean you're going to stay down here?"

"No!" The response was automatic, emitted without thought. "Of course not. I love my career—I'm good at it, I enjoy my success, and I've worked too hard to leave it all behind. And I hope . . . that we can still work together. That's one thing that I know we do well. Very well, in fact."

He wiped his hands over his face. "Don't do this, Cassandra. We had something great going between us. We just need to get away from here and get back to New York. You'll see things differently then."

Pushing herself away from the railing with a violent jerk, Cassie stepped toward him. "You just don't get it, do you? I *am* seeing things differently for the first time in years." She stared out at her mother's magnolia. "Did you ever play tag as a kid—you know, where there was one place called base where nobody could tag you? Well, you were my base. I clung to you to keep all that hurt and humiliation away from me, knowing that as long as I had you and my career, they could never touch me."

She faced him, feeling the warmth of the fading sun on her cheeks. "I don't need a base anymore. I'm okay with my past. I even feel like I want to

353

visit here often. But I don't want to marry you."

He stood before her, his balled fists on his hips. "Is that it, then? You don't want to marry me?"

She nodded, her voice too tangled with conflicting emotions.

His lips formed a thin line. "Fine. Then I'd better get packing." He turned away from her and yanked open the screen door. "Carolyn Moore needs me at the office."

The screen door slammed, leaving Cassie staring after him. She called out at his retreating back, "You forgot the ring!"

She waited a few seconds before the door swung open again and Andrew reappeared. He got down on his hands and knees, plucked it off the floor, then stood again as he tucked it inside his shirt pocket. "You'll regret this decision, Cassandra. All that fried food has turned your brain to mush. But maybe when you're back in New York and you need somebody intelligent to talk to and straighten you out, call me. I just might be available to talk some sense into you."

He left her on the porch, his footsteps disappearing inside the house.

Weakly, she shouted at him through the door, "And don't call me Cassandra. My name's Cassie!"

She sat back down on the swing and waited for the big, crushing blow of disappointment and sorrow to swallow her. But it never came. A small breeze teased the hair at her temples, and a little smile crept up on her lips. Kicking her shoes out of the way, she jumped down the porch steps and began running, feeling the soft grass under her feet and a freedom she hadn't felt in years. Hiking up her dress, she turned a cartwheel, landing solidly on her backside. Lying in the grass, she looked up at the early evening sky, a hint of stars glowing dully behind the sun's glare, and smiled to herself.

HARRIET SCRAPED THE REMAINS of a potato salad into a large Tupperware bowl and sealed the lid over it, trying not to lean too heavily on the kitchen counter. She knew she'd have to pay for all the energy exerted in getting the shower together, but she didn't regret one single moment. It was like she'd been waiting her whole life to welcome Cassie back home, to remind her sister of where she came from, and who would always love her best. But Harriet's favorite moment of the whole evening had been when Cassie had reappeared to tell everybody about her broken engagement.

Instead of shocked looks of disappointment, Harriet had been surprised to recognize looks of relief on the faces of many of the partygoers. Even Miss Lena had smiled brightly before turning her attention back to the detailed summary of her current novel she'd been delivering to a surprisingly large audience of matrons.

Cassie walked up behind Harriet at the sink and stuck her finger in the remaining salad still left in the serving bowl, then licked it off with childish enthusiasm.

"I saw that."

Startled, both Harriet and Cassie swung around and found Sam standing in the kitchen doorway.

Guiltily, Cassie lowered her hand. "I missed so much of the party—but I refuse to miss any of Mrs. Crandall's potato salad. It might pack one thousand calories per spoonful, but it's worth every one." She took the bowl from Harriet. "I'm taking over from here. You've already done way too much, and I want you to sit down and put your feet up."

Not even having the energy to argue, Harriet squeezed her sister's hand in thanks. She moved to the kitchen table, where Sam had already pulled out a chair for her to sit in, and then he helped lift her legs to rest in another.

Sam leaned against the counter and casually crossed his legs at the ankles. "Where's Andy?"

Cassie let the dirty bowl slide under the warm, soapy water in the sink, keeping her back to Sam. "Last time I saw him, he was packing."

"Leaving so soon?"

She shrugged, squeezing another dollop of dishwashing liquid into the sink. "No reason for him to stay, I guess." She began scrubbing the soggy salad out of the bowl.

"I'm sorry."

She scratched her chin on her shoulder. "No, you're not. You think he's a jerk."

"Yeah, that's true. But I'm sorry if you're hurting."

Harriet saw Cassie's cheeks color, and then her sister ducked her head to hide it. She'd always been afraid of showing her emotions, as if doing so would make her appear weak in the eyes of those who needed her to be strong. Harriet struggled to find the words to tell her sister that she didn't need to be strong for her anymore, that it was okay to show the rest of the world how big her heart really was. But her tongue tripped on the words as she realized that Sam knew it, too, and that if anybody was going to convince Cassie, it would be him.

Cassie lifted the bowl and rinsed it under the tap, finally turning around to face Sam as she stuck the bowl in the dish drain on top of the pile of clean dishes. "Actually, I'm feeling pretty good. It was almost a relief."

"Good. And I know what you mean about relief. I don't know how long I could continue coming up with Southernisms without going to the library for fresh material."

A reluctant smile crept up on Cassie's face. "You were going a little overboard with that stuff. If Andrew wasn't going to deck you one, I certainly was."

Sam smiled back. "Hey. It worked. I'd say you owed me one."

Her smile faded as she looked down at her empty ring finger. "Yeah. I guess so."

He lifted her chin and Harriet leaned her head against the back of the chair and closed her eyes so she could pretend she was sleeping. "I'm sorry your marriage plans didn't work out. But I think you'll find that it wasn't meant to be. You two weren't meant for each other, that's all. You'll find somebody. I know it."

Stepping back, Cassie picked up the dish towel. "I guess you're going to tell me the angelfish story again."

Harriet forgot she was supposed to be sleeping. "What angelfish story?"

With a roll of her eyes that reminded Harriet so much of Maddie, Cassie said, "Sam told me that angelfish mate for life, and that when one dies, the other just stops swimming and sinks to the ocean floor to die."

Harriet's fingers played with the gold band on her left hand, and she remembered the day Joe had put it there. "How beautiful. But how sad. I mean, it makes me think of Daddy. He never remarried after Mama died. And I can't imagine ever marrying anybody else besides Joe. But I'd like to think that there are second chances out there." She looked pointedly at a doubtful Cassie. "Yes, even for Andrew. I don't think anybody was really meant to be alone."

The sliding door leading to the backyard opened,

and Mr. Parker stepped into the kitchen. When he spotted Cassie, he came over to her and put an arm around her shoulders. "I hope your heart's not broken over this, Cassie."

Harriet knew Cassie's heart was far from broken, but Mr. Parker's sympathy nearly brought tears to Cassie's eyes. She sent him a bright smile. "No, I'm fine. Really. As everyone keeps telling me, it's better that it happened now rather than later." She put her arm around Mr. Parker's thick waist and squeezed. "I was hoping you'd let me keep your shower present, though. I could use a homemade ice-cream maker."

He winked at Harriet. "Sure, dear. You go on and keep it. Save me the trouble of getting you something else when you do decide to get married."

Sam coughed. "So, Dad, did you get the car running?"

Mr. Parker pulled out a handkerchief and wiped his forehead. His nail beds were stained dark with fresh grease. "Yep. Just finished. Parked it in front of Cassie's house so he'll have no trouble finding it."

Harriet sat up, taking in the grease and the perspiration still dotting Mr. Parker's forehead. "Wait a minute. Does this mean—"

Cassie interrupted her. "You fixed Andrew's car? Tonight?"

The older man looked sheepish. "I hope you don't take this the wrong way, but after I saw you with your fiancé earlier this evening, I went back to the service station to put in that part I had ordered. I didn't want to be the one responsible for keeping him here one minute longer than necessary."

Cassie's eyes widened as she looked at Harriet, then back at the two men, their matching blue eyes now sparkling with hidden mirth. Harriet let out a laugh, but by the time she'd covered her mouth with her hand, the other three were laughing, too.

Wiping tears from her eyes, Cassie hugged Mr. Parker. "Thanks. You're a lifesaver. I hadn't quite yet figured out how I could face him for the long drive to the airport tomorrow."

He grinned. "Glad I could help." He shoved his handkerchief back in his pocket. "Better go find the missus now, before she tans my hide for skipping out on her when the music started. She'll forgive me, though, when I tell her why." With a wink, he left through the sliding door, closing it gently behind him.

"There goes a very smart man." Sam lifted a stack of dirty paper plates and shoved them deep into the garbage can.

Cassie leaned back, her arms propped on the counter, a teasing grin on her face. "Too bad you're not more like him."

Sam quirked an eyebrow. "You think I should start wearing overalls?"

"Anything but linen pants and silk shirts."

Harriet raised her eyebrows at her sister, knowing she hadn't meant to say that, since it was a little like speaking ill of the dead. She figured Cassie must be scared of something, though, and let it be.

Sam stepped closer to the counter, picked up a clean fork, and stabbed it into Burnelle Thompkins's chocolate bourbon pecan pie. "Did y'all get to try any of this?"

Harriet nodded, feeling a little nauseous. "I had two pieces, then ate what was left on Knoxie's plate. I was happy to finally have an appetite, but I think I overdid it." She rubbed her stomach.

Cassie eyed Sam warily. "Is that what I think it is?"

With a look Harriet could only call seductive, Sam approached with the full fork held aloft. "Ten-time state-fair champion in the pie division and none other. Would you like some?"

She nodded eagerly.

Instead of handing her the fork, he held it in front of her mouth. "Take a bite."

Cassie opened her mouth and bit only half the piece off the fork. As she chewed slowly, Sam put the rest in his mouth, leaving a small crumb on his lower lip.

Harriet half closed her eyes again, wishing she had the energy to get up and leave the two of them alone before it got embarrassing for all three of them.

Cassie's finger and his tongue reached the crumb at the same time and collided, making Cassie jerk her hand back. "Get a room," Harriet muttered, but neither Cassie nor Sam seemed to have heard her.

Sam's voice rumbled in his throat. "Want some more?"

Cassie nodded, yet Sam made no move toward the pie, but just looked at her with an innocent grin.

The door slid open again, and Lucinda, her fuchsia jumpsuit looking a little crumpled, entered the kitchen. She smiled with relief when she spotted Harriet. "Just the people I needed to talk to." She leaned against the glass for a moment as if waiting for the scent of her Saucy perfume to reach them. "Harriet, you're beat—don't try to deny it. I'm going to spend the night here so you can rest in the morning while I get up with the children. Sam, would you mind driving Cassie home?" She smiled expectantly.

"If the lady doesn't mind riding in my truck, I'd be happy to."

Cassie swallowed. "Really, Aunt Lu. I can walk. It's only a few blocks. . . ."

Lucinda shook her head. "It's hotter than Hades out there, and you've got all those leftovers to cart back. Just let Sam take you."

"Absolutely," Harriet said, nodding in agreement and resisting the impulse to high-five

362

her aunt, and relieved beyond measure that she'd get the morning off. She'd been on the verge of asking Joe to get a substitute to teach his Sunday School class, and was glad now that she didn't have to.

Lucinda winked at Cassie. "Great. I'll see you in the morning." The door slid closed behind her.

Avoiding Sam's eyes, Cassie said, "Well. That settles that, I guess. All the dishes are done, so let me go get my purse."

They said their good-byes, and Joe entered the kitchen right after they left.

"Har—I've been looking for you." He looked around the empty kitchen. "Please don't tell me you cleaned all this up by yourself."

She reached out her hand and he took it, the old familiar spark still there. She brought his hand to her mouth and kissed it. "No, Cassie helped." She looked up at her husband. "It's good to have her back, isn't it?"

He knelt in front of her and cupped her face in his hands. "It is." His eyebrows furrowed. "You look exhausted."

She tried to brush his hands away but he wouldn't let her. "I'm fine. It's been a big party, that's all."

"I think you need to go to bed early tonight and sleep as long as you can tomorrow. Lucinda told me that she'd already let you know she's staying." Without warning, he lifted her in his arms, just as he'd done on their wedding night fifteen years before. "There are still a few stragglers outside. I'll tell your good-byes."

"Joe, put me down. I can walk."

He stood and began walking toward the stairs. "I know, but then I wouldn't be able to show you what a strong he-man I still am."

She slapped lightly at his arm before gratefully resting her head against his shoulder as he began to climb the stairs. "I love you, Joe Warner."

He kissed the top of her head. "I love you, too, Harriet," he said as he moved toward the bedroom they'd shared for so many years. She closed her eyes, comforted by the familiar scent of him, and was asleep before her head touched the pillow.

CHAPTER 17

After all the food containers had been stored neatly in the back of the truck, Cassie slid into her seat and waited for Sam to walk around to his side. She blinked hard at the dash. There, staring at her, and propped upright on its cardboard backing, was her old high school picture. The same one that had been in the garbage pile in her father's study. She yanked it off the dash and threw it at Sam as he opened his door.

"What in the hell is that doing there? Are you sadistic or something?"

He leaned down and carefully picked the picture

off the driveway. "What are you talking about? There's not a thing wrong with this picture. I saw you were planning on throwing it away and figured you wouldn't mind me taking it."

His smile almost made Cassie forget her anger. Almost.

"Why would you want that? To put it in your attic to scare the mice away?"

He slid in easily on the leather seat and closed the door. "No. I wanted to show it to Andy. I figured if that didn't make him run, nothing would."

She punched him on the shoulder, trying not to laugh.

He rubbed his shoulder, pretending that it hurt. "Actually, I wanted you to sign it. You promised me our senior year that I could have one of your pictures, and I guess you forgot. Now's my chance. I figured for my patience I could at least get it autographed."

She folded her arms over her chest, trying to remember promising him a picture, and couldn't. She couldn't even remember having had a conversation with him prior to the night of the ill-fated fall formal.

"I'm not signing that thing. It belongs in the garbage." Her chin jutted out.

Sam leaned back in his seat and started the engine. "Fine. I'll just set it up here on my dashboard to keep me company."

Leaning back in her seat, she stared out the open

window up toward the inky sky with its spattering of stars. "Funny, I don't remember asking you for *your* picture." She cringed at the petulant sound of her voice, wondering why she was being so mean.

"You didn't." He glanced over at her. "What's the matter? Feeling scared?"

She noticed she was clutching her necklace and quickly dropped her hand. "Of course not."

But that wasn't true at all. Being near him jangled all the nerves in her body, heating them like eggs sizzling in a frying pan. The sound of his voice alone sent her pulse skipping and humming in her veins. And that was what scared her. He was as much a part of Walton and her past life as the old house. He lived and breathed the place in which he had been born and the place he planned to be buried. But she had long since cut her tethers and was now leading a life she had worked very hard to obtain. The thought of returning to this place was as foreign to her as putting "y'all" back into her vocabulary and going barefoot. No, she wasn't scared. She was petrified.

Sam pulled into the drive and stopped the engine, but didn't move to get out. She faced him in the bright moonlight.

"Andrew's car is gone."

Sam's voice was quiet. "Yeah. I noticed."

He continued to look at her, his breath soft and rhythmic. A firefly, caught inside the cab of the truck, blinked between them.

Cassie smiled crookedly. "Horny bug. Hope he finds himself a date."

Sam's lips turned up. "Is my butt glowing, too?"

She gave a quiet laugh. "Not yet."

When his mouth touched hers, she sighed and allowed herself to be pressed against the back of the seat. She sighed again, tasting him, and thinking that a kiss had never felt this good.

What are you doing, Cassie? She opened her eyes, wondering if she'd said the thought aloud. She pushed away, sliding herself up against the door. "Stop. Please. What were we thinking?"

His eyes glittered from the faint porch light, his voice a low drawl. "I know what I was thinking, and if I were a betting man, I'd say you were thinking the same thing."

She pushed herself harder against the door, the handle digging into her back. "I . . . we can't."

He leaned closer, his lips brushing hers. "Why not? Are you and Andy still engaged?"

Breathless, she only shook her head.

He nibbled on her lower lip. "Do you still have feelings for the man?"

She barely managed two shakes of her head.

"I didn't think so." He pressed his mouth against hers again, and she even enjoyed it in spite of herself. She could have been in the middle of a hurricane but wouldn't have heard a thing for the roaring in her ears. Why was she letting this man affect her so?

She struggled to think clearly, and pulled back. "But I was engaged to the man when I woke up this morning. I don't think I . . ."

Sam raised his head, his breathing hard and heavy. "Now's not the time to be thinking with your head. Feel with your heart for a change."

She eyed him warily. This wasn't fooling around. This was like running with scissors. But her body thrummed at a high pitch just from being this close to him fully dressed. If she didn't have him now, she'd never get him out of her system, and she'd always wonder what it would have been like. Something was thinking for her, but it probably wasn't her heart.

He must have read something in her eyes, because he leaned down closer and touched his lips to hers for a brief, tantalizing moment before unlatching her car door.

With lightning speed, he jumped out of the truck and was helping her out. She had barely made it to a standing position before she found herself pushed against the side of the truck, and they were kissing again. Trying to catch her breath, she pushed away.

They stared at each other for a long moment, breathing heavily, the heat from their bodies rising like steam in the sultry night air. She recognized the need in his eyes, and something else there, too. Blinking slowly, she wondered if the same look was mirrored in her own eyes and prayed that it wasn't. She started to back away but Sam stopped her with his arm, then lifted her until she straddled him, their lips not breaking contact as he walked up the porch stairs and into the foyer. He kicked the door shut behind him with a booted heel, then headed for the stairway.

She stopped him at the foot of the stairs, pulling her mouth away from his and sliding down to stand on the bottom step. "Wait a minute. Where are you going?"

He arched an eyebrow. "To your bedroom." He lifted her and took another step before she slid down again.

"We can't . . . You . . . Gosh, Sam, not in my bedroom. That's like . . . like running naked in church or something."

While she spoke, his hand had moved to her back and slowly slid down the zipper of her dress. "Do you have a better suggestion?" Gentle fingers pushed the dress off her shoulders and helped the delicate fabric slide to the ground. He regarded her red slip. "A slip?"

She watched as his fingers relieved her shoulders of the thin scarlet straps and the slip joined her dress around her ankles. "Old habits die hard."

He lifted her onto the landing and she heard various clothing items being thrown into the hall somewhere behind him. He leaned over her, his hands propping him up. "You're so beautiful." He took a deep breath. "Do you have any idea how long I've waited to see Cassie Madison naked?"

She squirmed under him, wondering why he was wasting so much time talking. "Uh-uh."

"If you can't guess, I'm not going to tell you, because it's too embarrassing." He lowered himself just a little. "Say 'y'all.'"

"What?" She looked at him, incredulous.

"I'm not going any further until I hear you say it." His breathing was strained.

She pushed herself against him, crazy with her need for him. "You're nuts."

He didn't move. "Say it."

"Y'all." She could barely speak.

He slid against her. "Now say 'fried chicken and sweet tea.'"

"Sam, please! Don't make me wait."

He bent his head and kissed her neck, then looked up again. "Say it."

"Fried chicken and sweet tea."

He lowered himself with a long sigh. "That's my good ol' Southern girl. I just had to make sure."

She slapped him on his shoulder before entwining her arms around his neck and pulling him toward her. She needed him now—needed him to fill a void that until tonight she hadn't known existed. This man, this stubborn, know-it-all, good-ol'-boy, too-good-looking-for-his-own-good man completed her in a way she had never felt before. Falling into his arms was like falling home, a return to a place held precious and dear.

As Sam turned his attention to the matter at hand, she allowed herself to gaze out into the foyer. The moonlight spilled inside from the fanlight over the door, painting all with a blue-white light. She looked up at the shadows of the portraits on the wall, the pictures of all the Madisons who had walked up these very stairs for over a century. With a grimace, she closed her eyes, burying her face in Sam's neck, and hoping that Great-great-great-grandfather Madison wasn't watching.

CASSIE AWOKE SLOWLY in the early morning light, tired from lack of sleep but with her mind more at peace than it had been in years. Sometime during the night, Sam had carried her and their clothes to her bedroom, and it had seemed the most natural thing in the world to allow him to lie down next to her. She'd even found the strength to protest when he left her for a short while to move his truck to the back so that, according to Sam, she wouldn't get a "fast" reputation.

The curtains puffed gently into the room, and she gave a languid stretch, feeling the warmth of Sam's body pressed against her back. She thought about all the mornings she had awakened with Andrew. She would be cold and lonely on her side of the bed, and he would be curled up on his, facing away from her.

She turned toward Sam and was surprised to see

371

dark blue eyes studying her intently. Her voice was thick. "Don't you ever sleep?"

He cocked an eyebrow. "Only when I'm not otherwise occupied."

She placed the flat of her palm on his stubbled cheek, and he held it there. "I've never . . ." She stopped, unsure of what she wanted to say, of what she could say.

"I know," he whispered back.

He kissed her softly, his lips warm and inviting.

The front door slammed and the tapping of Lucinda's high heels floated up the stairs. Cassie jerked upright, feeling the heat of a blush envelop her body from head to toe. "Oh, my gosh. She can't find you here!"

Sam sat up, casually leaning back on his elbows. "And why not? Last time I checked, you were an adult."

She slugged him with her pillow. "Put your clothes on. I'm going to try to sneak you out the back door."

He responded by grabbing her around the waist and wrestling her back down to the mattress. The desire to get him out of her bed evaporated. "What are you doing?" she whispered halfheartedly.

"I'm trying to make love to you, but you keep talking and distracting me."

He began to kiss her neck, and she struggled to cling to what little reasoning she still possessed. "But . . . Aunt . . . Lucinda . . ."

Somebody knocked on the bedroom door, and they both froze. "Cassie? Are you awake? I was about to make breakfast and was wondering if you'd like something."

Cassie jumped out of bed, hitting Sam on the head with her knee.

"I'm awake, Aunt Lu. I just need to get dressed and I'll be down in a minute."

"All right. I'll be in the kitchen." Lucinda's heels tapped their way down the hall.

Cassie let out a sigh of relief and was about to collapse back on the bed when she heard Lucinda call back, "Tell Sam he'll have a plate waiting with the eggs over easy, like he likes them." After a short pause, she continued, "And please don't leave your underwear on the coatrack in the foyer, Cassie. It doesn't look nice." The heel tapping continued in the hallway and then down the steps.

Cassie fell back on the bed and folded her arms over her eyes. "I will never be able to look her in the face again."

Sam rolled over her, his body pressing hers into the mattress. "Did you ever stop to think that maybe we were set up? Why do you think Lucinda had me drive you home last night to an empty house?"

Her eyes widened as she thought back on the night before, of how eager Harriet was to agree to have Lucinda stay the night. She closed her eyes again and shook her head. "It's a conspiracy. I can't win." Smiling, she touched his earlobe. "Last night you asked me how long I thought you'd been thinking about seeing me naked. How long has it really been, Sam?"

His eyes darkened and narrowed. "I don't know if I should tell you."

"Why not?" She wished she could call the words back, suddenly sure that she didn't want to hear his answer. "Sam—" Her words were cut short by a sharp rap on the front door, and then, with a jangling of keys, somebody pushed open the door and walked into the foyer downstairs with heavy footsteps.

"Hello? Anybody home?"

Cassie recognized Ed Farrell's voice, and then Lucinda's calling up the back stairs for her to answer the door. She pictured her aunt in the kitchen up to her elbows in pancake batter. "I'd better go see what he wants." She put her feet on the floor, but Sam's hand held her back.

"Don't go." His voice was serious, and she knew he wasn't talking about staying in bed.

With a gentle shake of her head, she pulled away, somewhat relieved to have an excuse to distance herself from him. His hands on her seemed to scramble her brain and she needed her wits about her.

"I'm not going to lie to you, Sam. You knew before we even came into this house last night that whatever happened between us was only temporary. We're two different people. We want very different things in life."

Sam slid from the bed and Cassie tried to keep her eyes off of him as he bent to retrieve his pants and pull them on. He looked at her, his face a mask of restraint. "We're not so different. You're just so busy denying it that you can't see the truth." He slid his shirt over his head.

Her hands shook as she pulled on underclothes, shorts, and a shirt. "How can you say that? You don't even know me—not really." She straightened. "And as for last night . . ." She bit her lip, unable to go on. She had wanted to say it was because she was lonely, but they would both know she was lying.

He approached and stopped directly in front of her. "I have loved you ever since sixth grade, when you put that roach in Susan Benedict's lunch box. Only God knows why, but there has not been a day since that I have not studied you, thought about you, or loved you. I spent hours with your father talking about you in the fifteen years, three months, and eleven days since you left. It's a sickness, I know. But I can't seem to cure myself." Shaking his head, he walked toward the door. "Last night was a mistake. I told you before, it's all or nothing with me. I won't be your warm body for lonely nights."

He pulled open the door, not looking at her. "And don't worry. I'll take the back stairs."

She wanted to say something, but the threat of tears made her mute.

He shut the door gently behind him. She waited a moment, then left to go downstairs.

"Hey, Ed. I'm here. Sorry to make you wait."

Ed looked up, a flush of embarrassment flooding his face. "Gosh, Cassie—I wouldn't have just barged in like that if I thought you were here. Nobody answered the door, so I let myself in." He held out a stack of papers. "I wanted to drop off this stack of fact sheets to leave on the kitchen counter. Lists all the amenities and things that a prospective buyer might be interested in." A stray blob of white shaving cream clung to his chin as he smiled.

Cassie's gaze strayed to the letter box sitting on the hall settee. Scooping it up before Lucinda had a chance to be curious about it, she faced Ed, holding out her hand. "Thanks. I'll put them in the kitchen."

He handed them to her, his gaze catching sight of the box. "That's a beautiful antique letter box, Cassie. Where did you find it?"

"In my attic. It was my daddy's."

Ed nodded, rubbing his jaw. "Was there anything in it?"

She adjusted the bulky box in her arms. "A few letters. Nothing of any value."

"Well, I'm starting a little collection of American antiques and I'd love to have that. Let me know if you're going to get rid of it, because I'd like to call first dibs."

"Sure. I'll let you know."

He turned to go, but faced her again, his brows puckered. "Have you had any more calls from the Roust people?"

"Well, just one besides the original call I told you about. It was their marketing department. Wanted to find out how long it had been on the market and how long I might wait until changing my mind about keeping it residential. I hung up on them."

He smiled, the blob of shaving cream dangling precariously. "Good for you. I guess they're saving their hassling for me."

Cassie grabbed for the knob and held the door open for him. "What do you mean?"

He sighed heavily. "Well, one of my sites was vandalized last night. You know that condo development off of Route 1 where the drive-in movie theater used to be? Somebody came and stole all the bathroom fixtures last night. Just plain ripped them out of the walls. It's gonna set me back at least a month to get them replaced and reinstalled."

"I'm sorry, Ed. And you really think Roust had something to do with it?"

"Not that I'll ever be able to prove it, of course, but who else would want to do that? Well, maybe that Sam Parker. He's as bad as Jim Roust. One wants to destroy the town and the other wants to make sure it remains the armpit of the state." He stepped out onto the porch. "I don't blame you one bit for wanting to leave this one-horse town in your dust. Not one bit."

She leaned back on the doorframe. "I wouldn't exactly call Walton an armpit, Ed. Certainly it's no Manhattan, but it does have its charms."

Frowning, he faced her again. "Are you sure you're not changing your mind about staying here for good?"

The ghost of Sam's touch claimed her, making her skin tingle and her heart thud. Just as quickly, fear gripped her: fear of losing herself, of losing control and everything she had worked so hard for. The only thing she was sure of was that she could never go back to that vulnerable country girl she had once been. "No, I'm not staying—I just couldn't. I mean, there's just not a whole lot here to keep me—well, except for Lucinda, Harriet, and her kids. I'm sure I'll visit, but I'll never live in Walton again."

A congenial smile settled on his face. "Fine. I respect your decision. I just need to get back to work to find you a nice little family to move in here. Anything but having those Roust people in here trying to turn this into a shopping mall." He snorted, stepping heavily down the porch steps. "And if you see Dr. Parker, tell him that I've got two more council members on my side regarding that moratorium. Tell him to just give it up and stick to doctoring, like he's supposed to."

Cassie flushed, wondering if Ed had seen Sam's truck in the backyard. "I'll mention it to him."

He sent her a brief nod. "All right, then. I'll be seeing you. Think I've got another family interested in a showing and I'll bring them by later."

"I probably won't be here, but you know how to get in." He flushed, bringing back Cassie's memory of the skinny boy with the hungry look in his eyes. She stepped toward him and wiped the shaving cream off his chin. Showing it to him, she said, "I didn't think you'd want that there."

His eyes flashed with a mixture of gratitude and something else. "Thanks, Cassie. I appreciate that."

Saying good-bye, she closed the door.

When she went back inside and entered the kitchen, she was just in time to hear the back door slam and then the engine of Sam's truck start up. His barely touched plate sat on the table next to a half-empty cup of coffee. Lucinda stood by the stove, spatula in hand and a worried look on her face. "He said he wasn't that hungry after all. Said he had business in town he needed to see to."

Realizing he must have heard the entire conversation, she went running to the back door, flinging it open. "Sam," she shouted, scrambling down the steps toward him, and spotting all the food containers of the spoiled leftovers from the night before piled on the porch.

He lifted a hand to wave, but didn't stop as he drove past her, the dust from his wheels floating up over her, settling on her like a cloak of shame.

CHAPTER 18

Cassie's alarm clock rang, shrill and urgent, at six thirty Wednesday morning. She hadn't slept much since the night of the shower, her thoughts ricocheting between her feelings for Sam, her precarious job situation, and her worries over selling the house. She had counted enough sheep to fill the house and yard, but still sleep evaded her.

She had finally resorted to pulling the letter box from under her bed and reading until her eyes blurred. Most of the letters were simply written, the words of a young girl in love. Whatever had been between her father and this woman had been love—even if not the same as what her parents had shared. But a love, nevertheless, that had created a child. Feeling weary, but not yet ready to sleep, she pulled the last unread letter from the box.

February 14, 1973

My dearest Harrison,
I know your dear, sweet heart is breaking with mine, and I suppose it's just a part of growing

up. *I hope this is the last time for both of us, but as Daddy says in his preaching, we never know what the good Lord has in store for us.*

I'm not angry with you or with Catherine Anne for what has happened between you. I love you both dearly, and I can easily see why you both feel the way you do. And I had no intention of making my predicament stand between you two. You asked me to marry you, and it would be the greatest honor of my life to be your wife. But it is not to be. I will not be the one responsible for making your life one of "what-ifs." You love another, and I am setting you free.

I'm telling Daddy and Mama tonight, but I won't mention your name. They might guess, but I will never give up our secret. Your future children will be grateful for this.

I'm sure I will be sent away, but I'm all right with this. And please don't call me a saint— because you know well and true that I am not. I've prayed a lot about this, and no matter how painful it is, I know I'm making the right decision for all of us.

Love,
E

P.S. I'm returning the beautiful locket. Keep it safe, for it holds all my love for you inside.

Cassie's eyes stung as she picked up the envelope and turned it over. A thin gold chain with a small heart locket emptied into her hand, puddling in her palm. She turned the locket over to examine it more closely and spotted two sets of initials: HM and EL.

With a rush of excitement, Cassie slid from the bed and put the locket on her dresser. She'd discreetly ask around to find out whom the initials belonged to. And then, maybe, find her father's first love. She crawled back under the covers, shivering. Sam was right. It was like quicksand. If she wasn't careful, just a few more steps and she would be swallowed completely.

With a deep yawn, she turned her head into the pillow, jerking back suddenly as she recognized Sam's scent. No one was looking, so she buried her nose in it, taking a deep breath.

The last time she'd seen him had been at church the previous Sunday and it had been a lesson in torture. Just about every member of the congregation at First United Methodist had taken turns patting her arm and offering condolences over her broken engagement. That would have been fine if their sentiments hadn't been followed by broad hinting about Sam.

The man in question had done everything he could to remain aloof. He had been a portrait of politeness, but no teasing, no twinkling eyes or winks in her direction. She almost wanted him to make some comment on her behavior or appearance, even if it was mean and nasty, just so she could know that he was thinking about her. Not that it mattered. Things were best this way— and far less complicated.

She had sighed with relief when he walked past their pew with just a wave in her direction. The empty seat next to her had gone unnoticed, thank goodness. Until the tenacity of the Sedgewick twins made its presence known. With matching pillbox hats and white gloves, they had each taken one of Sam's arms and led him to sit next to Cassie, chatting the whole time as if to keep him from noticing what they were doing.

Beyond a polite "good morning," the only time she heard his voice was during the hymns, when he broke forth with a surprisingly strong tenor. When they sat down, their legs had accidentally touched, and he unobtrusively placed a hymnal on the pew between them.

Cassie had caught Harriet's gaze, and her sister's green eyes were full of concern. The fleeting memory of Harriet's face, staring up at Joe during a picnic following high school graduation, fluttered through her mind. As Harriet had shifted her gaze and seen Cassie, standing at the dessert table with a lemon bar halfway to her mouth, Harriet had worn the same expression. Whether it was concern or pity, Cassie didn't know. Lowering her eyes, she had spent the entire service staring at the notes and words inside the hymnal, not seeing them, but acutely aware of Sam's presence next to her.

The man would not leave her alone. Thoughts of him had chased her into sleep, then accompanied her dreams so that, once again, she felt as if they had spent the night together. With a heavy sigh, she struggled out of the pillow's depth and climbed out of bed.

Before her feet had even touched the ground, Harriet's cell phone rang. Harriet had let Cassie keep it for the time being to see if anybody would call about the classified ad, and because Harriet refused to use it. Cassie picked it up, her palm sweaty.

"Hello?"

She heard breathing on the other end of the phone, but nothing else.

"Hello?" she asked again. "Who is this?"

A distinctive click on the other line answered her.

Lowering the phone, she looked at the incoming number on the screen. It was a local number, but not one she recognized. Jotting it down, she put the phone on the night table, leaving it there in case whoever it was called back.

She looked at the paper in her hand, then folded it in half. She should get on the Internet and do a reverse search to find out whom the number belonged to, but that could wait for later. The image of quicksand again came to mind, making her drop the folded paper on the table.

Cassie sighed. Harriet's appointment was at eight, and she needed a run first to clear her head. Hugging the large stuffed pink elephant, she pulled the curtain at her window aside and peered out. Her mother's roses drooped in the heavy humidity, the sky thick with gray clouds and the scent of rain. A perfect day to fit her mood. She had every intention of finishing up the attic today, with no time allotment for old memories. She had to move on. Her hard-earned career lay in shambles, her relationship with her boss iffy at best. Yes, her stay in Walton had been long enough, and it was time to start making plans for a return to New York.

THE SMELL OF Saucy perfume hung heavily inside Lucinda's car. Cassie blasted the air-conditioning full-force and then cranked all the windows down to air it out. It was bad enough driving a pink car, but to smell like it was adding insult to injury. Grimacing at her thoughts, she noticed her hand fingering the charms around her neck. *What are you scared of, Cassie? It's only a checkup. Everything will be fine.*

Harriet opened the front door of her house before Cassie could ring the bell. Her blond hair was worn straight and tucked behind her ears like a teenager. Her gingham cotton sundress flapped like a shapeless tent over Harriet's body, but Cassie noticed a roundness to her arms and face that she hadn't noticed before. Cassie had to remember that her sister had gone through five pregnancies, and a softening of the figure was inevitable.

Harriet raised her fingers to her lips. "Shhh. The children are still sleeping. School starts soon and I want them to sleep in as much as possible."

Cassie nodded and led the way to the car and slid into the driver's seat. She waited for Harriet to open her door. After watching her sister struggle with it, Cassie reached across the seat and pushed it open from the inside.

"You need to start pumping some iron, Har. You're not getting any younger."

The fatigue in her sister's smile made Cassie want to call back her words. Silently, she put the car in reverse and backed out of the driveway.

"Joe wanted to come with me today, but I told him no. It's just a checkup. It would be silly to get up early on summer vacation for that." She worried her bottom lip.

Cassie frowned as she pulled onto the road but kept silent. They drove past Miss Lena's house and they both waved as they spotted the old woman on her porch. She wore a bright pink sweater over her housedress in spite of the heat, and the ubiquitous romance novel lay open on her lap. She waved and smiled as they passed, then

386

bent her head back to reading. Ed Farrell, shirtless, but wearing a red bandanna around his forehead and dark socks with his sneakers, pushed a lawn mower around Miss Lena's front lawn but didn't look up.

Harriet leaned back in her seat. "Do you think that'll be us when we're old and gray? Sitting out on the porch wearing sensible shoes and our stockings rolled down to our ankles and reading sex scenes to each other all day?"

Cassie laughed. "I hope so. It seems to me that Miss Lena's got a pretty good deal going." Her smile faded slowly as she drove, as she thought of their mother, and her own mortality, and what a blessing it was to be allowed to grow old. She pulled into a parking spot but stopped halfway with a start. The idea of sitting on a large porch with her stockings around her ankles and waving at passersby suddenly sounded amazingly appealing and like something to aspire to. Certainly more so than working herself into a heart attack and dropping dead at her desk at an early age. She shook herself mentally and finished parking the car.

Cassie helped her sister out and pushed open the glass door of the clinic. The waiting room was empty except for a large woman sitting against the wall and knitting. Cinnamon potpourri saturated the air, giving the space a warm, inviting air along with the cozy gingham curtains and matching upholstery. An empty reception desk filled one corner of the room, a box of lollipops propped on a corner.

The woman put aside her knitting and stood slowly, a wide grin splitting her face. "Cassie Madison—I heard you were in town."

Cassie allowed herself to be enveloped in a bear hug and then held out for scrutiny.

"My, my—you're as pretty as a picture. You look just like your precious mama, God rest her soul." Her dark eyes warmed. "You don't remember me, do you?"

Cassie smiled. "Of course I do, Mrs. Perkins." She held her hair back from her forehead. "My scar's almost gone, but I still remember you bundling me into your car and driving me to the hospital."

Mrs. Perkins's smile widened, allowing a gold tooth to shine through. "I'd never heard such caterwauling in all my days. You learned your lesson, though, didn't you? You played pranks after that but you never tried to climb on the courthouse roof again, no sirree."

Cassie smiled, feeling the warmth that emanated from this gentle spirit. Camellia Perkins had worked for her mother as a housekeeper, but she'd always been treated as more of a friend of the family. She had stayed on, taking care of the girls, after their mother had died, until Aunt Lucinda had moved in with them. Her soft bosom had absorbed many a tear from the Madison sisters.

Harriet gave the older woman a hug. "Good to see you again, Mrs. Perkins. I missed your birthday last month, and I've been meaning to mail a present to you. If I'd known you'd be back in town visiting, I would have brought it over. How long are you here for?"

Mrs. Perkins put her hand on Harriet's cheek. "You are always so sweet. You don't need to bring me nothing. Just stop by for a visit and that will be a treat enough. I'll be here for another week. I'm watching my grandbabies while their parents take a second honeymoon. Lord knows they need it!" She winked at Harriet, as if to show a camaraderie between mothers.

Harriet smiled. "Now, why are you here? You aren't sick, are you?"

Mrs. Perkins gave a deep, rich laugh, a sound like hot melted tar on summer asphalt. "No—I'm as healthy as a horse. I'm here with Patricia, my oldest granddaughter. She's getting her stitches out. What about you, dear? You look tired."

Harriet looked away, greeting Mary Janc as she walked into the waiting room. Mary Jane said hello to Cassic, then turned back to Harriet. "Sam's ready for you. Come on back with me."

Cassie touched her sister's arm. "Do you want me to come with you?"

"No, you can stay here and get reacquainted with Mrs. Perkins. I won't be long." She flashed a

389

bright smile, then disappeared behind the door with Mary Jane.

She sat down next to Mrs. Perkins, feeling restless. The older lady turned to her. "Is she sick?"

Cassie plucked at her skirt. "She's just tired. Sam's going to do some tests and I guess prescribe her some vitamins to perk her up."

Mrs. Perkins nodded, satisfied. "I just can't get over how much you look like your mama. I'd think you were her if I hadn't seen that sweet woman in her coffin with my very own eyes."

Cassie looked down at her hands.

Mrs. Perkins leaned closer. "Your mama was such a sweet lady to work for. So kind and gentle. Always had a nice word to say to everybody. I was with her when you came into this world, you know."

Cassie looked up, surprised. "I didn't know that." Lucinda had told her about the circumstances of her birth, but this was new.

The large woman leaned back, resting her knitting on her ample lap. "You've always been impatient—I remember you as a little child. But it started when you were born. I was helping your mama clean her silver and her water broke just like that—no warning or nothing. Thank goodness your aunt Lucinda was there. I left her with your mama and I ran as fast as I could to old Dr. Williams." She gave Cassie a gold-toothed smile. "I wasn't so big then and I could run fast."

A faraway look drifted across her face. "You were born right there on the dining room floor in the middle of your mama's wedding silver. We'd barely got you wrapped up and your mama on the parlor couch when your daddy came in for lunch. We'd been so busy getting you born that we'd forgotten all about him." She chuckled, then frowned. "My memory's getting fuzzy now, but I'll never forget what the judge said the first time he held you. It was just so peculiar."

Cassie straightened, her attention captured. "What did he say?"

Mrs. Perkins took a deep breath. "Well, he marveled over how pretty you were, of course. And then he said something like how he was going to spoil you something fierce, because he'd never know if his firstborn was being spoiled or not."

Cassie felt the air leave her lungs. "His firstborn? But I was the oldest."

Mrs. Perkins slapped her hands on her knees. "As sure as I'm sitting here, that's what he said. All of us there just sort of passed it off as new father's shock. We honestly didn't think he was in his right mind." A soft look came over her face as she regarded Cassie. "But, oh, how he loved you. I never seen a man make such a fuss over a baby before. You'd think you were the first baby ever born."

The door opened and Mrs. Perkins's granddaughter walked into the waiting room.

After a quick introduction, Mrs. Perkins hugged Cassie again and then left.

Cassie tried flipping through the magazines on the table, but couldn't concentrate. Mrs. Perkins's words kept echoing in her mind, as did the image of her and Harriet as old ladies wearing fluffy pink sweaters in the summertime.

The hands of the clock pushed across its face with each lethargic tick as Cassie paced the room. Her anxiety over Harriet mixed with her eagerness to share her news about the locket's initials and the possibility of a sibling. But her father's firstborn had died—isn't that what Miss E's letter had said? *Unless he or she hadn't.* Thunder rolled lazily in the distance, the room darkening by a degree.

The door handle rattled and Cassie spun around, her words drying in her mouth. Harriet's face radiated a quiet peace, an acceptance, and it chilled Cassie to the bone.

Cassie stepped toward her. "How did it . . . ?"

Harriet held her finger to her lips. "I need to be alone. I need time to think before I see Joe."

Cassie opened her mouth to say something but stopped as Sam followed Harriet into the waiting room.

Harriet continued. "I've asked Sam to talk to you now. He has my permission to tell you . . . everything. I . . ." Her voice trailed away. "Tell Joe I had to run some errands and I'll be home soon."

"Har, it's starting to rain. Let me drive you home. We can talk in the car."

Harriet shook her head and pushed open the door leading to the outside. Cassie walked toward her but Sam pulled her back. "Let her go," he said, his voice dry. He grabbed a large black umbrella in a stand by the door and handed it to Harriet as she walked out into the parking lot.

Cassie pushed away, intent on following her sister out the door. The first drops of rain began to darken the asphalt as she reached the parking lot and watched Harriet run down the sidewalk as if her life depended on reaching her destination.

She felt Sam's presence behind her, and waited for his touch. When it didn't come, she turned around to face him. "Are you going to tell me?" Something in his eyes made her step away. "What's wrong with my sister?"

"She's pregnant." The words fell flat, his voice carrying more meaning than the simple words.

Her relief was short-lived when she noticed his serious expression hadn't changed. "That's good, right?"

He shook his head. "In this case, not necessarily."

She touched his arm, then let it drop. "Tell me straight, Sam. Harriet said she wanted you to tell me everything, and I can take it. Don't give me any wishy-washy drivel. I can take the cold, hard facts." She stuck out her chin and forced it to stop trembling.

He regarded her closely. "All right, then." His eyes softened. "Harriet also has breast cancer. I know because I've just reviewed the results of the biopsy with her."

Cassie blinked. "Biopsy? What biopsy?"

The rain fell in a steady drizzle now, but neither of them moved. "Last week when Harriet went to Atlanta to get a few things for the party and refused company—she actually went to an appointment to have a biopsy done. I drove her myself. We'll need more tests to see if the cancer's spread." He wiped his rain-dampened hair off his forehead. "I'm sorry."

Her first impulse was to turn around and run as far away as she could. She even managed to take a step away from him, before she jerked around to face him again. "Biopsy? Last week? And you didn't tell me? My sister has breast cancer and you didn't think I should be told?"

Sam slowly shook his head as the rain plastered his white coat to his shirt. "You know I couldn't. My professional relationship with Harriet is strictly confidential. I'm sorry."

She slapped both palms against his chest, the sound sharp against the pattering of the rain. "My sister has cancer and you're sorry? You should have told me—you know you should have told me." She started to cry and was glad for the raindrops gliding down her face.

He placed his own hands firmly over hers,

keeping her close to him. "I am sorry, Cassie. It was Harriet's choice not to tell anybody until she knew for sure. Not even Joe knows. She . . . she wanted to decide for herself about the baby."

Jerking away from him, Cassie stumbled on the wet pavement. "The baby? Oh, God." She looked up at him, blinking at the raindrops, seeing things as if through a microscope. "She's going to try to save the baby first, isn't she?"

Sam hesitated for a moment, then nodded.

Cassie shivered, feeling cold all of a sudden. "How far along is the pregnancy?"

"Four months—almost five."

Cassie stared at her feet, at her neon green–painted toenails, and let her peripheral vision fade. "The baby will make treatment for her more difficult, won't it?"

He didn't pause. "Yes. It will. But we won't really know for sure until we know whether the cancer has spread."

Cassie looked at him square in the face, all of the fight in her gone. "Is my sister going to die, Sam?"

He reached out to touch her, but stopped midway. He slid his hand into a back pocket instead. "I don't know. Cases exist where both mother and child have survived, but again, it depends on what stage the cancer has progressed to. When I'm in Atlanta I'll be making appointments for her with the best people in the field. If there are treatments that will help her but won't harm the baby, we'll find them. But I won't lie to you. This will be difficult."

The wind picked up, whipping her hair across her face. "Harriet's always a mother first, isn't she?"

Sam nodded, his eyes dark. "She had a good example."

Cassie bit down hard, stilling her chattering teeth. "She hardly knew our mother."

"That's not who I was referring to. Despite your best efforts, your nurturing side still shows." He sent her a crooked smile.

Cassie took a deep breath and turned away. The rain had stopped, but the sky draped low, dark clouds over the summer-scorched earth.

"I'm not going to tell you to be strong, Cassie. You're strong enough for all of us. But I do want to tell you that it's okay to cry—that it's okay to ask for help or a shoulder to lean on. There're plenty of people in town who would be happy to have the honor."

She stuck out her chin and grabbed hold of the charms around her neck. Thunder growled in the distance, vibrating the ground.

He shoved his fingers deep into his lab coat pockets. "And I'm sorry if you think that relying on me or anybody else will make you unwillingly form attachments to us. But I'm here if you need me. As a friend, and nothing more, if that's what you want."

She searched her purse for her car keys. "I need to get going. A storm's coming."

Sam stood in front of her and gently lifted her chin. "It is. Just remember to take shelter when it starts to pour."

Pulling away, she headed toward Lucinda's car. The tall oaks swayed with the wind, shaking loose their acorns. Fading hydrangea blossoms edging the walkway bent over double, their large, withered heads dipped in sorrow.

"You know where to find me." The wind carried Sam's voice to her and she stopped. She wanted to rush to him, to have him hold her. She wanted to feel his heartbeat against her ear, to know his understanding. She faced him again and watched as the wind pelted his white coat and blew his hair into small tufts. But she could not take what she was not able to give.

Forcibly, she turned toward the car again. Thunder rumbled overhead as a large gust pushed at her, drying her eyes and bringing with it the promise of rain.

MADDIE FINISHED TWISTING the rope of the tire swing and picked her bare feet off the ground, not caring that she was flicking all the droplets off the tree's leaves and soaking her hair and clothes. Because it didn't matter. Nothing really mattered anymore. Lucy Spafford and Kevin O'Neal were going out, and Maddie couldn't help but wonder if her Aunt Cassie had felt the same way when her daddy ran away with her mama.

She watched as her daddy came out the front door of the house with baby Amanda on his hip, a worried expression on his face. "Have you seen your mama? Aunt Cassie called and said Mama was running a few errands, but she should be back by now. I wish she'd carry her danged cell phone." Amanda's dirty diaper drooped, and as her daddy got nearer, Maddie could smell it, too.

Maddie shook her head, not wanting to say anything she shouldn't. She was wondering when everybody was going to guess her mama's secret or if and when her mama was going to just tell everybody. They'd all know the truth soon, anyway. It was gross, really, thinking that her parents . . . Well, she didn't want to go there. But wasn't five children enough? They were old, for crying out loud, and Maddie was fourteen—way too old to have a baby brother or sister, much less two of them.

"Where'd she go?" Maddie asked, although she knew. She'd seen her mama go through four pregnancies, so it hadn't been that hard to figure it out.

"To see Dr. Parker for a checkup. Your mama's been feeling poorly lately, and needed some kind of supervitamins or something. Dr. Parker thought he could help."

Maddie leaned back on the swing, looking up at

the patterns of wet leaves against the gray sky. "I haven't seen her. Maybe you should call Aunt Cassie."

"I did. She's not answering her cell."

Maddie used a foot to push off the ground, moving the swing side to side. "They probably decided to stop and have lunch at the Dixie Diner and get out of the rain. And you know how Mrs. Thompkins doesn't like you to talk on the phone when you're eating."

Her daddy smiled, erasing some of the worry lines on his forehead. "Yeah, you're probably right." He looked at her closely. "What are you doing out here? It's pretty wet."

She rolled her eyes. "Just thinking."

"About Kevin O'Neal?"

She frowned.

"Football practice starts next week. I could make him run fifty laps around the field if you like."

She shook her head, although she wasn't sure if that wasn't a great idea after all. "That's all right. But maybe I can go back to New York with Aunt Cassie when she goes."

Her daddy was silent for a moment. "We'd miss you something fierce, Maddie. Especially your mama. I don't think she could stand to have both you and Aunt Cassie so far away from her."

Maddie snorted. "She's so busy with the little kids that I'm sure she wouldn't even know I was gone— except when she needed a babysitter."

Amanda gurgled and reached for her older sister, but her daddy switched her to his other hip instead. "You know that's not true, Maddie. Your mother loves you very much. You were our only child for five years, until Sarah Frances. And you remind your mama of your Aunt Cassie."

Maddie frowned again, not sure if that was a good or bad thing. "Do you think Aunt Cassie will stay here in Walton?"

He shrugged, jostling a drowsy Amanda. "I don't know. She's always been pretty independent and makes her own decisions. She'll do what she thinks is best."

Maddie looked up at the dripping leaves again. "But what if what she thinks is best isn't the best for everybody else?"

Amanda's head fell on her daddy's shoulders and Maddie saw that she'd fallen asleep.

Her daddy spoke quietly. "Life's full of decisions like that, and there's no book of rules that tells you how to play. You make the best decision you can at the time, and deal with the rest."

"Like you eloping with Mama?"

Her daddy gave her a hard look. "Something like that."

Maddie looked down at her bare toes in the grass, the neon green nail polish almost glowing in the cloudy light. "Granddaddy once told me that all of life wasn't like brain surgery, that not every mistake was fatal. I guess that's what he was talking about, wasn't it?"

He smiled. "Your granddaddy was a very smart man."

Sarah Frances opened the screen door and yelled out, "Daddy! Joey's putting boogers in his milk again!"

Hoisting Amanda one more time, he said, "I'd better get inside, and you, too, if you want some lunch. I expect your mama will be home soon."

She nodded, then remembered one last question. "Did Aunt Cassie play a lot of practical jokes on people when she was younger?"

"Boy howdy, yes, she did. There wasn't a bug or manure pile or nest or anything, really, that she was afraid to touch and put where it didn't belong. And that's just for starters. I have no intention of telling you anything else because I'm afraid I'll give you ideas." His eyes narrowed. "Why are you asking?"

She smiled sweetly. "No reason. Just wondering."

He looked as if he didn't believe her. "Well, Aunt Cassie did those things because she thought she needed the attention. But you get plenty enough, so you shouldn't have the need to put anything on the school roof or paint anybody's porch pink, okay?"

Maddie stared at him blankly, wondering how after fourteen years he still didn't know her that well at all.

"Daddy!" Sarah Frances screamed. "Now he's putting them on Knoxie!"

He began walking back to the house. "Come on back inside, Maddie. It looks like it's going to rain again."

"In a minute." Maddie stayed where she was and began twisting the tire swing as tight as it would go, then lifted her feet, sending her and the swing unwinding quickly, the leaves and the limbs and the gray sky above seeming to twist out of control while she stayed absolutely still.

CHAPTER 19

Cassie sped down the street, not seeing anything but the blurry pink of the car's hood. She blinked, clearing her eyes temporarily. The windshield wipers beat a rhythm: *Harriet is sick Harriet is sick Harriet is sick.* Desperate for a distraction, she flipped on the radio to Garth Brooks singing about friends in low places. She sang along for a few bars before switching it off in irritation. *Since when do I know all the lyrics from a Garth Brooks song?*

She sat in a parking space in front of the town square for a long time, hoping she'd eventually spot Harriet. When the rain became hard enough to obscure her vision, she started the car again and slowly drove through the downtown area. She was barely aware of where she was heading until she swerved the car into her sister's driveway. Not wanting to wait while she searched for an umbrella under the seat, she opened the door and ran to the porch. She pushed on the doorbell again and again until she heard footsteps approach.

Joe opened the door and greeted her with a smile that quickly changed to a worried expression. "Where's Harriet? I thought she was with you." Amanda cried inconsolably in the background.

Cassie forced herself to remain calm and pasted a smile on her face. "She had another errand to run. I was hoping she'd be back by now."

He shook his head, opening the door wider for her to come inside. "No, I haven't seen her since she left with you this morning." He shut the door as Amanda cried louder in the background.

Cassie looked past his shoulder into the hallway. "Do you need to see about the baby?"

He swiped a hand through his hair. "Um, yeah. I was just feeding her when the doorbell rang. Come on back."

Cassie followed him into the kitchen. Amanda sat in the high chair, with an upended bowl on the tray and baby cereal covering most of her hair and the floor beside her.

Joe surveyed the mess with a sad shake of his head. "I hope Harriet gets back soon. She's a lot better at this stuff than me."

The television blared from the family room, and Cassie peeked inside. The three youngest Warner children lounged around the room although it was almost noon, still wearing their pajamas. Cereal boxes, bowls with milk and spoons stuck in them, and various toys were strewn from one end of the room to the other. She turned back to Joe and forced a smile. "Hey, why don't you take the kids upstairs to get dressed and then straighten the family room, and I'll finish feeding Amanda and get her cleaned up." She glanced over at the baby, who was now making a face rub out of the cereal. "Harriet's probably on her way back."

Stricken, Joe's eyes went wide. "She'll have my hide. I'd better hustle, then. Thanks, Cassie—you're a peach." He hurried into the family room as Cassie surveyed the kitchen for the best plan of attack.

Thirty minutes later, trying to hide her impatience, she handed the fed and cleaned baby to her father. "I guess I should get going. Please have Harriet call me when she gets back."

Cassie stepped out onto the small porch, letting Joe catch the door before it swung shut. "I will. And thanks for the help. You probably saved my marriage."

He smiled affably, but Cassie had to look away. "See you later," she said, before returning to Lucinda's car and starting the engine, the tires squealing as she pealed out onto the road.

She didn't have to think about where she was going. The comforting and familiar scent of

404

mothballs and old cedar in the attic in the big house called to her. It had once been a place of sanctuary and refuge and Cassie figured that if Harriet ever needed such a place, it was now.

The rain slowed to a steady drizzle as she urged the car under the drooping oaks leading to the house. She spotted Aunt Lucinda immediately, hands clutching a fuchsia umbrella with ruffles, staring up at one of the trees. Lucinda wore a bright yellow jogging suit and matching athletic shoes, making Cassie smile. Trying to keep her girlish figure, Lucinda had taken up power walking. She still did her hair and wore full makeup before venturing outside, but it met with Cassie's approval. Slowing the car, Cassie rolled down the window.

"What's wrong with the tree?"

Lucinda faced her, a frown puckering her penciled eyebrows, her mascara smudged under her eyes from the rain. "Somebody's been stripping the bark off these old trees. Look." She indicated the bottom twelve inches of the tree trunk, where somebody had neatly shaved off the bark. Thick tree sap wept over the naked wood.

"Are they all like that?"

Lucinda nodded. "As far as I can tell." She leaned in the window, peering closely at Cassie. "You here to talk to Harriet? She's up at the house, waiting for you. Said she's had a good long think but wouldn't tell me a thing until she'd talked to you." Straightening, she slapped the side of the car, her metal rings making a pinging noise. "You go on and see about your sister. I'll see what sort of damage has been done to these oaks."

Cassie waved, then rolled up the window and drove to the front of the house. She ran up the stairs, taking them two at a time, until she reached the attic.

HARRIET STOOD IN front of a cracked cheval mirror, holding up the white satin-and-lace gown in front of her, and trying not to let her wet clothes touch it. She caught Cassie's reflection as she emerged at the top of the stairs and smiled.

"It's Mama's wedding gown, remember? I always thought I'd wear it when I got married." She sighed, lowering the dress. "At least you'll be able to."

Cassie tried to smile, but failed miserably. "Don't hold your breath on that one. I think I've screwed up things royally on all sides. Guess I'll just be an old maid like Miss Lena. Maybe she'll even let me move in with her."

Harriet smoothed the satin with her palm. "Promise me that you'll remind Maddie that this dress is here and hers to wear. She's so stubborn sometimes, but I think she'll listen to you. She looks up to you, you know."

Cassie swallowed. "Why don't you just tell her yourself?"

Without answering, Harriet gently laid the wedding dress back into the open trunk. Kneeling slowly, she began tucking yellowed tissue paper around the white gown. Cassie joined her as Harriet focused on placing the paper between the delicate folds of satin, each tuck and flip of the fabric like a gentle reassurance from their mother.

Harriet sat back on her heels, staring out toward the small window, where a new wave of rain was now forcing itself against the glass in sheets. The sound of a car door shutting drifted toward them. "Poor Joe, he doesn't even know where I keep the Christmas decorations. I don't know how he's going to manage."

"Stop talking like that, Har. You're scaring me."

Moving to a sitting position, Harriet leaned against the chest and breathed deeply. "Sorry. It's just that you've always been so strong. When we were girls, you were the one sticking your head under the bed to prove to me there weren't any bogeymen lying in wait." She closed her eyes, her hands resting on her abdomen, thinking of the baby inside. "I remember after Mama died, and you'd let me crawl into your bed because I was too scared to sleep alone. You told me there was nothing to be afraid of because Mama sent angels to watch over us." Harriet opened her eyes to look at her sister, a small smile crossing her lips. "You said you knew it was true because of my dimple. You told me that before I was born an angel kissed my cheek and left her mark, so you knew they were real. And now Mama was up in heaven to help watch over us when the angels had to go to sleep." Harriet sighed deeply. "I was never scared after that."

Cassie looked away, and when she spoke her voice was quiet. "The only reason I wasn't scared was because I believed it, too."

Harriet reached for Cassie's hand and held it. "You were a good big sister. You didn't deserve all the pain and hurt you suffered because of me. If it makes you feel any better, I was so jealous of you when you moved to New York."

Cassie wiped her eyes with her free hand and regarded her sister. "You jealous of me. Now there's a concept. You had everything you wanted right here. What could there possibly have been in New York for you to envy?"

"Snow. I've always wanted to see snow. I guess I'll probably die before ever getting to see the white stuff."

Dropping Harriet's hand, Cassie scrambled to stand. "Don't say that. It's bad karma and all that." She walked toward the window and stared out at the gray sky. "You're pregnant and they've found a few cancer cells. That's all we know right now, and that's all I'm considering." She turned around. "And what could you have been thinking, getting pregnant so soon after Amanda? Haven't you ever heard of birth control?"

Harriet pushed the dark thoughts away and regarded her sister from beneath lowered brows. "Honey, as a single woman I'm sure you don't know much about the baby-making business, but believe me, thinking has very little to do with it."

Despite the tears on her face, Cassie laughed out loud. "Please stop. I'm getting mental images and I just don't want to go there."

Harriet laughed, wanting to freeze this moment in time, stop its progression. The musty smell of the attic, the discarded remnants of their childhood strewn about in boxes and trunks, and laughter and confidences shared with her sister. They all combined to form a savory stew of memories, like the recollection of a long-ago Christmas.

Cassie picked up a tiny wooden cradle from the ancient dollhouse, forgotten in its dark corner of the attic. Its windows appeared as sightless eyes, watching the big people play at real life. She didn't lift her eyes from the small toy when she spoke. "I know you haven't told Joe about the baby. You know, it's not too late. . . ."

Harriet interrupted her with the slamming of the trunk lid. "Don't, Cassie. Don't even say it. Terminating this pregnancy isn't an option. Maybe it's hard for you to understand that because you're not a mother yet yourself."

Cassie dropped the tiny cradle, letting it hit the roof of the dollhouse. Her voice rose as it always had with anything that she couldn't control. "Not understand? No, you're wrong. You're the one who can't understand. You were too little to remember what it was like watching Mama die, and then being left to take care of a younger sister. Maybe I understand a little too much."

Harriet stared at her sister for a long moment, then struggled to stand. "I'm sorry, Cassie. I never knew how much of a burden I was for you. But I could never deliberately sacrifice one of my children, and no, you wouldn't understand that, because you've never been a mother. You've never heard the heartbeat of a child growing inside you, right under your heart. I could no more kill this baby than I could kill one of my older children." Her chest rose and fell with exertion as she leaned heavily against a stack of boxes, her heart hurting more than her body. She knew she'd have to have this argument again and again, but more than anyone, she needed her sister to understand.

Cassie took a deep breath, trying unsuccessfully to calm down and lower her voice. "I don't believe in terminating pregnancies any more than you do, and I've never even been pregnant. But give me a little credit here, Har. I don't have an MBA for nothing. You have to look at the pros and cons. Your existing five children need you—especially Maddie. Look at her—my God, she reminds me so much of me at that age it hurts. She needs a mother badly." Tears fell down her cheeks freely now, and she angrily wiped them away. "And what about

410

Amanda? Do you want her to remember you only from wrinkled photos Joe pulls out of his wallet?" She threw her hands in the air. "I don't understand you. You're making this decision with the same shoot-from-the-hip decision-making process you used when you eloped with Joe. You never seem to think about what's going to happen to those you leave behind."

Harriet crumpled onto the top of the closed trunk, feeling defeated, and unsure she could even defend herself. "That's not fair. I was just a teenager then, and it wasn't a life-or-death situation, either."

Cassie kicked a Raggedy Ann doll on the floor, sending it flying into the wall with a slight thud. "No, I guess it wouldn't have been life or death for you then. I was the only one who wanted to die after you married Joe."

Harriet stopped breathing for a moment, relieved yet terrified that Cassie had finally put her hurt into words. She knew Cassie hadn't meant to wound her, especially now, but old hurts died slow and hard, and the fear Cassie felt for her sister pulled out ugly thoughts from the darkest place inside.

Harriet swallowed, trying to find the right words. "If I haven't said it enough, I'm sorry. I really, really am. But I'm not sorry for marrying Joe. I make all my decisions from the heart, and I can't say I regret a single one. But I am truly sorry for hurting you and for being at least partly responsible for the mess your life is in right now. But you're a big girl, Cassie. And I think it's time somebody filled you in on a few things you've been missing." With a shuddering breath, she fixed her sister with a steady gaze. "Since Mama and Daddy aren't here to do it, I guess it's my job, so here goes. You've got this wonderful thing happening between you and Sam staring you in the face, but you refuse to acknowledge it because you've got it in your head that you're not sticking around here long enough to get involved with anything or anybody."

Harriet held up her hand, fending off her sister's objections. "Whether you know it or not, you're too stubborn to admit that maybe you need people in your life who know you well but love you anyway. Or that Walton really can be a great place to live—with the people who love you, even when you're being ornery. And you need these people, even if you're blind to it, and even if you're living in New York or Timbuktu or wherever you decide to live. If you're too stupid to see that, then you're not half as smart as I've always thought you were." Not having any more energy to continue, Harriet rested her head in her hands, hoping she'd said enough.

Cassie sank down on a dusty box and began crying. "I'm sorry, Har. I didn't mean those things—I really didn't." She bent and rested her elbows on her knees, the heels of her hands closing her eyes. "I'm just so damned scared. And I'm angry—angry that this has happened to you. For the first time in my life, I don't know what to do." She sniffed loudly, sitting up and wiping her eyes with the backs of her hands.

Harriet lifted her head and held her gaze steady on her sister. "What are you afraid of, Cassie? I hope it's not for me. Don't waste your energies—because I've got enough fear and uncertainty for all of us. Are you afraid of your feelings for Sam? Or maybe it's just admitting that you're wrong about how you feel about this town and what it means to you? Try it—you'll find that it's a lot better once you get it out of your system. And it's okay not knowing what to do—that's part of life. But don't close off any options. For instance, have you even considered remaining here? I think you need to just stop being so stubborn about everything and listen to your heart for a change."

Cassie jumped up off the box, her voice rising. "Why does everybody think that staying in Walton will solve all my problems? And it's going to take a hell of a lot more than the best sex I've ever had to keep me here in Walton."

A throat clearing had both sisters turning their heads toward the attic stairwell. Sam Parker stood on the top step, his lips drawn together in a tight smile, his jaw working furiously. His gaze sought Cassie's. "Thank you for clearing that up, Cassie.

And you shouted it so loud that I also thank you for the citizens of this town who needed clarification of what you were doing Saturday night."

Cassie kicked a trunk with her sandaled foot. "Dangnabit!" She clutched her foot while hopping on the other. Sam approached but she held out her hand to stop him. "Don't you touch me. Haven't you ever heard that eavesdropping is rude?"

"Hey, I've been standing here for a good ten minutes waiting for you to come up for air. I'm glad I finally got your attention, because I was afraid your head was about to explode."

Her mouth opened to reply, but she quickly shut it. Ignoring him, she turned to Harriet. Speaking calmly, she said, "I think I just broke my toe. I'm going to go find a real doctor to look at it. I'll find you later when I've calmed down so we can talk rationally about you and what our next step is going to be. I also have a feeling I'm going to need to do some apologizing." Turning her back on Sam, she hobbled down the stairs.

Harriet watched her go, not really sure whether she should laugh or cry.

CASSIE LEANED AGAINST the hallway wall, breathing heavily, her heart pounding. Her first urge was to call Andrew and discuss work. She needed to throw herself into a project, be lulled by columns of figures, negotiate and placate a

414

recalcitrant client. When working, she was competent, in control, and respected. There was no fear, no need to shout, and no feelings of inadequacy. She was halfway to the phone when she realized Andrew might not be the right person to soothe her worried mind right now.

With a heavy sigh, she limped through the house and out the back door and headed toward the gazebo. The sun shone in sporadic fits through scattering clouds as the wet grass soaked her feet through the sandals. With damp blades clinging to her bare toes, she collapsed on one of the seats and rested her forehead on her drawn-up knees. She wanted to cry or scream—but couldn't decide which. She longed for her orderly world in New York, but when she focused on the black-and-white sterility of her apartment or the stark white walls of her office, they left her cold.

Cracking open an eye, she stared at her throbbing big toe. She wasn't stubborn; she simply knew what she wanted. And sure—she was scared. Scared because her sister had cancer. But certainly not scared of admitting she was wrong. Wrong about what? That she didn't belong in Walton? Hadn't her phenomenal success in the advertising world of New York proven that?

She needed someone to talk to. But the first person who came to mind was the last person in the world she ever wanted to see again.

As if conjured, Sam came out of the back door,

striding toward her across the pricker-filled grass in those damned formfitting jeans and cowboy boots. He stopped at the bottom of the gazebo, one water-splattered, booted foot planted firmly on the bottom step. His eyes were guarded as he spoke.

"So, do you want me to look at your toe? It's either me or Dr. Clemens, the veterinarian. Then again, maybe a vet should be your first choice. You were shouting like a wounded animal back there. And at Harriet, no less. You should be ashamed of yourself."

To her complete surprise and humiliation, she began to cry. Not just tears, but fat tears spilling over her cheeks and accompanied by loud, gulping sobs.

Without a word, Sam sat down next to her and pulled her in his arms, resting her head on his chest. She didn't resist, but allowed herself to be held while she soaked his shirt.

"It's . . . my . . . toe," she blurted out between sobs. "It . . . hurts."

Sam held her closer and rubbed her back. "Yeah. I know."

They remained like that until she had no more tears left. Slowly, she pulled herself up and took the offered handkerchief. She sent him a quivering smile. "You're not going to have any left if you keep giving them away."

His teeth shone white as he smiled. "Well, you're not supposed to keep them. You're supposed to wash them and then return them to me."

"Oh." She wiped her tears and mascara off her cheek, then blew her nose loudly into the white linen square.

"Let me see your toe."

She stuck out her leg for him and watched as his gentle fingers removed her sandal and placed it on the bench. She grimaced as he manipulated the digit, but kept quiet. With a little smile, she said, "This is getting to be a bad habit—me with a hurt foot and both of us here in the gazebo while you try to make it better."

He didn't smile back as he let his hands rest on her bare leg. "Yeah—some habits are hard to break."

Not liking the look in his eyes, she hastily removed her leg from his lap. "So—what's the prognosis, Doctor?"

"It's not broken—just bruised. Try wearing open-toed shoes or going barefoot until it's better. No high heels."

She nodded and silence fell between them, the space filled with only the smell of cut grass and fabric softener blowing at them from the dryer vent at the back of the house. "I'm sorry, Sam." She wanted to add, *for the things I've said and the way I've treated you,* but her behavior appalled her, and she couldn't stand to be reminded of it just yet.

He stretched his arms out on top of the bench

and crossed his long legs. "Don't think twice about it. Besides, I'm going to bill you for the consultation."

Cassie looked down, embarrassed, realizing he was trying to save her the humiliation of an apology for her dreadful behavior. She felt like a child spared from a much-deserved spanking.

He looked toward the tops of the houses in Farrellsford as he spoke.

"Harriet wants you to tell your aunt Lucinda. Can you do that?"

Cassie nodded. "Yeah. It's the least I can do."

They were silent for a moment before Sam spoke again. "I'm heading out to Atlanta now. I've got Harriet's biopsy results with me and I'm going to schedule a few appointments for her." He uncrossed his legs and stood. "And I'm still planning on checking those records for you while I'm there."

She raised her head. "I totally forgot. I was speaking with Mrs. Perkins in your waiting room this morning, and she told me something really strange. She said that she remembered that on the day I was born, my dad mentioned something about not knowing if his firstborn was being spoiled or not, so he was going to make up for it by spoiling me."

Sam frowned. "Doesn't sound like he believed his child had died, despite what Miss E's letter said."

"That's exactly what I thought. I figure if I have another sibling out there, my dad either had more than one girlfriend, or, more likely, that his Miss E lied about the baby dying. And there's something else." She reached into her jeans pocket. "I found this in the letter box. Look at the initials." She let the locket and chain drop into his outstretched palm.

"HM and EL. Well, HM is most likely your father. But EL . . ." His forehead creased. "Nobody comes to mind right off. But I'll think about it and ask around. I'll let you know if I learn anything."

He handed her back the locket and she slid it into her pocket, next to the crumpled piece of paper with the phone number she'd taken from Harriet's cell phone.

"Sam, you don't have to do this, you know. I'm sure Harriet and I . . ." She stopped, no longer sure about Harriet at all.

"Look, Cassie, as I told you before, I'm doing it because I like mysteries. I like finding answers— maybe that's why I became a doctor. And I'm curious, too. I got to know the judge fairly well these past fifteen years." His eyes were filled with meaning as he looked at her. "I think he left those letters in the attic because he wanted you to find them."

"Well, thank you." Silence fell again, and Cassie looked away, completely discomfited. She wondered if Sam also saw her naked whenever he looked at her.

Sam stood. "I guess I'd better go. It's a long drive."

Cassie stood, too. "Thanks again, Sam. For everything."

He raised an eyebrow in reply.

She put her hands on her hips. "For what you're doing for Harriet. And for searching for the birth records. And my toe. I know I don't deserve any of your kindness, but I want you to know that I appreciate it." She felt the blood rush to her cheeks.

"You're welcome," he said, a slow grin spreading on his lips. "See, that didn't hurt too much, did it?" He moved before she could swat at him, his boots clumping down the steps of the gazebo, and heedless of the hard rain that had begun to fall again. "Good-bye, Cassie. I'll talk to you later."

"Sure. Talk to you later. Drive carefully," she added as an afterthought.

He walked several yards before turning around to face her again. "Best sex you ever had, huh?"

She picked up her sandal and threw it at his retreating back, narrowly missing him. She watched as he hiked up his pants and walked toward the back door with a deliberate and exaggerated swagger. Burying her face again on her drawn-up knees, she let herself laugh.

CHAPTER 20

Cassie waited for nearly half an hour for the rain to stop before leaving the gazebo and retrieving her shoe. She paused for a moment as she came around the front of the house, taking in the blue-and-white sheriff's car parked in the drive. The make and model of the vehicle was most likely a lot more recent than that of Sheriff Hank Adams, whom Cassie remembered from childhood. He'd once played football for the University of Georgia before a career-ending injury had derailed his career. Eventually, he moved back home to Walton, pinned on a sheriff's badge, and slid behind the wheel of a government-issue Crown Victoria. From her brief run-ins with Sheriff Adams during her youth, she knew his heart was as big as his bulldog chest. Still, the sight of his car gave her a start, and she ran up the steps, wondering what had happened.

She found her aunt pouring iced tea for the lawman in the front parlor. He rose and gave her a big bear hug.

"How ya doin', Cassie? Still up to tricks?" He winked, and she blushed, recalling the time he'd caught her raising Principal Purdy's boxers atop the high school flagpole. He'd promised to keep quiet if she'd return the article of clothing to the clothesline where she'd found it.

"I'm doing fine—thanks for asking." She wrinkled her nose. "And I'm not a teenager anymore, so no need to check up on me. I stay in bed at night now."

He winked again. "That's what I've heard." He turned to Aunt Lucinda and guffawed loudly. "Mrs. Crandall seems to recall Dr. Parker pulling out of Cassie's driveway Sunday morning wearing the same clothes he had on the night before." He sent Cassie a wink while Lucinda looked down into her tea and Cassie choked.

Finding her voice again, she asked, "Is this a social call or is something wrong?"

"Well, I hate to say it, but this is official. Your aunt called me about them trees. Seems like somebody's deliberately vandalized them."

"Are you sure? What kind of a person vandalizes trees?"

The large man shrugged. "Same kind of person who hunts an endangered animal—pure meanness, is all. I suspect it's some of those kids from that new neighborhood behind your property. Ain't got nothin' better to do until school starts."

Cassie crossed her arms. "Are there any other houses with damaged trees? I'm finding this a little difficult to believe."

"Yep—yours and two others: the Ladues' and the Pritchards'. Seems they skipped right over the Haneys'. Guess because they don't have any big trees ever since the tornado two summers ago wiped them all out. But whoever it was stripped the bark clean off the bottom of all twelve of your live oaks. I've told your aunt here to have them tarred just as soon as she can before all the sap runs out of them and they bleed to death." He beat his hat against his knee. "Those trees are over a hundred years old. It would be a real shame to lose them all."

Deflated from the day's events, Cassie sagged into an armchair. "This is unbelievable."

The sheriff rose to leave. "Yep. Sure is. I'll send a patrol car to keep an eye on your place at night, so don't be alarmed if you hear a car. But I doubt you'll have any more problems."

He stood to go, but Cassie called him back. "Sheriff, would you mind looking at this number and telling me if you're familiar with it?" She slid the paper from her pocket.

Sheriff Adams took one look at it and smiled broadly. "Yep. Know this one real well. It's the number of the pay phone outside the Dixie Diner. Used to use it all the time before I got my cell phone." He handed the paper back to her. "Why do you want to know?"

Cassie shrugged, crumpling the paper in her hand. "No reason, really. I had a phone call come in on Harriet's cell phone from that number and just wanted to know where they were calling from."

The sheriff nodded, drained his glass of iced tea,

then tipped his hat and said, "Ladies," and left.

Lucinda picked up the tray with the tea and glasses and headed toward the kitchen just as the phone rang. Cassie grabbed the phone in the foyer before the second ring.

"Hello, Cassandra? It's Andrew."

She paused for a long moment before answering. "Andrew? How are you? And why are you calling me on the house phone?" She wanted to smack herself on the forehead. She wasn't good at these surprise phone calls.

"I'm fine. I've been thinking about you." He paused. "And I'm calling on the house phone because I half hoped that you wouldn't answer."

"Really. You've been thinking about me." She wasn't going to lie and tell him she'd given him more than a passing thought since he'd left.

"Yeah, really. As a matter of fact, I was just talking to the VisEx people about you today."

"Oh." She tried to calm the excitement in her voice. She had been working on acquiring the VisEx account for over two years. It would have been a real coup to get them to jump ship from their current agency and sign with Andrew's. "And what did they say?"

"That they were ready to sign with me. On one condition."

A lump lodged in Cassie's throat. She had a sick feeling she knew what he was about to say. "They'll only sign if you manage the account."

She held the phone tightly, her gaze straying outside to the porch and then beyond to the magnolia, its glossy leaves winking in the wind. "I don't know what to say, Andrew. This would really be an excellent opportunity for me. But I meant it when I said we were finished, and I've been thinking about it, and I'm not sure if I can work for you now after all that's happened between us."

There was a long pause filled with empty air. "I know, and I can understand what you're saying. And even though I still don't understand your reasoning about us, I can promise you I'll back off for now. Because I want you to seriously think of the opportunity this would be for both of us. It would be the biggest account we've got—and you'd be calling the shots."

Just a month before she would have been beyond elated with this news. But now she could barely find even a drop of enthusiasm. She couldn't say that it was just Harriet's illness, although that was a large part. There was something else there—something she couldn't quite put her finger on. "I don't know, Andrew. This is all pretty sudden."

"Cassandra." His voice was stern, as a parent would speak to a recalcitrant child. "You worked too hard for this to give it up. And think about what it would do for the agency."

Her gaze wandered up the stairs and toward the portrait of Great-great-great-grandfather Madison.

His eyes seemed to narrow slightly as she studied it. "I . . . I really don't know. And I can't give you an answer right now. When do you need to know?"

"They're in their current contract until next January. But they won't sign without knowing you'll be here. Come on, Cassandra—do you want me to lose the account? And let's not forget that I'm still paying all the expenses on our apartment. I'm even forwarding all of your mail without complaint. I'm not looking for thanks, and I know you said you'd settle accounts when you returned, but I would hope my cooperation would encourage you to make a decision about the VisEx account a little faster."

Andrew's crowning glory was his ability to elicit guilt. And it almost worked. "I appreciate everything, Andrew. I really do. But like I told you, I can't give you an answer right now. I need time."

She could hear his chair slamming against the wall behind his desk, something he did frequently when upset. "How much time?"

"I don't know. A month. Maybe more. I just don't know."

"Cassandra . . ." She pictured him doing his deep-breathing technique. "Okay, fine. If time is what you need, then time is what you've got. I'll talk with the VisEx people and get back to you."

"Okay, fine. You do that. I'll talk to you later."

"And, Cassandra?"

Cassie waited, although she wasn't sure for

what. An apology? A reason to tell him about Harriet and share with him what it meant to her? But then she realized that the time for all of that had passed, if it had even ever existed.

"Never mind. Good-bye."

She kept the phone to her ear for a long moment, listening to the silence. Slowly hanging it up, she walked over to the screen door and looked out toward the row of oaks, her mind deep in thought. Her gaze traveled across the lawn past the live oaks and toward her mother's magnolia and her eyes widened with a start. Jerking open the door, she ran out of the house toward the tree. Running her hands over the beloved trunk, she checked for fresh scars, and was relieved out of all proportion that the tree was unscathed. She sank down onto the damp leaves beneath it and watched as Aunt Lucinda picked her way across the yard in her high heels.

"There you are, precious. I figured this was where you'd run off to."

Cassie peered at this sweet woman who had done so much for her. She knew Lucinda loved Harriet and herself as if they were her own daughters. And what she was about to tell her would hurt deeply. "Sit down, Aunt Lu. I have something to tell you."

Without hesitation, Lucinda sat down next to Cassie on the damp leaves. "It's about Harriet, isn't it?"

Cassie nodded, not surprised at her aunt's intuition. She'd always been like that. The woman had unseen radar that could detect a broken heart or hurt feelings from over a mile away. She'd been the source of comfort for all the bumps and bruises of childhood, and then, later, for the biggest heartbreak of all.

Before she could speak, Aunt Lucinda reached out and took Cassie's hand. "It's bad, isn't it? I've had one of my feelings for over a month now and I just can't seem to shake it."

Cassie squeezed her hand, seeking comfort. "Aunt Lu, Harriet has breast cancer. Sam's scheduling appointments for her with some specialists in Atlanta." A lump lodged itself in her throat and she swallowed. "But she's pregnant—which could complicate things."

She looked at her aunt, ready to lean her head on the familiar shoulder and wait for the comforting pats that had always made everything seem better. Instead, she watched her aunt's face crumple and tears erupt on the finely wrinkled face. When Lucinda rested her head on Cassie's shoulder, Cassie instinctively placed her arm around her and held tightly. She gave her gentle pats, remembering their powerful healing benefits, and waited for Lucinda's sobs to subside.

A leftover gust from the storm shook the magnolia, making the glossy green leaves weep raindrops down on them.

"Let's go inside." Cassie stood and offered her hand to her aunt. They walked back to the house together, Aunt Lucinda leaning heavily on her, and Cassie wondering exactly when it had happened that she had finally grown up.

THE BELL OVER the door at the Dixie Diner chimed brightly as Cassie pushed it open. At six thirty a.m. there was a surprising hubbub in the small restaurant. The sheriff, Senator Thompkins, Ed Farrell, and Hal Newcomb, the editor in chief of the *Walton Sentinel*, sat at a corner booth. They raised coffee cups in her direction. Cassie thought she caught a glance of sympathy from Sheriff Adams and quickly looked away. Already, Harriet's house was filling up with casseroles, pies, and hams. It reminded Cassie of a funeral and she wanted to shout at the top of her lungs from the town hall that Harriet was only sick and that Cassie had no intention of letting her die.

She spotted her old friend Mary Jane at the counter, a copy of the morning edition and a steaming cup of coffee in front of her. With a guarded smile, she waved Cassie to the place next to her.

Cassie smiled back, unsure of how things stood between them. Mary Jane had been her best friend for so many years while growing up, but things had changed—and Sam Parker wasn't a small part of that change. She air-kissed her old friend on the cheek, as she had learned to do in New York, wondering why as she did it. "Thanks for meeting me for breakfast. I know I promised you lunch, but I have a feeling I'm not going to have a lot of free time for the foreseeable future."

Mary Jane took a short sip from her mug. "I heard. I think it's a brave thing you're doing—watching all those kids while Harriet and Joe are in Atlanta." She grinned. "Whatever possessed you? Of all the people I can think of who would qualify. Like your Aunt Lucinda, for instance."

Cassie held up her hand. "I know, but Lucinda was already scheduled for a trip to Charleston with her senior group and I didn't want her to miss that. Besides, Harriet's my sister. And I love her kids. A bit rambunctious, sure, but they're great. Nothing I can't handle."

Mary Jane didn't comment, but raised an eyebrow. The waitress came to take their order, and Cassie placed hers. With a mere glancing thought toward fat grams and calories, she ordered the blue-plate special of fried eggs, bacon, hash browns, and grits.

As Mary Jane ordered, Cassie's gaze wandered over the restaurant toward the diner's window. The backward letters of the restaurant's name arched over the glass, transforming the yellow morning glow that shone through them into pink fingers of light reaching across the laminate tables. She recalled when she and Harriet were small and their father used to bring them to the diner for lunch. They would sit in the same corner booth and Harriet would always read the letters on the window backward, thinking it was a hoot. She hadn't understood they were just the backs of the letters. Cassie would call her stupid because Harriet couldn't figure it out.

The waitress said something to her, bringing her back to the present. Cassie handed her the menu, then turned toward Mary Jane. "Have you ever wanted to recall words you've said to your brother in the past?"

Mary Jane leaned close. "We all do, Cassie. Especially to our siblings. I think we learn what buttons to push while still in the womb. It just is. And remember, you're sitting next to the person solely responsible for her brother's lifelong nickname of Stinky. Now, that's something to be proud of."

The waitress filled Cassie's mug with coffee as the bell by the front door jangled again. Two men in heavy work boots, stained T-shirts, and overgrown beard stubble stomped into the diner and took seats at the other end of the counter. Cassie and Mary Jane eyed the group of men in the corner warily.

Mary Jane leaned over. "Those are Roust's men. They're working on the old Olsen property. Remember that big house? They're getting ready to level it and build a new Wal-Mart on the lot."

She wrinkled her nose as if the men sitting ten feet away already reeked of sweat and hard Georgia clay.

Cassie slid a look at the workmen. "What's wrong with the old Wal-Mart?"

Mary Jane nodded. "Exactly. That's what Sam's trying to knock into the council's thick skulls."

She thanked the waitress as her plate was put in front of her. "Sam's missing an important town council meeting this evening. They're taking votes on that moratorium—it'll save the Olsen home if it passes. At least for now." Taking a bite out of her toast, she daintily wiped her mouth with a paper napkin. "Sam's asked me to go and speak for him, but I don't have his powerful way of talking. He can be very persuasive when he wants to be."

Cassie felt herself coloring and took a bite of hash browns to hide it.

They continued eating, chatting about old friends and new clothes, waving to the stream of townspeople who flowed in and out of the front door. The bell chimed again and again, as if to remind the two women of the one subject looming between them that needed to be avoided.

When Ed Farrell got up to leave, he approached Mary Jane and Cassie at the counter. With a nod in Cassie's direction, he addressed Mary Jane. "I guess I'll be seeing you at the meeting tonight. I'm sorry Sam won't be here, but it will be a shorter meeting without him."

Mary Jane swiveled on her stool. "Don't be so sure of that, Ed. Sam has given me a ten-page speech of what he wants covered. I wouldn't schedule any early morning appointments if I were you."

He looked agitated. "Yeah, well. I gotta go. I'm supposed to trim Miss Lena's hedges, but first I've got an appointment to show your house, Cassie." He leaned closer to her. "Aunt Lucinda told me about the call from New York. I just want you to know that I've thought about it long and hard and I'd be willing to help you out by buying the house myself. Not to live in it, of course, but at least I could afford to sit on it—or lease it—for as long as it takes to sell." He held up his hand. "Just something to think about. It could be the answer to your problems. You'd be able to return to New York, and your beautiful house will be left in capable hands."

Cassie nodded. "Thanks, Ed. I'll definitely think about it."

He nodded, then left. Mary Jane looked at her like she'd lost her mind. "You've got to be kidding, right? I wouldn't sell that man my house if he paid me a million bucks. Don't you remember how mean he was in high school? How he used to pick on Sam?"

Cassie took a brief sip of her coffee. "That was ages ago—he's changed. What you don't seem to recall is how everybody used to pick on him. It's a miracle he didn't become a serial killer or something instead of a successful businessman."

Mary Jane shook her head. "There's something up with him; I just haven't figured out what it is yet."

Senator Thompkins left the other table and approached, turning to Cassie with a grim look. "I wish you'd talk Sam out of this foolishness. He's just wasting his energy fighting progress. And I'm sure you know how to distract him."

Cassie felt the heat flame her cheeks again as the grill sizzled behind the counter with another order of hash browns. She took a gulp of scalding coffee, burning her tongue but glad for the excuse not to answer. Choking down ice water, she waved the senator out of the door.

"Does the whole town know?"

Mary Jane put down her fork. "Please, Cassie. We might talk slow, but news travels fast here." She smoothed the paper napkin on her lap. "But what I'd like to know is, what does it mean? Was it a one-night stand or are you after a bit more?" Her voice held a note of forced lightness. "I wish you'd just go ahead and stake your claim or leave town, because the suspense is killing me. I'd like to know if I should start nursing my broken heart or give it another chance."

Cassie set her mug down with a quiet thud. "I . . . I don't know. . . ."

Mary Jane leaned closer. "Sam Parker is the

most stubborn, pigheaded man I know. I also know he's the most sincere, kindhearted man I've ever met—and a damned fine doctor. It doesn't hurt that he looks pretty devastating in a pair of Levi's, either. And I'd give my left arm for him to look at me just once the way that he looks at you." She wiped the back of her hand roughly over her eyes and turned her head. "I don't know why I'm selling his virtues to you. I should be selling you a one-way ticket out of town. But I just can't stand to see him suffer. He doesn't deserve it."

"Look, I don't want to hurt anybody. Sam knows how things stand between us. And, Mary Jane, you of all people should understand—you were with me all through my growing up. I never belonged here; I never intended to stay. Sam belongs here, and I belong somewhere else—somewhere everybody doesn't know, or care, where I sleep or with whom—end of story. I have no claims on him."

Mary Jane picked up the check from the aqua-colored Formica. She turned to Cassie. "You just pretended you didn't belong to separate yourself from Harriet. It made you stand out—like your outrageous pranks. But you're an adult now. It's time you started acting like one." She slid off of her stool and stood. "I love him, and I thought I had a pretty good chance with him until you came into town. So grow up and make your decision, because watching the two of you is killing me."

She pushed in her stool. "Thanks for having breakfast with me—but I've got to get to the clinic."

Cassie watched as her old friend paid her check and left through the door, the bell announcing her exit. She took another sip of coffee, trying to swallow the bitter taste in her mouth.

She stayed in the diner for another cup of coffee, waving to people as they came through the door and enjoying the last peace and quiet she would probably see in quite a while.

As she was going through her purse to pay her check, Harriet's cell phone rang. Flipping it open, she said, "Hello?"

Again, there was no answer, just light breathing on the other end and then a quick click from the other person hanging up. Cassie looked at the number registered on the screen, recognizing it as the same one used earlier. The pay phone outside the diner. She jerked her head toward the front of the building at the two huge windows, realizing that they did not afford a view of the corner where the phone was located.

Leaping from her stool, she ran to the door, almost running into the Sedgewick twins entering the building. Doing her best to squeeze by them, she plunged outside onto the sidewalk, only to find the phone abandoned, the receiver dangling by its cord.

Cassie glanced around, looking for anybody

running, appearing out of place, or watching her intently. All she saw were people going about their business at the slow, small-town pace she had come to recognize. With a sigh, she turned around and went back into the diner to pay her bill. Fortified now with both adrenaline and caffeine to get her through any difficulty, she drove Lucinda's pink car to Harriet's house.

MADDIE HEARD THE car outside and sat on the bottom step waiting for her aunt Cassie. Her dad, carrying Amanda, gave her one of his looks as he spotted Maddie not moving toward the door. The baby's diaper stank and Maddie glared at her father, daring him to ask her to change it.

He opened the door. "Hey, Cassie. Thanks again for this."

Aunt Cassie wrinkled her nose. "What's that smell?"

"Sorry. I haven't had a minute to spare." He held up Amanda. "Would you mind?"

Cassie hesitated for only a second. Reaching for the baby she said, "Sure. No problem."

Handing over the baby he said, "Thanks, Cassie. I've got a bottle in the refrigerator if she gets hungry. I'll be upstairs helping Harriet pack if you need anything." He closed the door behind Cassie, then, with a look of warning meant for Maddie, ran past them and up the stairs.

Her aunt looked at her. "Good morning, Maddie."

"Hmm."

She raised an eyebrow, then, holding the baby in front of her like a sack of dirty laundry, carried her up the stairs. "Come on, sweetie," she said to the baby. "Between the two of us, I'm sure we can figure this out."

Maddie followed her upstairs, her feet heavy on the steps. She leaned against the wall of the bedroom Amanda shared with Knoxie, and watched as her aunt laid the baby on the changing table, then studied the diaper like it was a science experiment.

Without looking at her, Aunt Cassie said, "I know your parents have told you what's going on. I know how hard this is for you and I'm sorry." She pointed to the rocking chair. "Why don't you sit down so we can have a chat?"

"I'm not in the mood to chat." Maddie shut the door harder than she'd planned, then slumped into the rocking chair, but only because she couldn't think of another place to sit. Besides, she didn't have an argument with her aunt. None of this was her fault.

Aunt Cassie untaped the dirty diaper and folded it down. Making a funny face, she turned back to Maddie. "How are you doing?"

Maddie folded her arms across her chest. "Life sucks."

With one hand, Cassie reached into the diaper-wipe box, grabbing hold of a handful. She shook the wad hard, trying to separate one from the bunch. "Yeah, sometimes it does, Maddie." She shook the wipes harder. "That's why it's nice to have family and friends who care for you. You know we'll be here to help one another with the rough spots." A clump of wipes fell to the floor, one of them sticking to Aunt Cassie's bare leg.

Maddie rolled her eyes. "Yeah, right. My mother's dying, my father's clueless, and you're leaving. Why can't this be happening to Lucy Spafford? Her mother's a witch, and Lucy doesn't have a million brothers and sisters. It's just not fair."

Maddie's voice caught but her aunt didn't turn to look. She was concentrating on getting the diaper in the right spot. "No, Maddie. Life is rarely fair. But you can't start thinking so negatively now. Your mother is going to need your support. Remember, she didn't choose to get sick."

"But she's choosing that baby over us. It's like she doesn't even love us—or why would she take such a risk?"

With one hand pinned on the baby's squirming stomach and the other one trying to pry the adhesive off the clean diaper, Cassie spoke in a calm voice. "There is one thing that you should never forget. Your mother loves you deeply—as only a mother can. She's making the best decision she knows how. Your mother told me that she could no more sacrifice that baby than she could sacrifice one of y'all. It's a mother thing. You'll understand it one day." She sighed deeply, her hands still. "And it's really too soon for us to be assuming there even has to be a choice. If the cancer is in its earliest stages it can be treated without harming the baby. We just have to wait, and be strong. And trust your mother's maternal instincts to do what's right for all of you."

Maddie scowled. "Like you know anything about maternal instincts."

Keeping her gaze on the baby, Aunt Cassie said, "I lost my mother when I was younger than you. I can pretty much relate to what you're going through. And I certainly share your anger. But this was your mother's decision, and it's up to us to support her." The baby gurgled and began to kick her pudgy legs like a frog, making it difficult for Cassie to close the diaper. Cassie stopped struggling for a moment and said very softly, "Be kind to your mother, Maddie. She needs your love and understanding right now as much as you need hers."

Maddie watched as her aunt resumed the diaper battle, feeling like she wanted to scream and cry at the same time. She was sad and angry, and she wasn't sure which one she was supposed to be feeling, so she just kept quiet. *Be kind to your mother.* Her aunt's words wouldn't go away, no matter how much she wanted to forget them, or how wrong she thought her aunt was.

Tired of watching her aunt struggle, Maddie

stood. "Let me do that. You've got the thing on backward." With a small smile breaking through her scowl, Maddie expertly diapered her baby sister and snapped up the playsuit. When she lifted the baby off the changing table, Amanda snuggled into Maddie's shoulder, rubbing her eyes with her little hands. "That means she's tired. I'll put her down for her nap. I don't figure you know how to do that, either."

Cassie sent her a grateful smile. "No, I don't. I'll watch you so I can learn."

When she was finished, she motioned for her aunt to follow her from the room, then closed the door quietly. Sarah Frances met them at the bottom of the stairs with a pathetic look in her eyes. "I'm hungry."

Maddie rolled her eyes again, but didn't say anything. Watching her aunt handle her brother and sisters might be the most entertaining thing going on in Walton.

Aunt Cassie smoothed Sarah Frances's hair. "Have you had breakfast?"

The little girl nodded solemnly. "Yes, ma'am. But we're still hungry. We need a snack."

Cassie looked at her watch. "It's only nine o'clock, but I guess that's a good time for a snack." She took hold of Sarah Frances's hand and led her into the kitchen. Knoxie and Joey were already seated at the table. "Okay. What do y'all have around here for a snack?"

Maddie hung back in the doorway, prepared to wait the whole thing out and see how long it took her aunt to catch on.

In a precise voice, Sarah Frances said, "Moon Pies."

Knoxie and Joey looked at each other, their eyes wide.

Cassie walked to the pantry. "All right then. Moon Pies it is." She found the box and pulled out four. "What would you like to drink with this?"

All three children looked at one another; then Sarah Frances said, "Co-Cola. Please."

"All right. Three Cokes coming right up." Aunt Cassie peeped around the corner at Maddie and held up the fourth Moon Pie. "You want some, too?"

Maddie scowled. "Like I would eat that at nine o'clock in the morning. Gross."

Aunt Cassie shrugged and went back to pouring the drinks. They were enjoying their snack when Maddie's mama and daddy entered the kitchen. Without looking in their direction, Maddie slunk off toward the back door and sat on a low stool. Aunt Cassie waved as she took a sip of her Coke while the children smiled, mouths full of Moon Pie.

"Aunt Cassie let us have a snack." Crumbs flew from Sarah Frances's mouth as she spoke.

"Don't speak with your mouth full, honey." Mama placed her hand on Sarah Frances's head and kissed her cheek. "I guess you didn't tell Aunt Cassie about the fruit bowl we use for snacks, huh?"

The little girl shook her head.

Cassie stood. "Sorry, Har. I think I was shanghaied."

"It's all right. A special treat isn't a bad thing. Besides, you're the one who's going to have to deal with their sugar high in about an hour." She turned to the children. "All right, everybody. Come and give me a kiss and a squeeze."

Maddie stayed where she was as chairs scraped the floor and everybody ran to hug and kiss their mama. When they were through, she straightened and turned to Maddie. "What about you?"

Maddie shrugged, finding it hard to stay really angry while trying not to cry. Mama came and stood next to her, then put her arms around her and squeezed, and Maddie fought hard not to hug her back. Finally, her mama straightened, then touched Maddie's cheek. "I love you. You'll always be my first baby, my big girl. Don't forget that."

Maddie nodded once, but didn't look up as her mama walked away.

Everyone moved to the front hallway and Maddie followed a good distance behind. She watched as her mama hugged Aunt Cassie tightly. "Thanks for letting the kids come to your house to stay. I've got all their bags packed and waiting by the door."

Cassie gave a half smile. "I feel so stupid—wanting to be home to watch over my trees. I hope the kids will be okay away from home."

Mama touched her cheek. "They're only a few blocks away. And I think it will be such an adventure for them that they won't think about missing me."

Cassie looked up at the ceiling, pretending to look at the light fixture, but Maddie knew she was trying to stop any tears from falling down her face, because Maddie was doing the same thing. "Oh, I've got lots of things planned for them. Painting porches, inflating condoms, dressing statues—all sorts of things. You just concentrate on getting well—I'll take care of everything else."

Maddie accidentally laughed, although it came out like a snort, and Mama and Aunt Cassie looked at her.

Smiling, Mama turned back to Aunt Cassie. "That's what I'm afraid of." She reached and took hold of Cassie's necklace. "I guess I should be buying you some more hearts to put on this chain."

With a shake of her head, Cassie closed her hand over Mama's. "Oh, no, Har. You just need to start your own necklace."

Mama hugged her sister again. "Really—thanks. And I mean it. This is a big thing you're doing for us, and we really appreciate it. And the hotel room, too. I don't know how you finagled all of your travel miles and hotel bonuses and whatnot to get us the room for free, but we'd have been sleeping in the car otherwise."

Cassie blinked hard. "Hey, it's the least I could do. Especially after what I said . . ."

Harriet put a finger to her lips. "Don't. We all get scared and angry and say things we don't mean. And you don't owe me an apology—ever. What you're doing for us speaks louder than any words ever could." With soft hands, she wiped the tears and smudged mascara out from under Aunt Cassie's eyes.

Daddy returned from putting the suitcases in the trunk, sweat already dripping down his forehead and upper lip. He gave bear hugs and loud kisses to the children, then turned toward Cassie and wrapped his arms around her.

"You have my cell phone number. If you have any questions, just call." He looked over at Maddie. "And I know Maddie will be your right-hand gal. She knows how everything works around here. Right, Maddie?"

Not knowing what else to say, she answered, "Whatever."

He rubbed her head as he'd done when she was a little girl, then turned to her mama. "We have to go if we're going to make your first appointment." Hoisting an overnight bag over his shoulder, he led the group out to the driveway, then helped her mama into her daddy's car, leaving the minivan behind for Aunt Cassie.

Maddie hung back, not wanting to see her mother waving or the car disappearing down the driveway. There was something final about that, like a movie where you didn't like the ending.

The doors shut, and then her daddy backed the car into the street with a crunch of gravel before driving away slowly. They all stood watching it go, staring silently at the empty road for a long time.

"Aunt Cassie, I need to go potty." Knoxie tugged on her aunt's shorts, breaking the silence.

With a crooked smile, Cassie herded the children back into the house, but Maddie remained outside focusing on the spot where the car had been. Slowly, she began jogging toward the street, then faster and faster until she couldn't breathe, her heart hurting so badly that she pushed her fist against it. Finally she stopped and put her hands on her knees, trying to get the air in her lungs and her heart to stop hurting, and all the time wishing that she'd hugged her mama good-bye.

CHAPTER 21

There's a possum in the house again!"

The shriek jerked Cassie from the window seat in the front parlor where she had been perched, watching for stealthy shadows on the front lawn of her house. Her only reward had been the twin circles of headlights making a slow dance across the yard as it turned around in the drive. The porch lights had illuminated a police car, and Cassie had sat back with relief.

With her adrenaline pumping again, she raced toward the family room, where the older children, with the exception of Maddie, were engrossed in a Disney movie. Making its slow, lumbering way across the Berber carpet, a large rodentlike animal twitched its nose in Cassie's direction.

"How in God's name did that get in here?"

The animal stopped for a moment, as if preparing to answer, then continued its stroll across the family room floor.

Joey, without taking his gaze off the television screen, said, "Got through the cat door in the kitchen."

With hopefulness in her voice, Cassie asked, "A cat?"

Joey shook his head. "Pop-pop had a cat, but she died last year. Daddy's not gotten around to fixin' that door yet, and Pop-pop didn't know how. The possum just sticks her snout around the screen door, pushes it open, and then crawls in through the little door. Aunt Lucinda doesn't like it neither."

Amanda, swinging contentedly in the baby swing, squealed and threw a rattle, barely missing the small animal. In response, it curled into a little fur ball and played dead.

"This happens a lot?" Cassie moved to stand between the possum and the baby.

Knoxie nodded. "Yes, ma'am. Are you going to cook it? Aunt Lucinda keeps saying she's going to make a pie out of it if it comes inside again, but she hasn't done it yet. Do you know how to make possum pie?"

Without turning her back on the animal, Cassie released the baby from the swing and propped her on her hip. "No, I don't. And I don't think a potentially rabid animal should be walking freely in the house, either. Since Aunt Lucinda doesn't cook it, I have to guess that you have another way to get it out of the house?"

Knoxie stuck her thumb in her mouth and twirled her red hair. Sarah Frances lifted her head from the sofa. "When Pop-pop wasn't home, my daddy'd come over with a big shoe box and just scoop it up and put it outside again."

Cassie eyed the still animal, wondering where she could find a big enough shoe box. In the five days since she'd been watching the children, she thought she'd dealt with it all. She had learned that peanut butter did not take bubble gum out of hair, that a small metal object could travel through the digestive tracts of small babies with little or no effect, and that plastic glow-in-the-dark yo-yos should never be put on top of burning lightbulbs to make them brighter. Learning to remove a wild animal from the house had not even been considered.

Maddie, who'd been upstairs, appeared in the

doorway. "I see the possum got in again. I guess you'll need to call Dr. Parker." She smiled innocently at her aunt.

"Whatever for? I'm perfectly capable of dealing with this. I did live in Georgia for almost twenty years, you know." Cassie looked at her watch. Through her frequent phone calls during the week with Harriet and Joe, she had learned Sam would be returning from Atlanta today.

"Besides, he's probably just getting in and it would be silly to bother him for something like this."

The animal stirred on the floor, its rear end twitching. Cassie glanced at her niece. "Here, take the baby and keep an eye on the possum while I go find a laundry basket." She returned with one from the laundry room and successfully tossed it over the frightened animal. With her foot, she began to nudge the basket and its prisoner across the floor inch by inch. Maddie disappeared into another room before Cassie had even made it to the edge of the rug.

Twenty minutes later, when she had finally reached the kitchen table with the animal and laundry basket intact, the doorbell rang.

Sam tipped an imaginary hat. "Ma'am," he said in greeting. "I understand you have a varmint that you need rescuing from."

"My hero." Cassie rolled her eyes as she shut the door behind him but was unable to stop her grin.

"I guess Maddie called you. I'm handling it just fine, thank you very much. But since you're here, be my guest." She motioned for him to follow. "Come on—the varmint's back here." She led the way to the kitchen.

He took a high five from Joey and patted the little girls on their heads. Baby Amanda got a peck on her cheek, and Madison got a wink.

Cassie took the baby from Maddie and juggled her on her hip. "I managed to move him from the family room into here, but I'm not sure how to get him out the door."

He nodded as his gaze fell to the upside-down laundry basket and its prisoner still curled up inside. "Mmm-mm-mm. Now there's some good eatin'."

She wrinkled her nose. "That's disgusting, Sam."

"I guess you've never had possum stew, then."

"No, I can't say I make a habit out of eating roadkill."

Sam snorted. "You just don't know what you're missing." He knelt in front of the basket. "And I guess you think eating raw fish isn't disgusting."

She fisted her free hand on her hip. "That's different."

He looked at her and raised an eyebrow. "Is it?"

"Yes, it is. And how do you know that thing's not rabid?"

He bent to look inside the basket. "Well, for one thing, it's not foaming at the mouth. And for another, it's acting like a possum is supposed to. If it were barking or chasing somebody, then I'd be concerned."

She looked at him, not sure whether he was joking or not.

"But you're right—rabies is something to think about. I'll seal that door permanently so we don't have to wonder next time."

"Aunt Cassie, Sarah Frances is breathing on me." Cassie stepped into the family room in time to see Joey throw a pillow at the sofa, neatly clipping the back of his sister's head.

Cassie flipped off the television. "Okay, everybody, movie's over. It's time for bed. Everybody upstairs to put on your jammies. I'll be there in a minute to tuck you in."

"And say our prayers." Knoxie's wet thumb hung poised outside her mouth.

"And say your prayers," echoed Cassie.

The little girl plopped her thumb back in her mouth and ran after her brother and sister, her feet padding lightly on the wood floors.

Amanda whimpered, so Cassie blew a raspberry on her neck, making the baby giggle. She turned to Sam. "I'm going to give the baby a bottle and get her ready for bed while you get rid of that varmint." She paused for a moment, trying to find her nonchalant voice. "There's beer in the fridge. Help yourself." Putting the baby on her shoulder, she went upstairs.

After putting the baby in her crib and turning on the monitor, Cassie made her rounds of the children's makeshift bedrooms. Suitcases and clothes still lay strewn over the floor, but Cassie had yet to find the time to help the children unpack and put everything away.

As she approached Knoxie's room, Cassie paused and watched as the little girl stood on the rug in front of the bed and made a huge leap to land on top of her covers.

"What are you doing, sweetheart?"

Wide green eyes stared up at her. "I don't want the bogeyman under the bed to grab my feet, so I jump." Knoxie crawled under her covers.

"Oh, honey, there aren't any bogeymen under your bed." She got down on her hands and knees and peered into the dark space. "Yep—all empty."

"My mommy uses bogeyman spray to keep them away."

"She sprays under the bed?"

Knoxie nodded, her red curls jostling.

Cassie crooked her index finger, got down on her hands and knees again, and made a hissing noise with her mouth.

Knoxie giggled. "No, Aunt Cassie. She uses a real bogeyman spray."

Cassie peeked up over the edge of the bed. "A real spray?"

"Yes, ma'am. And it really works."

Pulling herself up again, Cassie went across the

hall to the bathroom and retrieved a Lysol spray can. Returning to the little girl's bedroom, she held it aloft. "This is my own kind of bogeyman spray." She hunched down and spritzed the area under the bed thoroughly, lifting the bedspread at the foot of the bed to get an extra squirt. "Okay, sweet pea. That's guaranteed to keep away any and all nasty bogeymen."

Sitting on the edge of the bed, Cassie held her niece's hand, and with bowed heads they said their good-night prayers. Cassie hid her smile at the stridency in the little girl's voice as she called for God's blessing on every person, beast, and insect Knoxie had ever met. Just as Cassie began to nod off to sleep, Knoxie's words caught her attention.

"God bless Daddy and Mama and please take care of them on their trip. I miss them and want them to come back soon. And God bless Aunt Cassie for taking care of us and please let her know that we love her even when she shouts at us for putting our tennis shoes in the oven to dry. Amen."

Cassie stood, not sure she could trust her voice. Leaning over, she kissed the little freckled nose and tucked the sheets tightly around the small girl and assorted stuffed animals. "Good night, sweet pea. I love you, too. And I'm sorry I shouted."

She flicked on the night-light and let herself out of the room, careful to leave the door cracked open. Leaning against the doorframe, she closed her eyes, wishing for a moment that she could believe that the bogeyman could be held back with a household spray.

When she opened her eyes, she spied Sam waiting for her at the top of the stairs, leaning against the banister.

"You handled that well."

"Thanks." She rubbed the back of her neck, the exhaustion of taking care of five children all day finally catching up to her. She studiously avoided his eyes. "I'm pooped. I think I'll go straight to bed. Hang on a second and I'll walk you out."

She disappeared into her room and reappeared carrying her blanket and pillow, the cordless receiver of the baby monitor clutched in her hand. She headed down the stairs and felt him follow behind her.

"Where are you going with that stuff?"

She threw the blanket over her shoulder. "I'm going out to that old magnolia tree my mother planted. With everything going on around here, I'd hate to have something happen to it. I mean, it's pretty old and all, so somebody should watch over it. I've already told Maddie where I'll be, so she knows where to find me if anybody needs me." She held up the baby monitor. "Plus, I'll be able to hear Amanda if she wakes."

He opened the front door, then followed her outside. She stood awkwardly, her pillow held in front of her. "Good night, then. And thanks for taking care of Mr. Possum for us."

"You're welcome. My pleasure, as always." He tipped his imaginary hat, then slowly sauntered down the porch steps.

As he walked toward his truck, Cassie headed across the lawn to her mother's magnolia. Its leaves dully reflected the moonlight, making it almost glow. She propped the monitor against the trunk, then spread out her blanket and pillow. As she lay down, she spotted Sam walking across the lawn toward her, a blanket tucked under his arm.

She sat up. "What are you doing?"

"I thought you could use some company. Plus, I've been carrying around this blanket in my truck for over a year, and I figure it's time to put it to use."

"Well, I hadn't really thought I needed company. But if you haven't got anything else to do, then be my guest."

He spread his blanket on the ground by her feet, allowing him to peer out at the sky. The wind rustled the tree above them, making the leaves whisper like children sharing secrets. The summer scents of mowed grass and jasmine drifted on the humid air, cloaking them like a blanket. Sam crossed his arms behind his head and stared upward.

"By the way, I did have a chance to check birth records while I was in Atlanta. Even with the initials from the locket, I didn't find anything that might be a remote possibility. Of course, I'm not really surprised. I have a feeling this was all so hush-hush back then that Miss E's parents probably covered up the paper trail pretty well."

Cassie braced herself on her elbow. "Remember that ad Harriet and I took out in the paper—the one that listed her cell number but not any names? I got two calls—I'm pretty sure it was the same caller—but they never said anything. Just waited for me to speak and then hung up." She sat up completely. "I know that the phone used was the one outside the Dixie Diner, and the second call came when I was sitting inside. It was almost as if the person knew I was in there. But by the time I got outside, whoever it was had gone."

"Sounds like whoever it was wanted to check out who you were without returning the favor."

Cassie breathed deeply, smelling the sweet summer grass. "Yeah, that's pretty much what I thought, too." She rubbed her bare feet in the grass, the blades cool and damp on her soles. "I wish my father had trusted me with this before he died. I'm just amazed that he was willing to let this kind of secret die with him. Harriet thinks it's because Miss E is still living and he wanted to protect her still." She shrugged. "I don't really know what to do next. If she doesn't want to be found, then maybe I should just let it be. But what if the baby didn't die and we do have a sibling? I'd like to know. It's just that . . . well, I have enough to worry about now, especially with Harriet. . . ." She let her voice fall away and turned her head. "I suppose you've been told by Harriet and Joe not to tell me anything about what's really going on right now."

He was silent, answering her question.

"Everything they've told me so far is just so . . . I don't know, inconclusive. They're still running tests and looking at all the options, is what they're saying. What I really want is to be there with them, to help them make any decisions that need to be made."

Sam looked at her in the moonlight. "I know, and they know that, too. But this is their battle— not yours. You're doing what they need you to do right now, and you're going to have to accept that."

She nodded, gritting her teeth. It went against her grain to sit and wait, but she had five children who needed her now—almost as much as she'd begun to need them.

They were quiet for a while, watching the passing lights of a jetliner high above them. Eventually, Sam turned to face her. "Has Ed Farrell been by recently?"

Cassie nodded. "He's brought several couples through here in the last week. But they'd heard about the vandalism and Maddie's bike being stolen last Monday night right off the front porch.

I could tell the parents were a bit leery, and nothing I could say would make a bit of difference. One of the women actually said something about the neighborhood going downhill. Can you imagine? I wanted to open a can of whoop-ass on her."

He turned his head, a smile in his voice. "A can of whoop-ass?"

She clamped her hand over her mouth. "Oh, crap—it's contagious."

"Sounds like you've been hanging around Ed Farrell too much." He snorted softly. "That Ed—he's like a booger you just can't thump off."

She tossed her pillow at him, hitting him in the chest. "You are such a redneck."

"Right. And saying you're going to open up a can of whoop-ass on somebody is so much more refined."

"That just slipped out. Besides, yours was disgusting."

He propped himself up on his elbows, a smirk visible on his face. "Then why are you laughing?"

She slumped back down on top of her blankets next to him. "You can be so annoying, Sam Parker."

"So that's what you call it. I always thought 'annoying' was a negative term."

A laugh crept up her throat and bubbled over into the night air. She had the most outrageous notion to move closer and kiss him. Just once.

Cassie rolled over on her stomach, propping her chin in her hands. "Give Ed a break, Sam. He's not the same bully you knew in school. He's changed—a lot. I actually kind of like him. I mean, he's still a little rough in spots, but he's seriously trying to smooth them out. I respect that in him."

Sam's eyes glittered in the moonlight as he sat up to face her. "I'd respect him a lot more if I knew where all his money came from. How did he go to college and start his business? Those are expensive ventures, and he came from nothing. There's something that's just not right there. And then there's the matter of what he's trying to do to this town—make it into one of those damned planned communities." He lay back down, his face toward the sky. "I don't for one moment believe he has anyone's best interests at heart except for his own."

Cassie opened her mouth to tell him about Ed's offer to buy her house, but Sam interrupted. His voice carried a note of urgency. "Cassie—look up."

She tilted her head out from under the shelter of the leaves and looked up into the black sky. The tail end of a falling star skimmed past Orion's belt, glowed like spun gold for a brief moment, then faded into nothingness. Cassie stood and stared up at the dwindling light, realizing how long it had been since she'd last seen a falling star, and wondering where all those empty nights had gone.

"Make a wish," she whispered, remembering long-ago summer evenings spent with Harriet and their father, watching the sun set, the waxing moon rise, and the stars erupt with light. "Wishing on a falling star makes it come true."

Sam stood next to her, his eyes glowing brightly, the moon making them shine silver.

"Sometimes. I've been wishing on falling stars for a long time, and I'm still waiting."

"Be careful what you wish for." His warm breath stroked her cheek. Looking down, she noticed his feet were bare. "I'm going to wish that Harriet gets better and everybody lives happily ever after."

He didn't say anything, so Cassie raised her head. He was studying her carefully with a slight upturn of his lips. "You're such a Pollyanna. It's one of the things I've always loved about you."

She tucked a strand of hair behind her ear, feeling self-conscious. "Andrew called me a daydreamer. I think he said it was his job in life to break me of that bad habit."

"Then he failed. I'm glad."

Looking up at the sky again, she felt small and insignificant under its vastness. She took a deep breath, the great boundless sky somehow making her say the unspeakable, as if the atmosphere could swallow the words and take them away forever. "What if Harriet dies, Sam? How will any of us move on?"

Sam moved to stand behind her and put his hands on her shoulders. She resisted the urge to rest her head on his fingers.

"Well, you get out of bed, you eat your grits, say hey to your neighbor, you give extra love to her children, and you live your life. The sun is a pretty stubborn guy, and he'll rise each day just to spite you. But life does go on." He squeezed her shoulders. "You survived when your mother died. I suspect you still grieve for her. I know I do for Tom. But I think you've followed your dreams the way your mother would have wanted you to, despite the running-to–New York part, and you should be proud of that."

Her fingers idly tinkered with the gold charms around her neck. "No, I think she's crying with shame up in heaven. Maddie's almost fifteen and this summer is the first time I've ever laid eyes on her. I've never sent a birthday card or baby gift in all these years." She swallowed thickly. "I'm just glad I can be here now. I don't want to think of Mama crying anymore."

He turned her around to face him, his expression earnest. "She's not crying—I think she's just waiting. The book isn't closed on this chapter, Cassie. Now, I'm only going to say this because I know you've already thought about it." He stepped closer, his eyes searching hers. "If those children are left motherless, what will you do? Visit them twice a year and send presents

461

from New York every birthday and Christmas?"

She tried to pull away, but he held on to her. "I won't be blackmailed into staying here. And I'm not going to think about any of that now—but I do know that whatever decision I make, it will be made of my own free will. Not anybody else's— including yours, Sam Parker."

They stood facing each other for a long moment, their breath melding in the small space between them. The tree frogs thumped their rhythm into the night, echoing the loud beating of her heart. Their lips met, and she was unsure who had moved, only that she seemed to be where she was supposed to be.

For a long time she was unaware of the tree frogs, or the moon, or the world that continued to spin beneath her feet whether she wanted it to or not. And then Sam reached up and removed her hands that had wrapped around the back of his neck and stepped away. Slowly letting go, he said, "Good night, Cassie."

She let her arms fall to her sides, feeling suddenly boneless. "Good night?"

"I've already told you—it's all or nothing with me."

Grabbing a handful of dirt and dead leaves, she threw them at him. "Now's a damned fine time to start acting like a Southern gentleman!"

He reached over and held on to her wrist before she could throw another handful. "I want you,

Cassie. God knows how much. But I told you before—I won't be used. I want to be more to you than a nice roll in the hay." He released her and raised an eyebrow. "Even if it is the best sex you've ever had."

"I was just making that up. Besides, you started it."

"I did not."

Straightening her skirt she said, "Did, too."

"Did not."

She threw her pillow at him. "I can't believe you—you're such a child. I'm leaving." She gathered up her blanket and turned to go, mindless of the clinging leaves and twigs.

"I'll stay here and watch your tree if you like."

She turned to face him as he leaned against the tree, looking at her with a wide grin.

"Thank you." She turned around and stomped across the lawn. On the bottom front porch step she called back, "I'll bring you breakfast in the morning."

Quietly, she let herself into the house and crept up the stairs, dumping the blanket and pillow in the upstairs hallway. Then she checked on all the sleeping children, taking comfort in the soft rhythm of their breathing. Amanda had kicked off her blanket, so Cassie gently tucked it around her small body. As she left the room, she caught sight of the baby monitor on the dresser. Realizing she'd left the receiving end under the magnolia tree, she tiptoed over to it, leaned into the speaker, and whispered loudly, "Did, too."

Smiling with satisfaction, she let herself out of the room, closing the door quietly behind her.

CHAPTER 22

Harriet sat in the chair by the hotel window watching the growing Atlanta traffic pulse and swerve below her as she waited for the sun to crack the sky. Joe stirred in his sleep and she turned to look at him, all the lines and creases of worry in his face erased for a few short hours. It still amazed her that after all these years she still felt like a young girl in love for the first time: still breathless with anticipation when he walked in the door. But now, in this darkest part of their marriage, something had changed. The love was stronger, somehow. Yet different. It was as if by holding it to the fire they had given it a new shape and a brighter luster.

Her gaze drifted to the red glow of the alarm clock, the digital numbers reading six thirty. Harriet knew that if Amanda hadn't already awakened Cassie, Knoxie would in the next ten minutes. Picking up Joe's cell phone from the desk, she let herself into the bathroom and closed the door, then sat down on the side of the tub to call her sister.

Cassie answered on the second ring, her voice alarmed. "Har? Is everything all right?"

"Everything's fine. I just wanted to talk with you before the animals started rattling their cages."

Harriet could hear the smile in Cassie's voice. "The little darlings are all still asleep, thankfully. I set my alarm for five thirty so that I could be dressed and caffeinated before I faced them. Of course, this means I'll have to nap with Amanda after lunch, but Lucinda's back from Charleston and said she'd be happy to watch Joey and the girls, so it's all good."

Harriet closed her eyes, picturing the sweet faces of her children. "Despite what Joe said, I knew you'd be perfect for watching the kids. Thank you. Again and again."

Cassie's voice sounded defensive. "What did Joe say?"

"Nothing we need to talk about right now. How's Maddie?"

There was a pause, as if Cassie wanted to argue. Finally, she answered, "Maddie's great. A perfect angel, actually, which I didn't really expect. She does her chores without me asking her and has been a real help with Amanda."

Harriet frowned. "She's up to something."

"What?"

"Is she keeping her things tidy, and putting things away?"

"Yes, as a matter of fact, she is. Her dirty laundry has actually made it into the laundry basket every day, which is more than I can say about her brother. Joey seems to have a hard time with the dirty laundry–laundry basket connection."

Smiling, Harriet said, "Yeah, well, Joey comes by it honestly. Being his father's son and having that Y chromosome dooms him for life in the laundry department. But as for Maddie, a clean room means she's definitely up to something."

Harriet could sense Cassie's frown. "How can you say that? Maybe she feels sorry for me and is just trying to give me a break."

She shook her head. "Cassie, when you were Maddie's age and planning something, what did you do?"

There was a long pause. Then: "I'd be on my best behavior and keep my room clean so I was under Daddy's radar."

"Exactly."

"I'm so screwed."

"Yeah, well, you'll learn."

Cassie's voice rose a notch. "Don't say it like that, Harriet. It makes it sound like you're not coming back or something."

Something fluttered inside her abdomen and Harriet rested her hand there, sensing the child inside. "I'm sorry. I meant it for when you become a mother. You sort of learn things that you never thought would be important."

"Yeah, like that there's such a thing as anti-bogeyman spray?"

The thought of Knoxie and her fear of the dark

space under her bed made Harriet's eyes tear. "Something like that."

"So how's it really going there, Harriet? And tell me the truth. You don't have to sugarcoat anything with me."

Harriet rubbed her belly again and let her head rest against the side of the shower wall. "We're still talking with the breast-cancer specialist who mentioned the possibility of a couple of drug trials. We'll know more today or tomorrow. They want to run a few more tests."

"Dear God, Harriet. Why is this taking so long? You could be getting sicker and sicker every day that they wait; don't they realize this? I'll be here with the kids for however long it takes until you're better, so nothing to worry about there; you just need to tell those doctors to get busy."

Harriet's chin dropped to her chest and she wasn't sure she could keep talking without crying. She swallowed away the lump in her throat and forced a smile, hoping to fool the one person in the world who knew her best. "I'll do that. And I'll threaten them with giving you their phone numbers if they don't get on the ball."

Cassie's voice sounded almost cheerful when she spoke, and it occurred to Harriet that maybe Cassie was trying to fool her, too. "Okay. Whatever works."

Harriet kept looking up at the ceiling for a long moment before she could speak again. "I'd better go so you can have another cup of coffee while it's still hot." She smiled into the phone, ignoring the tears that dripped into her mouth, and recalled an old joke they had once shared. "Cassie?"

"Yes?"

"You're still my favorite sister."

Cassie made a choking sound. "So are you."

"Give the kids a hug and kiss for me and Joe, and tell Maddie to call me when she gets home from cheerleading tryouts. School starts in a week and she'll need new clothes since she's grown like a weed this summer." She swallowed. "She's never there when I call, it seems."

After a brief pause, Cassie said, "I will. And if you're not back in time, I'll take her into Atlanta to do her shopping. As a way of thanking her for all of her help."

They said their good-byes and Harriet closed the cell phone. After a while, she turned off the light in the bathroom, then returned to bed. Without opening his eyes, Joe reached for her and she slid up next to him, like two spoons in a drawer. He kissed her neck, then fell back asleep, his hand soft on her hip. His warm breath teased her skin as she lay awake and watched the sun lighten the wall in front of her and felt the flutter of the baby again, the touch as light as snow.

CASSIE STRUGGLED WITH the covered casserole dish and umbrella, the enticing aroma of fried okra making her stomach rumble. Joey sloshed behind her wearing a yellow rain slicker and matching boots. He held Mrs. Crandall's cake plate with Cassie's first pineapple upside-down cake perched on top and covered with plastic wrap.

A car horn honked and they both stopped and watched as Sam pulled up alongside the curb. "Lucinda called and said y'all might need a ride."

"We're fine." Cassie continued walking, lowering the umbrella to keep the wind from blowing the rain into her eyes.

"Aunt Cassie!" wailed Joey. "This cake's heavy and it's getting wet! Can't we have Dr. Parker drive us?"

Cassie stopped for a moment and eyed her waterlogged nephew, his brown freckles stark against the whiteness of his skin. "I'm sure Dr. Parker has other things to do, Joey. We're almost there anyway."

Sam hopped out of his truck and took the cake plate from Joey. "Get in the truck, big guy, and I'll put this on your lap."

Cassie resisted when he tried to take the fried okra out of her hands. "Don't you have better things to do? Like rescue a house or lance a boil?"

He wrested the casserole dish away from her. "Nothing so glamorous, I'm afraid. It was slow at the clinic, and I'm due for a medical visit with Miss Lena anyway." He held the door open for Cassie. "And what's this about Lucinda's car?"

She waited until he had seated himself inside the truck before answering. "Somebody slashed her tires last night—and it was parked right in front of the house. I heard Johnny Ladue's motorcycle suffered the same fate. I hate to admit it, but all this vandalism is starting to get to me. And with the way everybody's talking about it, I'll never sell the house."

Sam reached over and lowered the volume on the radio. "Who do you think's responsible?"

"Sheriff Adams asked me the same thing. Besides you, the most likely culprit would be the Roust people."

Sam raised an eyebrow. "Besides me?"

Cassie shrugged. "Well, yeah. You have some archaic idea of leaving my house untouched forever, which is pretty amazing, since you don't even own the property."

"Uh-huh." He didn't say anything else, but kept his eyes focused straight ahead.

"But I figured with all your boil lancing, baby birthing, town counciling, and tree babysitting, you wouldn't have had the time to do some vandalizing, too." Cassie paused for a moment, waiting for a response. When she received none, she continued. "Anyway, the sheriff at first thought it was kids pulling pranks—like the Haney boys. Ed said they're pretty wild, and now Richard Haney works for Roust, so that would make sense. Sheriff Adams found footprints in the mud around

470

the house, so we have our first clue to go on. He's working on it now and should be able to tell whether or not the Haney boys were involved."

She shifted in her seat, readjusting the fried okra in her lap. "And Jim Roust keeps calling me. At least that guy from *Preservation* magazine is polite when he calls. I actually tell him no, thanks, before I hang up on him. When Roust calls and I recognize his voice, I hang up right away. I guess that wouldn't really put me in his good graces, but it would be hard to believe that a man of his standing in the business community would resort to guerrilla tactics. Especially after what he did to Ed Farrell's construction site."

A dog ran in front of the truck, causing Sam to slam on the brakes. The fried okra nearly slid from Cassie's lap. A quick check of the backseat reassured her that the cake hadn't suffered the same fate.

Joey looked up at her with wide eyes. "I got it, Aunt Cassie. I was holding it real tight. It did slide a little bit, but I think it made it straighter."

Sam chuckled and Cassie elbowed him.

Clearing his throat, Sam asked, "What happened at Farrell's site?"

"He said that all the bathroom fixtures were taken out of the condo complex in the middle of the night. He was pretty sure it was Roust."

His brows furrowed. "Funny. I hadn't heard anything about that. And Ed told you this?"

Cassie nodded.

Sam started to say something when he caught sight of Joey in the rearview mirror. "What kind of cake is that?"

The little boy wrinkled his nose. "Pineapple upside-down cake. Aunt Cassie made it all by herself."

With a quick glance toward the backseat, Sam said, "I can see that. I don't think I've ever seen one with such an, um, interesting shape to it, though. Who's it for?"

Cassie fixed him with an evil look. "The fried okra's for Miss Lena, but the cake is for Mrs. Crandall. My mama always taught me that you shouldn't return a dish without something in it."

Sam tried unsuccessfully to hide a laugh. "Do you think I need to stick around for a while to make sure she's okay after she eats it?"

She slapped him on the shoulder with her wet umbrella, spraying water droplets all around the front cab of the truck. Still, she couldn't resist a smile, even though the news via phone from Atlanta was still not what she was hoping for. Despite the upbeat tone from both Harriet and Joe, and the ever-hopeful words of "more tests," Cassie knew she was not being told the whole story. She was almost glad. The truth would come, sooner or later, and she'd have to deal with it. But for now, she was enjoying being with her nieces and nephew, allowing them their last days of carefree bliss before their lives would be irrevocably changed forever. She glanced at Sam, noticing the crease lines in his face from smiling, and the bright blue of his eyes. Yes, it felt good to smile again.

Mrs. Crandall opened her front door and Cassie watched the older lady's frown as she examined the cake.

"It's a pineapple upside-down cake," explained Cassie.

Mrs. Crandall brightened, "Oh, yes. I see. And my favorite, too. Thanks very much, dear."

A small black poodle appeared from behind the door and began nipping at Cassie's ankles. Cassie almost suggested feeding the cake to the dog first, just to be sure. "You're welcome." With a small wave, she walked back down the sidewalk and hoisted herself into Sam's truck.

As she buckled her seat belt, she said under her breath, "You'd think some people had never seen a pineapple upside-down cake before."

"Well, Mrs. Crandall certainly has. She's a major contender in the kudzu festival bake-off each year with her own rendition. Maybe she'll be calling you later to find out how you did that interesting shape."

Cassie slid lower into her seat with a groan. "Well, at least Lucinda made the fried okra. I'd hate to be accused of trying to kill Miss Lena, too."

Joey laughed from the backseat, then joined in

with Sam to sing along at the top of his lungs with the man on the radio waxing poetic about a woman named Carlene.

Despite the rain, Miss Lena sat out on her porch, her ubiquitous pink cardigan over her shoulders and stockings rolled down around her ankles, a new romance novel clutched between aging hands.

Miss Lena looked up with a bright smile as Sam approached, Cassie and Joey following close behind with the fried okra. "Good afternoon, Miss Lena." Sam leaned down and gave the old lady a peck on the cheek.

"Well, good morning. What a nice surprise. Did I have an appointment today?" Her smile dimmed somewhat as confusion seemed to settle over her.

Gently, Sam said, "No, Miss Lena. But I wanted to give Cassie a lift in the rain, and figured I'd check in on you while I was here. You remember Cassie, Harrison and Catherine Anne's oldest. And this big guy . . ." He pushed Joey to stand in front of the old lady. "This is Joey. Harriet and Joe Warner's boy."

Miss Lena's eyes sharpened. "Joey?" She shook her head. "No, that isn't right. That's not what they called him." She looked down at her lap, her lips moving. "It was Frank or Fred. . . ." Her sparse brows furrowed, her fingers plucking at her pink sweater in agitation. "I . . . I can't remember. . . ." Her voice faded, her gray eyes staring intently at Joey.

"My name is Joey." The little boy stuck out his lower lip, then hid his face in Cassie's blouse.

Cassie rested her hand on Joey's shoulder. "We've brought you some fried okra for dinner. Aunt Lucinda made it. She said it's your favorite."

Miss Lena didn't seem to be listening. Her eyes seemed to focus somewhere behind Cassie's shoulder as she spoke. "I only got to see him that once, and then they took him away. . . ."

Sam took the casserole from Cassie. "I'll bring Joey more often, if you like. I've just always thought that little boys might be a little rambunctious for you."

A small smile wandered over her lips. "Oh, no. Little boys are wonderful."

Cassie helped the old lady up from her chair, then led her into the house behind Sam and Joey.

As Sam deposited the casserole in the kitchen, Cassie situated Miss Lena in her favorite armchair and made her comfortable. Joey sat as far away as he could on the faded chintz sofa and kept a wary eye on the old woman.

Miss Lena settled back in her chair and opened her book again. "This book is just wonderful. It's one of those Viking stories. I had no idea how lustful they were back then."

Cassie sent a quick glance at Joey and noticed him listening intently. As Miss Lena began to read from the book, Cassie quickly placed her hands over Joey's ears.

"Sorry to interrupt you, Miss Lena, but I noticed a few weeds in your front garden and I just want to take Joey outside to take care of that for you. I'll be right back." Firmly grabbing his arm and oblivious to the dissipating rain, she led Joey out of the house.

When she returned, Sam's bag lay open on the floor and Miss Lena had fallen asleep in her chair, the book having slipped to the floor at her side, and a gentle snore rumbling in her chest. Quietly, Cassie picked up the book and put it on a table within easy reach.

She sat on the ottoman and regarded Miss Lena closely.

"What are you doing?"

She jerked around at the sound of Sam's voice. He was holding his stethoscope, evidently left behind in the car.

Shrugging, she stood. "Just looking at her. And wondering. Wondering what her story is. She has no family except for her sister in Mobile, but lots of friends, and she's never been married. I wonder why."

Sam leaned against the console TV and crossed his arms over his chest. "From what I understand, it wasn't from lack of interest by Walton's young men at the time. Miss Lena was a rare beauty, by all accounts. Look at this."

He crossed the room in two long strides to a cherry curio cabinet. Opening it, he pulled out a framed picture and handed it to Cassie.

The woman in the Polaroid picture wore a late 1960s style polka-dotted dress with a hem slightly above the knee and a high neck. Her dark hair gleamed in a straight, blunt cut that framed an oval face with delicate features and large, almond-shaped eyes. Her seductive smile spoke of a secret yet to be revealed.

Cassie gently stroked the glass, wiping off dust. "She really was beautiful, wasn't she?" She looked back at the sleeping woman. "I can certainly tell there's a story there somewhere. I mean, look at this expression— she's definitely been up to something."

Sam nodded. "Yeah, I've always thought the same thing. I've tried to get her to tell me things, to write them down, but her mind doesn't stay on any one topic for very long. I really hate to think her stories might die with her."

An unexplainable, deep sadness rushed through Cassie like a wave at high tide, burying all under its force. She stared at the gnarled hands on the armrests and wondered if they had ever caressed a lover's cheek, or held another's hand at a movie, or clutched at a shoulder in passion. Had Miss Lena denied herself all these years, not willing to settle for good enough, or had she simply grown old waiting for the love of her life to show up?

Cassie looked at the portrait again, raising a finger to wipe off a smudge on the glass, then froze. The room seemed to fade from her peripheral vision as she lowered her head to examine the picture more closely. Her breath stilled as she studied the necklace the woman wore—a small gold locket.

"Sam."

He turned quickly, as if recognizing the urgency in her voice. Without a word, she handed him the portrait, pointing at the locket.

He stared at it for a long time, his forehead creased, until he finally looked back at Cassie. "I can't believe I missed it." He shook his head.

"Missed what?"

"Her full name is Eulene. Eulene Larsen. It's written on her medical charts in my office, and it never even occurred to me."

"EL," Cassie said, her eyes focused on the photo again.

"Exactly." Quietly, he replaced the portrait where he'd found it.

Cassie moved, as if awakened from a stupor, and pulled an afghan off the back of the sofa. Settling it gently on Miss Lena's lap, she tucked it around the sleeping woman's bare legs. Afraid to speak, she joined Joey on the front porch while they waited for Sam to finish up.

The ride back to Cassie's house was quiet except for Joey in the backseat singing along with the radio. A brief respite from the summer heat had blown in with the storm, and the windows were open to let them enjoy the coolness of the rain-sweetened air.

Finally, Sam spoke. "So, what are you going to do?"

Cassie continued looking out the window. "I don't really know. I think Daddy kept the secret to protect Miss Lena and her reputation. I'm not sure it would be the right thing to do to let her know that we know."

Sam's voice was quiet. "Not that she'll remember anyway. There's a good chance that she's blocked out all of that completely."

She rubbed her eyes with the heels of her hands. "Maybe it doesn't matter. Except that I might have a sibling out there, and Miss Lena might be able to tell me one way or the other."

Reluctantly, she met Sam's gaze. His eyes were hard and serious. "You do what you think is right, Cassie. Though I don't think a little bit of quicksand ever hurt anybody." Sam stuck his head out the window and sniffed. "I smell something burning—like leaves. But it's too early and way too wet for that."

Cassie sniffed, too, and was about to comment when she spotted the fire truck coming out of her driveway and passing them on Madison Lane. Unlatching her seat belt, she clutched the door handle. "Hurry, Sam."

He had barely stopped before Cassie opened her door, jumped out of the truck, and started to run. Without stopping, she called out over her shoulder, "Sam—stay with Joey."

Aunt Lucinda and a small group of people hovered around the old magnolia in the front yard. She recognized a few of the neighbors, too, and they were all shaking their heads.

"Are the children all right? What happened?" Her breath came in heavy pants.

Lucinda touched her arm. "The children are fine, and everything is okay now—thank God. But somebody set fire to the dry leaves under the magnolia. Thank goodness so many of them were damp from the rain, or this whole part of the yard would have just gone up like tinder."

Cassie stared at the blackened leaves at the base of her tree, smelling the acrid stench of wet leaves and something like gasoline. Her throat tightened. "Is the tree . . . damaged?"

Richard Haney, her father's old neighbor, stepped forward. "I don't think so—it just appears to be singed a bit. I'd have a tree surgeon look at it just in case, though. Hate for you to lose such a fine tree." He shook his head sadly.

Mrs. Haney peeked out from behind her husband's shoulder. "I just don't know what's happening to our neighborhood. It used to be so peaceful. Maybe we should have moved farther away." She cast a glance in the direction of

Farrellsford. "And to think I slept last night with my doors unlocked. Don't think I'll be doing that again."

Cassie eyed the Haneys carefully, wondering why they were there. "How did this happen?"

Aunt Lucinda wiped her hair off her forehead, watching Sam approach with Joey. "I was in the study, going through your father's things just like you asked, when I smelled smoke. I looked out the window and stared out at the lawn until I saw smoke rising up from this tree. I didn't even think. I called nine-one-one and got all the children out of the house. Madison had just come home from school and she went and got a hose, but the fire truck came before she even had a chance to get it all the way out here. The fire chief says it's definitely arson. Said something about detecting an accelerant, whatever that is." A small sheen of perspiration shone through Lucinda's flawless makeup.

Cassie stared at the singed base of the tree, a small furrow between her eyebrows. "Why would anybody want to hurt my tree?"

The small crowd began to disperse, giving Cassie pats and smiles of sympathy as they left. Mrs. Haney mentioned something about a neighborhood watch group and said she'd call.

Cassie faced the Haneys, fists on her hips. "You do that. And you can also tell Mr. Roust that no matter what he does, I'm not selling him my land.

The guys who are doing this for him are bound to be caught sooner or later, so you might want to pass along that message to your boys."

The Haneys both looked at her with stunned expressions. Richard Haney stepped forward, his face grim. "I've known you too long, Cassie, to seriously believe that you'd think our boys had something to do with this! Sure, they're wild and all, but they'd never do something like this. And as for Roust being behind all this, believe me—he's got much bigger fish to fry than you. If he wanted this land, he'd have had it long ago." Grabbing his wife's elbow, he stalked away.

Sam crouched in front of the magnolia. "Your tree will be fine, Cassie—don't worry. Maybe you could rig a spotlight from the house to illuminate this part of the yard. Unless you want to camp out again tonight."

Sarah Frances came racing out the front door. "Aunt Cassie—telephone. It's Principal Purdy." She looked at her older sister with an impish grin and began to chant, "Maddie's in trouble, Maddie's in trouble."

"Hush, child." Lucinda grabbed the young girl by the shoulders, hugging her with her face pressed against her side to muffle the girl's voice.

Cassie sighed. She wondered if it could have something to do with Maddie not making the cheerleading squad again. High school had been in session for a week and the disappointment hadn't even seemed to faze Maddie. She even seemed almost cheerful.

"Let me go take that phone call. Would you mind coming with me, Sam? I've got a check for your dad to pay for Andrew's car. I keep forgetting to bring it by."

As they walked across the lawn, Cassie noticed Maddie disappearing around the corner of the house. She seemed to be in a hurry.

She took the phone in her father's office, after first hunting for it amid the piles of papers and boxes. Sam lifted a golf club off brackets on the wall and started practicing his swing.

Cassie held the receiver to her ear and said hello. The principal's voice seemed strained as it came through the phone. "Hello, Cassie. I'm afraid this isn't a social call. I understand you're in charge while Joe and Harriet are in Atlanta."

"Ah, yes. That's right. What can I do for you?"

"Well." There was a long pause. "This is about Maddie. There's been a sort of . . . incident, and I need to sit down and talk with you about it."

"What kind of incident?"

"It involves Lucy Spafford. And, um, I'd rather not discuss it over the phone but would like you to come down to my office. Would you be available in an hour, say about five o'clock?"

"Yes, sir. I'll be there." She frowned into the receiver, wondering why a thirty-five-year-old professional was still afraid of her old high school principal.

After hanging up the phone, she went to the desk drawer and handed Sam the check for the car repair. He took it, staring at her with a curious expression. "What's wrong?"

She crossed her arms over her chest. "I'm not sure. But it involves Maddie and Lucy Spafford. Principal Purdy wants me to come to his office to discuss it. I was wondering . . ."

She stopped and Sam tilted his head, eyes narrowed. "What?"

"Well, if you could come with me. I'm not good at this parenting thing, and I think I'll be needing moral support."

Sam hung the golf club back on the wall. "It's not you who's in trouble, you know. But if you think it will help, I'll be glad to go with you. I am Maddie's godfather, after all. Just let me call the clinic and let Mary Jane know where I am."

She touched his arm. "Just don't tell her why, okay?"

He raised an eyebrow, but didn't say anything.

Maddie was conspicuously absent as she and Sam got in the truck. Cassie had a nagging feeling that she'd soon find out why.

Principal Purdy was cordial enough as Cassie and Sam entered the familiar office. Except for the desktop computer and fax machine, not much had changed since the days she had been a frequent visitor. Mr. Purdy accepted Sam's presence and ushered them both inside before motioning for them to sit in two chairs facing his desk.

After he sat, the principal steepled his fingers and was quiet for a few long moments, as if hunting about for the correct words. His hair, now completely white, had thinned considerably, with only sparse strands spread over his balding pate like a spider's web.

Finally, he spoke. "I think the best way to get through this is to just start, so let me begin." He cleared his throat. "As you are probably aware, Mrs. Anderson's freshman advanced civics class took a field trip to the state capitol last Thursday. It's an honor to be placed in that class, which is why we allow Mrs. Anderson to introduce her subject matter by taking these select students to the capitol the first week of school. As a treat, you might say, before they begin the challenging course work. Your niece"—he indicated Cassie with a dip of his head—"was on that trip, along with Lucy Spafford."

He stood and took a paper cup from a table next to a water dispenser. "Water anyone?" Cassie and Sam declined and waited for the principal to fill his cup and return to his chair.

"Anyway. At the entrance to the capitol building there's a metal detector where all visitors to the building must pass through." He took a long drink of water, draining the cup. "When Lucy Spafford put her purse through the detector, it beeped. The security personnel, as is their job, then had to manually examine the purse to find the cause of the beeping." He stopped speaking, then lowered his head, looking up at Cassie through heavy eyebrows.

"What was it?" Cassie's voice cracked and she swallowed. All of a sudden she had the clear image in her head of Principal Purdy's red-and-white-striped boxer shorts flying high atop the flagpole. She bit down on her lip, hard.

He cleared his throat again. "It was a . . . um . . . a sexual device. I believe the term is a vibrator. A battery-operated model."

Sam coughed but Cassie continued looking at the principal with a straight face. "And what has this got to do with Maddie?"

"Well, Lucy's best friend, Lauren North, said she's seen an, ahem, Adam & Eve catalog in Maddie's locker. Seems anyone can just call their eight-hundred number and request a catalog." He cleared his throat. "You'll want to check your credit card statements for the charge, and tell Harriet and Joe to do the same." Sam and Cassie waited while the principal helped himself to another cup of water. He sat down again and continued. "When I questioned Maddie, she admitted to putting the uh, device, into Lucy's purse. She didn't even try to deny it. I think she enjoys the attention." He looked pointedly at

Cassie, who tried to keep a bland expression on her face.

Cassie crossed, then recrossed her legs. "This happened last Thursday? Why wasn't I notified about this earlier?"

"I, well . . ." He coughed again into his rounded fist. "I was waiting for Harriet and Joe to return, but I understand they're expected to be gone for some time." With a short pause, he continued, "And Lucy and her parents are eager to move beyond this . . . this incident."

Cassie nodded, her grown-up expression plastered seamlessly on her face. "I will discuss this with Maddie and come up with a suitable punishment."

Principal Purdy nodded, his expression one of relief; then he slid back his chair in a clear signal that the meeting was over. "I don't think this calls for a suspension—not this time, anyway. I'm sure a lot of this has to do with Harriet's illness, and it's natural for a girl such as Maddie to act out. And your niece is a very spirited girl, Cassie. A good student, too. Reminds me of another student we used to have." He winked in Cassie's direction. "She just needs to rein in that energy—focus it in some other, more productive direction."

"Yes, sir. I understand. I'll be sure to bring this up with Harriet and Joe when they return." Rising, she leaned forward and shook the principal's hand; then Sam followed suit.

They left the office quietly, only the soft tapping of their heels following them down the deserted after-hours school halls and out the door. They remained stoic and poised until Sam's truck had turned out of the school's parking lot. Barely past the intersection, they both burst out laughing.

Sam pulled the truck to the side of the road, howling with laughter. Cassie leaned her head against the seat back, trying to catch her breath. "Oh, my gosh—I have such a mental image here. Can you just see Lucy Spafford looking at what they pulled from her purse? It's just so damned funny."

Sam leaned his forehead against the steering wheel. "Man, I'm just picturing all those kids staring at that thing and wondering what in the hell it was." He shook his head and looked at Cassie. "That's the funniest damned prank I have ever heard of. I think you're going to have to retire your crown—she's got you beat."

"I'll gladly relinquish it. She's a worthy successor." They were silent for a moment before Cassie suddenly turned toward Sam. "Oh, my gosh! I just remembered her asking me if batteries were metal. That was when Andrew was here. To think she's been conniving all this time!"

Sam elbowed her gently, still laughing. "She comes by it honestly."

Cassie grinned. "Yeah. She does. Just a chip off the ol' block."

"Are you going to tell her parents?"

Cassie shook her head. "No—at least, not right now. I think they have enough on their plate for the time being. Besides, I don't want to be the one to have to explain to Harriet what a vibrator is."

"Are you going to at least punish Maddie?"

Cassie watched a convertible full of teenagers whiz by them on the road. "You bet. Besides an apology to Lucy, I'd say the whole first floor of my house needs waxing, wouldn't you?"

Sam started the engine. "I seem to remember you with wax under your fingernails a few times."

Cassie nodded. "And I'm a damned fine floor waxer, too, I'll have you know." She flipped down the overhead visor and fixed her hair. "But if she's anything like me, this won't make her sorry in the slightest. It'll just make her try harder next time so she doesn't get caught."

Sam chuckled. "I can't believe she's Harriet's child. She's you made over, through and through. Poor Har." He shook his head, a wide grin on his face. "I just keep thinking about Maddie explaining to her mother what a vibrator is. If it ever comes to that, I want to get it on tape so I can upload it to YouTube."

That made Cassie start laughing all over again, barely able to contain herself. She laughed until she started to cry, thinking of the marvelous girl who was her niece and of the girl's mother, who might not be there to see her daughter grow into womanhood.

As if sensing the change, Sam slid his arm over her and let her nestle in his shoulder. No more words were spoken, but his warmth and understanding were enough. She buried her face in his denim shirt and cried for her own motherless childhood, for Harriet, and mostly, for Maddie.

CHAPTER 23

Cassie hopped on one foot as she struggled to put on her swimsuit as quickly as she could. Sarah Frances and Joey were already downstairs in the foyer, suited up and with sunscreen-coated faces and bodies, waiting impatiently for her to come down and take them to the creek.

As she fastened the tie on her back, she spotted a deep gash in the wood of her bed's footboard. It was a fresh wound, the wood pale and splintered, and it was apparent that something large and heavy had fallen and hit it, taking out a chunk of cherrywood. Leaning to press her fingers on the mark, she noticed three envelopes half-hidden under the dust ruffle of the bed. Kneeling, she picked them up.

One by one, she slid out the letters and examined them. The first two she recognized as having read before from the stack inside the letter box. But the third envelope was smaller than the others and completely blank on the front: no handwriting, postmark, or stamp. The flap was open, apparently never sealed, but it was ripped on one corner, making her think it might have been inadvertently stuck to the back of another envelope and easily missed. She was fairly sure that she hadn't seen it before. Turning it over, she pulled out the letter inside and unfolded it. Her heart squeezed when she recognized her father's handwriting with the heavy strokes and large capital letters.

August 18, 1985

My Dearest Child,
I'm sorry not to be addressing this to your name, but despite my best efforts, I've never been able to find out whether you're a boy or girl or what they have named you.

In the possibility that I might die before ever seeing you, I am writing this letter so that you might understand why we have never met. It is likely that you will never read this, and that I'm merely writing it to ease my own mind. It is small comfort, but it is the only one I can seem to find.

Your mother, with your best interests at heart, gave you up for adoption without my knowledge. She told me you had died, and I had no reason to believe otherwise. Please know that I would have found you and made

491

you my own if I had any knowledge of your whereabouts. The only secret I would have kept would be your mother's identity. She's a good woman, and I would never want to compromise her reputation, even if it meant allowing your identity to remain a secret to the outside world.

You were almost three years old when I found out that you had not died at birth and that you'd been adopted. Your mother only told me right before the birth of your sister, Cassandra. I suppose she thought it would heal the old wounds, but it did not. It made me want to find you, and to be a part of your life. But you'd already been adopted and your mother thought it best not to divulge your whereabouts or any other information about you that would have made you easier to find.

Since then I've been trying to find you— not to take you away from a family who has no doubt grown to love you and accept you as their own, but to make sure that you are happy. But your maternal grandparents, who by then were gone, handled the adoption privately and there are no records that I can find. But I will keep trying.

I have an idea in my mind of what you must look like. I can only hope that one day I will be able to see you face-to-face and tell you that you have your mother's eyes, or my nose, or my father's hands.

Know that I love you—as much as I love your two sisters—and my greatest wish is that we will be reunited. I will keep that hope alive until I am blessed enough to see your face or until I go to meet my maker and will have to atone for my wrongs against your mother. Please forgive me for not giving you a name. I would give up my very home just to be able to hold you in my arms but once.

Yours always,
Harrison R. Madison III

Cassie held the letter for a long moment, relief flooding through her. Relief that her father had known about his child, and that he'd never given up looking. She felt excitement, too. *I have another sister or brother out there. Somewhere.* Her gaze caught sight again of the gash in the footboard, and she stood so suddenly her head swam. *The letter box. The letter box is gone.*

She had left it on the bed, and could still see the indentation on the bedspread. Dropping to her knees, she peered under the bed but found it empty except for her slippers.

She slipped the letters into her purse, then allowed her gaze to scan the room one last time to make sure the letter box wasn't there before running downstairs shouting Lucinda's name.

Her aunt stuck her head out from the kitchen, flour from her homemade biscuits smeared on her nose. "What's wrong, sweet pea?"

Cassie struggled to calm her voice. "Have you seen a large wooden letter box? I left it in my room and it's gone."

Lucinda's penciled brows furrowed. "No, I haven't seen it. And you know I wouldn't take anything out of your room without your permission. Are you sure you didn't misplace it?"

Cassie shook her head. "No. I know I didn't."

"Aunt Cassie—can we go now?" Joey's voice from the foyer carried each consonant in a drawn-out whine.

"I'll be there in just a minute." She turned back to Lucinda. "It was Daddy's writing box—it has his initials on the top." She thought for a moment. "Did anybody come look at the house this morning while I was out?"

Lucinda shook her head. "Nope. Not that I know of, anyway. I was in the back, weeding my vegetable garden."

Cassie frowned, deep in thought. "Well, if you do come across it, could you please put it back in my room?"

Lucinda nodded and Cassie slowly left the kitchen, wondering what had happened to the letter box. Maybe because she was so preoccupied she'd moved it from the bed and just forgotten where. Or maybe someone had taken it, dropping it first and allowing the three letters to fall out. She shook her head, afraid to think of the implications.

She turned the corner into the foyer and spied her niece and nephew sitting on the bottom step already wearing their masks and snorkels, and she couldn't resist a smile. She'd think about the letter box later. It hadn't walked off by itself and would surely show up.

CASSIE STOOD PERCHED on a rock by the creek, her bare toes gripping its slippery surface, her hair slicked back off her face and dripping water down her back. The temperature had been hovering in the high nineties all week and the coolness of the water felt heaven-sent.

"Shark attack!" she shouted as she jumped into the water. When she emerged, eyes tightly shut, the delighted screams of the children in the creek alerted her as to where her victims were hiding.

"Shark!" she shouted again, diving for a nearby squealer who sounded suspiciously like Sarah Frances. Grabbing a small wet body with plastic floaties encircling her upper arms, Cassie tickled the girl mercilessly until the child shouted, "Shark bait!" Cassie hugged her, then let her go. "Your turn to be the shark."

As the dripping Sarah Frances climbed up onto the rock, Cassie skimmed under the surface again, delighting in the cool sluicing of the water over her body. She opened her eyes and stared up at the mottled sky, the surreal sun casting an uneven light under the surface. It was quiet and peaceful under there: no worries, no sickness, nobody clamoring for her attention. And no Sam to mess with her mind. She blew bubbles from her mouth, round little troubles that rose to the surface and exploded into light and air. A shout from the bank brought her crashing up to reality.

Blinking the water out of her eyes, she spotted Ed Farrell approaching.

"Hey, Ed," she said, waving with an arc of water.

"Hey, Cassie." He smiled broadly and waved back. "I saw Lucinda walking with Knoxie and Amanda and she told me where to find you. Thought I'd go for a swim, too." He stopped near the edge of the water, his hair sticking to his forehead in sweaty streaks. His wore a T-shirt, a floral swimsuit that reached almost to midcalf, and faded blue flip-flops, and he carried an Atlanta Braves towel. "Mind if I join y'all?"

"Sure, come on in."

Dropping the towel, he pulled off his oversize shirt and stepped slowly into the water. "Just trying to get in my daily workout, and swimming is as good as any exercise." He quickly squatted down, immersing himself completely. "As a matter of fact, I'm planning a fitness facility in downtown Walton, and I can guarantee we'll have an Olympic-sized swimming pool in it. Easier to do laps and all that stuff than in a creek."

Cassie nodded. "Sure would be," she said, although she didn't voice her stray thought about how sterile an indoor pool would be compared to Senator Thompkins's creek. "Hey, Ed. Remember my father's letter box—I was holding it one day when you stopped by and you admired it?"

Ed nodded. "Sure do. Beautiful antique. Why? Have you changed your mind about selling it?"

"No. I just can't find it. I don't think I misplaced it, but can't figure why it isn't where I put it. If somebody you brought to the house took it, you'd notice, right?"

Ed splashed water on his face. "Absolutely. It would be kinda hard sneaking something like that into my car without me noticing, you know?"

Cassie breaststroked away from him, enjoying the cool sluice of water on her arms and chest. "Yeah, I guess so. I just can't understand what happened to it."

Joey let out an earsplitting scream before landing in the water with a perfect cannonball and successfully drenching everybody.

Ed sucked in his breath as the cool water hit his skin. "Hey, kid—watch who you're splashing."

Cassie sent the boy an admonishing glare that wasn't quite successful. Joey stifled a smile, issued a perfunctory, "Sorry, Mr. Farrell," then swam over to his sister.

Cassie shook her head, counting again the days until school started for the younger children. Even though Maddie had been in school almost two weeks, Joey and Sarah Frances attended a small church-run elementary school, and they started later, much to Cassie's chagrin. Her days were filled with entertaining three boisterous children and a baby, refereeing fights, and feeding the kids endlessly. At three thirty, when Maddie returned home from school, the homework battle began. It had taken Cassie three whole days to realize that her oldest niece could be bribed with stories about her life in New York or the promise of trying on some of her clothes.

Ed waded his way to the middle of the creek, then treaded water to keep his head above the surface. "I had another couple express interest in your house today, but when I told them where it was located, they said no. Said they'd been talking at a party with an old neighbor of yours about all the vandalism problems and weren't interested in moving into a questionable neighborhood."

Cassie let her feet touch the gravelly bottom. "Questionable neighborhood? Was that neighbor perhaps Richard Haney?"

"I'm afraid so. And whether or not it's true isn't at issue. Either way, it's getting harder and harder to find somebody for your house."

She regarded him closely, wondering again who it was he reminded her of. "You know, Ed, I was thinking about your offer to buy the house. I think I've decided to go with keeping it and just renting it for a while—at least as long as it takes us to find a single-family buyer."

He dipped his head in the water, slicking the hair back off his face. "Well, that might make things easier, that's for sure. And it would also give you time to think and reassess what you really want to do with the house." He turned on his side and began sidestroking across the creek. "I'm assuming you heard about the town council meeting. Sam may have won the battle for an ordinance against more teardowns, but he won't win the war. It's just a matter of time. We're having a referendum in January, and I can guarantee the people will vote down the ordinance. The majority of our citizens are pro-progress, and a few sticks-in-the-mud like Sam Parker won't make a bit of difference."

He put his face under the water again, and when he came up, he spewed a mouthful of water out through his teeth. "But you just tell me what to do, Cassie. I know how eager you are to return to your career and maybe patch things up with that fiancé of yours. I am here to do your bidding."

Cassie stopped treading water and just stood still for a moment, contemplating going back to New York and confronting Andrew again. She hadn't heard from him about the VisEx account, and she assumed he'd either dropped her completely or had managed to buy her more time. Strangely, it didn't seem to matter to her— it was as if that life

499

were one thousand light-years away from the docile creek and splashing children. She flipped over onto her back, letting the water over her ears muffle sound.

It seemed that everybody these days was trying to force her to make a decision about something. Even the reporter from *Preservation* magazine was relentless with his weekly requests for a feature article and a photography shoot.

She did the backstroke over to the bank and crawled out of the creek, pulling herself over to the large diving rock. Grabbing her towel, she began drying herself off. "Ed, how much monthly rent do you think I should—" Her words were cut off by a scream from Sarah Frances.

Cassie jumped back into the water and swam as quickly as she could to her niece. The girl was clutching at something under the water, making it difficult to hold her head above the surface. She was screaming and choking on water when Cassie reached her and pulled her to the bank.

An ugly gash, about two inches wide, bisected the bottom of her left foot. Blood ran freely from the wound, washing pink down her drenched skin. When she saw the blood, Sarah Frances began to scream louder, and continued her wail as Joey held up the rusty can lid out of the water.

On autopilot, Cassie reached for the shirt she had worn over her bathing suit. It was a crop top with spaghetti straps and the perfect size for wrapping around a small foot. She tightened it as much as she could, trying to calm the hysterical child at the same time.

Ed threw on his shirt. "Come on—put her in my car. I'll drive y'all to the clinic."

Cassie nodded. "I'll wrap towels around her foot so we don't get blood on the upholstery."

He nodded as Cassie carried the sobbing girl and settled her in the backseat. She quickly gathered the rest of their belongings before she and Joey piled into the car. Ed drove a little faster than she would have liked, but they got to the clinic in record time, even with dropping Joey off at home with Lucinda first.

To Cassie's surprise, Ed carried Sarah Frances inside the empty waiting room himself. Mary Jane stared with amazement at Ed carrying the little girl, but quickly adjusted her expression. Cassie, wearing just her bikini top and cutoff shorts, explained the situation, and Mary Jane disappeared into the back to get Sam.

Sam appeared and took the little girl from Ed. Her sobbing quieted once she was in Sam's arms, and Cassie couldn't help but notice how he seemed to have that effect on most women.

She followed Sam and Sarah Frances into an examining room that resembled an underwater adventure. Blue walls with painted bubbles and pudgy fish swam around the perimeter, with bright rays of sun covering the ceiling. The little girl sat on top of white paper in the middle of an examining table, her skinny legs stuck out in front of her, and her tearstained face a mask of childlike suffering. Cassie put her arms around the girl's shoulders. "She stepped on a rusty can lid in the creek."

Sam nodded before bending to examine the little foot. "You did a good job with this bandage," he said as he unwrapped Cassie's shirt from the foot and stared at it for a moment before discarding the shirt on the floor.

He sent a reassuring smile to Sarah Frances as he examined her foot. When he was finished, he pressed a button on the wall, then addressed the little girl. "I don't think we'll need stitches. I'll send Miss Harden in to clean it and bandage it, and then you can pick something out of the goody box, okay?" The little girl nodded, her cheeks pale and stained with drying tears.

He turned to Cassie. "You wouldn't happen to know if her tetanus is current, would you?"

"Actually, I do—and it is. I had Harriet go over all that stuff with me before she left." She shrugged, trying not to look too proud. "You know, just in case."

It looked like he was about to say something, but he was interrupted by Mary Jane's entrance. Sam gave her instructions, then asked Sarah Frances for permission to speak with her aunt in private. With a promise to be quick, he ushered Cassie out of the examining room to his office at the end of the hall.

He went to a small refrigerator and pulled out two Cokes, handing one to Cassie. The air-conditioning blew strong from the overhead vent, making Cassie all too aware of her barely dressed state. She pulled the tab on the can and took a long swallow.

Sam continued to watch her closely without speaking, so she turned her back to him and examined the small but well-furnished office. "So. This is where you work."

"Yep. When I'm not lancing boils or saving houses, that is."

She sent him an arch look before returning to admire the neutral tones interspersed with bright colors on throw pillows, curtains, and a quilt hanging on the wall. Cassie walked over to the quilt and touched it, admiring the tiny, handmade stitches. "Did your mother make this for you?"

He took a long swallow from his Coke. "Actually, Mary Jane did."

"Oh." She turned back around to face him. "So. What did you need to talk to me about?"

He leaned against the wall and took a deep breath, just like a man ready to open a box he knew contained something unpleasant. "I just got off the phone with Joe right before you got here. They're coming home tomorrow."

"Tomorrow? Why didn't they call me to let me know?"

"They did. You must have left your cell phone

someplace where you couldn't hear it, and you haven't been home. Gallivanting with Ed Farrell, I expect."

"I don't gallivant with anybody—especially not Ed. I was just at the creek and he showed up." She crossed her arms over her chest, hugging herself. "So, that's good news, right? That she's coming home?"

Sam sat on the edge of the desk nearest her. "Why don't you take a seat."

His voice had turned suddenly serious, and she obeyed without question.

"Harriet wanted me to speak to you first, before they got home. I guess they need you to know, so you can help them with the children. Especially Maddie." His blue eyes were gentle as he regarded her, but they did nothing to still the rising tide of fear inside her.

Unbidden, her fingers reached up to the gold charms around her neck and began touching them one by one. She held his gaze and kept her voice strong. "What do they need me to know?"

"They had her charts and test results faxed over to me, and I was on the phone with her oncologist for over an hour this morning, discussing her care. So." He looked down at his hands for a moment. "So, I can explain this to you in black-and-white terms, in medical terminology, in words that won't make a lot of sense to you. Or I can tell you what you don't want to hear."

Cassie stood, walked over to the window, and jerked up the venetian blinds, sending a small cloud of dust motes into the late-afternoon sunshine. "Tell me. . . ." She cleared her throat, her voice stronger now. "Tell me everything—medical and otherwise. I need to know everything." Her voice sounded far away to her, reminding her of the same voice her father had used when he told her that her own mother had gone to heaven. She felt small and scared again, and the need to run away and hide made her foot twitch. But she reached inside herself and found the inner reserve, her particular brand of stubbornness, and clung tightly to it. "Shoot," she said with false bravado.

He took a deep breath. "She has breast cancer with lymphatic invasion—a stage-four cancer. Aggressive, multimodality therapy is warranted, but we have to be careful because of the pregnancy. Radiation is out of the question because of how widespread the tumors are, and Harriet won't consider chemotherapy because of the chance of miscarriage or fetal damage—however small the risk at this stage of the pregnancy. Surgery is also not an option at this stage because of how much the cancer has spread." He paused for a moment, as if gathering strength. "She, with her doctor's knowledge, will wait until the baby is born before beginning treatment—if any is even warranted at that point."

Cassie made her way back to the chair and sat

heavily, her legs no longer able to hold her, and began to shake with small trembles at first, which then erupted into visible limb movements. She realized she still held her Coke can and let Sam take it out of her shaking hand. Then he moved to stand next to her, draping his lab coat over her bare shoulders.

Cassie stared at the wall. "If she's at stage four now, but waits four more months for treatment, what's her survival probability?"

He squatted by her chair and looked her in the face. "It's already pretty low, Cassie. Cancer cells have spread everywhere—including her liver. Even without the pregnancy, her chances of survival are very, very small. And aggressive treatment would most likely only give her a few more months, while possibly harming the baby."

Her voice was calm, belying the trembling in her arms. "And the baby?"

"The baby is healthy. There have been no known instances of a maternal-fetal transfer of cancer cells." He touched her arm, a glimmer of light in his voice. "It's another boy."

"A boy." She gripped the coat around her arms, unable to control their shaking. Squaring her shoulders, she sat up straight in the chair and looked directly at him. "So, after the baby is born, what do we do then?"

He stared at her for a moment before speaking. "This isn't an advertising plan, Cassie, where there's a solution to everything. This is the human body, and I'm afraid it just doesn't work like that. We're in a wait-and-see mode right now."

She stood so quickly her chair flipped on its back. "So what do we do?" she repeated, her voice rising and cracking. "What's the next course of treatment?"

He stood, too, but slowly and deliberately. "We make her comfortable. And we . . . manage the pain. The baby will be born by C-section as soon as it is medically feasible to do so where it won't compromise his health."

The overhead air vent shut off and all was silent inside the office except for the muffled voices down the hall and Sarah Frances's childish laugh. Cassie gripped the edge of the desk, unable to move or form words. Yanking the coat off her shoulders, she threw it to the ground.

"So there's nothing we can do?" She slapped her hands on the surface of the dark wood desk, making a piece of paper slide off the top, then slowly drift down to the floor.

She tried to move, but he held on to her with both hands on her shoulders. "At this point, no. But this is Harriet's decision, and she needs your support."

Cassie struggled, not even trying to keep her voice down. "Am I the only one who wants to fight this?" Biting her lip, she struggled to get away from him.

Gently, he said, "No, Cassie. I think we realiz when it's time to pick up the pieces and go home—wherever that might be. Harriet has made her choice—let her do this in peace."

"No!" She jerked away and headed for the door, leaving Sam behind.

She ran to the examining room and found it empty. In a panic she started opening all the doors down the corridor, shouting Sarah Frances's name. When she came to the waiting room, she stopped. The little girl was at a kid-sized table coloring. She looked at her aunt with a smile and held up the picture she had been working on. It was a picture of a house with seven stick people in front. One of the figures with long blond hair held a small baby in her arms.

"I'm drawing this for Mommy. I'm going to give it to her when she comes home."

Cassie knelt by the child and hugged her tightly.

As if sensing something, the child stiffened and began to cry. "I want my mommy."

Cassie patted the back of the girl's head and whispered softly to her, "I know, sweetheart. Let's go home."

Then she lifted the little girl, the picture clutched tightly in the small fist, and carried her out the door.

CHAPTER 24

On Saturday afternoon, Maddie sat on the porch swing at Aunt Cassie's house with her aunt and wiped the sweat from her nose again with the inside of her elbow. Aunt Lucinda kept calling this heat wave the dog days of summer, and everybody was looking for a way to cool off. In what Maddie could only think of as sheer desperation, that morning Aunt Cassie had taken them all to the Piggly Wiggly for a breakfast of Moon Pies and Cokes and they had lingered in the chilly frozen-food aisles until they had goose bumps on their arms and legs.

The ceiling fan whirred overhead and a metal tub of peas sat between them. Mama and Daddy were on their way home, and Maddie had a feeling that Aunt Cassie was using the dreaded chore of pea shelling to keep them both too busy to worry. Not that it was working, seeing as Maddie had plenty of time to worry, but at least it kept her hands busy.

Aunt Cassie tried to hide a yawn as she struggled to shell a pea. Maddie had found her aunt hunched over her laptop at the kitchen table around three o'clock in the morning when Maddie had gotten up to get a drink of water. At first, Aunt Cassie had tried to shield the screen from her, and then she'd given in when Maddie wouldn't go away.

Maddie's mama had always told her that she was as stubborn as her aunt, and she'd just proved her wrong: Maddie was apparently a lot more stubborn.

Aunt Cassie had stayed up most of the night researching breast cancer on the Internet, hoping to find mention of some new drug, some miracle cure. A lot of what she'd shown Maddie had been mostly gibberish to both of them, but she'd printed it all out anyway, sure, she explained, that it would mean something to somebody. Maddie wanted to share her aunt's sense of hope, but couldn't. The difference between reality and fantasy was very clear to her, having been raised around framed photos of an aunt who never visited despite Mama's promises that she would one day. And she'd never believed in Santa Claus, either.

Maddie threw a handful of peas at the tub on the floor, missing the bucket and sending the small green projectiles scattering across the floorboards. As she bent to pick up the annoying peas, she heard the sound of tires on gravel and looked up to see her daddy's car, followed closely by Dr. Parker's truck. Aunt Cassie stood and walked to the screen door, opening it and shouting to the younger children to come outside.

Maddie continued to shell peas, confused at how so much anger and so much love could live inside her at the same time. Her fingers continued working as she watched the two vehicles park in clouds of dust. Her daddy and Dr. Parker got out and went to help her mama get out of the car.

Her mother seemed smaller, somehow, more frail. They had been gone only three weeks, yet the woman who stepped out of the car hardly looked like the mother Maddie knew. The baby bump was bigger, sticking out of the shapeless dress, and made Maddie look away. She focused on the peas as she followed her mother's progress to the bottom step, where she sat down with a heavy sigh. The sound of running feet could be heard in the foyer right before the screen door slammed, and Maddie watched as her mama spread her arms wide.

Knoxie, Joey, and Sarah Frances fought over their mother's limited lap space, but were all given turns before being handed over to Daddy for bear hugs and big kisses. Aunt Lucinda appeared with Amanda in her arms. When the baby saw her mother, she squealed and reached with chubby arms.

Maddie stayed on the swing, shelling peas and letting them plop into the bucket, until her father approached. "Hey, peanut. Aren't you going to give your favorite daddy a big hug and kiss?" His eyes were full of concern, but he kept the warm smile on his face.

Maddie shrugged, which made Aunt Cassie prod her on the arm. Reluctantly, Maddie reached up and gave her father a hug and a quick peck on the cheek before returning to her shelling. She really wanted to throw herself at him and cry into his shoulder like she'd done as a little girl. But she couldn't. She was too old for that now, and far too angry.

Mama stood with Amanda in her arms, wobbling slightly. Lucinda took the baby as she approached Maddie. "Hey, Maddie. Can I have a hug, too?"

Maddie looked up far enough to see the little baby bump under her mother's dress, but couldn't go any farther. She resumed shelling peas, hoping her mother would just go away.

Aunt Cassie stepped between them and gave her sister a big hug, then held her at arm's length. "Welcome home, Harriet." Dropping her sister's hands, she turned to Maddie's daddy and gave him a hug, too. Maddie looked up then and saw the expression on Aunt Cassie's face and it made her want to cry all over again. It was like seeing a fast-forward movie about the last fifteen years of her parents' and Aunt Cassie's lives, spent apart, and how now that it was too late they could see only wasted time.

Aunt Cassie told everyone to go into the kitchen, where Lucinda had prepared a homecoming lunch. Maddie threw in her last handful of peas and followed behind the rest of her family. After the little kids finished fighting over who got to sit next to Mama, Maddie squeezed into a spot on the other side of the table between Dr. Parker and her aunt, holding hands with both of them as her father said grace.

Maddie watched as her mother took a single bite of her chicken salad and chewed slowly. Dropping her fork, she stood, leaning heavily on the table. "Excuse me, everybody. But I've got to go lie down on the sofa in the parlor. I'm just so tired from the trip."

Cassie excused herself and followed her. Maddie, having lost her appetite, too, followed but stood back in the doorway, unsure of where she belonged.

"Are you all right?" Aunt Cassie grabbed an afghan off her father's reading chair and tucked it all around Mama's small body on the couch.

"Besides the cancer, yes, I'm fine. Just tired is all."

Maddie winced at her mother's words and saw from her aunt's expression that she felt the same. "I'm sorry, I didn't mean . . . Well, I can't believe you can joke about this."

Mama leaned back and closed her eyes. "I'm sorry, Cassie. It's just that if I don't laugh . . ." Her voice faded.

Aunt Cassie went to the bookcase to take out a stack of papers. Pulling up the ottoman in front of the sofa, Cassie held them up. "I printed these off the Internet last night. It's a whole list of clinical trials you can sign up for. There're also a few articles on drugs that they expect the FDA to approve in the next year. I think you, Joe, and Sam need to look at these."

Mama nodded, her eyes soft, and reached out her hand. Cassie gave her the pages, looking like she expected them to be read and examined right away. Instead, Mama dropped them on the sofa beside her.

"I'll give you some time to look at those while I go make sure the kids eat their lunches, all right?"

Mama nodded, her eyes already closing before Aunt Cassie had left the room. Maddie watched her mother sleep, seeing how her skin almost matched the beige of the sofa and how her hair didn't seem so shiny anymore. Lying on the couch, Mama looked as small and helpless as Knoxie. She knew her mama was short, but it had never occurred to Maddie until now to see her mother as anything else but big and strong—her protector in all the little hurts of life. Sliding down the wall, Maddie sat on the floor, where she could keep an eye on her mother and still follow the conversation in the kitchen, and allowed the tears to slip silently down her cheeks because nobody else could see them.

Aunt Cassie seated herself where Mama had been, and began mashing bananas to feed to the baby. She didn't speak to Daddy or Dr. Parker until the other kids had run out of the kitchen because of Aunt Lucinda's promise of homemade ice cream. As usual, they left the back door open and Dr. Parker got up and closed it.

Aunt Cassie wiped Amanda's mouth, then sat up. "I've been doing a lot of research on the Internet. I think there may be options Harriet doesn't know about yet." She glanced up hopefully, her gaze moving from one man to the other.

Maddie's throat tightened as the two men exchanged a look and Daddy shifted uncomfortably in his chair. Even Maddie knew the truth; her father had told her everything over the phone from Atlanta. Her mother had made her choice, and Aunt Cassie had been away far too long if she believed she could change her mind.

Dr. Parker put down his sandwich. "We've already gone over every viable possibility, Cassie. We've looked down every avenue, and this is the course of action that Harriet and Joe and her doctors have chosen. And you need to remember it's *her* life we're talking about."

Cassie put down the fork she'd used to mash the bananas and dumped the food on the high-chair tray. Amanda immediately dived into it with both hands. "So what you're telling me is that those five children—soon to be six—don't need their mother. You're giving up."

Dr. Parker slid back his chair, leaning forward on the table as he spoke to her with precise words. "We're not giving up—we're making the best decision we know how with the situation we are given."

She slid back her own chair, bumping the wall behind her. The baby stopped shoveling food into her mouth and instead stared up at Aunt Cassie. Lowering her voice, Cassie said, "There has to be something else. Some treatment somewhere. If you would only look."

Dr. Parker spoke with a great deal of control, keeping his voice low. "Damn it, Cassie. Don't you think I already have? Maybe if you saw the CAT scans yourself, you'd understand the situation better."

Aunt Cassie stood and slapped her hands on the table. "I don't want to see any CAT scans. What I do see now is my sister and those children. I just can't accept that she won't be here for them—am I the only one who can't? It's wrong. And I need you to help her." She swiped her hands over her face as if she were ashamed to show her tears.

Amanda began to whimper and her daddy took her out of the high chair and left without a word out the back door, Lucinda following close behind.

Maddie slid up the wall to stand, sure she'd never seen Dr. Parker so angry. He came around the table in two steps and stood really close to Aunt Cassie. "You're not the only one upset here, Cassie. Don't you think that Joe would go to the ends of the earth to help her if there was just the slightest chance? Don't you think we're all angry

516

at what has happened? Because I'm angry as hell. I'm angry that this has happened to Harriet. To her whole family." He turned to face the wall, and pounded a fist on pale blue wallpapered cornflowers that Maddie had helped her mother pick out. "You should be thanking God that this wasn't a decision you had to make, and respect Harriet enough to comply with her wishes and not make this any harder for her." He took a deep breath, facing Cassie again. "Don't fight her on this."

Aunt Cassie tried to walk away, but he blocked her path. Her voice trembled when she spoke. "I can't give up, Sam. It's not in my nature."

She made a move to get by him again, but he held her back with his hands on her arms and shook her gently. "Now, listen to me, because I'm not going to tell you again. Let Harriet die in peace. And if you feel you can't, then go back to New York. It's where you think you belong anyway."

A quiet sob erupted from Maddie's throat. *Die.* It was the first time she'd heard the word spoken out loud, and despite having thought about it for a long time, hearing it made it seem real somehow, like needing to see a shooting star before believing they existed.

Maddie followed her aunt into the parlor, where they both noticed that all the pages Cassie had printed out the night before had slid off the couch in a white waterfall and were now covering the rug under the coffee table.

"Cassie?"

Stopping, Cassie knelt by the sofa and took her sister's hand. "Do you need something?"

Mama nodded. "I need your understanding."

Cassie looked down. "I thought you were sleeping. I'm sorry that you heard all that."

"I'm glad I did, because I need to make sure you understand something. Even without the pregnancy, my chances of survival are almost nonexistent. I could fight it with everything the oncologist throws at me, but it would only prolong my life by a few months—if at all. Why risk the life of my unborn child only to give me a little more time?" She swallowed, closing her eyes for a long moment. "Maddie?"

Maddie pressed herself against the doorway, trying to become invisible. Her aunt caught her gaze and motioned her over to the sofa. Slowly, Maddie walked to where her mother lay and allowed her to take her hand.

"Sweetheart, I know you're angry about the baby. That you think I'm choosing him over you and the others. But I want you to know something." Her chest rose and fell in shallow breaths, her skin so pale it seemed almost see-through. "I have been blessed by being allowed to give life to you and your sisters and brother, and you are all my greatest accomplishments.

And life is all this baby is asking of me, and all that I will ever be able to give him. Allow me this, please." She closed her eyes again. "Please," she said again, her voice barely louder than a whisper.

Maddie dipped her head, hot tears spilling on their clasped hands, wanting to argue and to shout and to put her head in her mother's lap. She had so much to say but was unable to find the right words. And then her mama closed her eyes and went to sleep, and Maddie didn't need to say anything at all.

THE PHONE RANG and Cassie rushed to get it in her father's study before it could disturb Harriet.

"Hello, Cassandra. It's me."

"Andrew." She waited for a rush of emotion—any emotion—but none came. She was completely tapped out. "How are you?" The background noise of pulsating music and laughing people made it hard to hear. She wiped the tears from her face and searched to find a stronger voice.

"Never been better. As a matter of fact, I'm in the midst of celebrating."

She leaned against the desk, feeling so very tired all of a sudden. "Celebrating what?" The sound of a woman's voice came from close by. It sounded a lot like Carolyn Moore's.

"We closed the VisEx deal today—it's mine."

Cassie felt a faint tingle reminiscent of the old

adrenaline rush course through her veins. "That's wonderful, Andrew—and congratulations."

His voice broke through the background noise. "I couldn't have done it without you, Cassandra. You were the one who made the initial contact and set the groundwork. You deserve as much credit as anyone."

"To be honest, I'm surprised. When you didn't call back after our last conversation, I assumed the deal had fallen through. I guess you got them to agree to it without having my name attached."

There was a long pause and the woman's voice again, faint but insistent. Then Andrew spoke. "Actually, that term of the agreement didn't change. I told them you'd be back in January to manage the account."

She stared at the phone, speechless for a moment. "You told them what? Andrew—but that's not true. I told you I wasn't sure. How could you do this?" She rubbed her temple, feeling the beginnings of a headache. She almost welcomed it. It was so much easier to deal with than heartache.

"Because I knew you'd come back when I offered you a partnership."

The air seemed to leak out of her like a punctured beach ball. "A partnership? As in 'Wallace and Madison'?"

"Yes. That's exactly what I mean. What do you think?"

"What do I think? My gosh, what could I think? I'm . . . flattered. More than flattered, really. I don't know what to say." She tried to force enthusiasm into her voice.

"How about just saying, 'Okay, Andrew, I'm on the next flight out'?"

She brushed the hair off her face, feeling her hand shake. Why couldn't she just say yes? She felt powerless here, helpless to do anything to save Harriet. Instead, she heard herself say, "It's just . . . well, things are complicated here. I need more time." She was reluctant to tell him about Harriet. Maybe because she didn't want him to trivialize it, as she now realized he'd done through other personal turmoil. Or maybe because she thought that if she kept it to herself, it would go away.

Another pause now, with the distinct sound of clinking glass coming through the receiver. "The Cassandra Madison I knew wouldn't take more than a second to think about it."

Irritated, she said, "Well, maybe I'm not the same Cassandra Madison you remember."

"Yeah, well. The thing is, you don't have to decide right away—although I was hoping you would so I can put all my people in place. But the VisEx people won't be able to make the move until after the first of the year. How about if I give you until January first to decide? Will that give you enough time to sort through your complications?"

Her gaze rested on the family picture of Harriet and Joe with the kids, then moved to the framed crayon rendering of her with her nieces and nephew catching fireflies. "Yeah. That should be plenty of time." As if Harriet's life were a complication. As if January could even be looked forward to without thinking of the intervening months and the specter of diminishing life that haunted the time between.

"Great. Because there's also the matter of the apartment. We need to sit down and talk about it—among other things. I feel we haven't really settled everything between us."

She nodded, then remembered she was on the phone. "Yes, you're right. We've a lot to talk about. I'll let you know."

"Cassandra?"

"Yes?"

"You don't sound like you anymore. I hardly recognize you."

She strummed her fingers along the charms at her neck, oddly comforted by their presence. "Yeah, I hardly recognize myself anymore." She sniffed, hoping he didn't hear it. "I've got to go. We'll talk soon." She hung up the phone, then stared at it for a long time, her blood pumping heavily in her brain. When she looked up, she spied two familiar hats through the sidelights of the door, and she ran to open it before the Sedgewick twins had a chance to ring the doorbell.

Their orange lipstick matched the plastic flowers on their hats and the antiquated Corning Ware casserole dishes in their gloved hands. Thelma spoke first. "We hear that Harriet is back, so we brought some food. We stopped by their house first, but figured they were probably still here. It's backbone and dumplings and macaroni mousse ring."

Selma patted Cassie on the arm before marching past her with what appeared to be the mousse ring. "We don't want you or Lucinda or Joe having to worry one single minute about anything else but taking care of Harriet and those precious children. Let us do the rest. The garden club has already set up a list of ladies to bring fresh flowers to her house, and the Daughters of the Confederacy have already got a meal schedule started." She turned an orange smile on Cassie. "We got to go first, since we're copresidents of both associations."

Seeing Harriet asleep on the sofa, the ladies, with their practical navy pumps, tiptoed past her and into the kitchen.

Feeling strangely defeated and utterly useless, Cassie climbed the stairs slowly, ignoring the reproving glare from Great-great-great-grandfather Madison.

CHAPTER 25

Cassie grabbed the top of the plastic garbage bag and hoisted it on top of the already full trash can outside the back door. She caught sight of her college freshman picture staring out at her through the thin sheet of plastic, the mousy hair and goofy grin preserved forever. With two fists, she smashed the bag into the can and closed it.

Harriet and Joe had been back for almost two weeks. Even though Cassie played her role of dutiful sister by watching the children or running errands, she had avoided any more serious discussions with Harriet. She hadn't seen Sam at all, through unspoken agreement. She wanted to apologize for insinuating that he had failed Harriet somehow as her doctor, but his words about her allowing Harriet to die in peace still stung.

As she pulled open the screen door to go back inside, the distinct sound of somebody humming nipped past her ears. It was so faint at first that she thought she was imagining it until she heard it again. Lucinda had been staying at Harriet's, so Cassie knew she was alone. Gently, she closed the door, careful not to make a sound.

She crept to the side of the house and stuck her head out. An old tire swing just like the one in Harriet's yard, and strung to a low branch of a towering oak, moved back and forth, the young girl who sat snug inside of it oblivious of her audience.

"Maddie?"

The girl stopped the swing abruptly, making the rope vibrate wildly. "Hey, Aunt Cassie."

Cassie walked toward her niece, her hands behind her back. "Aren't you supposed to be in school?"

Maddie gripped the sides of the tire swing and hung backward, her light brown hair falling behind her and touching the tips of the dried grass. "I didn't feel like it."

"Um-hm." Cassie leaned against the tree trunk and regarded her niece carefully. "Does it have anything to do with Lucy Spafford getting back at you for that trick you played on her?"

Maddie sat up, her face flushed red from being upside down. An impish grin lit her face. "Heck, no. It's actually made me pretty popular." She tilted her head while one bare toe propelled the swing in a wobbly fashion. "How do your floors look, by the way?"

"Very nice, thank you. The upstairs needs doing, too—so just be aware that I'm looking for the first opportunity to get that done."

With a little snort, Maddie began twisting the swing, making the rope bunch on the tree branch. "How come you didn't tell my parents?"

Cassie reached up and plucked a leaf from a limb. "Because I didn't want to see you get in trouble.

And because I don't think your parents need to be worrying about something like that right now."

Maddie lifted her foot, allowing the swing to twist her around in tight circles. With her head dangling and her hair over her face, she said, "Thanks."

"So, really, why aren't you in school?"

Maddie answered with a shrug.

Letting the shredded leaf drift from her hand, Cassie said, "Is it because of your mother? Are you trying to punish her?"

Maddie kept her head down, her hair a confessional curtain. "Maybe."

Cassie slid down the trunk to a sitting position at its base. "I wish you'd talk to me, Maddie. I might be able to help you. I know what it's like to be the oldest child and to have a mother who's sick."

There was a long pause, but Cassie waited patiently for her niece to speak. Maddie kicked a stone with her toe. "Yeah, but at least your mother didn't *choose* to die. My mother doesn't love me enough to want to fight." Her voice broke, but her hair still obscured her face.

Cassie looked up toward the lower branches, fighting the stinging in her eyes. "I'm having trouble understanding all of this, too. Your mother has had to make the most difficult decision of a lifetime. Neither you nor I can know what she's going through—and I hope we never do. But I'm trying really hard to put myself in her shoes, and you might want to try it, too. She's made this decision without thinking of herself. To her, it's not a matter of her life or the baby's—it's a few stolen months versus an entire lifetime. Can you understand that? And that takes more courage than I know I've got in my whole body."

Cassie closed her eyes. *Courage.* It was the first time she'd defined her sister's struggle that way. But it made her see things more clearly—made her finally acknowledge that none of this was about Cassie and some misplaced need she had to make amends for fifteen years of stupidity. This was about the depths of a mother's love, and of finding the courage to say goodbye instead of fighting against the vagaries of the universe. And, Cassie now realized, fighting it had been the easier path.

Cassie grabbed a dead leaf nestled among the roots of the ancient tree and let it rest on her open palm. She said a brief prayer of thanks for her newfound wisdom, and let its grace settle deep inside her. With renewed fervor, she faced Maddie. "You need to go to your mother. Talk to her." She reached out and touched the young girl's knee. "There will be times, later in your life, when you will wish you had. Do it now, so there will be no regrets."

A sob came from Maddie, and Cassie rose, her need to comfort making her heart ache—not just for Maddie, but for the lost girl she herself had once been. Maddie reached out for her, and Cassie met her halfway, clutching her tightly and letting Maddie's head fall on her shoulder. Her hand cradled Maddie's head, and she felt as if an unseen hand cradled hers, too. She was a girl of eight again, and through her own hurt and anger, she felt her mother's love.

"You'll never be alone, Maddie. As long as I'm alive, you'll never be alone."

Maddie's body shook with sobs. "But I'm so angry—angry at Mama for dying, and angry at the whole world for letting it happen. I know it's not her fault, but I can't help it. I can't help it if I think this lousy life is so unfair." She choked, and Cassie held her tightly, her own tears falling lightly on the brown head that reminded her so much of her own.

"You're damned right it's not fair. But we're not always given choices. Sometimes these awful things get plunked down in the middle of our lives and we're left to just deal with them. Some people handle them better than others, but we all find a way. You're strong, Maddie—you'll find your way. Just like I did."

Maddie looked up, her face red and streaked with tears and sweat. "You ran away."

With the pads of her thumbs, Cassie smoothed away some of the tears. "Yeah—and that wasn't the right thing to do. I think I've almost come full circle now, but it would have been a lot easier if I'd taken a more direct route."

Her niece looked at her with confusion. Cassie smiled. "What I mean to say is that running away is usually the easiest thing to do—but rarely the right thing in the end."

"But you've had such a great life in New York. Would you trade that for anything?"

Cassie stilled, the answer that popped into her head too frightening to confront. "If you'd asked me that last year, I would have said no. I love my career. I love New York and all the people I've met and the things I've experienced." She moved a wet strand of hair from Maddie's cheek. "But it all came at a very high price. My decision to run away cost me fifteen years with your mother."

Maddie sniffed loudly, then banged her fist against the side of the tire. "I'm so mad I could just spit."

The rope groaned as it slipped on the tree branch. "Go ahead and spit, Maddie, if it makes you feel better, but you do need to talk to your mother. She loves you and is worried about you. I think she could use your forgiveness and understanding right now."

"I don't know . . . how. It's too hard."

Cassie blinked, fighting the strange urge to laugh. Maddie was as stubborn as a rock when it came to asking for or giving forgiveness. The apple certainly didn't fall far from the Madison family tree. "All we can ask of ourselves is that we at least try. Sometimes it's all we can do. And it's definitely a step in the right direction."

Maddie sighed. "So what should I do?"

"Go to your mother. You don't even have to say anything, and I doubt she'll notice that you're skipping school, because she'll be too glad to see you." She tugged on her arm. "Just go. Now."

Maddie continued to stand there, uncertain.

"Remember—all you have to do is try. It's a start. Everything else will fall into place."

Maddie shook her head. "I can't. I can't! Not now—but maybe later. I promise—I'll try later." She hugged Cassie, then left with a slow gait, her brown hair swaying softly behind her.

Cassie wrapped her arms around herself, feeling goose bumps bead her skin. Her own words reverberated in her head and she felt like a hypocrite. Giving advice to others had always been easy; taking it never had been. Grabbing the swing, she threw it in a wide arc, watching it spiral into ever-tightening circles.

Without even realizing where she was headed, she followed her own feet across the lawn and down the drive. Harriet had told her that Sam had just bought the old Duffy house and was beginning the restoration, planning on doing all of the work himself. In the last week he'd moved out of the second-floor apartment he'd been renting from Mrs. Cagle and had moved into his new house the same day. Neighbors said he worked like a dog on it whenever he wasn't at the clinic or on call.

As Cassie approached, she spotted Sam standing

in the front yard working over a sawhorse. His bare chest glistened with sweat and she noticed he wore work boots and shorts—the first time she'd ever seen him wear anything except cowboy boots and jeans.

George barked and made a move to run to her, but Sam restrained him. He returned to his work, his back turned toward her.

She had to shout above the sawing. "I've come to apologize."

He turned off the saw. "Well, gosh, that's certainly news. Did you call the *Walton Sentinel*?" Without waiting for an answer, he turned the saw back on.

"Sam," she shouted again, moving closer so he could hear her.

He turned off the saw and put it down, then straightened. He lifted his eyebrows expectantly.

"I had a call from Andrew. He's offering me a partnership in the agency."

His face remained rigid. "Congratulations. When are you leaving?"

"I haven't given him an answer yet. I have until January."

He pulled a handkerchief out of his back pocket and wiped his forehead. With a forced lightness, she said, "I see you still have one left."

"Yeah, guess so. You can mail the other ones from New York. Just make sure you wash them first." He leaned down and hoisted another two-by-four onto the sawhorse and began marking measurements on it.

"Sam, you're not making this easy for me."

"That's a first." He clamped a pencil in his mouth, as if to effectively shut off all conversation, and flipped on the circular saw again.

She stared at his back, bare and brown from the sun, and she suddenly realized how very much she needed to touch him. The moment her fingertips touched his bare flesh, he stiffened and took a deep breath, flicking the saw off and dropping it on the table.

Stepping closer, she said, "I wanted to say I'm sorry—and you know that's not easy for me. I'm sorry for the way I talked to you about Harriet. You were right—I see that now. I know I need to focus on her needs and not what I want or think would be best." She rested her cheek on his back, feeling his intake of breath. "And . . . I need you. You're one of a very few number of people who understands me and puts up with me anyway. Harriet's dying, and I can't face it alone." She closed her eyes, tears teasing her eyelids. "I can't promise you what's going to happen in January, but . . ." She stopped, trying to find enough air in her lungs to continue.

His breathing came in long, deep, deliberate breaths, his muscles tense. "But what?"

"I need you. I need you now. And I can't imagine

not always feeling this way." She pressed her lips against the smooth skin on his back between his shoulder blades. "You do something to me, Sam Parker, that makes me forget all reason. Maybe I could stand to eat grits every morning for the rest of my life, or maybe I'm destined for a bagel from the corner deli—I don't know. But every time I picture a future without you in it, I feel more lost and alone than I've ever been in my life."

Her arms reached around his torso, rubbing his ribs, but still he didn't speak. She could feel the tightness in every single one of his muscles. "Please tell me that's enough—for now."

Finally, he turned around in her arms. His eyes were dark blue and brooding, but she recognized the glint of hope in them. He studied her face, as if weighing his words. "It's enough—for now. But I won't wait forever. Even Job had his limits." He stared down at her, his gaze dropping to her lips. He glanced in the direction of the neighbors' houses. "I have a feeling that these trees have eyes. Would you like to go inside for a glass of sweet tea?"

She licked her lips, but not because she needed anything to drink. Nodding, she led the way, trying to ignore the rubbery feeling in her legs. He followed her into the small foyer, closing the door with a booted heel while simultaneously pinning her to the wall.

She looked up at him, trying to stay calm and

reasonable. "We don't have to do anything right now—if you think I'm toying with you. I might die of frustration, but I'd rather do that than for you to think my feelings for you are anything less than serious."

She read the answer in his eyes as he brought his face closer. "I need you, Cassie Madison. You're stubborn, bullheaded, and mean to boot, but, God help me, I need you." He lowered his mouth to her neck and lingered there for a long moment. "I also need to take a shower."

She responded by slipping out of his grasp and taking his hand. "Come on then," she said as she began to lead him up the stairs. "You're going to need more than a spit shine. So let me see if I can help."

She heard the rumble in his throat as he laughed. "Yes, ma'am," he said as he lifted her off her feet and carried her the rest of the way up the stairs.

THE PHONE RANG at four thirty the next morning. Sam came fully awake immediately, reminding Cassie that being awakened in the middle of the night was something he did with regularity. He answered the phone, then gave it to Cassie.

She recognized Lucinda's voice immediately. "How did you know I was here?"

Lucinda's voice sounded groggy with sleep. "Diane Eames next door to the Duffy place. She called me last night to let me know she had seen

534

you and Sam in the front yard at about three o'clock and then hadn't seen you leave."

Cassie ran her hand over her face. "So are you calling me to tell me to come home?"

"No I wanted to let you know there's been another incident and the sheriff wants to talk to you again. He figured I'd know how to reach you. You left your cell on the kitchen table, by the way, in case you were missing it. I saw it when Joe brought me over to find out why you weren't answering our calls."

Cassie sat up and Sam flipped on a bedside lamp. "Is Mama's magnolia—"

"It's fine. But the grass in the middle of the yard isn't."

"What happened? Is anybody hurt?"

She heard Lucinda yawn into the phone. "No, luckily—nobody's hurt. Somebody used gasoline or something to spell out an obscene word in the front yard, and then set it on fire. I don't know what stopped it from spreading across the lawn and to the house, since nobody was home to notice it. Richard Haney was out walking his dog and saw it, thank goodness. He was the one who called the fire department."

Cassie ignored the tone of reproach in her aunt's voice. "An obscene word? Which one?"

"Really, Cassie. I don't think I can say it."

"Aunt Lu." She rolled her eyes. "Can you at least spell it?"

"It's the one that starts with 's-h.' But you'll see it soon enough once you come home. And Joe's fit to be tied, wondering where you are and trying to field questions from the fire department and the sheriff."

"For crying out loud, Aunt Lucinda! I'm thirty-five years old. But, if it will make everybody happy, I'll come home now, all right? One more thing—when you see the sheriff, make sure he knows it was Richard Haney who called the fire department. I find it interesting that the man would be walking his dog at this hour."

"He's always walked his dogs in the middle of the night, sugar." She yawned into the phone. "But I know Hank has already questioned him. He's off the hook, but I don't think his sons are. Somebody spotted the oldest one running down the street shortly before the fire was spotted."

"That's great. If you see the sheriff, tell him I'll call him first thing in the morning and we'll talk about it."

Lucinda yawned into the phone again. "Is Sam going to drive you?"

"I imagine he will. I'll be home soon, so you and Joe can go back home to Harriet. I'll have Sam keep me company."

They said good-bye and Cassie hung up the receiver.

Sam bent to kiss her neck. "What's wrong?"

"Well, the whole town will soon know that I've

slept with you again, and somebody has burned an obscene word across my front lawn."

His lips moved down to her collarbone. "At least I have an alibi. And to think you used to find New York City exciting . . ."

She knocked him over the head with her pillow, then kissed the spot where it had landed. "Come on. I need you to drive me home." She slid out of bed, taking the covers with her. "I just can't understand why my personal life should be fodder for over-the-fence gossip."

Sam's eyes darkened as he regarded her. "Maybe I'll have to make an honest woman of you instead."

She looked away, reaching for her pile of clothes. "Sam . . ."

He stood, too close to her, but not touching. "What if I told you I loved you enough to let you go?"

Shaken, she turned to face him, searching his eyes. "You told me the story about the angelfish for a reason, didn't you?"

His finger traced the line of her jaw. "Yeah, but don't forget the one about the black widow. Maybe loving somebody else would be safer, if not as exciting."

Cassie felt the stillness of the night and heard the crickets singing to the dark sky outside. "Would you marry Mary Jane if I left?" She shivered, but she wasn't cold.

"I could," he whispered.

"You'd be willing to settle, then? Be happy with good cnough?"

"Sometimes we have to make the most of what we're given and make compromises."

She moved away, slipping into her blouse. "Like your medical career. You settled for Walton when you could have gone anywhere."

He took a deep breath. "Sometimes you have to reach deep down in your heart and decide what road you're going to take. And all choices involve some sort of sacrifice. But in the end, you know whether or not you made the right decision." He bent down to pick up a pair of jeans from a chair. "And, no, I didn't settle by coming here. I used to think that I had, but now I know I made the right decision."

She attempted a light tone. "When did you figure that out?"

He regarded her calmly, his blue eyes searching hers. "When I saw you at my dad's service station the first night you came back. I thanked God that I hadn't stayed in the city long enough to become like you."

She sucked in a mouthful of air. "I guess that means you wouldn't consider coming to New York with me."

He looked at her across the room and said simply, "No." A lone car sped by on the street outside, its radio blasting a heavy beat into the dimly lit room.

"We could be happy there. With your degree and

experience here, you could pick and choose which medical practice you joined."

He took a pair of underwear from the drawer and slid them on, followed by the jeans. "You don't believe that any more than I do. If I really thought that's where we belonged, I'd start packing now. But I don't. Nor will I stand in your way if that's what you want." He pulled a boot over his foot. "Like I said, maybe I love you enough to let you go." He faced her, a failed attempt at a smile on his face. "Besides, I just don't think I could ever eat sushi or start using words like 'suppose' and 'do lunch.' It's just not me, Cassie." He slid on the other boot.

She sighed. "This isn't something we have to decide right now." Rubbing her hands over her face, she said, "Come on. Let's go." Without waiting to see whether he followed, she left the room and went down the stairs, the old wooden steps creaking under her weight. The sound, familiar and haunting, crept around her heart. Pushing any nostalgic thoughts away, she let herself out the front door.

CHAPTER 26

The heat of summer gradually gave way to the cooler temperatures of fall, although it stayed warm enough for the children to wear shorts to school. The grass in the yard turned the shade of weathered wood, except for the newly seeded spot in the middle where the ugly word had been burned. The Bradford pears throughout Walton gave a last breath of life with brilliant red and orange leaves before they, too, gave way to the season and their leaves settled one by one onto the ground beneath.

But the magnolia tree in the yard of the old house, where Harriet and Cassie had played as little girls, stayed a vibrant green, as if mocking autumn and all the other lowly plant species not strong enough to face the colder months.

Each passing week Harriet's belly grew larger while she felt herself growing weaker. It was odd, really. Her mind seemed to get sharper as her muscles and bones softened, as if her body were slowly giving up. Harriet managed the weekly trips into Atlanta for tests and progress reports, but refused to stay in the hospital even as her delivery date neared. She wanted to be home with Joe and the children, and Cassie and Lucinda helped make that possible by filling in at Harriet's Skirts 'n' Such.

Despite Harriet's fatigue, she and Cassie found themselves rediscovering the closeness they had once shared, sometimes staying awake late into the night and just talking. At times, Harriet would doze off, and Cassie would still be holding her hand when she woke up. Then Harriet would remember something about their childhood, and they would talk again, whispering and giggling like the young girls they had once been.

Thanksgiving came and went with only a nod to the usual holiday preparations. Harriet didn't have the energy and no one else even mentioned it. Harriet understood why when she overheard Aunt Lucinda telling Cassie that she didn't feel much in the mood for celebrating, since there wasn't too much to be thankful for. And Maddie had skipped coming to the dinner table completely, and no matter how Harriet tried to understand, seeing the empty chair every night was like having her heart broken a little at a time.

Even with Harriet's illness, there was no reprieve from whoever had been tormenting Cassie for the last six months. The fall annuals Cassie had spent an entire weekend planting, with Harriet's direction, had been dug up with incredible brutality. The flowers hadn't just been uprooted; they had been shredded. Bright fuchsia petals littered the flower beds like pink teardrops and scattered over the lawn with every teasing fall breeze.

Sheriff Adams had been by to investigate, and had a deputy to work the case full-time. But, like the other incidents, few, if any, clues had been left behind, and he and his department had no more answers for Cassie than they had when the vandalism had begun with the stripping of the oak trees. As for the oldest Haney boy seen running down the street the night of the fire, the account had come from Mrs. Ladue, who was legally blind and admitted to not having her glasses on at the time. Footprints had been found, and they matched the first set found, but there seemed to be no connection with the Haney boys.

Now that it was December, Harriet tried her best to push all other thoughts aside and focus on what had always been her favorite time of year. The streetlights downtown were wrapped in red and white like candy canes, with big red bows crowning their tops. Every store window blinked colorful lights along with the required faux snow dusting the storefront displays. The weather obliged by sending a cold blast south from Canada, making the Walton residents break out their heavy woolens for the first time in over two decades. The weathermen threatened snow, sending everybody to the grocery store for milk and bread. Snow had been as scarce as shoes in summer ever since Harriet could remember, and she wished on every star in the sky that it would snow just this one winter.

Since Harriet couldn't muster the energy to go out into the cold and select a Christmas tree, she suggested that Joe ask Cassie to go instead, trusting her eye. They'd had the same mother after all.

Joe and Cassie piled into the van with all five kids, Maddie included by much pressure and bribery on Cassie's part, and drove to the gas station, where several rows of fresh-cut pines from the Georgia mountains waited to be chosen and taken home. They ended up with the largest one they thought they could squeeze under the ten-foot living room ceiling.

Harriet clapped her hands as they drove up to the house, the tree riding on top like a trophy. From her chair by the fire, she hustled the children inside to direct them as to which nook or cranny to find the decorations. She'd found a notebook in the kitchen desk, and began to make a list of what decorations they had, and where they were stored.

"What are you doing, Har?" Cassie paused by her chair, staring at the notebook with a frown.

"Just in case," she said, not meeting her sister's eyes.

"We won't need it," Cassie said, but even Harriet could hear the uncertainty in her voice.

With Harriet and the children in the living room, Joe motioned Cassie into the kitchen to help him find scissors to cut the rope holding the tree to the van. But Harriet, with more than fourteen years of motherhood under her belt, was able to listen to their conversation amid the various conversations of her three youngest children.

Joe spoke first. "I need to talk to you about something."

Cassie's voice was full of concern. "What? Is it about Harriet?"

"No. It's about you and Sam."

There was a short pause before Cassie answered. "Um, what about us?"

Joe coughed. "Well, I, um, understand he's been spending every night at your house. I'm not judging you or even saying anything's wrong with that. I was just wondering if it was going to lead anywhere."

"Joe, I appreciate your brotherly concern. But it's not necessary. We're just living day by day right now. If anything changes you'll be one of the first to know, all right?"

Harriet heard several kitchen drawers opening. "I was just wondering. I worry about Sam. We've been friends a long time, and your leaving is really going to hit him hard."

"We've been very open with each other, Joe. We can handle it. And how do you know he's been spending the night at my house?"

There was a pause and Harriet pictured Joe giving Cassie one of his looks before Cassie spoke again. "This town doesn't need telephone lines, does it? Just hang out at the backyard fence."

"That's not such a bad idea, if you think about it."

When they walked back into the room, Harriet couldn't wipe the smile off her face in time and hurriedly busied herself with untangling metal ornament hooks instead of pumping her fist in the air as a sign of victory that maybe Cassie had finally come to her senses.

After cutting two feet off the bottom of the monster tree, they brought it in and settled it in the newly rediscovered tree stand, following Harriet's meticulous directions on the perfect placement. She'd always known, and hoped she'd passed it on to her daughters, that the tone of the Christmas decorations was set by knowing exactly where to place the tree.

With the exception of Maddie, the children watched like vultures, ornament boxes held in each hand, until the tree was ready to be decked out in all its holiday finery. Lying back against the sofa, Harriet gave the sign for them to begin hanging the ornaments. This was the only time she let the holiday decorations go without a plan, knowing that the secret to the perfect Christmas tree was in how oddly spaced the homemade ornaments were, and how the highest ornament was only as high as the tallest child could reach.

Harriet watched as Maddie sat slumped in a chair in the corner, looking as if half of her wanted desperately to join in with the other children while her other half just wanted to be miserable. Harriet looked at the ornament in her lap from her box of favorites Joe had handed to her and took a steadying breath. "Maddie, sweetheart, come here."

Maddie sighed heavily, then slowly moved from her chair and stood next to the sofa. Harriet lifted the tissue butterfly ornament, the wings iridescent with multicolored glitter. "Do you remember making this in kindergarten?"

A reluctant smile crossed Maddie's face before she could hide it again. She shrugged. "Yeah, I guess."

Harriet handed it to her and Maddie took it, holding it up to the light to make it twirl and sparkle. She bent her head closer to read the inscription on the wings.

"What does it say?" Harriet asked, although she'd long ago memorized all the words.

Softly, Maddie read, " 'Butterfly, flutter near my mother; please tell her that I love her.' " Her voice cracked and she looked back at her mother, her beautiful green eyes pooling with tears.

She knelt by Harriet, the butterfly held carefully in her hands, her voice very quiet. "I still love you, Mama. I never stopped. I didn't. And I'm so sorry. . . ." Maddie placed her hands gently around her mother, as if holding a glass doll, then laid her head on Harriet's shoulder and began to sob.

Harriet bent her head, her tears melting into her daughter's hair. "Shh, Maddie. There's nothing to be sorry for. I never thought you'd stopped loving me, okay? Not for one minute." She continued patting Maddie softly, feeling her own pain ebb. "I remember when you made that butterfly, and when you gave it to me it made me cry. And you didn't understand when I told you that sometimes beautiful things make people cry." She pulled Maddie up so she could look into her face. "Now promise me something. Promise me that when you see this butterfly you'll remember how much I love you, and if it makes you cry, I want them to be happy tears."

Maddie nodded, sniffing, then wiped her nose with the back of her hand. "You're not mad?"

"No, sweetie. I'm not mad. Now go hang your ornament in a spot I can see."

Maddie kissed Harriet on the cheek, then stood, examining the tree closely. Finding a spot in the front of the tree, she hung it on a high branch, a butterfly fluttering over a candy-cane reindeer and a toilet-roll angel. Harriet squeezed her hands together, finally assured that everything was going to be all right.

With a sigh, Harriet leaned back on the pillow and Cassie stooped to take the ornament box from her hand before she dropped it. Harriet pointed at the box. "These are my favorites—all made by the children. I keep this box in the linen closet upstairs. Make sure that's on my list for Joe."

Cassie was about to argue with her when the doorbell rang. Harriet tried to sit up, aware of what she must look like. "I'm a wreck. Quick, Cassie—hand me my lipstick in my purse over there."

Joey ran to answer the door as Joe turned to Harriet. "You're always beautiful in my eyes, Har. You don't need any lipstick."

Harriet grinned and rested her hand on the bulge of her abdomen. "Did I mention I'm having a torrid affair with Gus Anderson over at the hardware store?"

Joe sat down next to her and cradled her in his arms. "If I didn't know how crazy you already were about me, I'd believe it."

Harriet buried her face in his arm.

Knoxie sidled up to the sofa and squeezed in between her parents, snuggling deeply into their embrace. Amanda, just learning how to toddle, grabbed a glass ornament in the shape of a peach and threw it just as Sam walked into the room, Joey wedged tightly under his other arm. He caught the ornament and held up his prize. Putting the glass peach down and out of reach from the baby, he swooped down on the little girl and scooped her up in his other arm, making her squeal with delight.

Cassie stood. "I was about to go get some leaves from Mama's magnolia to spray-paint gold and use to decorate the tables and mantel. I could use some help."

Sam nodded, setting Amanda and Joey on the floor. "Sure, Martha Stewart. I'll go."

Bending to kiss Harriet, Cassie said, "We'll be right back, and then we'll make your house worthy of a spread in *Southern Living*."

Harriet grabbed her hand and winked. "Just don't do anything I wouldn't do."

"It's a little too late for that," Joe said, and Harriet laughed as Cassie elbowed him in the ribs.

"Now, quit, Joe. Don't make them mad or they won't decorate our house." She waved her hand back and forth. "Shoo, you two. And make my house glamorous."

Harriet watched as Sam and Cassie left, then leaned back on the pillow and focused her attention on the children decorating the tree, her hand falling to her stomach as the baby inside began to kick.

AFTER SLIPPING ON her jacket, Sam ushered Cassie out of the house, and they walked the few blocks in silence. Her cheeks stung from the wind, and she bundled more tightly into her coat. Sam put his arm around her, drawing her close, until they reached the old house.

Maneuvering a wheelbarrow under the tree, Cassie and Sam began picking up the fallen leaves, now brittle with frost.

One spiraled down from the tree, and Cassie caught it. Bending her head, she examined it closely, observing how the sinuous veins ran to the edge of the leaf, then disappeared, like a fragile life reaching its end. Opening her gloved hand, she let the leaf drift into the wheelbarrow. She sifted her hands through the pile, searching for the glossiest ones she could find, and remembering her mother doing the same thing as she and Harriet stood back with their dresses held out in front, ready to collect their treasures.

"Just think, Sam—this time next year Harriet's baby will probably be walking. Hard to believe, isn't it?"

He nodded, then reached down for another handful of leaves.

Cassie watched him while her fingers searched in vain for the chain under her jacket. She stopped, and stood very still. "She's not going to be here to see it, is she?"

Straightening, he fixed her with a gentle look, his eyes reflecting the scattering clouds. Slowly, he shook his head.

"How much longer?"

His hands fell to his sides. "I think she's living to bring that baby into the world full-term, although we've scheduled a C-section for the day after Christmas. Either way, it'll be soon."

She stared at him, feeling her face crumple, and he gathered her in his arms.

"I'm sorry. I know that's not what you wanted to hear."

She buried her face in the soft suede of his jacket, inhaling deeply. "No, it's not. But . . . thanks for being honest with me." She bent her head back to stare into his face. "And thank you—for being there. For me."

He took her face in his hands, his eyes soft. "I love you, Cassie, and I guess I always will. I'll always be here for you, whatever you decide to do."

Fresh tears filled her eyes, and she took a deep, shuddering breath. She stared into his face as if seeing it for the first time, with all its beloved curves and angles. "I love you, too, Sam Parker. You're stubborn, and irritating, and you make fun of me way too much, but I do love you. Now kiss me before I start crying again."

His eyes bright, he lowered his lips to hers and held her in his arms while the wind whipped at the old magnolia, its leaves shaking in applause.

LONG AFTER THE LAST ORNAMENT had been hung on the tree, the children were tucked into bed, and the final present was wrapped and beribboned, the men retired to the back porch for a beer and cigar, and the two sisters bundled up and headed for the front porch swing.

The sky had cleared, the wisps of clouds giving birth to brilliant stars and a rising moon. It rose, full and heavy, pregnant with untold stories. Harriet sat close enough that Cassie could feel the bones of her hip, her headscarf soft against Cassie's skin. Cassie reached her arm around her sister and stilled. She was so fragile, as if so much of her had already gone. How would they ever bear saying good-bye to what remained?

Their breaths came in little puffs and Harriet shivered. Cassie pulled her closer. "It's too cold out here for you. Let's go inside."

Harriet closed her eyes and shook her head.

Cassie noticed how translucent her eyelids had become, almost like those of an infant. "I like the cold." Harriet's voice sounded tired. "It reminds me that I'm alive."

Between them their gloved hands entwined, squeezing tightly. Cassie turned to her sister. "Are you scared?"

With teeth chattering, Harriet shook her head. "No. I'm not." She touched her forehead to Cassie's. "But I'm worried about you."

Cassie moved back. "About me? Whatever for?" She gave the swing a shove with her foot, letting it sway gently.

Harriet smiled, her teeth almost bluish in the light. "Because you don't know your own heart. You're almost thirty-six years old, Cassie. It's time you started listening to it."

Cassie shook her head and laughed softly. "I can't believe *you're* giving *me* advice. When did that happen?"

Leaning her head back against the swing, Harriet smiled softly. "I think I've gained a lifetime of wisdom these last few months. I guess dying does that to a person."

With a jerk, Cassie faced her sister. "Don't say that, Harriet. I can't stand to hear you say that."

Harriet touched her sister's cheek. "I've accepted it. And I've had a good life, Cassie. I've had the privilege and the honor of loving and being loved by the most wonderful man and bearing our children. It's been a full and happy life, and I have no regrets—except for those years without you. Promise me . . ." She took a deep breath and clenched her eyes shut, as if in pain. After a pause, she continued, "Promise me that you will live your life without regrets. Find your heart, and listen to it, and you can't go wrong."

Cassie laid her head on Harriet's shoulder and let the tears freeze on her cheeks. Finally she said, "I love you, Har."

Harriet placed her hand gently on Cassie's cheek. "I love you, too."

They stayed outside for a while longer, watching for shooting stars to wish upon. But the sky lay still and cold, the faceless moon climbing in the interminable sky. Cassie stood, pulling Harriet with her, and they went into the house, shutting the door firmly behind them.

CHAPTER 27

Harriet went into labor in the frigid morning hours of Christmas Day. While the town of Walton slept, and the children dreamed, Harrison Madison Warner came into the world, kicking and screaming. Cassie and Sam had to rush back to the house they had just left so Cassie could stay with the children and Sam could drive Harriet and Joe to the hospital in nearby Monroe. Sam called at shortly after six a.m. to tell her about her new nephew, who had all ten fingers and toes and, as he put it, was in fighting form.

As the children awoke one by one, Cassie told them about their new baby brother, whom Harriet wanted called Harry, and then everybody joined her in blowing up light blue balloons and draping blue and white streamers over every stationary object in preparation for his homecoming. The blend with the red, green, and gold was controversial, but the two events had to share the limelight.

Sam appeared around nine o'clock, and he, Cassie, and Lucinda celebrated Christmas with the children, videotaping them unwrapping and squealing over their presents. Harriet had to stay in the hospital for a few more days, and Sam wanted her to be able to share this Christmas with her children.

Harry came home first, a small bundle in a blue blanket, and a delight to his older siblings—except for Maddie. Reserved at first, she soon succumbed to his charm and began vying for a chance to hold him.

Three days later, Joe brought Harriet home to die. It was never spoken of, but it was plain to the adults that it was time to prepare and to let go. Joe moved a bed into the living room next to the Christmas tree, and that room became the heart and soul of the family. Sam came daily to visit and to administer her morphine drip, and life seemed to hang on a tenuous web for Cassie and the rest of the family as Harriet slowly slipped away from them.

Cassie spent the week between Christmas and New Year's at Harriet's. She was sensitive to Joe's need to be with his wife by staying away at times, but always close enough to be available if Harriet needed anything. Most of the time, she sat by Harriet's bed and held her hand and talked or read to her. The ebb and flow of family life moved the days forward, each single hour interminable in its pain and grief, but each close of day gone far too quickly.

On New Year's Eve, the bleak winter sky had darkened to a charcoal gray, sending frigid winds through the town of Walton and urging the people to stay inside. Those lucky enough to have fireplaces stacked on the pine logs and enjoyed the novelty of a roaring fire to warm a cold winter's evening. Harriet kept her face turned toward the flames, a small smile on her lips.

Cassie was reading aloud to Harriet an article on holiday cooking from *Southern Living* magazine when she felt the air shift. It was nothing tangible, and nothing that she could describe, but it was there. She glanced at Harriet, whose half-opened eyes, glazed from pain and morphine, were now focused on Joe feeding baby Harry a bottle.

Cassie let her gaze move across the room to Sam, who sat cross-legged on the floor, playing

Go Fish with Joey, Sarah Frances, and Knoxie, while Maddie sat curled up in a chair by herself, listening to her iPod and busily scribbling in her diary. Amanda was upstairs, being put to bed by Lucinda, and the peace of a day's end had settled over the house.

Quietly, Cassie closed the magazine, but nobody seemed to notice. It was as if she were an audience in a play, and she wanted nothing more at that moment than to close the curtain and prevent the final scene from playing out.

She stood and crossed to the window and looked out into the night sky. The moon lay murky and swollen behind the cover of clouds, laying a silver blanket over the slumbering garden below. She moved to the door and stepped out, sniffing deeply.

Excitedly, she ran back into the room. "It's going to snow. I'd bet old Grandma Knox's red hair that it's going to snow tonight." As soon as she spoke, great white flakes began to fall from the sky.

The children squealed, and even Maddie put down her pen to rush to the window and peer out. In unison, they turned to their father. "Daddy, please can we go out in the snow—please, please?"

Joe, out of years of habit, turned to Harriet. When she didn't answer, he turned back to the children and then to Cassie.

"If it's okay with your dad, I say go get

yourselves all bundled up and we'll go out and watch the snow fall."

All four children ran out of the room and headed toward the hall closet. Cassie made to follow them when a small sound came from the bed. Harriet's voice had grown so weak that Cassie had to bend close to hear. "I want to see."

Cassie looked at Joe, then at Sam. "Harriet wants to go out, too."

Joe stood, a wavering smile on his face. "I think she should. She's always talked about going skiing someplace so she could finally see snow. Who would have thought she could do it right in her own front yard." He knelt in front of Harriet and kissed her forehead. Turning to Cassie, he said, "I'll go put the baby down, and if you'll get Harriet bundled up, I can carry her outside."

Cassie nodded, and Joe brought the baby over so Harriet could kiss him. She touched his cheek, then buried her nose in his neck before saying good night.

Sam removed the IV drip, then helped Cassie with getting Harriet into enough layers for her to be able to stand the frigid cold. She had lost so much weight since Harry's birth, and the pain medication made it difficult for her to hold anything in her stomach. She hardly weighed more than Sarah Frances, and it scared Cassie to her core.

Joe came down the stairs, and after he had put on

his coat and hat, he bent to pick up Harriet. He scooped her up with ease, but when he asked her to hold on to his neck, she couldn't find the strength. Instead, Sam tucked her hands between her body and Joe's; then he and Cassie followed them outside.

The snow came down in hard, heavy swirls, like God's fingerprints on the landscape. The withered grass and bushes now glistened with springlike fervor, wearing fresh coats of new-fallen snow. Joey and Sarah Frances crunched their feet on the frozen ground, trying to make tracks as Maddie stared up in wonderment. Knoxie raced around the yard, her tongue hanging out like a puppy's in an open car window, trying to catch a flake.

Icy snowflakes coated Harriet's hat and coat, sticking to her eyelashes and brows. Cassie touched her arm. "Open your mouth, Harriet—see if you can catch one."

With mouth wide open, Harriet turned her face to the sky, her eyes clear and reflecting the joy that emanated from her. She caught one and smiled, her eyes reflecting the night's glow. "It tastes cold."

"Yes, it does, doesn't it?" Cassie laughed and Joe joined her, the sound hollow in the snow-dusted air.

Joe bent his head to say something to Harriet but seemed to stop in midsentence. Slowly, he raised his face, a look of bewilderment shading his eyes as the snowflakes landed on his nose and eyelashes before vanishing just as quickly as they had appeared.

Sam stuck out his arm, holding Cassie back, and she stepped away without resentment. What passed on Joe's face as he realized his beloved wife was gone cut into her heart at the same moment she realized that she had just lost her sister, her Harriet. She bent her head and wept until Sam pulled her into his arms and they cried together.

First Maddie, and then the other children, one by one, stopped and came to stand around their mother, still cradled in their father's arms. The weeping started but nobody thought to go inside yet, as if to do so would make what had just happened to them too real. Joe bent his head to protect Harriet from the snow, his body shaking as his tears fell on her face.

And still the snow continued to fall, covering the houses and trees with a thick white blanket, and whispering a gentle hush to the grieving family.

THE SNOW FELL for three days, paralyzing five counties. Without anything to clear the roads, life came to a virtual standstill. Power and phone lines were down in several areas and not expected to be repaired for a week. Cassie's deadline came and went, but she found relief from the reprieve of the downed telephone service. Her cell phone battery died and she couldn't recharge it but found she didn't really care. She felt as if she were walking in a dreamworld, with no beginning and no end, and could not even imagine thinking about her future, much less making plans for it.

Harriet lay at Murphy's Funeral Parlor, her service on hold until the snow cleared and the ground thawed. But every evening during visitation hours, the home was packed with mourners. They brought poinsettias, holly, and evergreen wreaths, since no fresh flowers could be found, and Joe brought a small Christmas tree, decorated with the children's ornaments, to rest at the foot of the coffin. The whole effect was a fitting tribute to a woman who had loved the Christmas season with the bright-eyed wonder of a child.

The food began piling up again in Cassie's kitchen as the citizens of Walton rallied around Harriet's family. Cassie had gone several times to Joe's to see him and the children, but the house was always swimming with visitors or the children were at friends' houses. She felt useless and unneeded and craved the calming distraction of work. She even practiced saying the name Wallace and Madison, and the ghost of the old rush came back to her, beckoning her. She longed to be in charge, in control again; even the cool anonymity of the city pulled at her. She wore her grief on her face here, and everyone knew it. But in New York, she could hide beneath her business persona and push the grief far away.

Harriet had told her to find her heart and follow it. Work had been her heart for so many years. It was black-and-white, and easily understood, and she knew how to navigate it. Wallace and Madison. She'd be foolish not to follow this opportunity, especially when she wasn't really needed here. The town took care of its own, and Harriet's family was safely tucked into the security of that knowledge.

Sam. Hadn't Harriet once said that love was about sacrifice? He would be her sacrifice, for surely whatever was between them now would be destroyed if he were to come with her to New York or she were to stay in Walton. She'd be sure to visit often to see Harriet's children and Lucinda, and maybe even see Sam until he married Mary Jane. Then she'd wait until the pain went away, because none of it would matter in New York, where she'd be a partner in a top advertising firm. It was what she had always wanted.

She sat at the edge of her bed and looked around at her pink rosebud bedroom, listening to the silent house around her as the fire in the fireplace did little to dissipate the cold in the room. Lucinda had moved into Harriet's house to help Joe with the children, and now Cassie's empty house sat creaking and muted by the unfamiliar mantle of snow. Cassie spoke aloud to the quiet around her.

"Harriet, you were wrong, you know. Love's not just about sacrifice. It's about making tough decisions, isn't it?" She took a deep breath, then moved to the closet, dragging out her suitcase and a handful of clothes on hangers.

She had to call Ed. She needed to find a tenant for her house, as well as somebody who could put everything the tenants didn't want into storage. But she would definitely hold on to the house. It was her family legacy, and all that she had left now of her childhood with her parents and Harriet. She imagined leaving it to Maddie one day, and hanging her own portrait in the stairwell to scare future generations of Madison children.

After speaking with Lou-Lou Whittaker to make an appointment with Ed at nine o'clock the following morning, Cassie left the room and wandered through the house, visiting old memories and replaying past conversations. She paused on the threshold of Harriet's old bedroom, seeing the girls she and Harriet had once been, sitting on the bed and sharing secrets. Clenching her eyes shut, she listened carefully to hear girlish voices, but only the bereft sound of the winter wind whistled through the empty room. Slowly, Cassie closed the door, clutching the brass knob tightly.

She returned to her room, her resolve to leave renewed. Dumping clothes on the bed, she opened her suitcase in the middle of the floor, then emptied out a dresser drawer and jewelry box and stacked the contents next to the suitcase. Lifting a pile of underclothes, she placed them into the suitcase. A drop of moisture hit her hand and she realized she was crying. *How am I going to tell Sam?*

She sniffed loudly, using her sleeve to wipe her nose. Pushing herself up, she sat on the bed, facing the wall, and allowed her fingers to play with the charms around her neck.

Headlights raced around her room, followed by the slamming of a car door. Peering out of the window, she recognized Sam's truck, and walked slowly down the stairs to meet him. She opened the door before he could knock, then waited for him to stomp the snow off his boots before coming inside.

He reached for her, but she pulled back, causing him to draw himself up. "Are you all right?"

She nodded, her eyes avoiding his. "I'm fine. I've been thinking about Harriet. . . ."

He touched her cheek softly, then let his hand fall. "That's what I came by to tell you. The snow's still on the ground but not falling anymore, and the power is back on downtown so they scheduled the funeral for Saturday. Joe wanted me to tell you."

She nodded, feeling very much like a third party. "Thanks. For letting me know."

He tilted his head. "Are you sure you're all right?"

"I'm sure."

"I've got power and heat at my place if you'd like to come back with me. Central heat has got to be better than a fireplace."

"I'll be fine—thanks. I've got the propane heater, too, if I get too cold."

He stood in the foyer in his jacket, as if waiting to be invited in. Finally, he said, "The referendum on further development is tomorrow night at town hall. It seems that this snowstorm could be a blessing in disguise. Everybody's stuck here with no place to go and nothing to do. We'll have a packed house. Anyway, I was wondering if you could come and maybe offer your support."

She swallowed, offering him a lopsided grin. "Are you sure I'm going to support the right side?"

He raised an eyebrow. "Well, since you haven't bulldozed this place, I have to assume you're in favor of preservation."

"Yeah. I'll be there."

They stood facing each other awkwardly for a long moment. Finally, Sam spoke. "What's wrong, Cassie? Why won't you let me touch you?"

Something halfway between a laugh and a sob erupted from her throat. "I've decided to go back to New York."

His face went absolutely still, but his eyes glittered in the dim light from the window. He stared at her for a moment without speaking. "So,

Cassie Madison does yet another great disappearing act. As soon as the going gets tough, she runs away. I guess I should have expected this."

She straightened her shoulders and faced him. "I am not running away. I've just been visiting here, remember? I have a career in New York and a great opportunity. I'd be an idiot to turn it down."

Sam slammed his fist on the wooden doorframe, making her jump. "Damn you, Cassie. What about Harriet's children? Don't you think you're needed here, too?"

Cassie fingered the gold chain around her neck, her fingers popping up and down along the charms in agitation. "They don't need me, not really. They've got Joe and Lucinda. And the rest of the town is lined up at their door to offer aid or food or whatever it is they think the children might need. I'm pretty much superfluous." She dropped her hand to her side.

"Superfluous? Your nieces and nephews have come to love you and depend on you. And what about me?" He kicked at the entryway rug, folding a corner of it over. "I guess I never even crossed your mind." Raking his fingers through his hair, he shook his head before leveling his gaze at her. "You want to know what's superfluous? It's your heart. You don't seem to use it, so why's it there?"

Cassie stood, stilling her shaking hand by clutching the banister. "You're not being fair, Sam. You just don't understand."

He shook his head and stared at her for a moment. "You're like a crop duster. You just dump your stuff in a puff of smoke and then you're gone into the wild blue yonder. You're right, Cassie. I don't understand you." He leaned in closer, his face flushed red, and spoke very quietly. "Yes, you've a great opportunity waiting for you, and you should be proud of everything you've accomplished. But your sister has died, leaving six motherless children, and you're planning on leaving them, and you don't seem to see anything wrong with that. Go then. We don't need you here."

He turned on his heel and, with long, angry strides, left the house.

Unmoving, she watched the empty space where he had stood, listening to his heavy footsteps cross the porch. It wasn't until she heard his footsteps crunching in the snow that her breath came back to her.

"Sam!" she shouted to the empty house. She couldn't let him go. Not like this. Forcing her feet to move, she ran after him, not bothering to put on her shoes.

She burst through the front door, letting the screen slam behind her, and cried his name again. He stopped by his truck and faced her in the dim light.

She shivered as her feet sank into the cold snow blown onto the porch. "Please don't go." Tears threatened behind her eyes, but she held them back, fighting for her precious control—the one thing she could always depend on.

He took a step forward, his breath coming out in big puffs in the frosty air. "What else do you want from me? Do you want me to rip out my bleeding heart and lay it in your lap? Because that's the only thing I have left to give that you don't have already. And I won't do it, Cassie. I won't." He turned back to his truck. Speaking over his shoulder, he said, "It'll hurt for a while, but we'll get over it. This town has a wonderful way of coming together and helping one another in bad times. I don't expect your departure to be any different." He opened the door.

"Sam, please!" Her voice held a desperation that she had never heard before, and it frightened her. Why had admitting weakness always been so hard for her?

Sam looked back.

She clambered down to the bottom porch step, her arm clutching the railing and holding her steady. Her teeth chattered. "Don't go. Please. I . . . need you."

Leaving the door open, he walked toward her. "You what?"

She looked at him with narrowed eyes brimming with tears. "You heard me."

He retraced his steps back to the truck and got in. He was about to slam the door when she shouted his name again.

Cassie had stepped off the bottom step and away from the railing's support. Without it, she swayed. "Sam, please! I . . . need . . . you." She fell to her knees in the cold snow, her control gone and her heart hammering in her chest. She felt herself drowning in her own desolation and knew only Sam could pull her out. Her body shook as she screamed at him, "I'm so afraid!"

Sam left the truck and came to stand in front of her, his face in shadow. "What are you so afraid of?"

She dropped her head into her hands. "That . . . that I'm going to die from this grieving. That I'm going to lose control. That I'm making the wrong decision." She shook her head. "God, Sam—I don't know what I want! I thought I had all the answers when I came here, and now I don't. And I'm so afraid I'm not smart enough to figure it out."

He knelt in front of her and held her shoulders, his hands two welcome spots of warmth. "Bullshit, Cassie. You're plenty smart enough to figure it out." He shook her shoulders. "And the only thing you've ever been afraid of in your life is admitting you're wrong. Try it, Cassie. The world won't end."

She sat back in the snow, and he let her go. "How can she be gone, Sam? Who's going to tell the children too young to remember what a wonderful mother they had? And about their grandmother and grandfather and about how to care for roses and make sweet potato pie and why it's important to wear a slip?" She sniffed loudly, her tears freezing on her face.

He stood slowly. "If you don't know the answer to that question, then I give up. I've done everything I know to help you. There's nothing more I can do." He shook his head. "But nobody's going to blackmail you with those kids, Cassie. That would make it too easy for you."

She shuddered, her voice stumbling between words. "It's hard . . . I can't . . . say . . . what I want." Looking at him with a fierce frown, she shouted, "It's too hard for me."

Gazing down at her, his eyes were unforgiving. "I love you, Cassie, and that's why I'm not going to say it for you. You're on your own with that." He turned and headed back toward his truck.

She felt like a small child in the midst of a tantrum, but she couldn't seem to stop herself. She was too miserable. "What if I wanted to say that I'd made a mistake, that maybe I've been wrong about some things?"

Sam stopped, but didn't turn around. "Then you'd better come right on out and say it." He waited for a moment, keeping his back to her, but Cassie kept silent. With a swift kick, he sent a tightly packed drift of snow flying before climbing into the cab of his truck and gunning the engine. With a long look at Cassie, he dipped his head, then took off out of the drive, the crunching snow a terrible, final sound.

• • •

HER POWER CAME back on around nine o'clock and Cassie spent the remainder of the night alternating between crying, doing laundry, and packing. By four o'clock in the morning, she was nearly finished. Pulling the last load from the dryer, she plucked out three handkerchiefs and began ironing. She cried some more as she moved the hot iron over the crisp linen, her tears sizzling into steam under the iron's hiss. Folding them neatly, she tucked them into her purse, next to the letters she'd found under her bed.

The first rays of dawn were streaming through the fan window as she wearily made her way up the stairs, a stack of clean and folded laundry in her arms. Dust motes flitted through the air, tracing a path to Great-great-great-grandfather Madison's portrait. She leaned against the banister on the landing, staring at her ancestor in the murky light. Setting down the laundry, she moved closer, and her eyes widened.

Why had she never noticed it before? In the millions of times she'd climbed up and down those steps, not just in the last several months, but in all the years she'd spent living in this house, she never once noticed. The shape of the eyes, the curve of the nose and jaw—it was just so obvious. And if Great-great-great-grandfather Madison didn't have all that hair, she'd bet he had large ears that slightly protruded from his head.

She sat down on the steps for a few moments, letting her newfound knowledge sink in. In the long run, it didn't really matter anymore. It was just one more loose end to tie up before she left. One more person to say good-bye to.

With heavy steps, she climbed up the steps to her room. She had three hours to sleep until her appointment at nine o'clock. She lay down on her bed and waited for the slow ticking of the hall clock to put her to sleep.

CHAPTER 28

Lou-Lou greeted Cassie warmly, her pink lips curved in a sympathetic smile. "Hey, Cassie. I'm so sorry about Harriet. Ed's closing the office on Saturday in honor of her funeral. We'll both be there."

"Thanks, Lou-Lou. It'll be good to see her friends there."

Lou-Lou's lip trembled a little. "I know the whole town's going to turn up. I mean, she knew just about everybody, and everybody loved her. And those poor kids . . ." Her voice cracked and Cassie had to turn away, knowing that if she didn't, she'd start crying again and wouldn't be able to stop.

"Is Ed here? We have a nine-o'clock appointment to talk about the rental agreement for the house."

Lou-Lou pressed a tissue into the corner of each eye. "He sure is. I'll just let him know you're here."

Before she had the chance to press the intercom button, Ed opened the door to his office. Cassie stared at him in surprise. He looked like he'd slept in his clothes, with his tie undone, his shirt hanging out, and his hair standing at attention in short brown bristles. Dark circles hovered under his eyes, and his jaw was shadowed with whiskers. He helped her take her coat off, then ushered her in, and she followed him, allowing him to close the door behind her.

He sat down behind his desk, indicating the chair opposite for her. She sat down, regarding him closely.

He cleared his throat. "I've got all the rental agreement papers—and all are in accordance with what we discussed. The rental rate is on there, as well as my commission. I will act as your agent and as your landlord in absentia. You shouldn't have to worry about a thing except for any large repairs and general maintenance. Just check on the last page that your New York address is correct so I can make sure you're getting your monthly rent checks—as soon as I find a tenant, of course."

She nodded and began to read through the sheaf of papers, initialing the indicated paragraphs and signing at the bottom of each page. When she was finished, she laid the pen down and slid the papers over to him. Then she sat still, facing him.

"You took Daddy's letter box, didn't you?"

A look of shock was quickly replaced by one of relief. "Yes. I did."

She was surprised at his candor. "And I think I know why."

He didn't say anything, and Cassie thought that maybe he'd grown tired of hiding and wanted the truth to come out finally, regardless of the circumstances.

"You're my brother, aren't you?"

Ed looked down at his desk and toyed with a pen. "I was wondering how long it would take you to figure it out. You almost caught me that once—when I called you outside the Dixie Diner. I wanted to make sure it was you who was trying to find me."

Cassie leaned forward. "Why didn't you just tell me? Why all this deception?"

He slid his chair back and swiveled it to face the large picture window, his profile illuminated by the bright morning sunshine reflecting off the snow. His resemblance to Great-great-great-grandfather Madison was more apparent than ever. He shrugged. "Because I didn't think it would be news you'd be too happy about." He glanced at her briefly. "I still remember how pathetic I was in school. And how I bullied Sam. Didn't think you'd take too kindly to finding out I was kin."

Cassie looked down at her hands, still reddened from her long walk in the snow. "You're not that boy anymore, and that has nothing to do with now. We share a father. And I'd be honored to call you my brother."

A dark flush covered his face and he shifted in his chair. "Yes, well, I thought it best."

Lou-Lou knocked briefly, then brought in coffee and cups on a tray. Cassie welcomed the interruption, using the time to study Ed with fresh eyes. She noticed again his unkempt state, and mulled over the reason why.

She emptied a yellow packet of sweetener in her cup, noticing that her hands shook. "How long have you known?"

Ed held his cup in front of him, the steam distorting his features for a brief moment. "When I was twenty, my parents died. I found some papers in their things that spelled out who my real parents were. And that I wasn't really even legally adopted. I was just given to the Farrells by my grandfather like an unwanted puppy."

He turned back toward the window and took a long sip of coffee. "You can imagine how shocked I was."

Cassie nodded. "Probably as shocked as I was when I read the letters and found out that my father had a lover before he met my mother, and that they'd conceived a child. I never would have believed it if I hadn't read the letters myself."

"Yeah, well. I was steamed, too. My father was rich and lived in a big house with the two kids he wanted, and I was living on some dirt farm with a man who beat me and a woman whose spirit had been crushed too long ago to care."

Cassie winced. "Daddy didn't know—at first he thought you'd died at birth. If he had known he would have taken you in. And when he did find out you were alive, he tried to find you, but I guess the trail had grown too cold by then and Miss Lena wouldn't tell him anything. You could have been anywhere in the world, as far as he knew. I bet the last place he would have thought to look would have been right on the outskirts of Walton."

Ed snapped around in his chair, spilling coffee over the brim of his cup. "Don't you stand up for him. If he'd really wanted to, he could have found me and taken me away from there. But he didn't. I was left there to nearly starve to death."

"That's not how it was, Ed—"

He cut her off. "Don't try to defend him. You weren't there when I approached him after my parents died. He pretended to be excited to see me, but he wouldn't acknowledge me publicly—he was too embarrassed about me. He gave me money for my education, and even set me up in business, but the deal was I couldn't come out with who I really was."

Cassie leaned forward. "I've read the letters, Ed. It wasn't about you—it was Miss Lena's reputation. It would have killed her for people to know she had had an illegitimate child. He did it to protect her. Can't you understand that?"

Ed swiveled away from her and rubbed his hands over his face. "Those letters. God. I wish I'd seen them years ago. It would have changed a lot of things."

"Like what?"

He faced her, his eyes wide. "Nothing. It's nothing."

Cassie sat back. "Does Miss Lena know that you're her son?"

Ed shrugged. "I wanted to wait until I was successful before I told her who I was, but by then it was too late. I've tried talking to her about it, and sometimes she even seems to understand, but most times her mind just drifts away and I don't think she understands anything. It's almost funny, though, because I've had the most lucid discussions about my business with her. And then she'll look at me in the next minute like she's never even seen me before."

Cassie set her cup gently on the desktop. "I'd like to acknowledge you as my brother. If you think Miss Lena would still be embarrassed, it could just be between us and a few friends—for now. But I'd like to. Besides Lucinda and Harriet's children, you're the only family I've got now."

He turned away from her, giving an almost imperceptible shake of his head. "I wouldn't go sharing the news with anyone just yet. You might find it's something better kept inside."

"What do you mean?" She leaned forward, wondering again at his rumpled clothing and hair. It seemed he'd been in the office all night, wrestling with demons.

He shook his head and stood, a clear sign of dismissal. "It doesn't matter. It's nothing that can be fixed anyway."

She stood too, a questioning look on her face. "Maybe, since we're family, I can help with whatever problem you're having."

He strode away from his desk toward the door, pulling it open for her. "I don't think so. Now, don't get me wrong—I like you and all. In fact, I like you a lot. But you're still your daddy's daughter, and I'm just not ready to trust you."

Touching his arm lightly, she said, "Well, you know where to find me if you change your mind." She walked through the door, then turned around, reaching into her purse. "I almost forgot. It's a letter to you from Daddy. It must have fallen out of the letter box when you dropped it on my bed. I found it under the bed with two other letters from your mother."

He colored again and took the envelopes.

"I don't know why he didn't give it to you when he learned of your existence. It was written so long ago, I'm wondering if he simply forgot about it."

Ed fingered the envelopes gently, but didn't move to open them. "Did you read it?"

"Yes. I did. And I hope that any doubts you have about our father's love and concern for you are answered in there."

He nodded, and she felt him watching her as she turned around and headed for the door. She stopped halfway and faced him again. "I'd like you to sit with me and Joe at the funeral, if you're comfortable with that."

Slowly, he shook his head. "No. I can't do that. But thank you. I do appreciate the thought."

"All right. But if you change your mind, you'll be welcome there." She said good-bye again and waved to Lou-Lou, then let herself out.

It didn't occur to her until later to ask for the letter box. And then she was glad she hadn't. She had been given many happy years with her father, sharing his life. The least she could do was give his lost son his old letter box and the letters inside that spoke of a child born of love and then given up.

MADDIE OPENED THE FRONT DOOR of her aunt's house, listening to the quiet inside. Since her mother had died, her own house had been louder and more crowded than usual, the freezer and refrigerator crammed with hams and casseroles and Jell-O rings, as if their neighbors thought the world was ending. And, Maddie thought, in a way they were right.

"Aunt Cassie," she called, and waited, but heard

only the ticking of the grandfather clock. Slowly, she walked from room to room, enjoying the silence but feeling a little unnerved by how alone she was. She'd just had to get out of the house, away from all the sympathetic stares and hugs and words that would never bring her mama back.

"Aunt Cassie," she called again, pausing in the study. Most of the books and papers had been boxed up and lay stacked against one wall. But the pictures in the frames had remained, and Maddie looked at them, recognizing her mother's high school graduation photo. She picked it up and felt herself crying again but couldn't seem to stop. She wasn't angry at her mother anymore; she was just lost. Her life at the moment felt like driving for the first time and not knowing where the gas pedal was.

She looked at a picture of Aunt Cassie and saw what Mama had always said about the resemblance between her aunt and herself. Even the freckles, Maddie thought as she leaned forward and saw the ones on Aunt Cassie's face. They weren't as thick anymore, so it was encouraging to know that Maddie wouldn't have to have them forever.

She examined several more framed pictures, seeing her mother's life from when she was a baby to the picture from the hospital bed holding a tiny Maddie, noticing for the first time how similar her own growing up had been to her mother's—family vacations at the beach, swimming in the creek, piggyback riding on her daddy's shoulders. Maddie even recognized Bitsy's in the background of a photo of her mother getting an updo, presumably for the Kudzu Festival parade. So little had really changed over the years, but she was no longer sure whether that was such a bad thing. It even made her feel closer to her mother somehow, even though it seemed her mother had never wanted anything more than a household full of children, and Maddie was pretty sure she wanted anything but that.

Not feeling hungry on account of the jelly rolls, vegetable casseroles, and cold chicken she'd been eating nonstop for days, she skipped the kitchen and meandered upstairs, wandering down the hallway and peeking her head into each room before moving on. But when she reached her aunt's room she stopped, her mouth going dry.

In the middle of the room was her aunt's suitcase, brimming over with clothes and shoes, most of them high heels Maddie hadn't seen on her aunt's feet since the first few weeks she'd been in Walton. Walking into the room, Maddie went to the dresser and saw the printout of an airline reservation from Atlanta to LaGuardia, with her aunt's name on it.

Maddie sank down on the bed, feeling completely empty. Betrayed. Aunt Cassie hadn't told her she was staying. But with her mother gone, Maddie had assumed her aunt would somehow want to stay, like Aunt Lucinda had done when Cassie's own mother had died.

She fell back on the bed, her head hitting the lid of the suitcase, but she didn't care. A little bruise on her head was nothing compared to what her heart was feeling. Why would Aunt Cassie want to stay in Walton, anyway? It wasn't like she didn't have a more exciting life someplace else. Maddie closed her eyes, picturing what it must be like in a place like New York, where nobody knew your name, or looked at you with pity because you were fourteen years old and your mother had just died.

Slowly, Maddie sat up, her eyes focused on the bright silks and cashmeres inside the suitcase but not really seeing them. She was seeing instead the hours and days that lay ahead of her, white-washed days tinted gray. Days of watching all of them stumble through life without the person who always seemed to steer them in the right direction. Mama had once said that she was the captain of their ship, and Maddie could only see them foundering now, her daddy having no clue how to manage the sails.

She eyed a notepad and pen on the nightstand and picked them up. Then, thinking of the right words, she began to write. When she was finished, she replaced the notepad and pen, then carefully folded the note and stuck it in her back jeans pocket.

On her way out of the house, she paused by the photo of Aunt Cassie, finally understanding why her mama had always said that Maddie was just like her aunt, and realizing that it had nothing to do with how they looked.

Maddie opened the door and felt the cold blast of air hit her face. Sticking her hands into her coat pockets, she looked up at the thick clouds above and prayed it wouldn't snow.

CHAPTER 29

Christmas lights still glistened in the snow outside the town hall as the square and available parking spaces quickly filled. Clouds had been threatening more snow all afternoon, and the smell of it was thick in the air as Cassie pulled into a parking spot in front of the Statue of Liberty.

The weather didn't seem to deter Walton's citizens as they streamed in from all directions. Cassie recognized most of the vehicles, including Sam's and Ed's, both parked near the town hall steps as if they had been the first to arrive. She waved her gloved hand in response to shouted greetings, and climbed the steps.

The meeting room was quickly becoming standing room only as Cassie made her way down the center aisle, looking for a place to sit. The radiators spewed out a thick heat, as people in sweaters and coats seemed to melt as quickly as the snow on their shoes.

"I didn't expect to see you here."

Cassie spun at the sound of Sam's voice close to her ear. "I told you I would be."

His face was closed to her, unreadable. "Thank you. Hope it doesn't take you away from your packing."

She pulled off her gloves. "Sam—"

"When are you leaving?" His words were clipped and impersonal.

"After Harriet's funeral. Lucinda's taking me to the airport at five. I . . . I called Andrew and accepted the partnership."

"Congratulations." He looked over her head, watching as the town council members took their seats up on the podium. "I've got to go."

"Wait." She put her hand on his arm and he stopped, a small flash of hope in his eyes. "I've been meaning to return these to you. I ironed them myself." She reached in her purse and handed the small stack of pressed handkerchiefs to him.

The flash in his eyes flickered, then died. He took the handkerchiefs from her. "Thank you. And good-bye. I hope you'll be happy."

Without waiting for her to respond, he turned and left her. Feeling a hundred pairs of eyes staring at her, she looked around for a vacant seat and was surprised to see Miss Lena with an empty chair next to her.

Cassie stepped over feet to reach her, then settled herself into the seat, trying not to bump anybody as she slid out of her coat. Miss Lena had on her ubiquitous pink sweater over a flowered dress, and navy blue woolen hose covered her legs. She reached over and squeezed Cassie's hand. "I'm so sorry to hear about Harriet. How sad you must be." She squeezed Cassie's frozen fingers. "I'm keeping you and her husband and darling children in my prayers."

Cassie coughed to clear out the lump in her throat. "Thank you, Miss Lena. Thank you very much." She looked into the older woman's eyes and saw that they were clear and bright.

The room gradually quieted as people shuffled into spots and the meeting started with the usual formalities. And then one by one people stood up and began talking about their town and using their words to hopefully sway an opinion one way or the other.

Senator Thompkins stood up and spoke about his great-great-grandparents, who had settled the town almost two hundred years before and were now buried in the cemetery behind the old Methodist chapel—the same chapel that was slated to be destroyed by a new industrial complex constructed by Roust Development.

A half dozen more people stood to tell similar stories. And then Richard Haney stood to speak about the areas of neglect and decay on the outskirts of town that had been rejuvenated and renewed, courtesy of Roust Development. Several other respected town members approached the podium to state their support of Roust and the terrific job he was doing for the town.

Cassie looked around for a man in a dignified suit, or at least somebody she didn't recognize, to be able to pick out the representative from Roust Development. She couldn't believe that somebody from Roust wouldn't be present at this important town meeting. But she saw no one she didn't know, and wondered if Jim Roust could be so conceited that he thought his pillaging of her town a done deal and this meeting inconsequential in the grand scheme of things.

Finally Ed Farrell stood. His tie was askew and he looked uncertainly around the room before gathering up an easel and approaching the podium. He set a large poster-board town representation up on the easel, then stepped back for everyone to see, an uncomfortable smile on his face.

Ed cleared his throat and began to speak. "Ladies and gentlemen, I offer you the great compromise. I suggest that we say no to the grand development scheme of Roust Development and instead let one of our own plan a new and more vibrant Walton. Sure, Walton was a great place for our great-grandparents. But that was back then— before computers and highways and super- markets." He took a handkerchief out of his back pocket and wiped his brow. "Yes, we know everybody in town, we go to church with our neighbors, and we marry the girl whose pigtails we used to pull back in fourth grade." A small chuckle rumbled through the gathered people. "But that's not what is going to keep Walton from becoming an economic disaster in the next few decades. We need revitalization—we need it to keep our young people here as much as we need it to bring in new people who can inject capital into Walton's economy." He stepped aside so people could get a better view of the easel. "This is what I'm suggesting—a new and improved version of Walton."

Cassie sat up in her seat, mesmerized. The map on the easel shouted with color and beauty and perfection—the ideal Walton. Nice cars traveled the wide boulevards of the town as people pushing baby carriages and walking dogs strolled down the pristine sidewalks. There was even a group of children flying kites in a park—a park that currently housed a block of businesses that included the Dixie Diner.

There was something so wrong about it—so unreal and incomprehensible. The rendering wasn't her Walton—it was some dreamer's idea of the perfect town. Whatever it was, it wasn't the Walton where people knew one another from birth, and neighbors helped one another and chipped in to bring food and care to an elderly woman. It wasn't the town where children swam in the old creek behind Senator Thompkins's house or had church picnics in the park where a new Piggly Wiggly was now drawn on the map. Whatever that town was on the map, it bore no relation to the wonderful place she'd grown up in. From the look on Sam's face, she could see that he was thinking the same thing.

Slowly, Sam stood. He had no easel or pointer, nor did he wear a suit. Instead, he sauntered to the podium wearing his jeans and boots, and waved to neighbors and friends. He leaned toward the microphone.

Very succinctly, he said, "Pardon my French, people, but this is all bullshit." A murmur passed over the crowd and Miss Lena giggled. "Just because Ed here says he's one of us does not mean he's got the town's best interests at heart. Sure, this town could use revitalization in areas—but not mass destruction of historic homes and businesses. We need to focus our efforts on preservation and finding new uses for existing structures. Because that is the only way we can hold on to the integrity of this town."

He paused for a long moment, his eyes scanning the room and meeting the gazes of individuals sitting out in the audience. "And if you decide to vote against preservation, I don't think it's going to matter who does the construction in the town—Ed Farrell or Jim Roust. Either way, they will ruin

Walton. They will ruin it just the same as if they burned it like General Sherman did on his march to the sea. People will move out, and strangers will move in. We'll start keeping our doors locked and won't know our neighbors anymore. There won't be any more Dixie Diner or Bitsy's House of Beauty or Harriet's Skirts 'n' Such. Everybody will be going to the mall for those services—and the empty shops will be boarded up and abandoned."

Cassie sat up even straighter, feeling the passion of his words. Sam continued. "And I ask you all this—where are Jim Roust and his people? Don't you think somebody who wants to change this town so much would be here tonight? At least to listen to what the town's citizens had to say about proposed changes? Don't you think he'd care?"

Cassie watched in surprise as Miss Lena stood, her gnarled hands gripping the seat in front of her. Her high voice rang out over the quiet crowd. "But he is here. He's standing right there in front by that easel."

Ed's face seemed to drain of all its color as he gazed up at his mother. He took a step forward, forcing a smile. "Now, Miss Lena, I think you're getting confused. Why don't you have Cassie take you outside the room for some fresh air?" A tic began in his jaw, belying his otherwise calm expression.

Miss Lena did indeed look confused as she tilted

her head and stared down at the men near the podium. "But, Ed, you told me yourself that you'd bought Roust Development and that you're the big boss now. Right, Ed?"

Ed sent an apologetic shrug to the audience. "I'm sorry for the outburst, ladies and gentlemen. Perhaps Miss Lena just isn't used to being out so late."

The old woman began to shake, her expression wiped clean of any confusion. Her voice, though trembling, came out clear and compelling. "No, Ed. I'm not used to being lied to—especially by my own son." She ignored the gasps and whispers coming from the audience around her, and continued to stare straight ahead at Ed. "I'm sorry if your childhood was not what it should have been. I only did what I thought was best at the time. Punish me, then, Ed, instead of these people—the same people who take care of me now and made sure you had clothes on your back and food on your plate when you were a child. Look at yourself! It doesn't look like your upbringing or this town held you back from becoming a big shot." She paused for a moment, taking a deep, calming breath. "I just wish that you were a little younger and I was a little stronger, because you deserve to have a switch taken to your backside."

Her voice seemed to falter for a moment as she glanced around at her rapt audience before turning back to Ed. "Since I was never able to give you motherly advice, perhaps you'd indulge me just this once." She wagged a gnarled finger at him. "Be nice to people—because all mean acts always come back later to bite you in the butt."

Miss Lena sat down with a thud as a stunned silence permeated the room. Her eyes seemed to cloud over as she regarded the people nearest her, as if trying to figure out where she was and why she was speaking. Cassie put her arm around her shoulders, pulling her close.

Ed stuck out his arms, his hands turned palms-up in supplication. "Come on, y'all. She's obviously confused." He stopped for a moment as a steady murmur began in the room, accompanied by accusatory glances. Ed's expression became belligerent. "Hey, even if I did own Roust, so what? I'm still the guy with all the great ideas for this town. I mean, look at the Dixie Diner." He pulled out a large, glossy picture from a portfolio by his feet and propped it on the easel. "It's ugly as sin. Yeah, they've got colorful awnings and window boxes, but it's still just an ugly old building. That whole block is. There are some major national retailers who are just chomping at the bit to get ahold of that real estate. Imagine the business that will bring into Walton—and the jobs."

Sam studied Ed, a new understanding reflected in his eyes. "Sure—low-paying, minimum-wage jobs. All the higher-level jobs will be filled by the companies on a corporate level. The people now owning and working for those businesses on the block will be unemployed." Sam took a deep breath in an obvious attempt to control a rising temper. "What it comes down to, Ed, is that you want to destroy this town little by little so we don't notice it right off. You're trying to cut us down to our knees because of something that happened almost forty years ago. I'm sorry, Ed, but I just can't seem to be able to let you destroy Walton without a fight."

Sam strode toward Ed, stopping not a foot away. "Because I will fight you, Ed—I will fight you to my last penny and my last drop of blood. This town and its people are my life—and more precious to me than all the money in the world. I feel real sorry for those who sneer at it and who feel they've outgrown the need to belong. For all the education and wealth in the world, they're just too damned stupid to know what a gold mine they have sitting right here in this room."

A tight lump lodged itself in the middle of Cassie's throat, and she knew Sam's words had been aimed at not just Ed.

Ed looked around, his mouth open, a hostile look on his face as his gaze scanned the crowd. When his eyes met Miss Lena's he stopped. Their gazes held each other for a long moment before she narrowed her lips and turned away, burying her face in Cassie's shoulder.

Sam spoke softly, but his words carried out over the mesmerized crowd. "And don't think that we'll forget that you've lied to us. Look out at the people of Walton, Ed, and see if you can look any of them in the eye without flinching. See if you're man enough now to tell us the truth."

Ed actually looked chagrined as his shoulders slumped and he looked back at his mother. She refused to meet his gaze. Then he turned to Cassie and she saw again the skinny kid wearing hand-me-downs. She offered him a reassuring smile, then mouthed the words, *Tell them the truth.*

With a brief sigh of resignation, Ed collapsed into a chair, holding his handkerchief to the beads of perspiration on his upper lip. The crowd began to murmur as he shook his head as if to clear it. Finally, he gave Cassie a quick nod and said in a weak voice, "It's all true." With a prompting look from Sam, he continued. "I'm behind all the proposed development in Walton by Roust Development."

People stood and began shouting and waving their arms while Miss Lena just shook and buried her face in Cassie's shoulder. A councilman banged a gavel, silencing the room once more.

Sam's voice was calm as he faced Ed, but Cassie could see his jawbone working furiously. "Why, Ed? I think we all need to hear why."

Ed kept his gaze focused on Cassie. "My reasons are personal."

Sam stepped forward, his face screwed up in a menacing cast. "I suggest you get real personal, Ed. We're listening."

Ed glanced up at the doctor for a moment, looking as if he'd just emerged from a come-to-Jesus revival. Quietly, he said, "I never intended to go forward with my planned town. I wanted to bulldoze Walton and build over it."

A stunned silence captured the audience, and Ed looked as if he wished the ground would open up and swallow him whole. But Sam was relentless in his inquisition. "Keep going, Ed. We're not leaving until you've told us the whole story."

Ed coughed and took a drink of water. A look of what Cassie could have sworn was relief crossed his face. With a deep breath he began speaking, the easel standing between him and the people of Walton like the screen in a confessional. "For almost twenty years I have lived my life feeling as if I had been done a great wrong. And it has only been recently that I have found out the truth, and that I have been the one wrong all these years." His gaze fastened on Cassie and she thought back on the letters between his parents and from his father to him.

"And the one person I have deceived the most is Cassie Madison. I lied to her about my intentions for her house—abusing her trust—and only because she had the great misfortune to be her father's daughter." He looked around the quiet room. "It was her father I was after—and everything he loved. His house, this town. I thought I could only feel peace if his beloved house was buried under a huge shopping mall."

Glancing at the bowed head of Miss Lena, he said, "I also seem to have lost the trust of the dearest, sweetest woman I have ever had the pleasure to know, and I am ashamed. For the first time in my entire life, I feel horribly ashamed." His head dropped lower. "And now I've lost a sister that I never let myself get to know, and I look around at all the people who knew Harriet and loved her and realize what a huge loss that is. And for what purpose?"

Miss Lena had finally stopped shaking and Cassie hugged her tighter.

Ed faced Sheriff Adams. "And it was me and men I hired who've been doing all that stuff over on Cassie's property—not Mr. Haney or anybody else. Yes, Richard Haney worked for Roust—but he never knew I was behind it. I take full responsibility for all damage and will take whatever punishment is due." He rubbed his hands over his face, hiding his eyes for a long moment. "I guess I should be thanking you all. I haven't felt this relieved in years." When he moved his hands away, Cassie could see the bright sheen of tears.

The poster board slipped off the easel and slid, face down, across the wood-plank floor, stopping at Sam's feet. Sam left it there, not looking down.

Sheriff Adams began walking toward Ed as Ed addressed the room again. "I'm sorry. I really am sorry—as pitiful as those words must sound to you all. I have tried for so long to ignore the evidence, but Miss Lena, and those of you who care for her, have done your dangedest to make me see the stuff this town is made of. Tonight has taught me that I can't ignore it any longer. Miss Lena has shown me what a special place this is. Y'all truly care about each other—and for each other. It's something special and rare, and with people like me in the world, it will be a dying breed. If anything I say here tonight is going to have any weight—I hope it's this." He faced the town council members. "I hope you vote no to more development and yes to preservation. I hope you vote no to people like Jim Roust and Ed Farrell who want to indiscriminately tear down old buildings. Sure, Walton could use some improvement—but it should be done smartly. I hate to say this, but on this point, I agree with Dr. Parker."

Before the words had time to sink into Cassie's ears, the double doors at the back of the meeting room flew open, and Joe stood on the threshold. He was bundled in a ski jacket, snow clinging to the hood and his eyelashes. "I'm sorry to interrupt everybody, but I've got an emergency and I need your help."

Her mind reeling from the recent turn of events,

595

Cassie handed Miss Lena over to Mrs. Crandall, who sat on her other side, and got up to go to Joe.

He continued, his face a mask of worry. "Maddie's run away from home. She left a note." He pulled a crumpled-up piece of notebook paper from his pocket and handed it to Cassie. "It's starting to snow real bad out there and I'm afraid. . . . We need to find her fast. Can I have volunteers to do a search party?"

While men and women streamed into the aisle toward Joe, Cassie bent her head to read the note.

I can't live here anymore. Nobody seems to realize that things will never be the same again without Mama. I don't know how Daddy is going to manage with all us kids, so I figured I'd make it easy for him by leaving. I've never felt I belonged here anyway. I've decided to move to New York. I look old for my age and I'm sure I can get a job waitressing or something—anything just to get away from this stupid little town where nobody will miss me anyway.

It wasn't signed, but there was no doubt as to who had written it.

Quietly, Cassie gave the note to Sam, who had come to stand by her, and watched as he read it. He handed it back to Joe, then quickly began organizing search teams and giving out his cell phone number.

He turned to Joe. "Is Lucinda with the children?" Joe nodded.

"Good. I want you to go with Hal Newcomb and go door to door to Maddie's friends' houses. Insist that the parents physically check the girls' bedrooms to see if Maddie is there. She could be hiding."

Ed managed to shoulder his way through the crowd. "Let me help. Please."

To Cassie's surprise, Sam nodded. "You can go with Hank. I don't think he wants you far from him anyway." He pointed at Hank. "I want you to head out toward the interstate. God forbid she thinks she's going to hitchhike her way up north, but I wouldn't put it past her, either."

Hank and Ed headed toward the door and Cassie grabbed her coat, running after them and calling to Sam over her shoulder, "I'm going with them."

Without waiting for a response, she followed Hank and Ed out to Hank's truck, the four-wheel drive easier to handle in the snow than his patrol car. They trudged out to the truck, and as Ed held the door open for her, he said, "I am sorry, Cassie. For what I've done to you and your house—and for lying to you. If it hadn't been for those letters—"

She held up her hand, cutting him off. "I'd be lying if I said I wasn't angry—because I am. And we've got lots to talk about—and we will talk, later. But right now, we have to focus on finding Maddie and bringing her home safely."

Ed nodded and they both climbed in as Hank started the engine. Cassie forced a smile. "I never thought I'd see the day where I was grateful for a four-wheel-drive truck."

Hank's face was grim. "Yeah. Let's just hope we don't get stuck on any icy patches. Nothing but ice skates can get you off of that."

They pulled forward on what used to be the paved road in front of the town hall but that was now just a flattened ribbon of white, winding its way around town.

Cassie spotted Sam's truck pulling out behind them, his face illuminated briefly by the flash of another set of headlights. People walked quickly out of the building, hurrying to spread the word that young Maddie Warner was lost somewhere out in the snow. If there had been time, Cassie would have hugged each and every one of them for not once considering their own safety. They had come together in a time of need to help one of their own, and it filled Cassie with pride to be among them.

Hank headed out toward the interstate, flipping on his high beams and illuminating snow and more snow and the occasional flakes blown off a tree branch.

Ed spoke from the backseat. "Why would she want to go to New York, do you think?"

Cassie looked out the window. "For some reason, she puts me on a pedestal. She thinks she'll find all the answers to all of her questions anywhere but here."

Ed leaned forward, resting his arms on the back of the seat in front of him. "Just like you, huh?"

She didn't answer and he eventually sat back.

Hank flipped on his scanner. "I'm sure with the snow falling like it is there won't be too much traffic on the highway. That might be a good thing for us."

Cassie clutched her knees tightly, not wanting to think about the implication. "Does she expect to walk all the way through the snow?" She leaned her head back against the seat. "My God, she doesn't even have boots." Tears welled in the back of her throat but she swallowed them down. "What could she have been thinking?"

Ed waited a moment before answering. "When you were fourteen, do you remember ever thinking things through? Heck, I don't think I've had a clear thought for almost twenty years."

Cassie didn't answer, her eyes remaining focused on the empty road in front of them. Hank drove slowly as their gazes scoured the sides of the road. Twice, Cassie thought she saw something, but both times what she thought was a leg or a head peeking out of the glaring white had turned out to be either a fallen branch or an icy rock.

When they reached the access ramp to the interstate, Hank slid to a stop. "I'm afraid to go any farther in the truck. It's all icy here and we might just flip over and end up upside down on the road below."

Cassie strained her eyes to see the six-lane highway, but no car lights or light source of any kind came from the road. Her gaze came to rest in front of the truck in the yellow arc of the headlights. She sat forward. "What's that?"

Hank squinted. "I can't tell from here. Stay in the truck and I'll go look."

Ignoring him, Cassie jumped out, reaching the object at the same time. Picking it out of the snow, she shouted, "It's Maddie's backpack. See? It has her name tag on it." A foot away lay a headband, the glassy beads covering it reflecting the lights from the car.

"Maddie!" Hank and Cassie screamed her name at the same time and were quickly joined by Ed. Hank took a step forward and slipped, his legs flying out from under him, and he landed awkwardly on his arm. The sound of snapping bone echoed in the snow-dusted air.

Hank grunted, then lay still, his face contorted in pain in the broad beam of the headlight.

Cassie knelt. "Don't move, Hank. I'll call Sam on Ed's cell phone, okay? Just try not to move."

Ed had crawled his way to the edge of the road, moving slowly. He tossed his cell phone to her and she caught it. "Be careful—it's all ice under the snow. Maddie must have slipped over the embankment."

A small whimper came from the bottom of the hill. "Help me! My ankle—I can't move it!"

Hank grunted again as he struggled to sit up before collapsing in pain. Cassie put a restraining hand on his good shoulder. "Don't move, Hank. We don't need another casualty. And if that's Maddie down there, Ed and I can bring her up. Just lie still."

She dialed Sam's number while she watched Ed flatten himself on his stomach and peer over the embankment where a broken guardrail offered no prevention against a potential fall. "Is that you, Maddie? It's Mr. Farrell—and your aunt Cassie. We've come to get you out of there, okay?"

"Please hurry—I'm so cold." Maddie's voice sounded faint and far away, as if being absorbed by the surrounding snow.

Sam answered on the first ring. "Sam—it's Cassie. We're at the northbound entrance ramp to the interstate. We've found Maddie, and she might be hurt—but she's talking. And I think Hank's broken his arm."

There was no emotion in his voice when he answered back. "I'll be right there." His good-bye was the click of the phone.

Ed looked back at Cassie. "Go inside the truck and look on the floor of the backseat. There's some kind of rope back there. Grab it, and bring it to me. I might need it to tie Maddie to me to bring her up."

Cassie nodded and did as she was asked, also bringing a blanket she'd found on the seat to put over Hank.

Ed stood rubbing his arms with his hands, trying to generate heat. "I'm going to go down and see if she's seriously injured. If she's not, I'm going to try to bring her up. I need you to stay here with Hank and wait for me—and let Sam know where I am when he gets here."

Her teeth chattered uncontrollably. "Okay. Be careful."

Wrapping the length of rope over his shoulder, Ed began to move slowly down the embankment, scooting down on his backside and using his heels for traction.

"Maddie—I'm coming down. Don't try to move."

Again, they heard the whimpering, but nothing more.

The short minutes it took for Ed to reach her seemed like hours. When Ed had completed a cursory examination and announced he would be bringing Maddie up, Cassie shouted with relief.

He tied Maddie to his back—piggyback style—while he dug through the layers of snow in search of handholds to grab onto. He slipped several times, once almost back to the bottom where he had begun, but eventually made it to the edge. Cassie grabbed Maddie's arms while Ed untied her and, after two failed attempts, pulled her off of Ed's back before waiting for Ed to roll forward onto level ground again.

As soon as they were both up, glaring headlights and crunching snow announced Sam's arrival. He smiled with relief when he spotted Maddie. After examining her ankle, he directed Ed to bundle her in a blanket he had brought and put her in the backseat of his truck.

He then turned to Hank. The sheriff's face now appeared as white as the snow around him and he'd begun to shiver. Sam knelt in the snow next to him. "Always have to be the center of attention, don't you, Hank?" Leaning closer, he said softly, "I'm going to have Ed help me put you in the backseat of your truck to keep you warm while I immobilize your arm. Then Ed's going to drive you and your truck to the hospital to have it set properly. The snow's tapering off and he won't have any trouble with it in your truck."

Hank nodded weakly, then allowed himself to be helped back to his truck. Cassie climbed into Sam's truck next to Maddie and wrapped her arms around her, waiting for her own teeth to stop chattering. And when they did she wasn't sure what she'd do first—yell at Maddie for scaring her or tell her how much she loved her.

She watched as Ed drove away with Hank and

then waited as Sam climbed in behind the wheel and turned his own truck toward town.

Cassie was amazed at the calmness in her voice. "Maddie—why did you run away? Don't you know that your family loves you and that we were worried half out of our minds?" She remembered the anguish on Joe's face when he announced the news about Maddie running away, and Cassie wasn't sure whether she should kiss or strangle her niece.

Maddie started to cry. "Don't be angry, Aunt Cassie. I didn't think anybody would miss me."

"Oh, I'm not angry, Maddie. I was just so worried about you." She squeezed her tighter. "And nobody miss you? Did you know that half the town is out there in the snow, searching for you—or that your father is going crazy with concern over you?"

Maddie just sobbed louder. "No, I didn't. And I'm only crying now because my . . . ankle . . . hurts."

"Yeah, yeah, yeah." Cassie smothered a grin, relieved that she could still smile.

Sam turned around in his seat, eyebrow raised. "Gosh, she sounds like somebody I know."

Cassie sent him a hard stare.

"I'm sorry," Maddie sobbed, burying her face in Cassie's shoulder.

Cassie's eyes misted, her heart swelling for this girl who reminded her so much of herself. She touched Maddie's cheek and spoke softly. "Sweetheart, all the love and belonging you could ever want in your life is right here; if you'd only stop for a minute to look around you'd know. They will love and accept you even if you decide to grow spots and join the circus. They're your people, Maddie. And most people spend their whole lives searching for what you've already got in this little town. Don't you ever forget that."

Sam's eyes met Cassie's in the rearview mirror and in that moment her mind cleared. As if watching a movie in vivid color and exaggerated detail, she saw Joe, the children, Lucinda, Sam, her beautiful house with the magnolia in the front yard and creaking wood floors—and the longing in her heart that she had carried around like a suitcase all these years disappeared. She had what she wanted; she'd had it all her life. And, finally, she knew what it was.

CHAPTER 30

Harriet's wake was held at Cassie's house to accommodate the large number of mourners. As if by divine intervention, the skies cleared, and the temperature rose to the high fifties. Gutters overflowed with melting snow as cleverly made snowmen became nothing more than disfigured lumps of carrots and hats in the middle of yards.

Cassie was pleased to see Ed and kissed him on

his cheek. He fidgeted awkwardly in his new suit, the result of a shopping trip to Atlanta with Cassie. "I'll be at your hearing next Thursday—and so will Joe and a bunch of other people, to support you."

He flushed, the white skin of his forehead, exposed by a recent haircut, turning a deep red. "I appreciate it, Cassie. Sheriff Adams says that I'll probably just get probation and community service. Plus I'll have to pay restitution to you for the property damage." He blushed deeper and shifted his feet. "I know I'll never really be able to apologize for everything I've put you through, but, well, I thought that as part of my community service I'd like to build a park. I was thinking of putting it over there off of Sycamore Street, where the Kobylt house used to be. And I'd like to name it the Harriet Madison Warner Memorial Park, if that would be okay with you."

Impulsively, she hugged him and blinked back tears. "I think it's a wonderful idea. Especially a park for children—it would be such a fitting tribute to her. Thank you, Ed. Thank you." She looked around the room for a moment before her gaze rested on her brother-in-law. "I'll let you tell Joe. I know he'll be as thrilled as I am."

Ed nodded and headed toward Joe.

Sam came to stand next to her. "How are you holding up?"

She smiled, feeling shy with him. They hadn't

spoken since the night Maddie ran away. It seemed as if Sam were giving her time for the words that she had spewed out in the backseat to her niece to sink in. "I'm doing fine. I can almost feel Harriet here with us, celebrating her life with us. When I think that, it's not as hard to . . . to face that she's gone."

He nodded and looked down, a quirky smile on his lips. "Lucinda told me that you'd unpacked your things and put the suitcase in the attic. Like you were planning on staying awhile."

Cassie busied herself by picking up a few paper plates and stacking them. "Well, gosh, I guess I can tell Joe to disconnect his phone service. He won't be needing it anymore, since Lucinda's moving in with him. She's better than a town crier."

He lifted her chin to face him. "Were you ever going to tell me?"

She felt lost for a moment as their eyes met. "Yes. Of course. I just wanted to get the details worked out first."

"Details?" He dropped his hand.

"Yes. It appears that I'm going to be the Southern partner of Wallace and Madison. I'll be establishing new accounts in Atlanta and the Southeast and handling them from my home office."

"Home office? As in this house?"

Cassie concentrated on lining up the silverware on top of the dirty plates. "Yep. The one and only."

"Cassie?"

She looked up at him. "Yes?"

"I'm glad."

"Glad?"

His eyes twinkled. "I'm pleased as a pig in mud."

She tried to hide her smile. "Don't be so cocky. I'm not doing this for you."

He raised an eyebrow. "No?"

"I'm doing it for me. And my family."

He took the plates from her and dumped them in the kitchen. When he returned, he joined her with his arm around her shoulders and they faced the mourners as a unit, accepting condolences and sharing their grief. Maddie, having suffered a sprained ankle during her fall down the embankment, hobbled around on crutches, bending over now and then to take a kiss on the cheek from one of her mother's friends or to hug someone's neck.

Joe still seemed to be in a daze, but was surrounded by his and Harriet's friends. They talked about her as if she were still alive, telling stories of her thoughtfulness, her kindness, and her love for her family. Joe smiled, and the aura of unbridled grief that surrounded him lifted slightly. Cassie walked over to where he sat with Harry in his arms and put her hand on his shoulder. They would get through this. With the help of all those who loved them, they would get through it.

After the last mourner had left, Joe led her outside to the porch. "Harriet asked me to give this to you." He reached into his coat pocket and pulled out a square black jewelry box.

Cassie took it and slowly opened the lid. Six gold heart charms lay nestled against black velvet, each one winking at her with the sun's reflection. Her other hand went to her mouth. She looked up at him, afraid to speak.

"These are for her children. She said you'd know what she meant." His voice cracked, and neither one could speak. He hugged her while they wept, and when they were finished, she drew back and looked at the hearts again.

"I'm going to need a larger chain to hold all these." A small laugh bubbled at her lips as she clutched the small box to her chest.

Cassie and Joe sat down on the swing and stayed there until the sun set, its long golden rays waving its last good-bye.

TIME MARCHED SLOWLY in Walton, and Cassie sometimes wondered if it marched at all. She watched the winter of her sister's death pass into the brightness of spring and then the heat of summer. And then it was the autumn of the year again, with old leaves falling, shedding their brilliant plumage, and her magnolia still resplendent with its glossy green leaves.

The children grew, lost teeth, and shed tears, and

Cassie was there at school plays, cheerleading tryouts, and late-night algebra sessions. Joey lost his first tooth, Harry learned how to crawl, and Knoxie decided she didn't want red hair anymore. Cassie treasured each milestone, each one made more poignant with the memory of the mother who couldn't be there to share them.

Maddie struggled the hardest with the loss of her mother, but Cassie made it clear that her niece would always have a warm shoulder to lean on when she needed it. Cassie looked back on that first year with both grief and joy, realizing life would always be a mixture of both, but also knowing that her little town would give her whatever she would need to cope.

And then it was December again, filled with bittersweet memories. It had been Maddie's idea to hold the wedding at Christmas time, and Cassie had agreed. Harriet had always loved Christmas, and it was now Cassie's duty to bring back happy memories of the season to her sister's family.

In the confusion and hustle and bustle of Christmas and wedding preparations, Harry's first birthday was almost overlooked. But Cassie remembered and baked the cake herself, following the advice of Mrs. Crandall, who was more than happy to lend a hand.

As if to thank Cassie for her trouble, Harry decided it was time to walk, and took his first steps, landing in the outstretched arms of his beaming aunt. She held him tightly for a moment, silently thanking the woman who had given birth to him.

The ceremony itself was small, with Reverend Beasley officiating. Cassie grinned at his sign in front as she was driven into the parking lot of First United Methodist. FEELING TIRED? RISE WITH THE SON. And, below that, CONGRATULATIONS, SAM AND CASSIE.

Joe and Lucinda left the limousine first and then Mr. Murphy helped her out, making sure she didn't step on the antique lace train of her gown. She hadn't been crazy about riding in the funeral director's limousine, but it had either been that or the sheriff's cruiser if she wanted to arrive at her own wedding in style. With a smile, Joe offered his arm, and she took it, trying to ignore the frigid winter weather that had once again descended on Walton and blew up her billowing skirts. Around her neck lay a longer gold chain, now filled with shining gold hearts and one golden key.

Joey, his shirttail hanging out of the back of his tuxedo jacket, proudly bore the rings down the aisle. Following him to the bright thumping of the church's organ, played by Burnelle Thompkins, came Knoxie and Sarah Frances in forest green velvet dresses, dropping white rose petals as they walked. Finally, the wedding march began and a brightly beaming Maddie, as maid of honor, preceded her aunt, who wore the ivory wedding gown that had been worn by her mother, then packed away with love and hope in the attic of the old house.

As Cassie marched down the aisle on Joe's arm, she wondered if her mother had felt even half the joy that was now filling her as she approached Sam and contemplated the life that lay before them. An escaped ray of sun peered through the stained-glass window over the altar, and it seemed as if her parents and sister were announcing their presence. Joe kissed her cheek, then handed her over to her groom.

Following the reception, held at the house, Cassie stood on the front porch with her new going-away outfit hidden under a heavy wool coat and tossed her bouquet into the waiting crowd of women. It landed in Lucinda's outstretched hand, who sniffed it with a coquettish smile. Cassie wondered if anybody else noticed the bright red blush suffusing the sheriff's face.

In a hail of rice, they ran to Sam's waiting truck, brightly decorated with red and green streamers and beer cans tied to the bumper. They pulled out of the drive, then headed for the cemetery.

Harriet's marker had been placed next to their parents', and both had been decorated with potted poinsettias draped with homemade ornaments from Harriet's children. From her pocket, Cassie took a gold tree ornament in the shape of a heart and tied it securely to a poinsettia. She stood as a chill wind blew down from the north, making her shiver, and Sam put his arms around her.

"I miss her, too," he said.

Cassie nodded and looked up at the graying sky above them, the cloud edges heavy and thick. "If I didn't know any better, I'd say it's going to snow."

Sam followed her gaze and nodded. "I guess you did learn a thing or two while up north."

She elbowed him gently, then rested her head on his wool jacket.

"Do you think Harriet and my parents are watching over us?"

He squeezed her tightly. "Hopefully not all the time." Then, his eyes serious, he kissed her lightly on the lips. "Yes, I'd like to think so."

As she looked up at him, three snowflakes drifted down from the sky toward them, twirled and buffeted by the whim of the wind before settling on the barren winter grass. Cassie watched them melt, then turned her face to the sky in search of more. "Snow in Walton for the second year in a row. What's the world coming to?"

Sam laughed, then took her hand and began walking toward his truck.

They drove through the town on the way to the interstate, hoping to make it to the airport before everything shut down. Bermuda in December held enormous appeal to Cassie as she flipped the heater in the truck to the max position.

The old oaks on the tree-lined streets bowed

over them in greeting, their leaves winking and swaying, as if celebrating a homecoming. Cassie sighed, turning her head to watch a group of bundled children playing tag on the front lawn of the Harden property, her warm breath fogging the window. She touched the gold necklace around her neck, reveling in the abundance of gold hearts, and she smiled. Home no longer seemed like a place where one was born, and then outgrew, along with skinned knees and childhood dreams. Instead, it seemed to her, it was a place that lived in one's heart, waiting with open arms to be rediscovered.

They drove through the town slowly, the cans and streamers tittering gently behind them. They passed Madison Lane, and the old high school, and Principal Purdy's house with the front porch, long ago painted a bright pink. They drove past Miss Lena's and found her with Ed helping her up the porch steps. They'd been at the wedding and reception, with Miss Lena's pink sweater over her Sunday dress, and loving the opportunity to talk to so many people about her beloved books. The Dixie Diner and Lucinda's Lingerie, formerly Harriet's Skirts 'n' Such, slid by their window, and two blocks later the Harriet Madison Warner Memorial Park, the playground equipment hibernating under a kiss of frost.

As Sam and Cassie turned into the town square the flakes fell heavier, dusting the grass and leaves like little blessings from above.

"Stop, Sam."

He pulled the truck over to the curb. "What's wrong?"

"Just a minute." She climbed out of the truck and crunched through the frozen grass to the Statue of Liberty, her driftwood head now a pale green under the smattering of snow. Hoisting herself up onto the base, Cassie stared into the face of Miss Liberty, with her perpetual come-hither look aimed at the Confederate soldier on horseback at the opposite end of the green.

Taking off her red knit cap, Cassie slipped it onto the crown, then jumped down and returned to the truck.

Sam pulled away with a laugh as she turned around to see the effect of Miss Liberty's new look and grinned broadly. Yes, Cassie Madison had returned. It had taken her fifteen long years, but she had finally found her way home.

A CONVERSATION WITH
KAREN WHITE

Q. Falling Home *is a very intriguing title—how did you come up with this particular phrase?*

A. This title came to me fairly easily. It's a coming-home story but "Coming Home" seemed so passive. Cassie's return to Walton, Georgia, after so many years away was a lot more forceful—hence the word "Falling."

Q. Cassie, the protagonist in Falling Home, *is a Southern girl who left home as soon as she could. Does her choice reflect any of your personal experiences?*

A. My parents are both from Mississippi, so I've always considered myself a Southern girl—although I lived all over the world while I was growing up and didn't actually live in the South until I moved to Georgia eighteen years ago. But I spent most of my childhood wishing I had a Southern town to call home, learning to be satisfied with yearly visits to my grandmother's house in Indianola, Mississippi.

Q. Could you see yourself living anywhere else but the South?

A. I suppose I could, since I've done it before. Being Southern is so much more than geography, though, and I imagine I'd carry my "Southernisms" wherever I went. But I do have an aversion to cold weather, so I couldn't stray too far above the Mason-Dixon line for that reason alone!

Q. *Is the town of Walton, Georgia, a real town or based on any real town?*

A. There's a Walton County, but no Walton, Georgia (as far as I know). However, a friend of mine from college is from Monroe, Georgia, and she and her mother took me on a lovely tour (including the antebellum house the family still lives in) of the town, and I knew that I had the basis for the fictional town of Walton. But all characters are completely fictional!

Q. *When you decided to revise the earlier version of* Falling Home, *how did you find marrying your current writing style to a book originally written nearly a decade earlier?*

A. My books are always about the story and the characters, and I loved both in *Falling Home*, which made the prospect of reworking the book exciting. It was a very organic process starting at the beginning and looking at each scene with the experience of twelve books under my belt. I let the characters talk to me, and simply went from there.

Q. How are you different now as a writer versus when you first wrote Falling Home?

A. Believe it or not, I was so relieved to see how I'd grown as a writer in the eight years between the first *Falling Home* and the new version. Not that I thought the original version was bad, but I certainly saw opportunities for better pacing, deeper characterization, and much less melodrama!

Q. What are some of the things that changed between the two versions?

A. The biggest change was adding two additional points of view. The original version was told solely in Cassie's point of view. Since my more recent books are focused on the relationships between women—friends, sisters, mothers—I added the viewpoints of Cassie's sister, Harriet, as well as of Harriet's daughter Maddie. I was so pleased with how this deepened the emotional impact of the story for the reader.

QUESTIONS FOR DISCUSSION

1. Have you ever lived far from your childhood home? If so, what was your experience like? What drove you to relocate? Could you sympathize with Cassie's yearning to redefine herself and her destiny?

2. What does the author have to say about living an urban life versus a more rural one? What positives and negatives are there to each? Which seems to suit Cassie when we first encounter her versus the Cassie we come to know at the end of the novel?

3. Do you think Cassie's father did the right thing by leaving her the house—thereby tying her to Walton? Do you think he still knew what was best for her after all these years? How do the other characters conspire to keep Cassie in Walton, too?

4. What are some of the stereotypes that the characters have of "city people" and of "country folk"? How do these perceptions influence their behavior? How are these ideas challenged?

5. Cassie and Andrew. Cassie and Sam. What does each relationship offer her? Did you find yourself rooting for one man over the other? Who seems a

better match for her—and did her transformation affect your answer? Were you surprised when Cassie broke off her engagement?

6. How does the past continue to influence the lives of Cassie, Harriet, and Sam? How do they each react to change—in Walton, in their family, in their lives?

7. Why do you think the author chose to keep Joe in the background? What effect does this have on the story—letting the sisters' relationship be the focus? Did you want to know what exactly unfolded fifteen years prior?

8. How does Harriet and Joe's early relationship mirror that of Lena and the judge? Why do you think the girls' father seemed to take Harriet's "side" in the love-triangle drama?

9. The residents and the town of Walton certainly had an effect on Cassie—bringing the past back to her through the moonlit nights, the magnolias and kudzu, the "Statue of Liberty," old romances and friendships, plus the integral new relationships with her nieces and nephews. What effect does Cassie's presence have on the town? On Maddie?

10. What are some of your most cherished childhood memories? Do you have a "sacred"

scent, food, or object that transports you back to those moments? What do you think gives them that power?

11. Do you think the sisters did the right thing by reading the letters? How did that change things? Would you have been curious, or been able to resist reading about the affair and the child?

12. Were you shocked to learn the identity of "E.L." or the love child? What reasons does Lena have for keeping the secret? Do you think Ed had a right to feel the resentment he did?

13. Harriet's decision to delay treatment for her cancer until after the baby's birth is heartbreaking. Do you think her choice is controversial? How might you consult a loved one in a similarly tragic predicament?

14. Walton is a prime example of a small town wrestling with tradition and the challenges and necessities of staying competitive for its working families and young people now and in the future. Development and modernizing involve real risks to the character that makes these towns so special. How has your town (or the place you live) tackled such challenges?

Karen White is the award-winning author of twelve previous books. She grew up in London but now lives with her husband and two children near Atlanta, Georgia. Visit her Web site at www.karen-white.com.

Center Point Publishing
600 Brooks Road ● PO Box 1
Thorndike ME 04986-0001 USA

(207) 568-3717

US & Canada:
1 800 929-9108
www.centerpointlargeprint.com